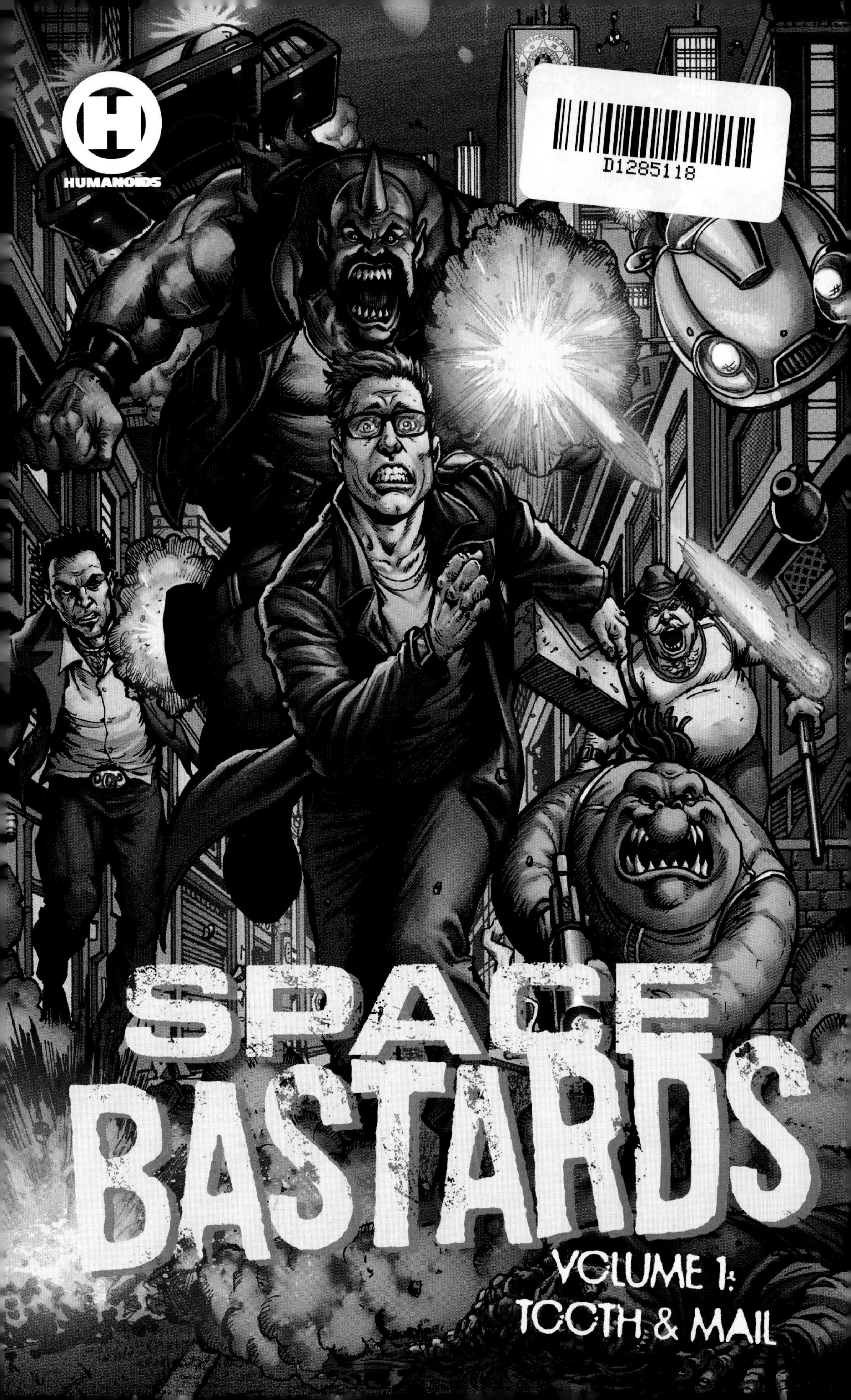
HUMANOIDS
SPACE
BASTARDS
VOLUME 1:
TOOTH & MAIL

SPACE BASTARDS

VOLUME ONE - TOOTH & MAIL

ERIC PETERSON & JOE AUBREY | Writers
DARICK ROBERTSON (EP. 1-5) and SIMON BISLEY (CHUCK WAGON) | Artists
DIEGO RODRIGUEZ (EP. 1-3), PETE PANTAZIS (EP. 4-5), and
SIMON BISLEY (CHUCK WAGON) | Colorists
SIMON BOWLAND (EP. 1-3) and TAYLOR ESPOSITO (EP. 4-5, CHUCK) | Letterers

DARICK ROBERTSON & DIEGO RODRIGUEZ | Cover Artists

SPACE BASTARDS created by ERIC PETERSON,
JOE AUBREY & DARICK ROBERTSON

MARK WAID | Publisher
ROB LEVIN | Editor
JERRY FRISSEN | Art Director
RYAN LEWIS | Designer

FABRICE GIGER | CEO
MATTHIEU COPPET | GROUP COO
ALEX DONOGHUE | COO, U.S. Operations
GUILLAUME NOUGARET | CFO
JERRY FRISSEN | Senior Art Director
ROB LEVIN | Executive Editor
RYAN LEWIS | Junior Designer
AMANDA LUCIDO | Operations Coordinator
BETH YORK | Development Director, Film & TV
EDMOND LEE | Director, Licensing
BRUNO BARBERI | CTO
licensing@humanoids.com | Rights and Licensing
PR@humanoids.com | Press and Social Media

To Rick (taking a Caddie). **—Joe**
To Tiberius and Rose. **—Eric**
To Marc Greenberg, for always having my back. Special thanks to Jeff Johnson and Stephen J.B. Jones. **—Darick**

WWW.SPACEBASTARDS.COM | The Official Site for Limited Edition Hardcovers

HUMANOIDS

SPACE BASTARDS VOL. 1: TOOTH & MAIL. First printing. This title is a publication of Humanoids, Inc. 8033 Sunset Blvd. #628, Los Angeles, CA 90046. Copyright © 2021 Eric Peterson & Joe Aubrey & Humanoids, Inc., Los Angeles (USA). All rights reserved. Humanoids and its logos are ® and © 2021 Humanoids, Inc. Library of Congress Control Number: 2021935216
This volume collects SPACE BASTARDS Issues 1-6.

"*Space Bastards* is one of those comics I love because it's clear from the first page that everyone involved just turned the volume up to 11 right at the start and never once turned it down. The new Humanoids series from Joe Aubrey and Eric Peterson and Darick Robertson is filled to bursting with the kind of manic energy its title and cover suggests, and if you're looking for a mature readers sci-fi thrill ride, look no further... This book is a blast."

—SYFY WIRE

"Exciting... A celebration of cosmic badasses and deathmatch-style dystopian adventures, *Space Bastards* provides plenty of thrills.... If you're a fan of *The Boys*, *Space Bastards* definitely is a sci-fi heir apparent and is quickly shaping up to be a good time."

—CBR

"Robertson brings all the raunchiness, chaos, and hilariousness that made *The Boys* such a great series to *Space Bastards*... *Space Bastards* is a gut punch parcel ride that makes you laugh and keeps you guessing until the end."

—AIPT

"It's REALLY over the top. The blood flies. The heads splatter. The violence is ultra... [It's] a lot of fun."

—GRAPHIC POLICY

"A rip-roaring fun story... An utterly bonkers action romp with a wildly unique premise and a legitimately engaging plot beneath its surface appeal. Give the Big 2 a break and check out this amazingly fun comic!"

—COMIC WATCH

"If you're into an action-packed space adventure with a lot of death and no guilt, complete with characters that say and do offensive stuff, Eric Peterson and Joe Aubrey's *Space Bastards* is for you...with artist Darick Robertson delivering comedy and blood through attention-grabbing visuals."

—THE GEEKIARY

"A dark, comical space opera... Artist Darick Robertson seems to be having a blast in delivering the dense and detailed artwork for this book, while writing partnership Eric Peterson and Joe Aubrey are themselves having a grand old time of it providing the dark humour and requisite over-the-top violence.... It goes without saying—so I'll write it instead—that if you enjoyed *The Boys*, you'll definitely dig this too."

—COMICON.COM

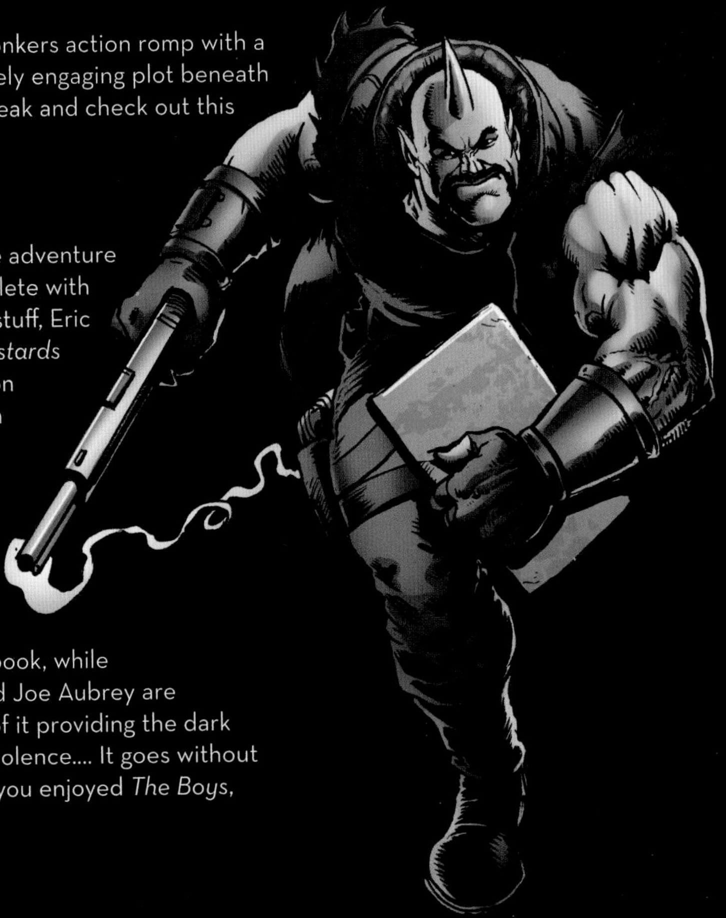

INTRODUCTION

by Mark Waid, **Publisher Responsible**

That *SPACE BASTARDS* came across my desk, as drawn by my old friend and collaborator Darick Robertson, made me eager to read it. That *SPACE BASTARDS* came across my desk at the same time a prominent government asshole was doing his best to destroy the U.S. Postal Service only made me love it more.

But I'm not here to sing Darick's praises. He's got a piece of three separate TV shows, while I have a piece of zero separate TV shows, so let him pat his own damn back. Let's talk, instead, about authors Joe Aubrey and Eric Peterson, who likewise annoy me. (I'm in a mood.)

When I originally quit my job as a lamplighter to break into comics writing, I thought I was pretty good. I wasn't. It took me years to achieve even a mild level of competence. That this is Eric and Joe's earliest comics work and is this good and this professional is just not right. Yes, they got a lot of great advice and encouragement from Robertson in between his Hollywood lunches, and they'll be the first to admit what an integral part of the creative process he could be when they could actually get past his publicists. But words still needed to be put to paper. Ideas had to flow, themes and characters needed to be generated, and the history of toilet humor had to be—wait for it—plumbed. (Please, hold your applause for the end of the intro.) What I'm saying is that two tyros leveled up really, irritatingly fast, and my only worry for this book is that the gags and the madness and the spectacle and the flat-out cleverness within is the flashy stuff that may overshadow the clear evidence that these are sincerely well-told stories, so much so that even the legendary artist Simon Bisley got pulled in to play along.

Know what you're getting into. These stories are, in fact, about bastards. Hardly a redeemable soul in the bunch. But it's a film-teachers' myth that a protagonist has to be "likeable." Bullshit. You just have to want to spend time with them. Readers will put up with (or page giddily through) no end of bad behavior, violence, sex, and raunch if they're sufficiently entertained. (No judgment here—comedy wouldn't be comedy if it were always in good taste.) I can prove it. Take off your clutching pearls, steel yourself for a case of the vapors, and go meet David S. Proton and his co-workers. You'll be glad you did.

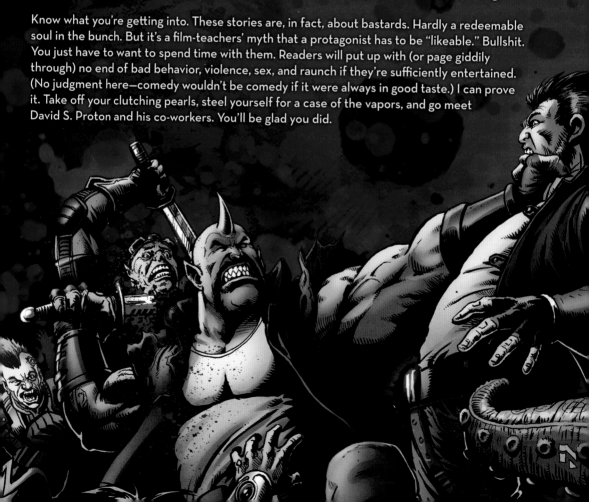

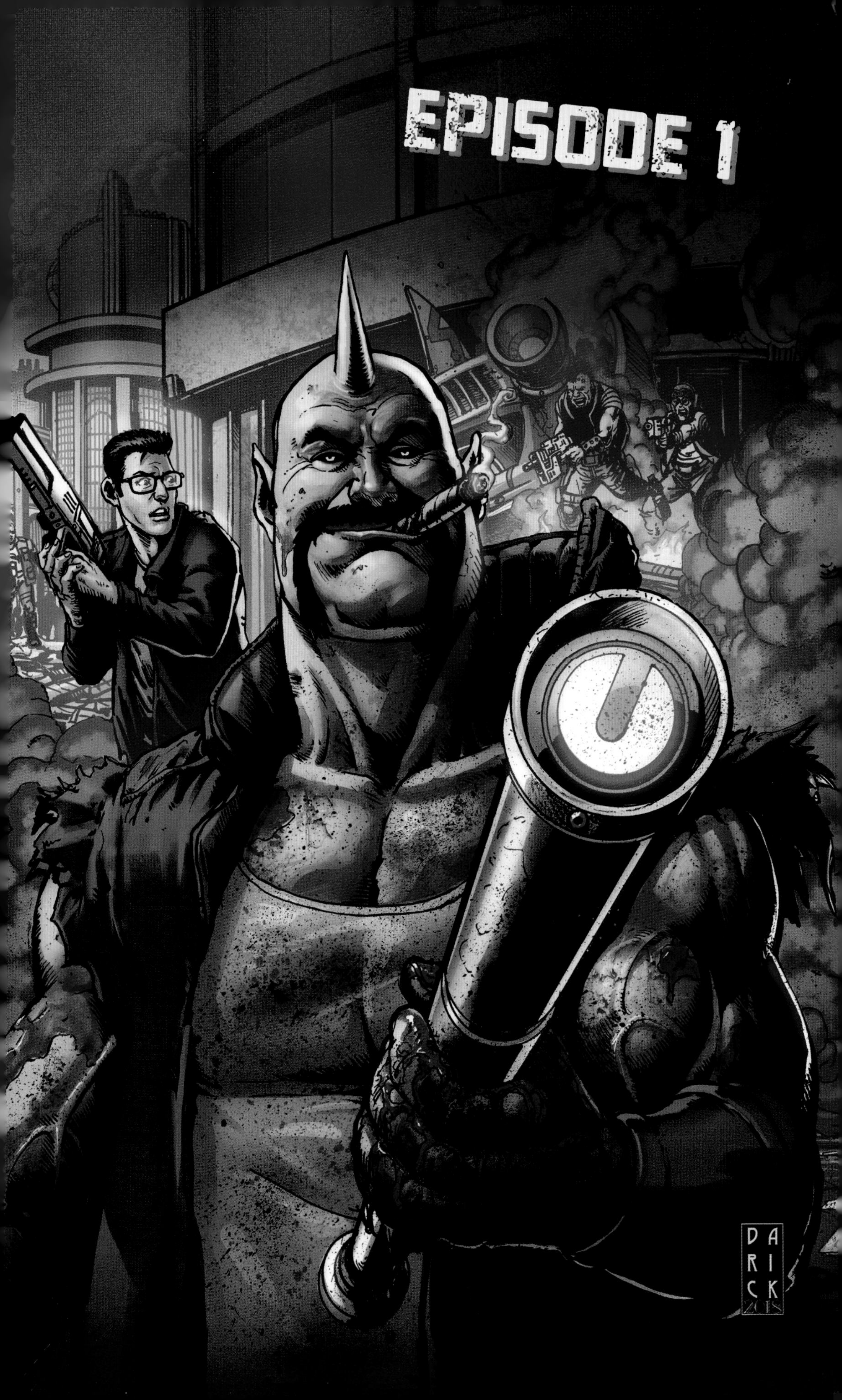
EPISODE 1
DARICK
2018

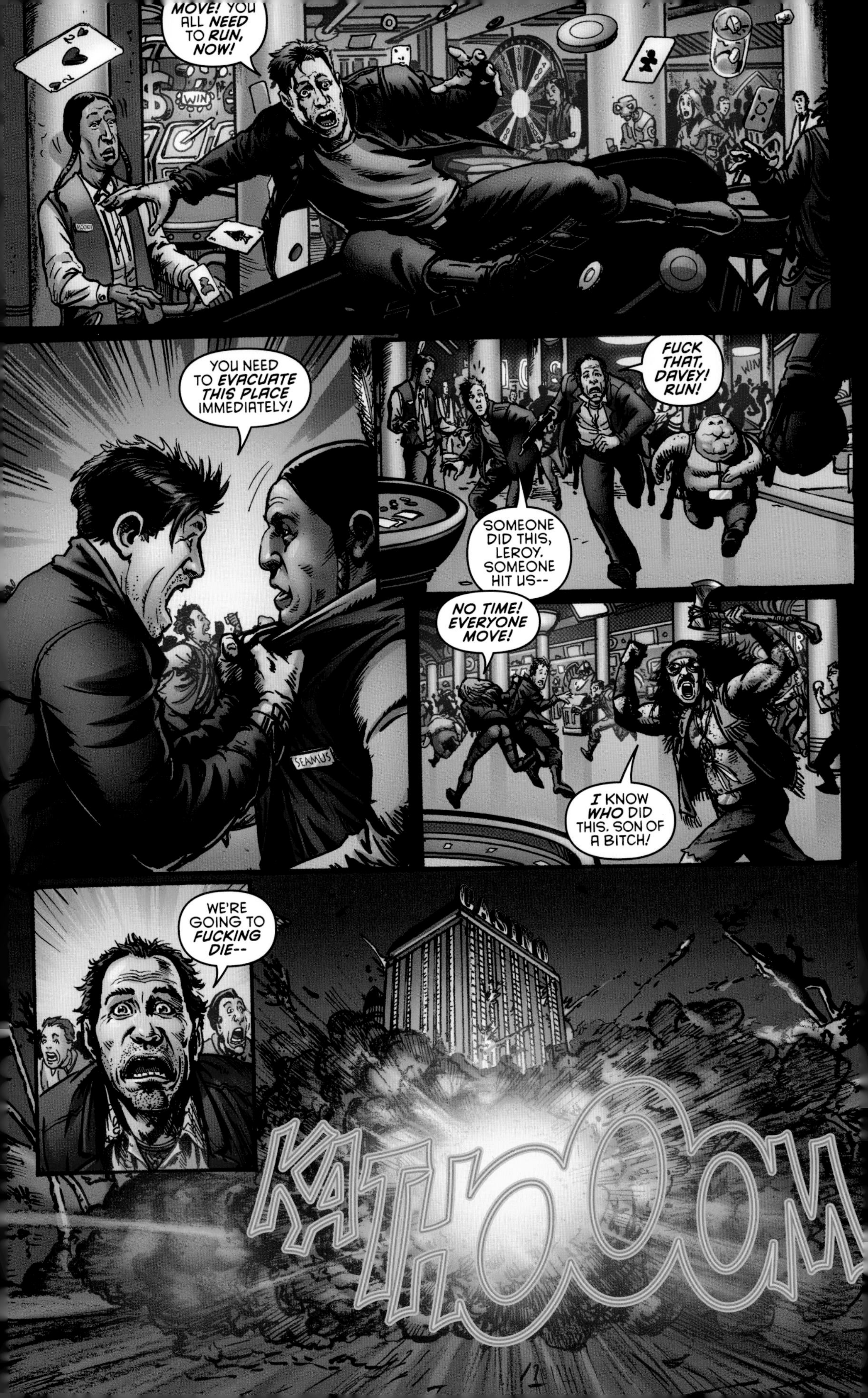
MOVE! YOU ALL NEED TO RUN, NOW!
WIN
YOU NEED TO EVACUATE THIS PLACE IMMEDIATELY!
SEAMUS
FUCK THAT, DAVEY! RUN!
SOMEONE DID THIS, LEROY. SOMEONE HIT US--
NO TIME! EVERYONE MOVE!
I KNOW WHO DID THIS. SON OF A BITCH!
WE'RE GOING TO FUCKING DIE--
CASINO
KATHOOOM

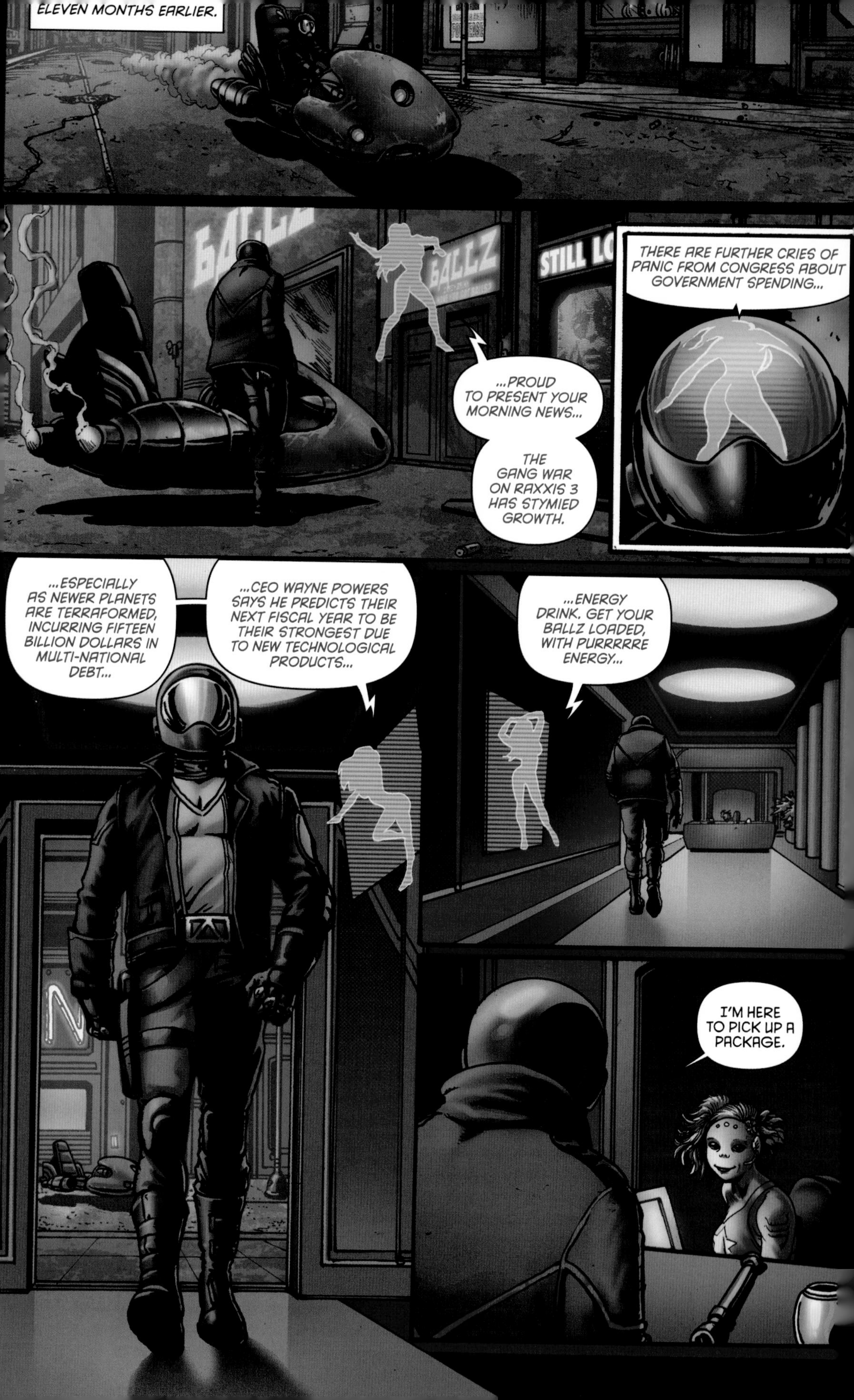
ELEVEN MONTHS EARLIER.
BALLZ
BALLZ
STILL LO
...PROUD TO PRESENT YOUR MORNING NEWS...
THE GANG WAR ON RAXXIS 3 HAS STYMIED GROWTH.
THERE ARE FURTHER CRIES OF PANIC FROM CONGRESS ABOUT GOVERNMENT SPENDING...
...ESPECIALLY AS NEWER PLANETS ARE TERRAFORMED, INCURRING FIFTEEN BILLION DOLLARS IN MULTI-NATIONAL DEBT...
...CEO WAYNE POWERS SAYS HE PREDICTS THEIR NEXT FISCAL YEAR TO BE THEIR STRONGEST DUE TO NEW TECHNOLOGICAL PRODUCTS...
...ENERGY DRINK. GET YOUR BALLZ LOADED, WITH PURRRRRE ENERGY...
I'M HERE TO PICK UP A PACKAGE.

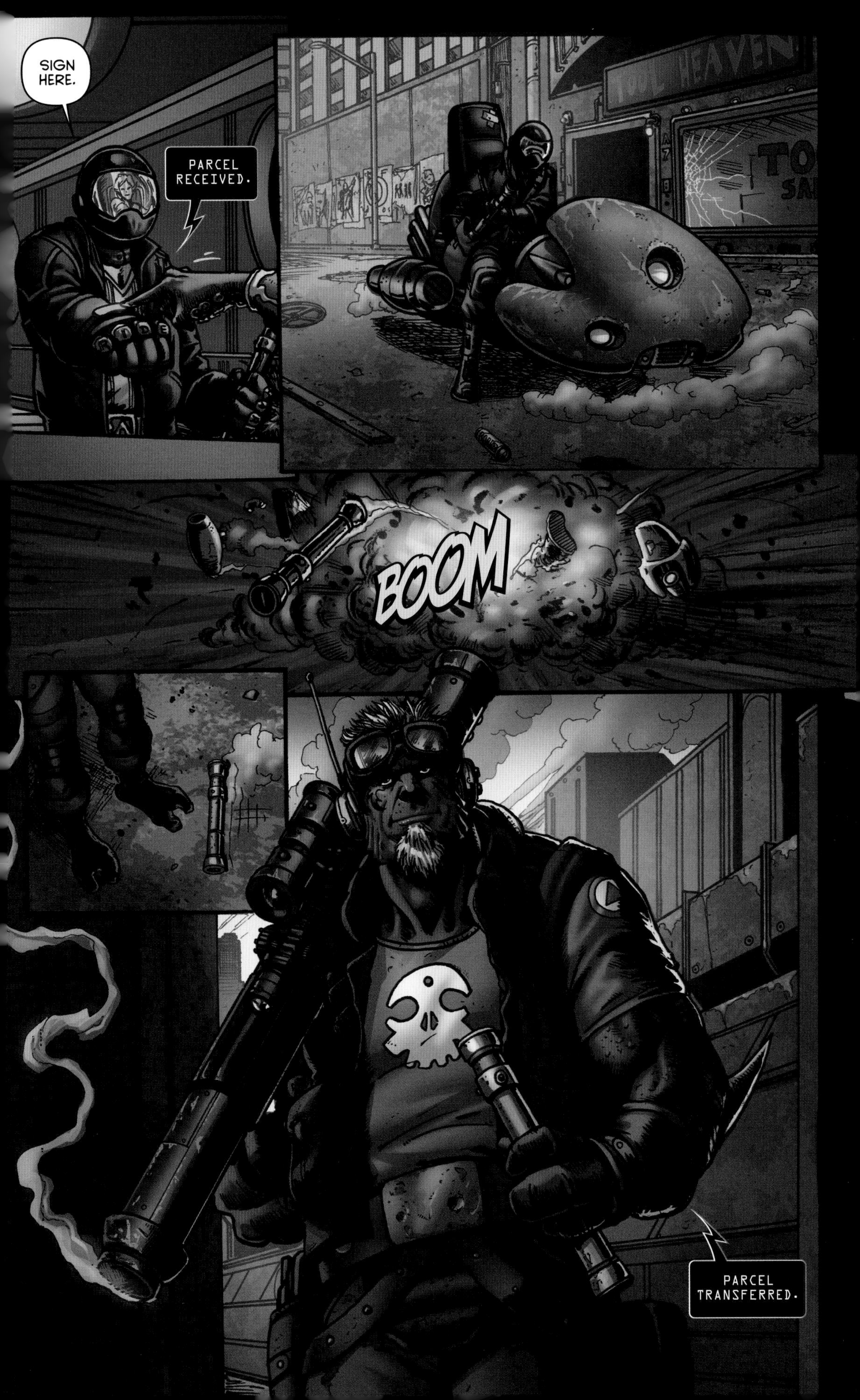
SIGN HERE.
PARCEL RECEIVED.
TOOL HEAVEN
BOOM
PARCEL TRANSFERRED.

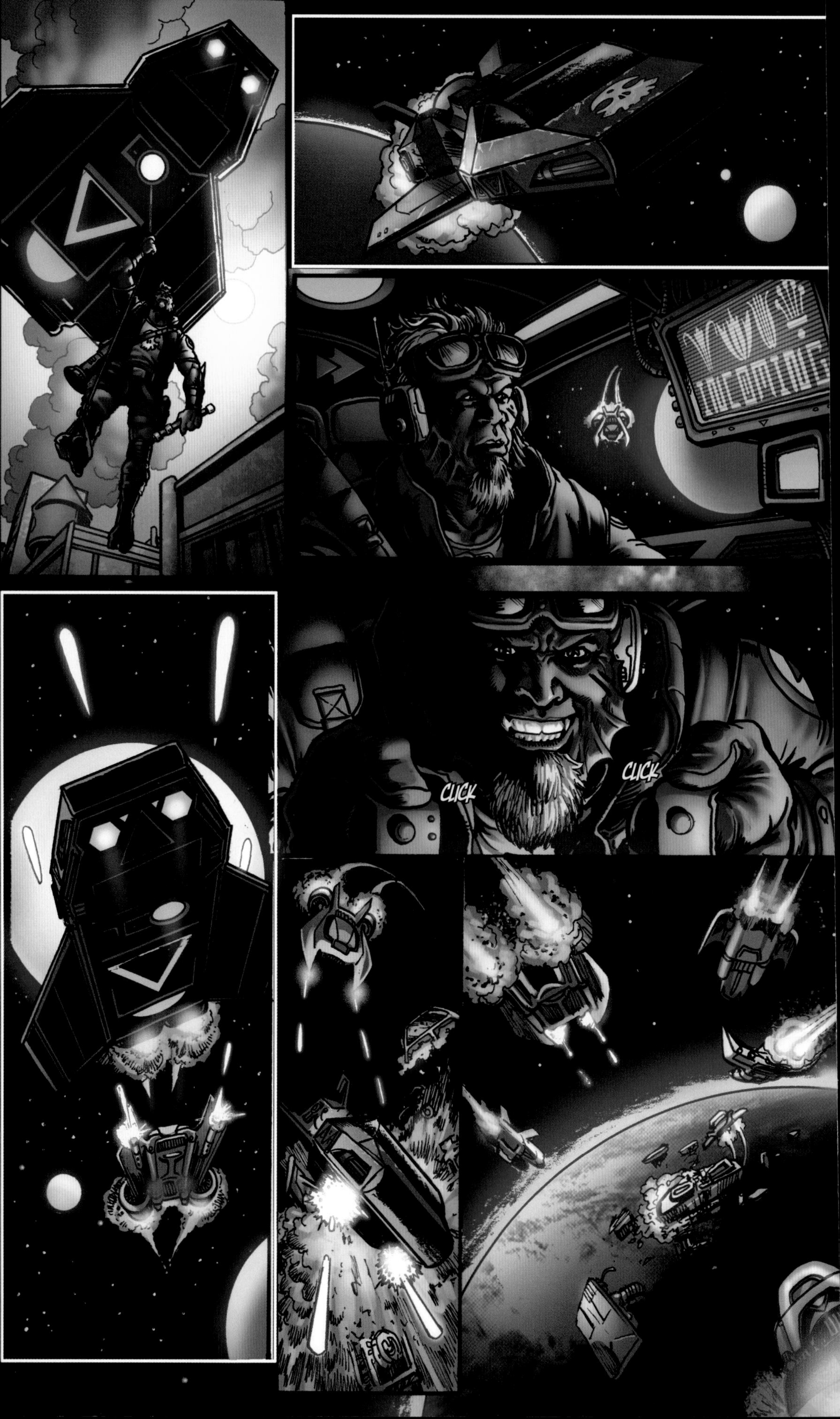
INCOMING
CLICK
CLICK

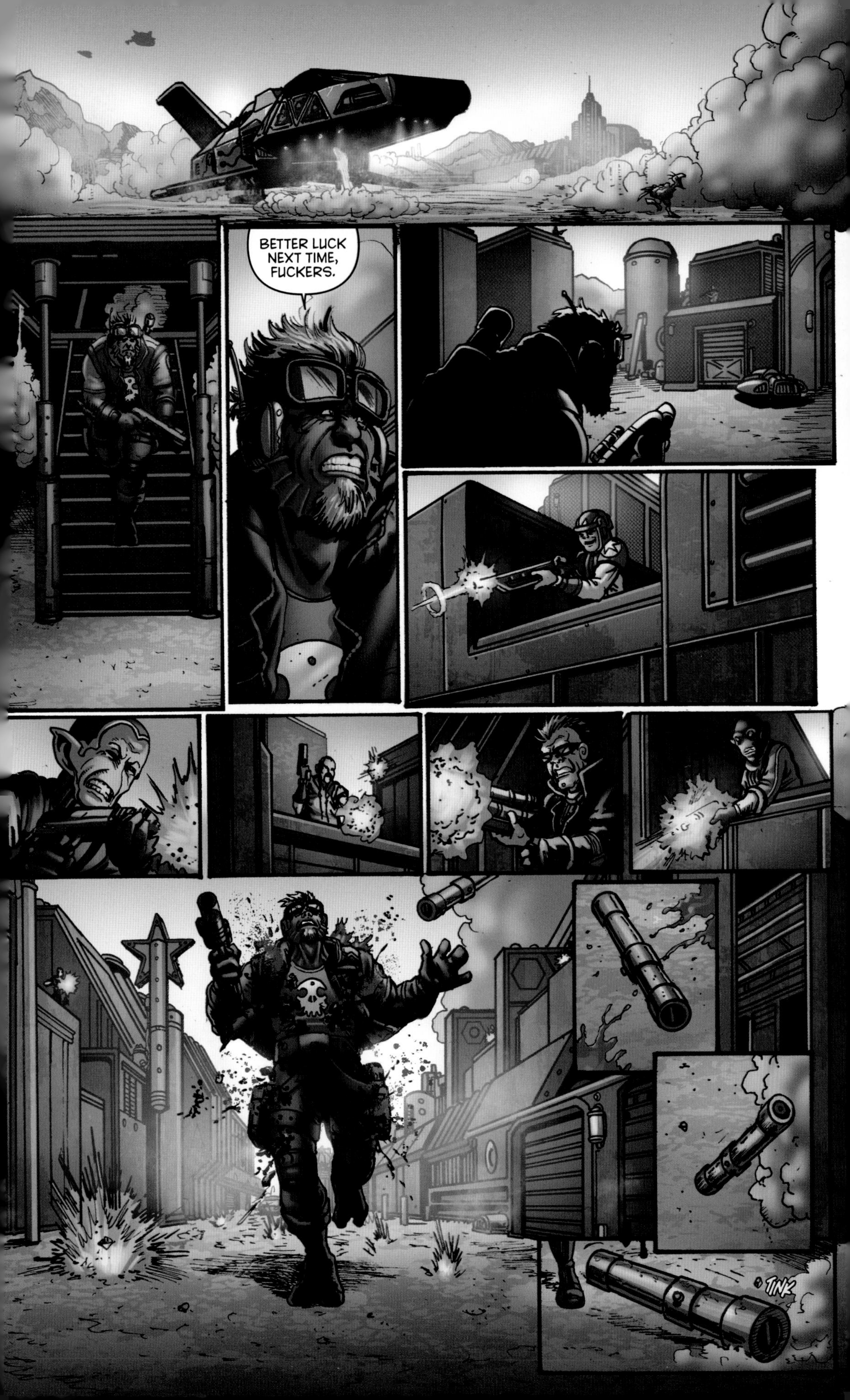
BETTER LUCK NEXT TIME, FUCKERS.
TINK

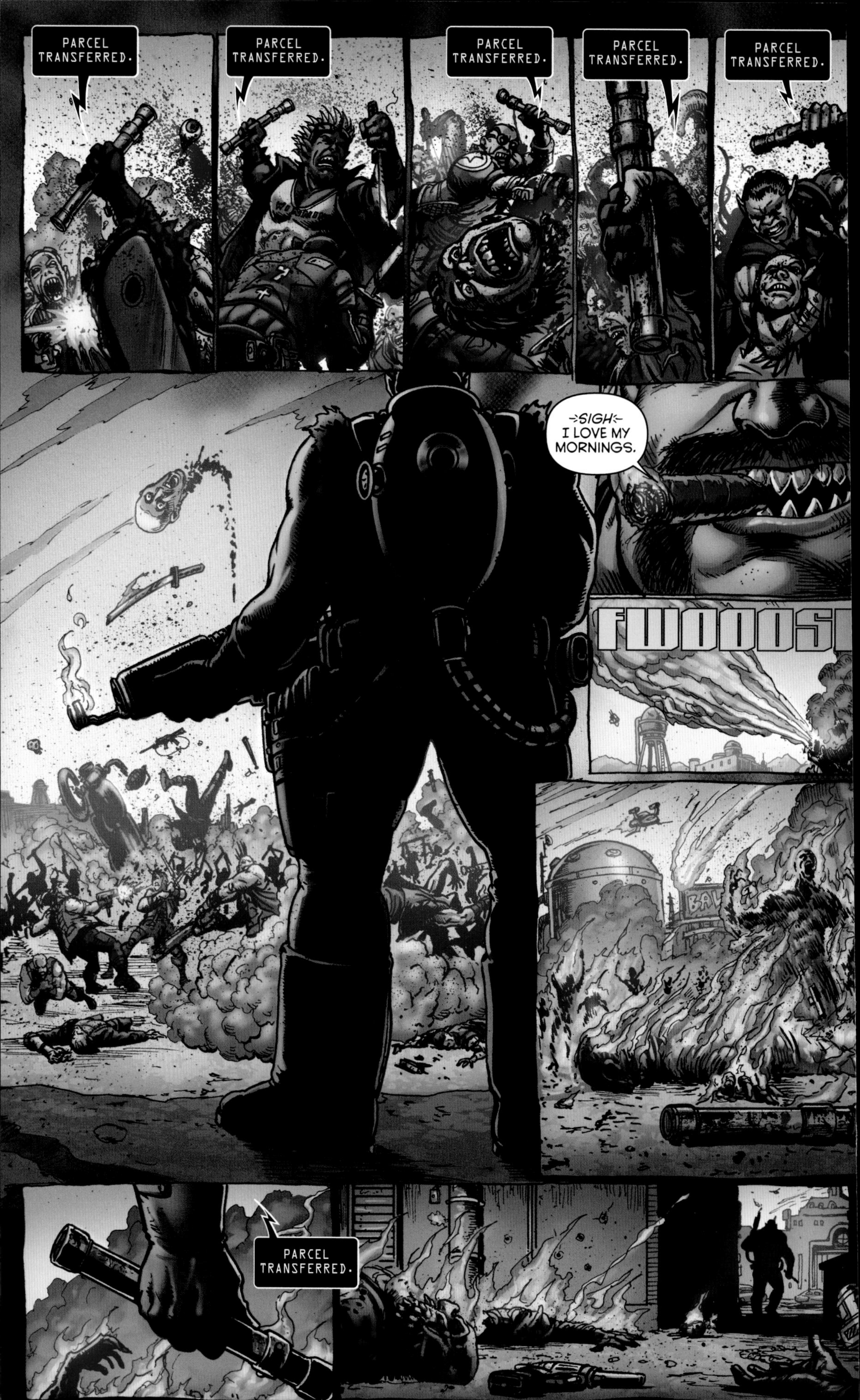
PARCEL TRANSFERRED.
PARCEL TRANSFERRED.
PARCEL TRANSFERRED.
PARCEL TRANSFERRED.
PARCEL TRANSFERRED.
-SIGH- I LOVE MY MORNINGS.
FWOOOSH
PARCEL TRANSFERRED.

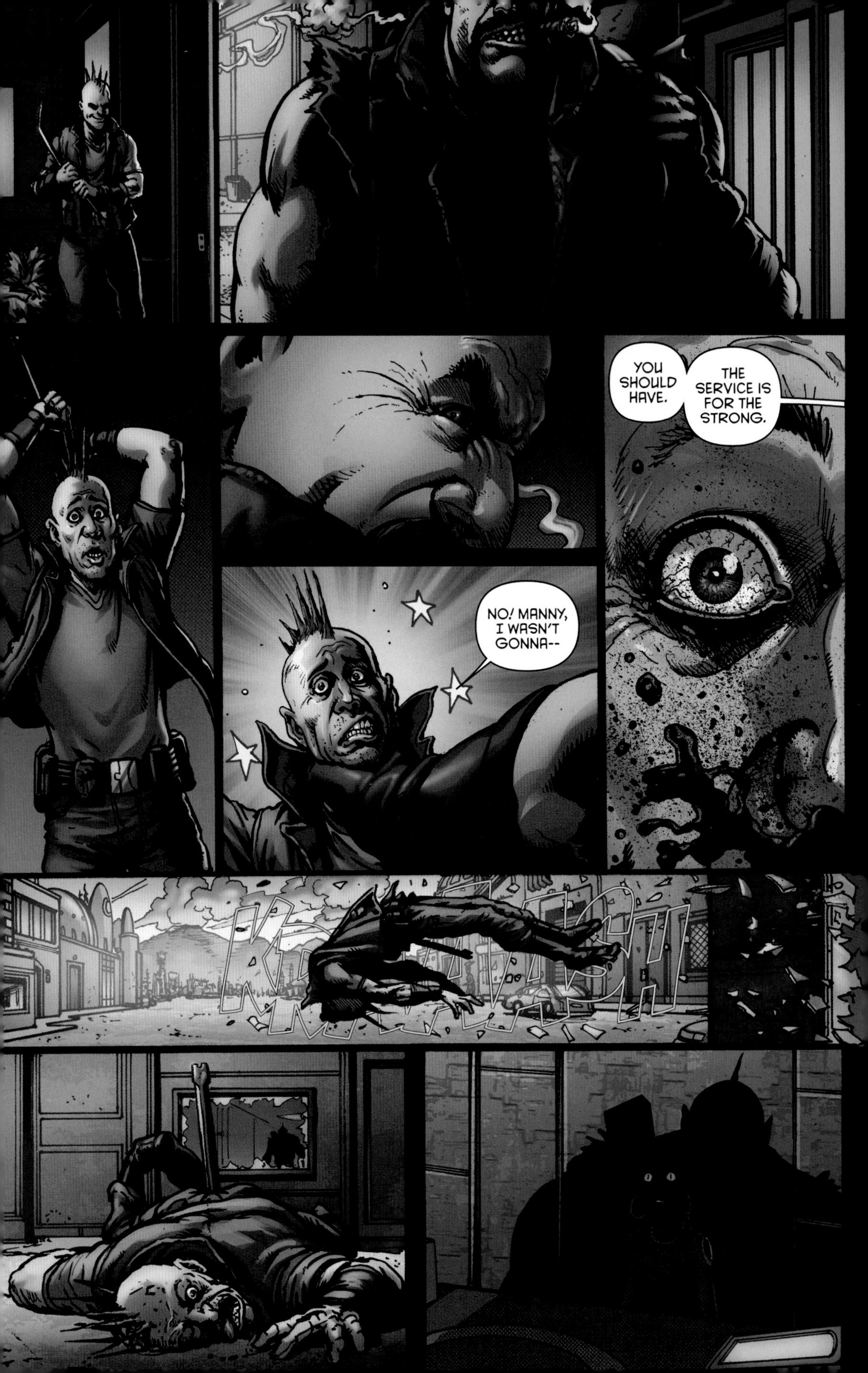
NO! MANNY, I WASN'T GONNA--
YOU SHOULD HAVE.
THE SERVICE IS FOR THE STRONG.

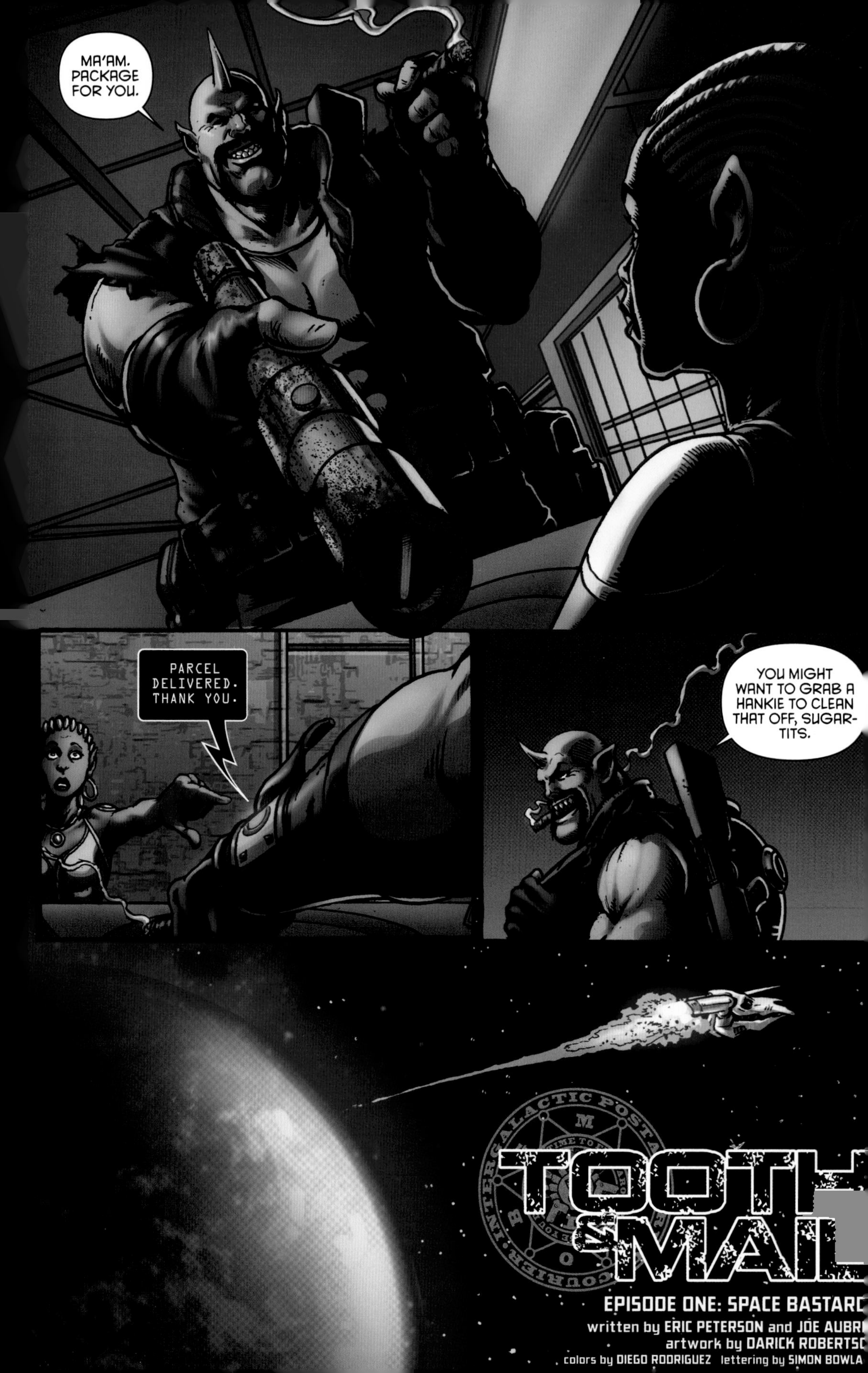
MA'AM. PACKAGE FOR YOU.
PARCEL DELIVERED. THANK YOU.
YOU MIGHT WANT TO GRAB A HANKIE TO CLEAN THAT OFF, SUGAR-TITS.
TOOTH & MAIL
EPISODE ONE: SPACE BASTAR
written by ERIC PETERSON and JOE AUBR
artwork by DARICK ROBERTS
colors by DIEGO RODRIGUEZ lettering by SIMON BOWLA

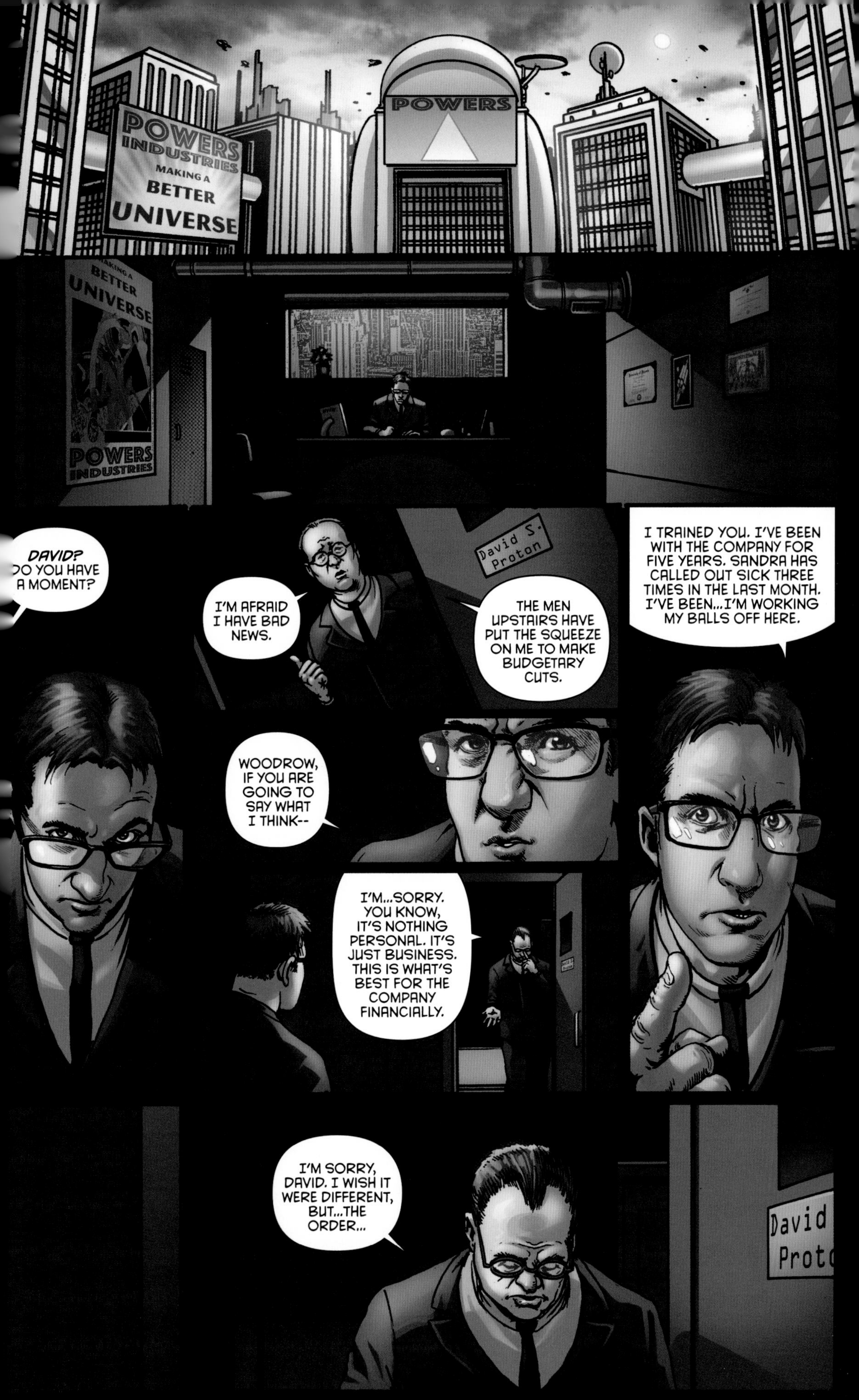
POWERS
POWERS INDUSTRIES MAKING A BETTER UNIVERSE
MAKING A BETTER UNIVERSE POWERS INDUSTRIES
DAVID? DO YOU HAVE A MOMENT?
David S. Proton
I'M AFRAID I HAVE BAD NEWS.
THE MEN UPSTAIRS HAVE PUT THE SQUEEZE ON ME TO MAKE BUDGETARY CUTS.
I TRAINED YOU. I'VE BEEN WITH THE COMPANY FOR FIVE YEARS. SANDRA HAS CALLED OUT SICK THREE TIMES IN THE LAST MONTH. I'VE BEEN...I'M WORKING MY BALLS OFF HERE.
WOODROW, IF YOU ARE GOING TO SAY WHAT I THINK--
I'M...SORRY. YOU KNOW, IT'S NOTHING PERSONAL. IT'S JUST BUSINESS. THIS IS WHAT'S BEST FOR THE COMPANY FINANCIALLY.
I'M SORRY, DAVID. I WISH IT WERE DIFFERENT, BUT...THE ORDER...
David Proto

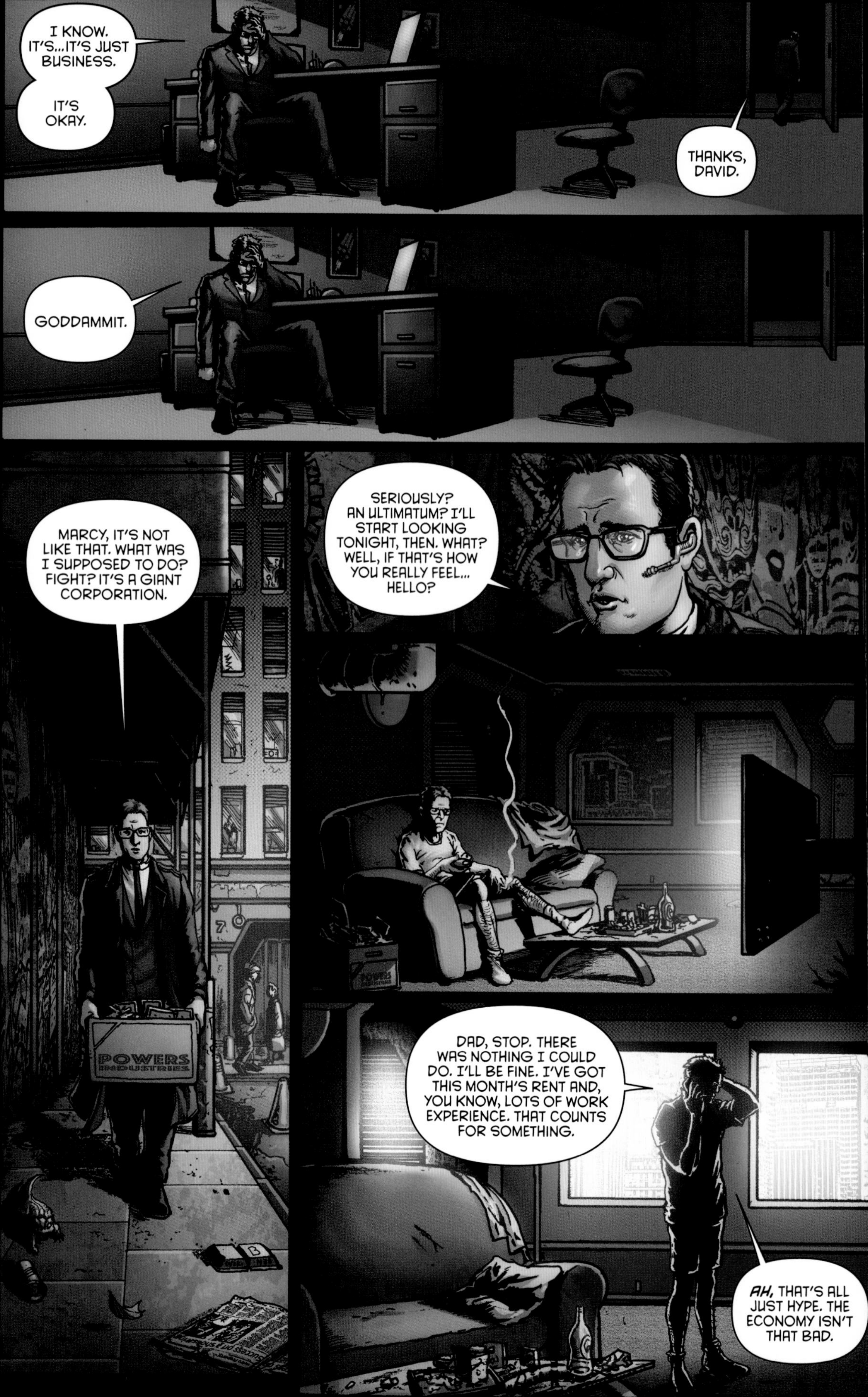
I KNOW. IT'S...IT'S JUST BUSINESS.
IT'S OKAY.
THANKS, DAVID.
GODDAMMIT.
MARCY, IT'S NOT LIKE THAT. WHAT WAS I SUPPOSED TO DO? FIGHT? IT'S A GIANT CORPORATION.
POWERS INDUSTRIES
SERIOUSLY? AN ULTIMATUM? I'LL START LOOKING TONIGHT, THEN. WHAT? WELL, IF THAT'S HOW YOU REALLY FEEL... HELLO?
DAD, STOP. THERE WAS NOTHING I COULD DO. I'LL BE FINE. I'VE GOT THIS MONTH'S RENT AND, YOU KNOW, LOTS OF WORK EXPERIENCE. THAT COUNTS FOR SOMETHING.
AH, THAT'S ALL JUST HYPE. THE ECONOMY ISN'T THAT BAD.

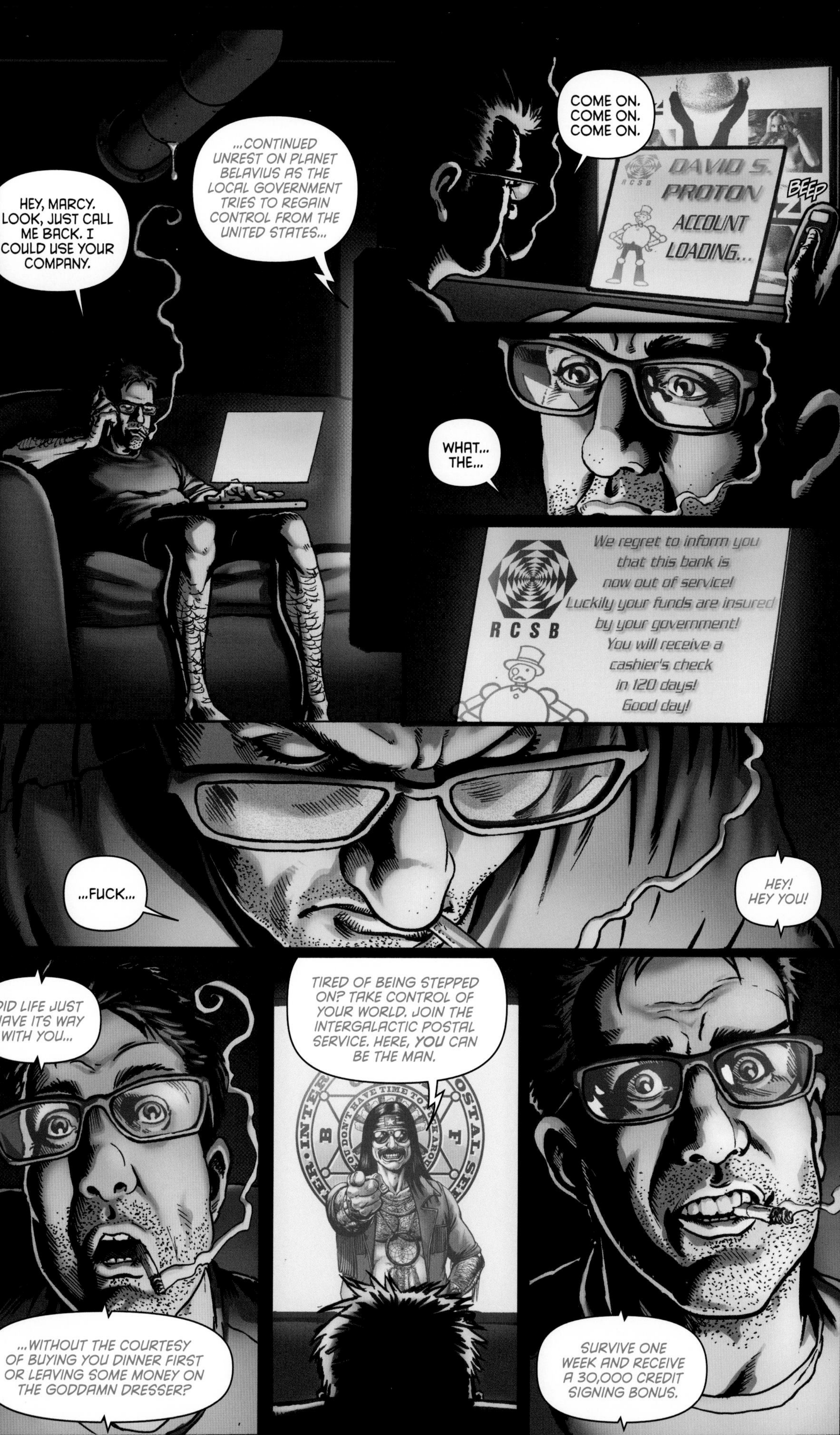
HEY, MARCY. LOOK, JUST CALL ME BACK. I COULD USE YOUR COMPANY.
...CONTINUED UNREST ON PLANET BELAVIUS AS THE LOCAL GOVERNMENT TRIES TO REGAIN CONTROL FROM THE UNITED STATES...
COME ON. COME ON. COME ON.
DAVID S. PROTON
ACCOUNT LOADING...
BEEP
WHAT... THE...
We regret to inform you that this bank is now out of service! Luckily your funds are insured by your government! You will receive a cashier's check in 120 days! Good day!
RCSB
...FUCK...
HEY! HEY YOU!
ID LIFE JUST AVE ITS WAY WITH YOU...
...WITHOUT THE COURTESY OF BUYING YOU DINNER FIRST OR LEAVING SOME MONEY ON THE GODDAMN DRESSER?
TIRED OF BEING STEPPED ON? TAKE CONTROL OF YOUR WORLD. JOIN THE INTERGALACTIC POSTAL SERVICE. HERE, YOU CAN BE THE MAN.
SURVIVE ONE WEEK AND RECEIVE A 30,000 CREDIT SIGNING BONUS.

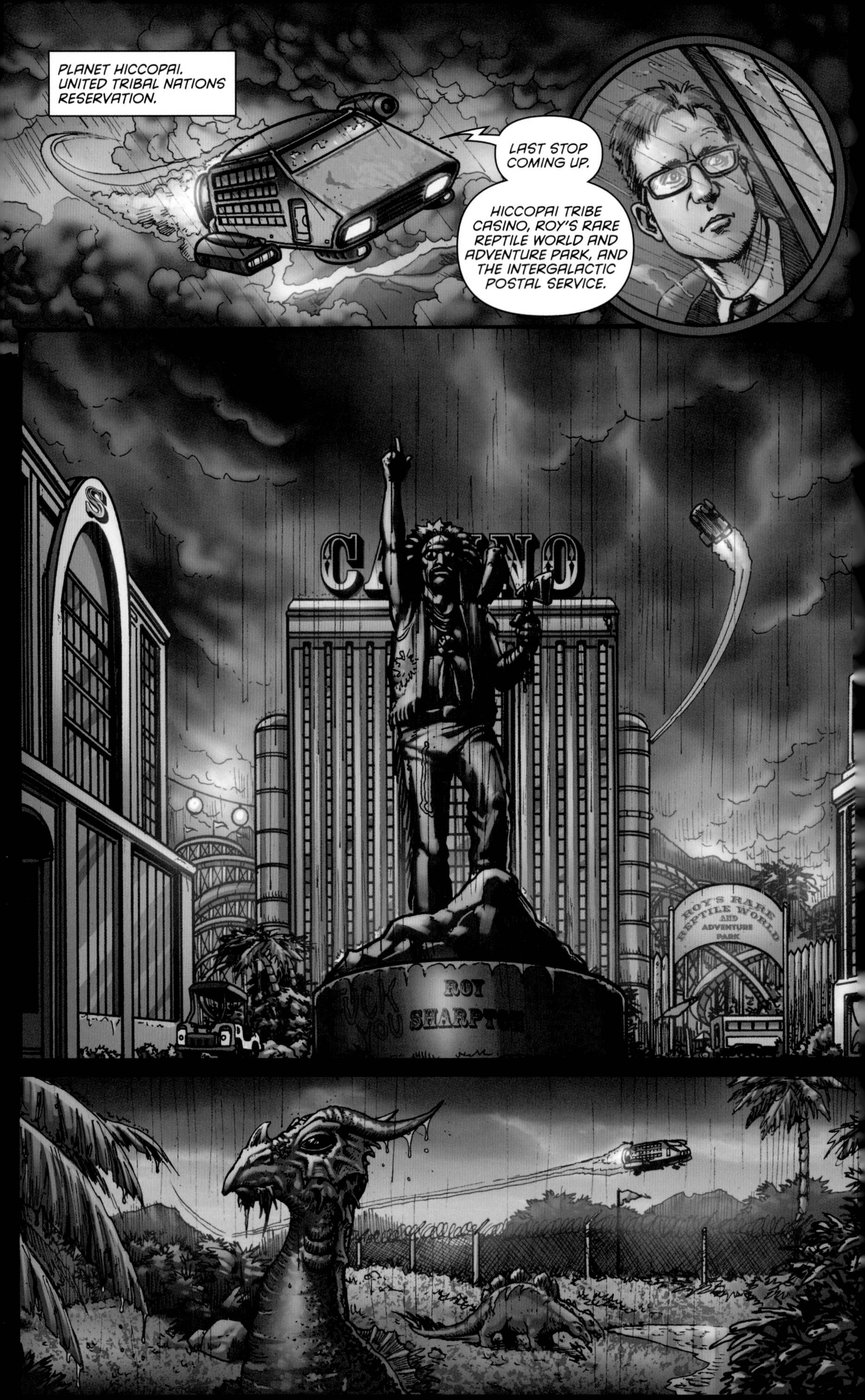
PLANET HICCOPAI. UNITED TRIBAL NATIONS RESERVATION.
LAST STOP COMING UP.
HICCOPAI TRIBE CASINO, ROY'S RARE REPTILE WORLD AND ADVENTURE PARK, AND THE INTERGALACTIC POSTAL SERVICE.
ROY'S RARE REPTILE WORLD AND ADVENTURE PARK
ROY

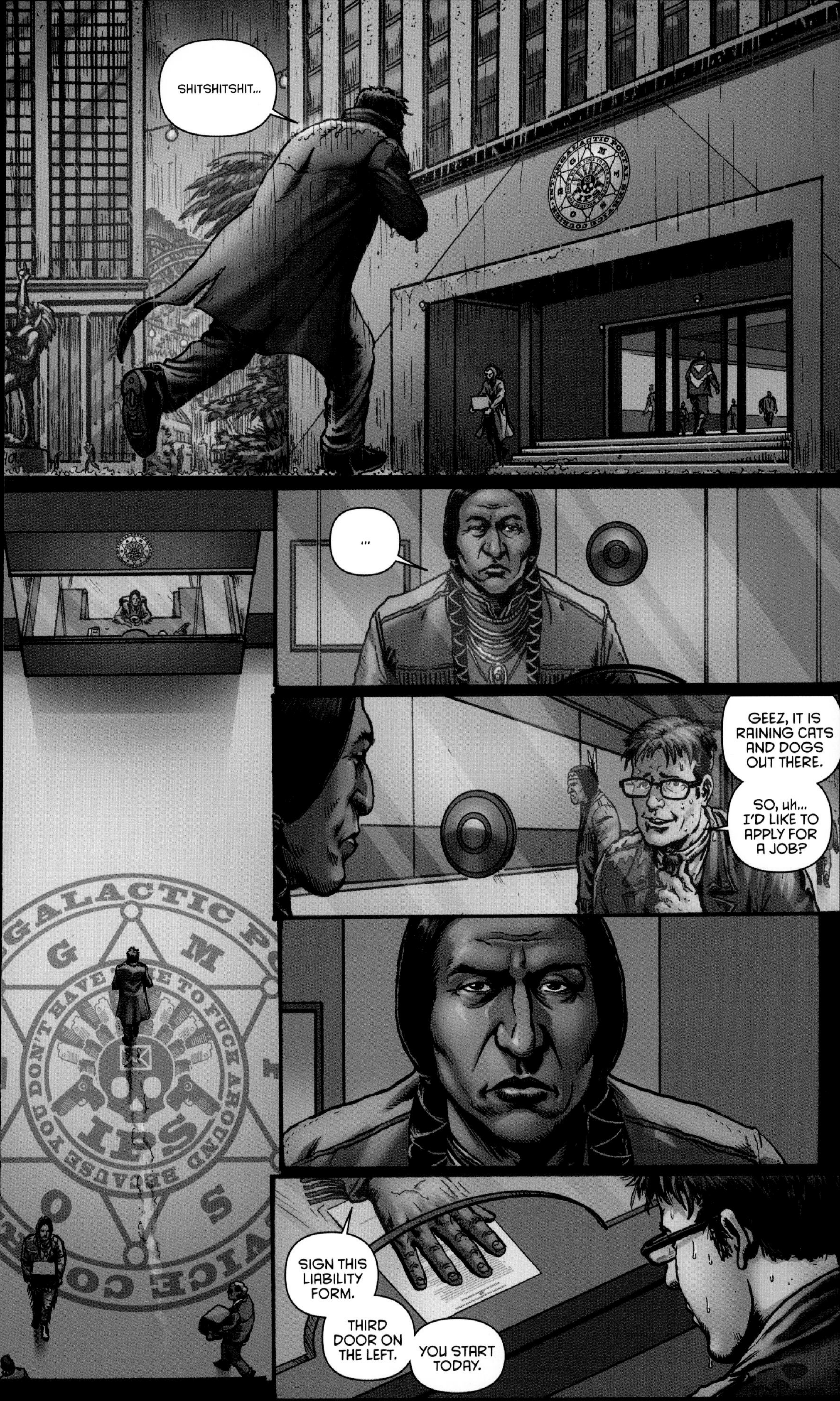
SHITSHITSHIT...
INTERGALACTIC POSTAL SERVICE COURIER
IPS
...
GEEZ, IT IS RAINING CATS AND DOGS OUT THERE.
SO, uh... I'D LIKE TO APPLY FOR A JOB?
GALACTIC P
G M
IPS
SIGN THIS LIABILITY FORM.
THIRD DOOR ON THE LEFT.
YOU START TODAY.

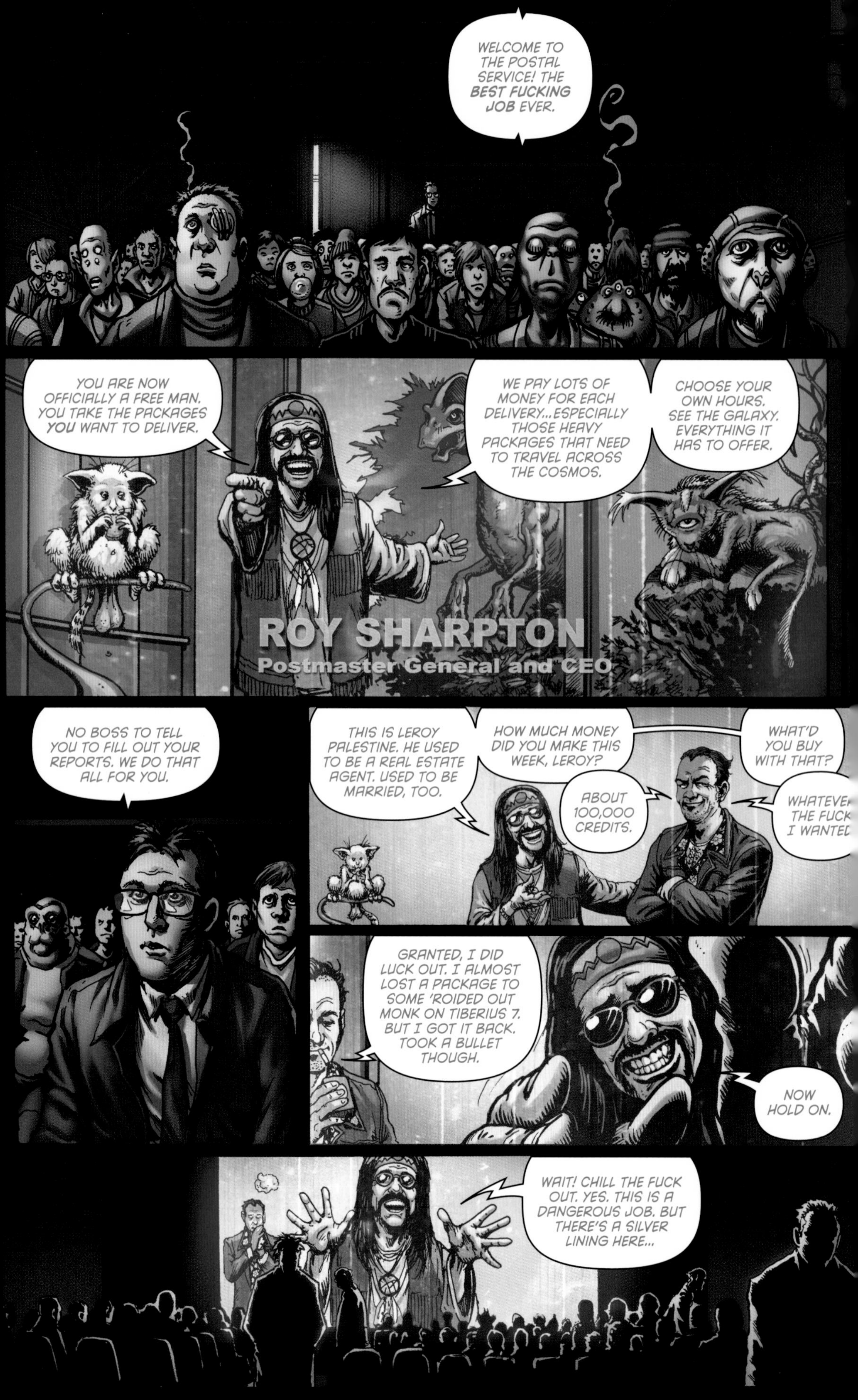
WELCOME TO THE POSTAL SERVICE! THE BEST FUCKING JOB EVER.
YOU ARE NOW OFFICIALLY A FREE MAN. YOU TAKE THE PACKAGES YOU WANT TO DELIVER.
WE PAY LOTS OF MONEY FOR EACH DELIVERY...ESPECIALLY THOSE HEAVY PACKAGES THAT NEED TO TRAVEL ACROSS THE COSMOS.
CHOOSE YOUR OWN HOURS. SEE THE GALAXY. EVERYTHING IT HAS TO OFFER.
ROY SHARPTON
Postmaster General and CEO
NO BOSS TO TELL YOU TO FILL OUT YOUR REPORTS. WE DO THAT ALL FOR YOU.
THIS IS LEROY PALESTINE. HE USED TO BE A REAL ESTATE AGENT. USED TO BE MARRIED, TOO.
HOW MUCH MONEY DID YOU MAKE THIS WEEK, LEROY?
ABOUT 100,000 CREDITS.
WHAT'D YOU BUY WITH THAT?
GRANTED, I DID LUCK OUT. I ALMOST LOST A PACKAGE TO SOME 'ROIDED OUT MONK ON TIBERIUS 7. BUT I GOT IT BACK. TOOK A BULLET THOUGH.
NOW HOLD ON.
WAIT! CHILL THE FUCK OUT. YES. THIS IS A DANGEROUS JOB. BUT THERE'S A SILVER LINING HERE...

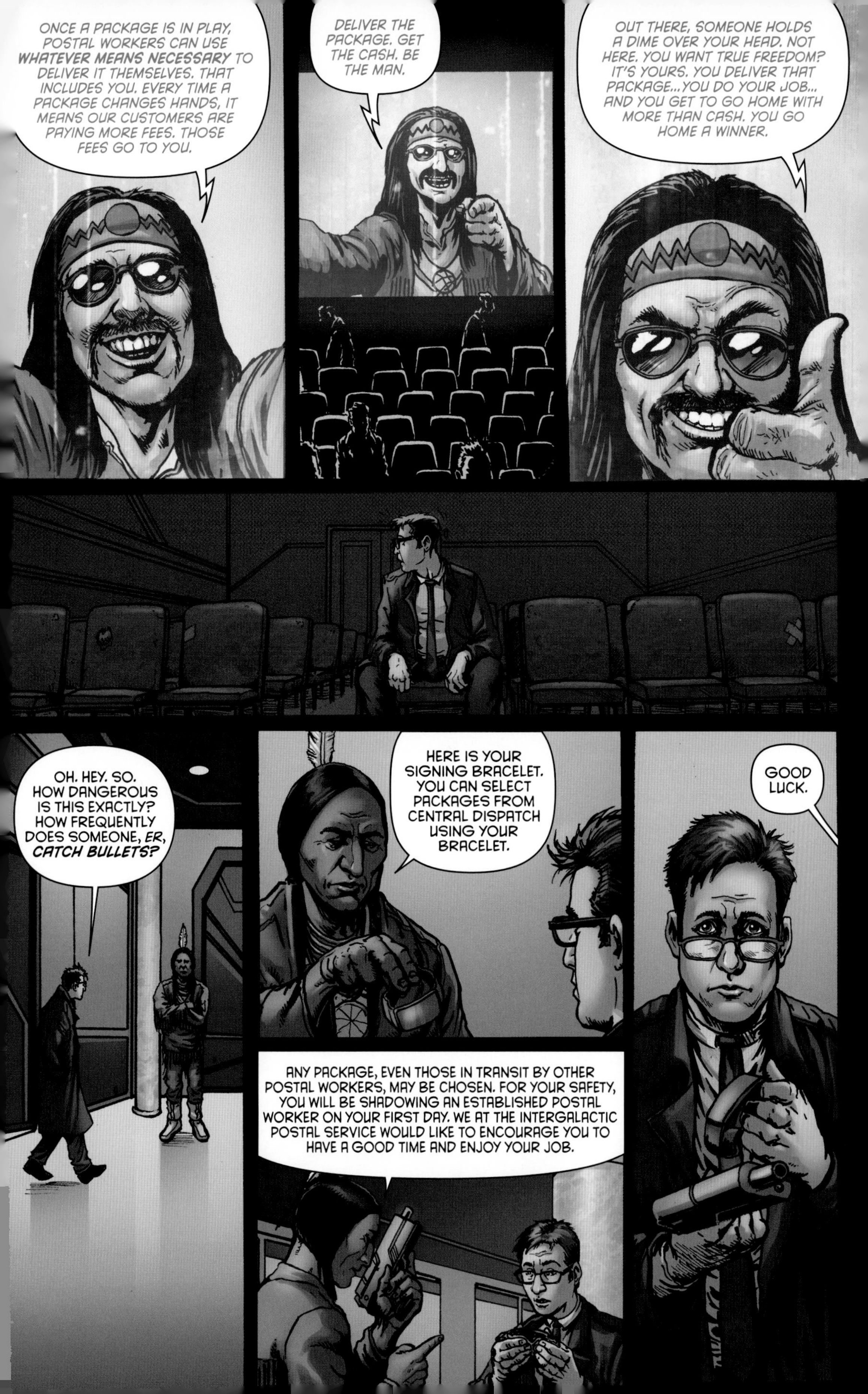
ONCE A PACKAGE IS IN PLAY, POSTAL WORKERS CAN USE **WHATEVER MEANS NECESSARY** TO DELIVER IT THEMSELVES. THAT INCLUDES YOU. EVERY TIME A PACKAGE CHANGES HANDS, IT MEANS OUR CUSTOMERS ARE PAYING MORE FEES. THOSE FEES GO TO YOU.
DELIVER THE PACKAGE. GET THE CASH. BE THE MAN.
OUT THERE, SOMEONE HOLDS A DIME OVER YOUR HEAD. NOT HERE. YOU WANT TRUE FREEDOM? IT'S YOURS. YOU DELIVER THAT PACKAGE...YOU DO YOUR JOB... AND YOU GET TO GO HOME WITH MORE THAN CASH. YOU GO HOME A WINNER.
OH. HEY. SO. HOW DANGEROUS IS THIS EXACTLY? HOW FREQUENTLY DOES SOMEONE, *ER*, ***CATCH BULLETS?***
HERE IS YOUR SIGNING BRACELET. YOU CAN SELECT PACKAGES FROM CENTRAL DISPATCH USING YOUR BRACELET.
ANY PACKAGE, EVEN THOSE IN TRANSIT BY OTHER POSTAL WORKERS, MAY BE CHOSEN. FOR YOUR SAFETY, YOU WILL BE SHADOWING AN ESTABLISHED POSTAL WORKER ON YOUR FIRST DAY. WE AT THE INTERGALACTIC POSTAL SERVICE WOULD LIKE TO ENCOURAGE YOU TO HAVE A GOOD TIME AND ENJOY YOUR JOB.
GOOD LUCK.

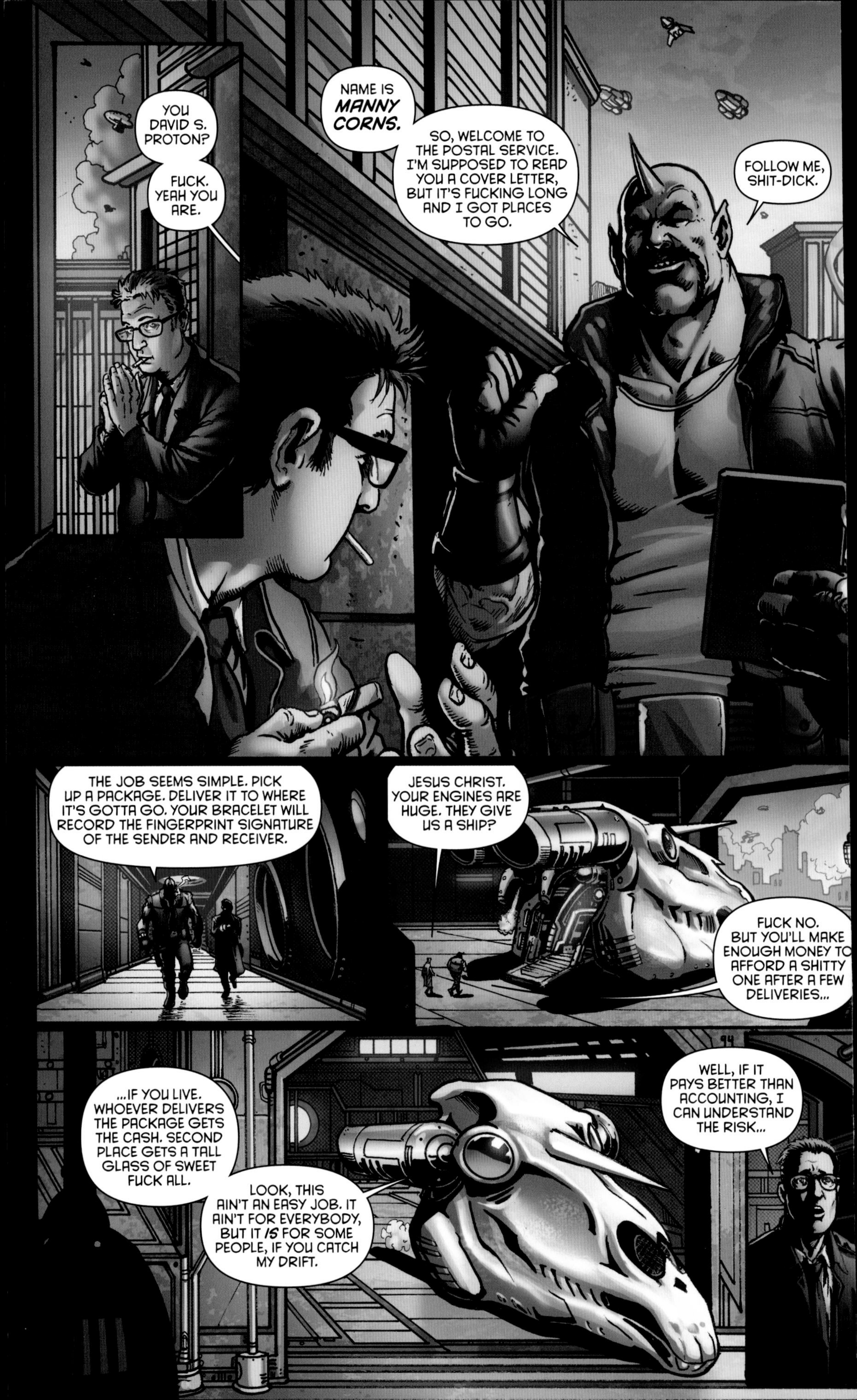
YOU DAVID S. PROTON?
FUCK. YEAH YOU ARE.
NAME IS MANNY CORNS.
SO, WELCOME TO THE POSTAL SERVICE. I'M SUPPOSED TO READ YOU A COVER LETTER, BUT IT'S FUCKING LONG AND I GOT PLACES TO GO.
FOLLOW ME, SHIT-DICK.
THE JOB SEEMS SIMPLE. PICK UP A PACKAGE. DELIVER IT TO WHERE IT'S GOTTA GO. YOUR BRACELET WILL RECORD THE FINGERPRINT SIGNATURE OF THE SENDER AND RECEIVER.
JESUS CHRIST. YOUR ENGINES ARE HUGE. THEY GIVE US A SHIP?
FUCK NO. BUT YOU'LL MAKE ENOUGH MONEY TO AFFORD A SHITTY ONE AFTER A FEW DELIVERIES...
...IF YOU LIVE. WHOEVER DELIVERS THE PACKAGE GETS THE CASH. SECOND PLACE GETS A TALL GLASS OF SWEET FUCK ALL.
LOOK, THIS AIN'T AN EASY JOB. IT AIN'T FOR EVERYBODY, BUT IT *IS* FOR SOME PEOPLE, IF YOU CATCH MY DRIFT.
WELL, IF IT PAYS BETTER THAN ACCOUNTING, I CAN UNDERSTAND THE RISK...

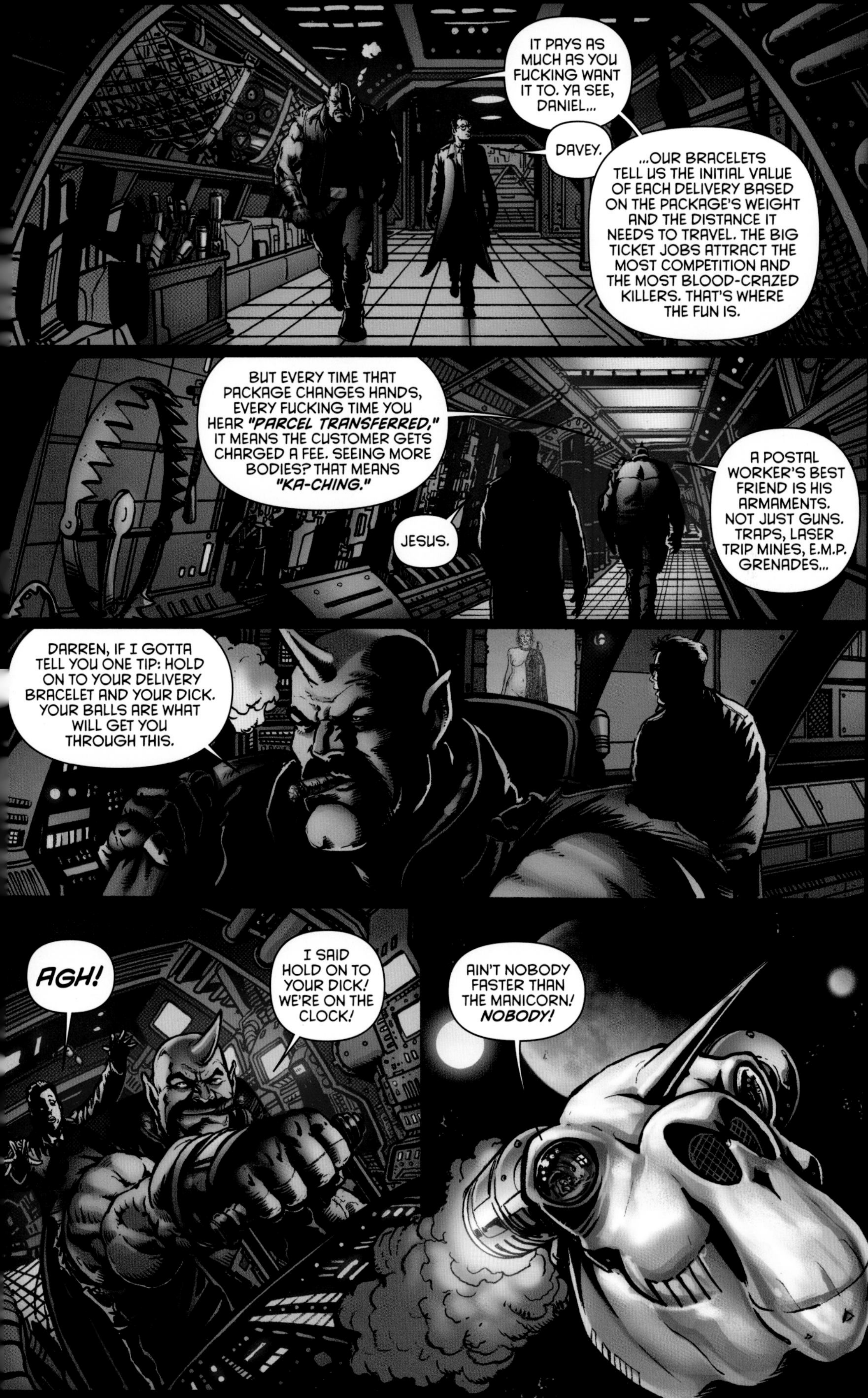
IT PAYS AS MUCH AS YOU FUCKING WANT IT TO. YA SEE, DANIEL...
DAVEY.
...OUR BRACELETS TELL US THE INITIAL VALUE OF EACH DELIVERY BASED ON THE PACKAGE'S WEIGHT AND THE DISTANCE IT NEEDS TO TRAVEL. THE BIG TICKET JOBS ATTRACT THE MOST COMPETITION AND THE MOST BLOOD-CRAZED KILLERS. THAT'S WHERE THE FUN IS.
BUT EVERY TIME THAT PACKAGE CHANGES HANDS, EVERY FUCKING TIME YOU HEAR "PARCEL TRANSFERRED," IT MEANS THE CUSTOMER GETS CHARGED A FEE. SEEING MORE BODIES? THAT MEANS "KA-CHING."
JESUS.
A POSTAL WORKER'S BEST FRIEND IS HIS ARMAMENTS. NOT JUST GUNS. TRAPS, LASER TRIP MINES, E.M.P. GRENADES...
DARREN, IF I GOTTA TELL YOU ONE TIP: HOLD ON TO YOUR DELIVERY BRACELET AND YOUR DICK. YOUR BALLS ARE WHAT WILL GET YOU THROUGH THIS.
AGH!
I SAID HOLD ON TO YOUR DICK! WE'RE ON THE CLOCK!
AIN'T NOBODY FASTER THAN THE MANICORN! NOBODY!

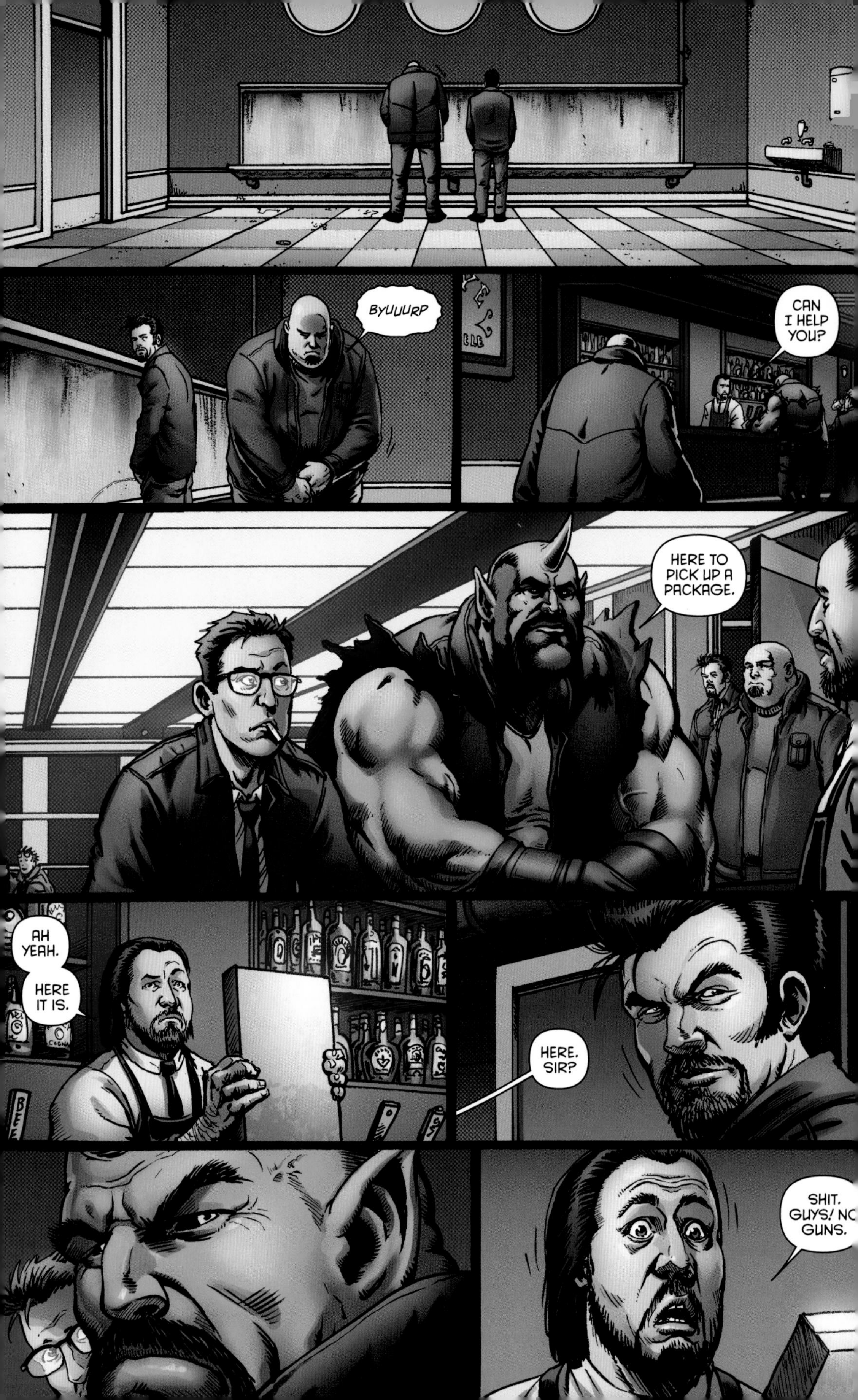
BYUUURP
CAN I HELP YOU?
HERE TO PICK UP A PACKAGE.
AH YEAH.
HERE IT IS.
HERE. SIR?
SHIT. GUYS! NO GUNS.

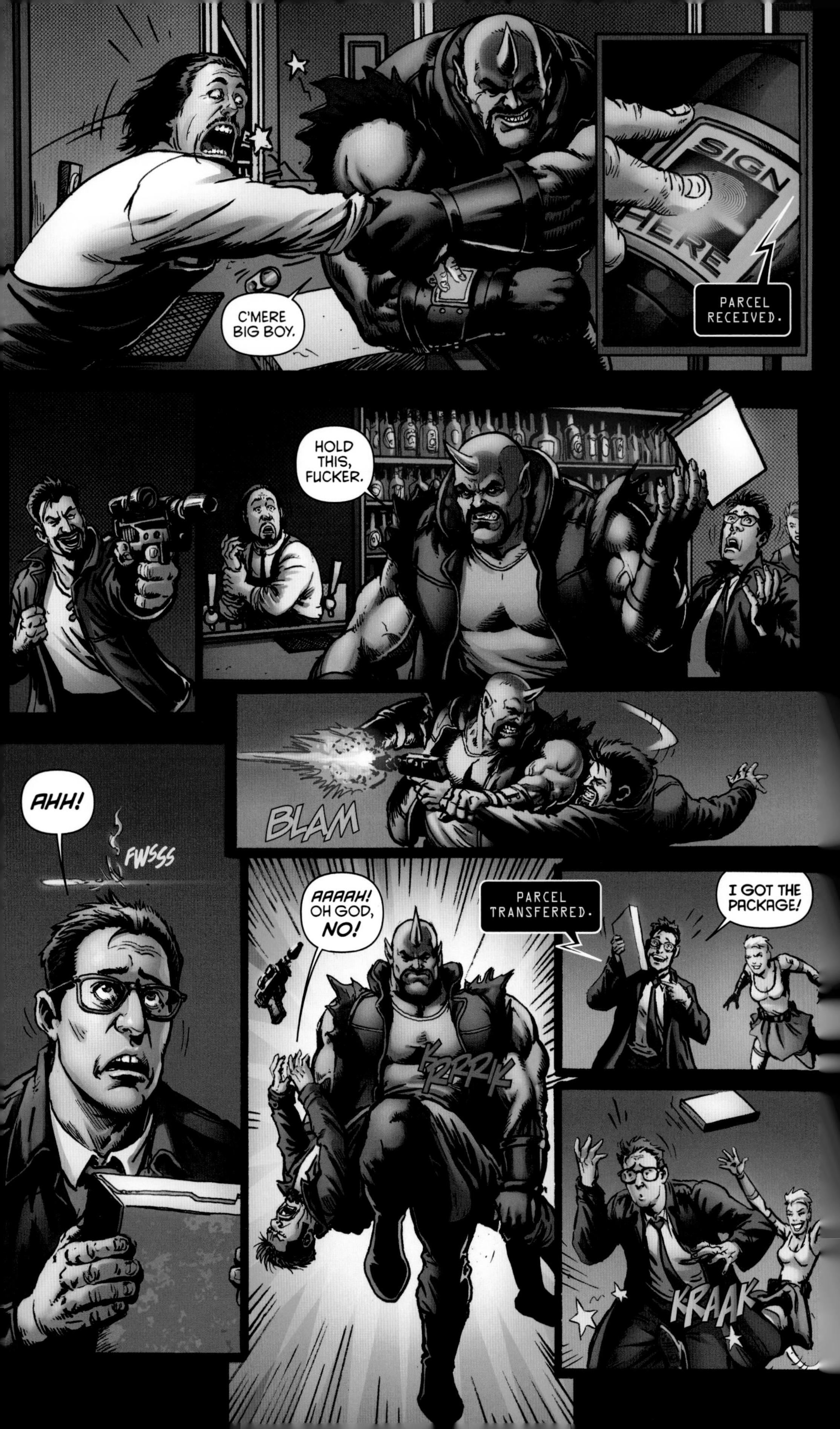

SIGN HERE
C'MERE BIG BOY.
PARCEL RECEIVED.
HOLD THIS, FUCKER.
BLAM
AHH!
FWSSS
AAAAH! OH GOD, NO!
PARCEL TRANSFERRED.
I GOT THE PACKAGE!
KRRRIK
KRAAK

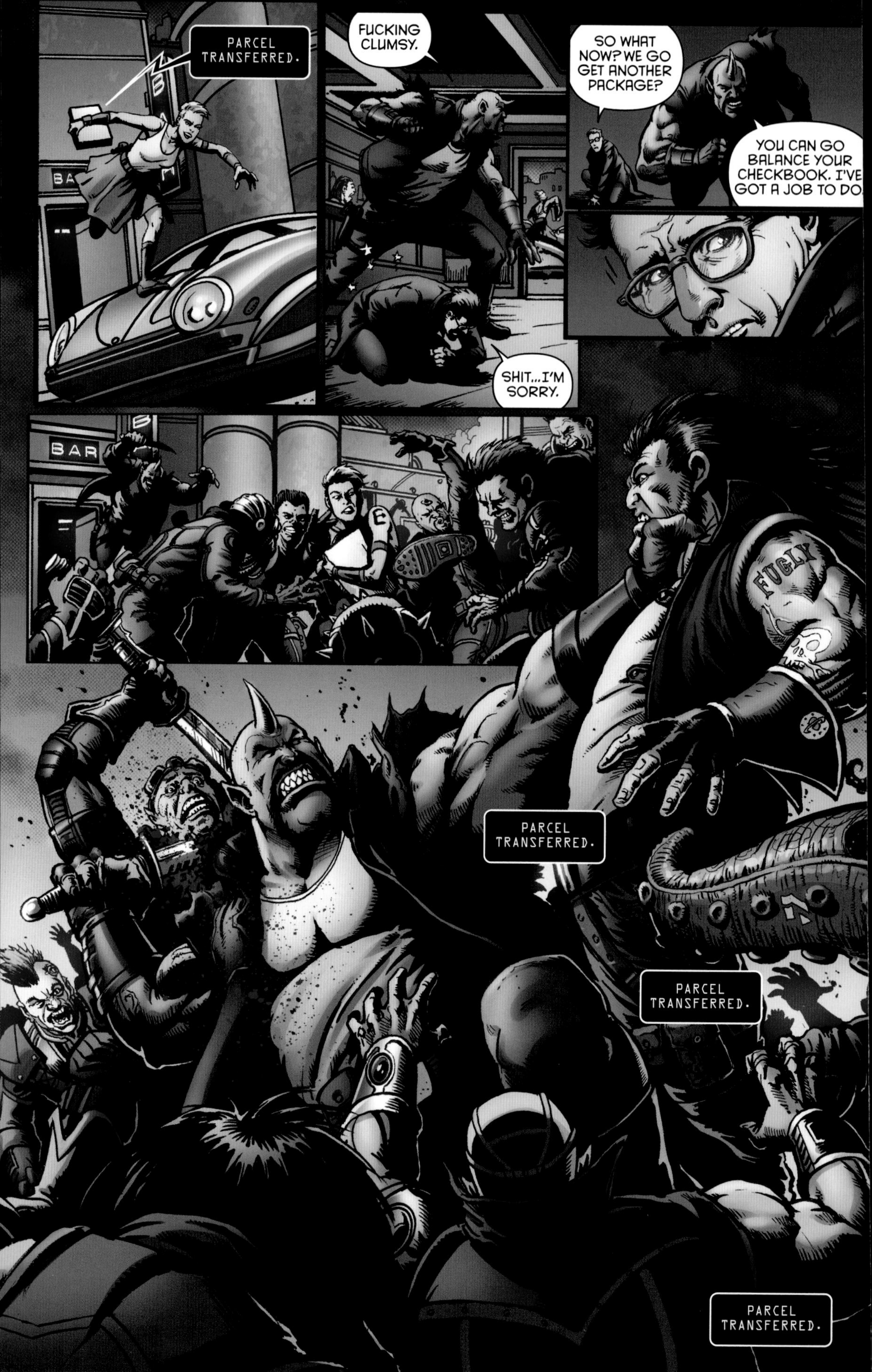
PARCEL TRANSFERRED.
FUCKING CLUMSY.
SHIT...I'M SORRY.
SO WHAT NOW? WE GO GET ANOTHER PACKAGE?
YOU CAN GO BALANCE YOUR CHECKBOOK. I'VE GOT A JOB TO DO.
BAR
FUGLY
PARCEL TRANSFERRED.
PARCEL TRANSFERRED.
PARCEL TRANSFERRED.

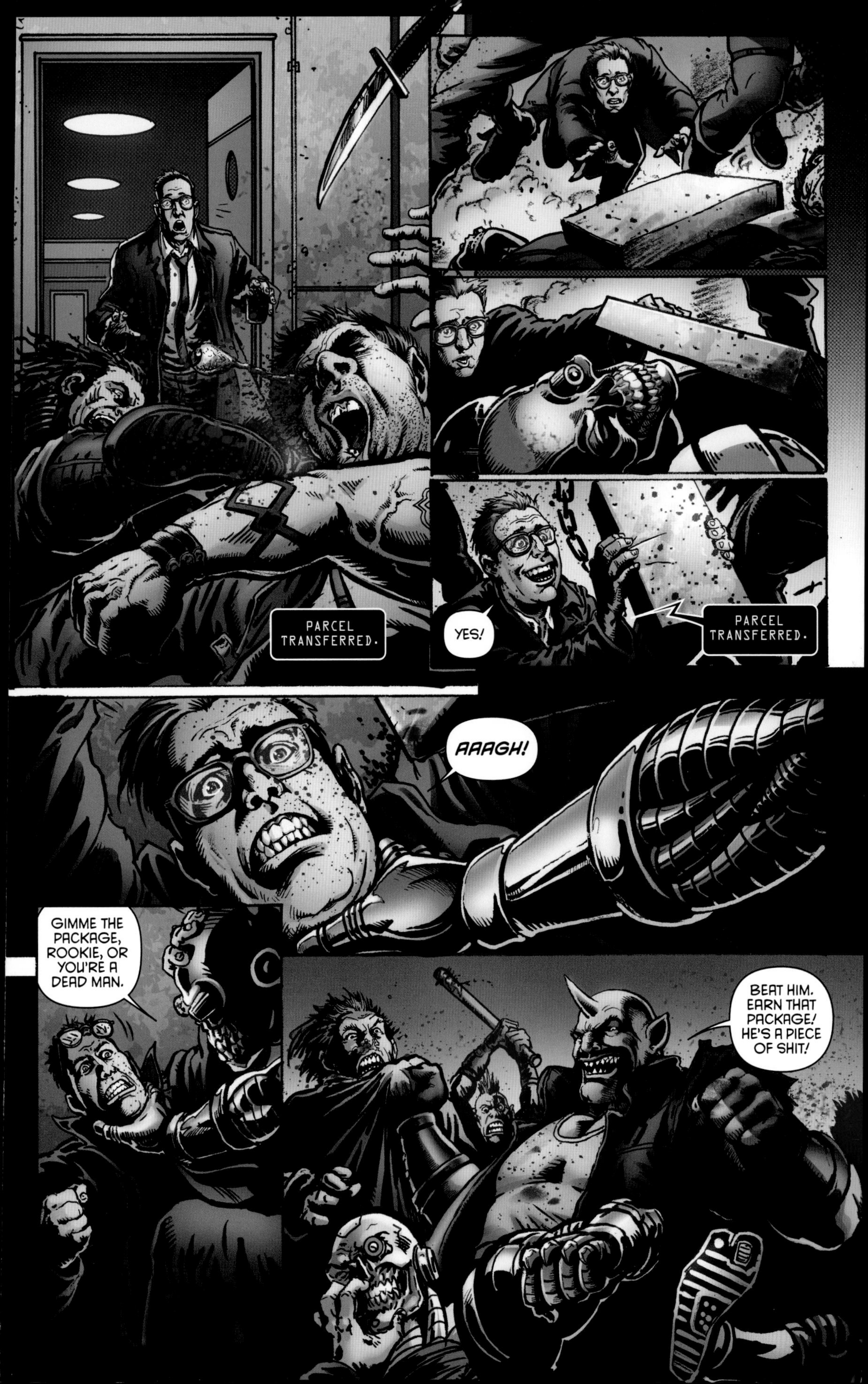
PARCEL TRANSFERRED.
YES!
PARCEL TRANSFERRED.
AAAGH!
GIMME THE PACKAGE, ROOKIE, OR YOU'RE A DEAD MAN.
BEAT HIM. EARN THAT PACKAGE! HE'S A PIECE OF SHIT!

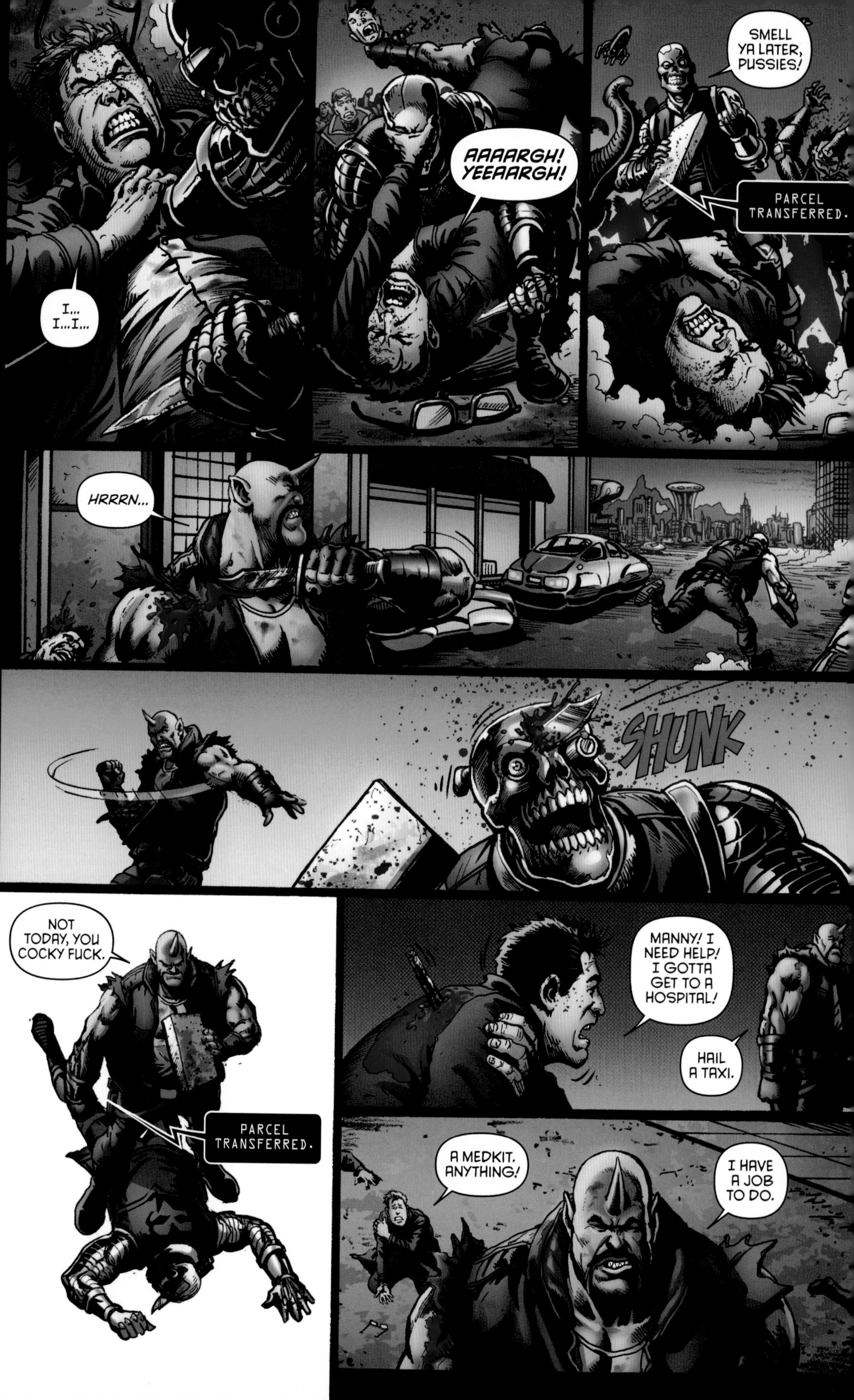
I... I...I...
AAAARGH! YEEAARGH!
SMELL YA LATER, PUSSIES!
PARCEL TRANSFERRED.
HRRRN...
SHUNK
NOT TODAY, YOU COCKY FUCK.
PARCEL TRANSFERRED.
MANNY! I NEED HELP! I GOTTA GET TO A HOSPITAL!
HAIL A TAXI.
A MEDKIT. ANYTHING!
I HAVE A JOB TO DO.

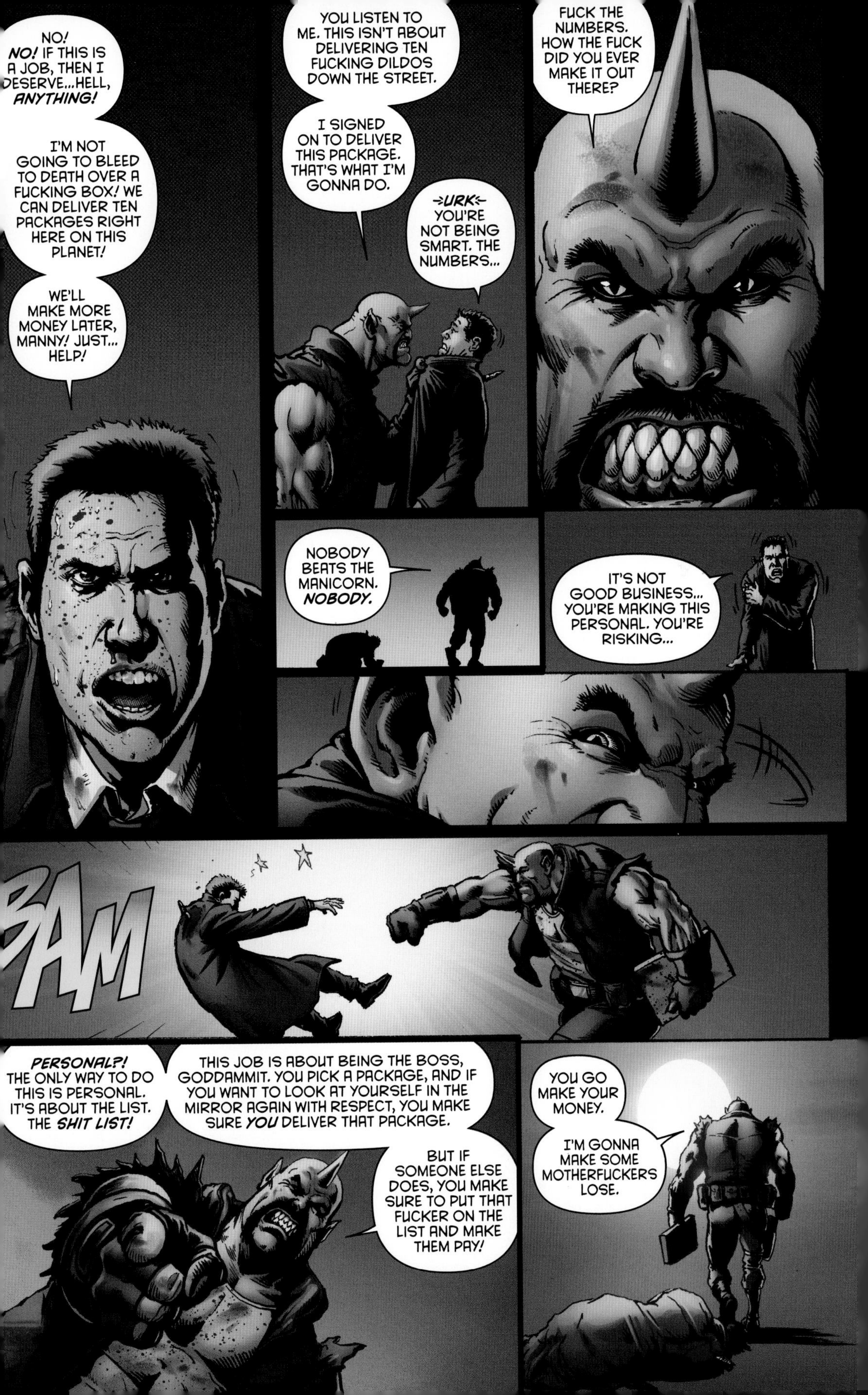
NO! NO! IF THIS IS A JOB, THEN I DESERVE...HELL, ANYTHING!
I'M NOT GOING TO BLEED TO DEATH OVER A FUCKING BOX! WE CAN DELIVER TEN PACKAGES RIGHT HERE ON THIS PLANET!
WE'LL MAKE MORE MONEY LATER, MANNY! JUST... HELP!
YOU LISTEN TO ME. THIS ISN'T ABOUT DELIVERING TEN FUCKING DILDOS DOWN THE STREET.
I SIGNED ON TO DELIVER THIS PACKAGE. THAT'S WHAT I'M GONNA DO.
URK
YOU'RE NOT BEING SMART. THE NUMBERS...
FUCK THE NUMBERS. HOW THE FUCK DID YOU EVER MAKE IT OUT THERE?
NOBODY BEATS THE MANICORN. NOBODY.
IT'S NOT GOOD BUSINESS... YOU'RE MAKING THIS PERSONAL. YOU'RE RISKING...
BAM
PERSONAL?! THE ONLY WAY TO DO THIS IS PERSONAL. IT'S ABOUT THE LIST. THE SHIT LIST!
THIS JOB IS ABOUT BEING THE BOSS, GODDAMMIT. YOU PICK A PACKAGE, AND IF YOU WANT TO LOOK AT YOURSELF IN THE MIRROR AGAIN WITH RESPECT, YOU MAKE SURE YOU DELIVER THAT PACKAGE.
BUT IF SOMEONE ELSE DOES, YOU MAKE SURE TO PUT THAT FUCKER ON THE LIST AND MAKE THEM PAY!
YOU GO MAKE YOUR MONEY.
I'M GONNA MAKE SOME MOTHERFUCKERS LOSE.

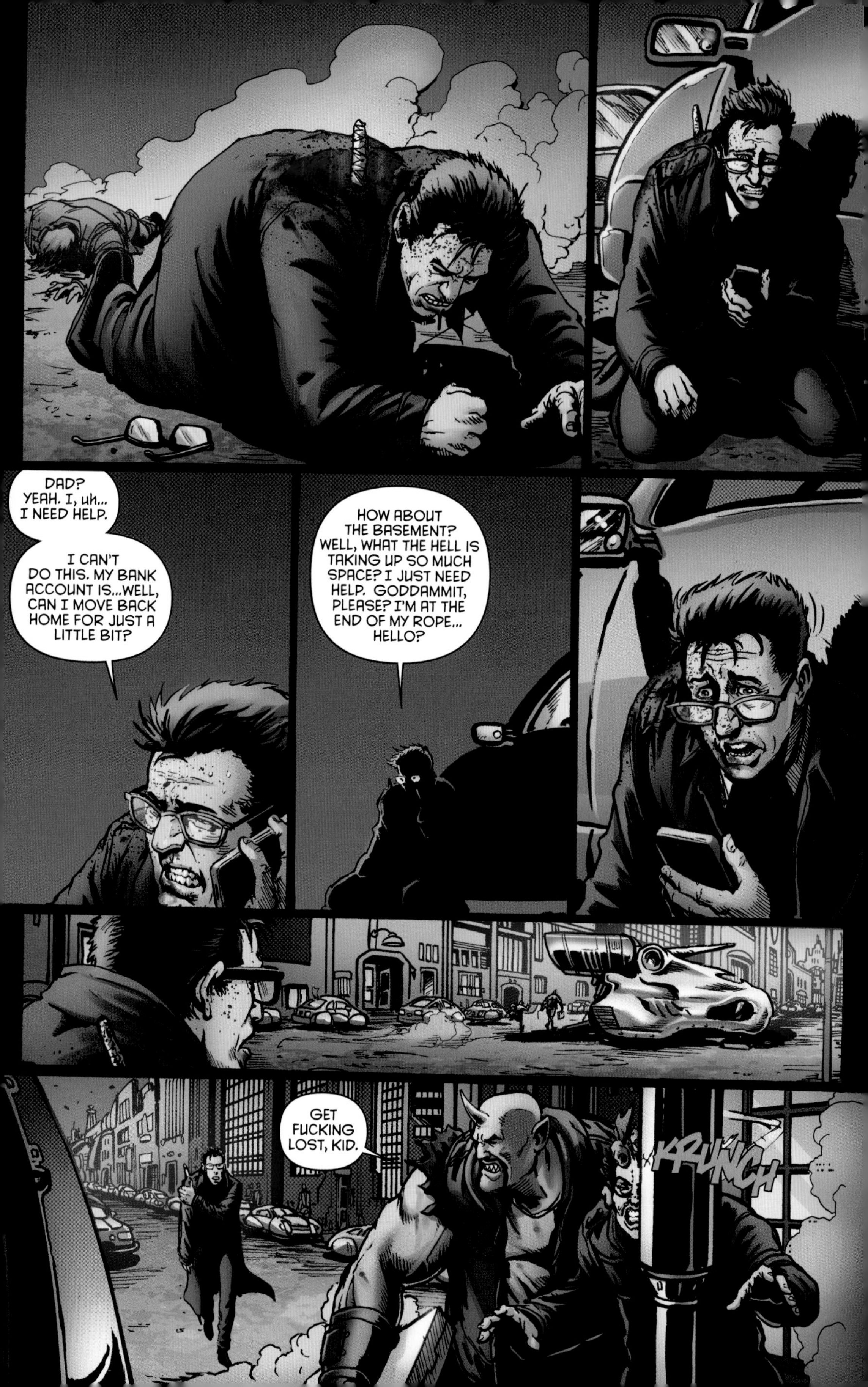
DAD? YEAH. I, uh... I NEED HELP.
I CAN'T DO THIS. MY BANK ACCOUNT IS...WELL, CAN I MOVE BACK HOME FOR JUST A LITTLE BIT?
HOW ABOUT THE BASEMENT? WELL, WHAT THE HELL IS TAKING UP SO MUCH SPACE? I JUST NEED HELP. GODDAMMIT, PLEASE? I'M AT THE END OF MY ROPE... HELLO?
GET FUCKING LOST, KID.
KRUNCH

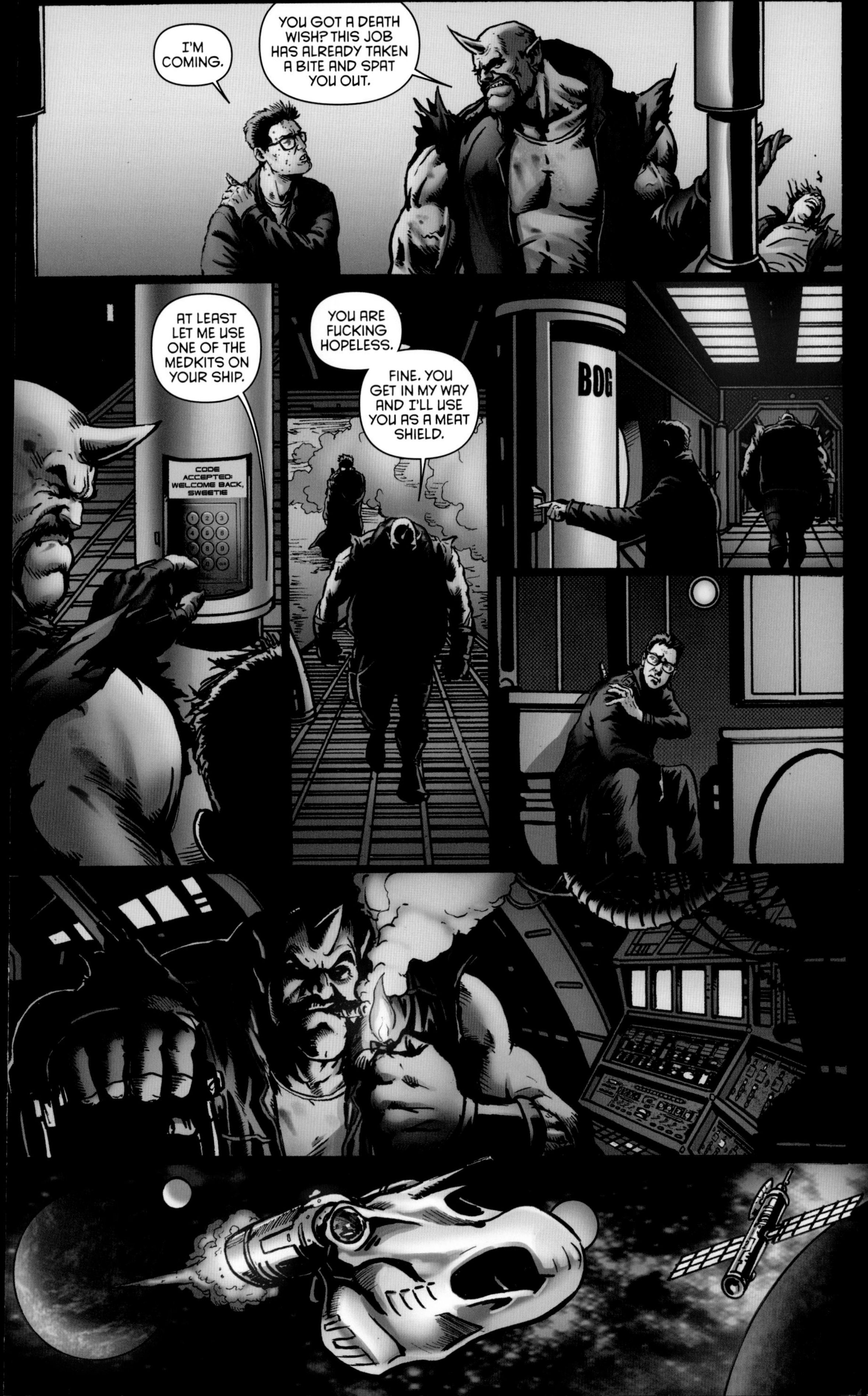
I'M COMING.
YOU GOT A DEATH WISH? THIS JOB HAS ALREADY TAKEN A BITE AND SPAT YOU OUT.
AT LEAST LET ME USE ONE OF THE MEDKITS ON YOUR SHIP.
CODE ACCEPTED: WELCOME BACK, SWEETIE
YOU ARE FUCKING HOPELESS.
FINE. YOU GET IN MY WAY AND I'LL USE YOU AS A MEAT SHIELD.
BOG

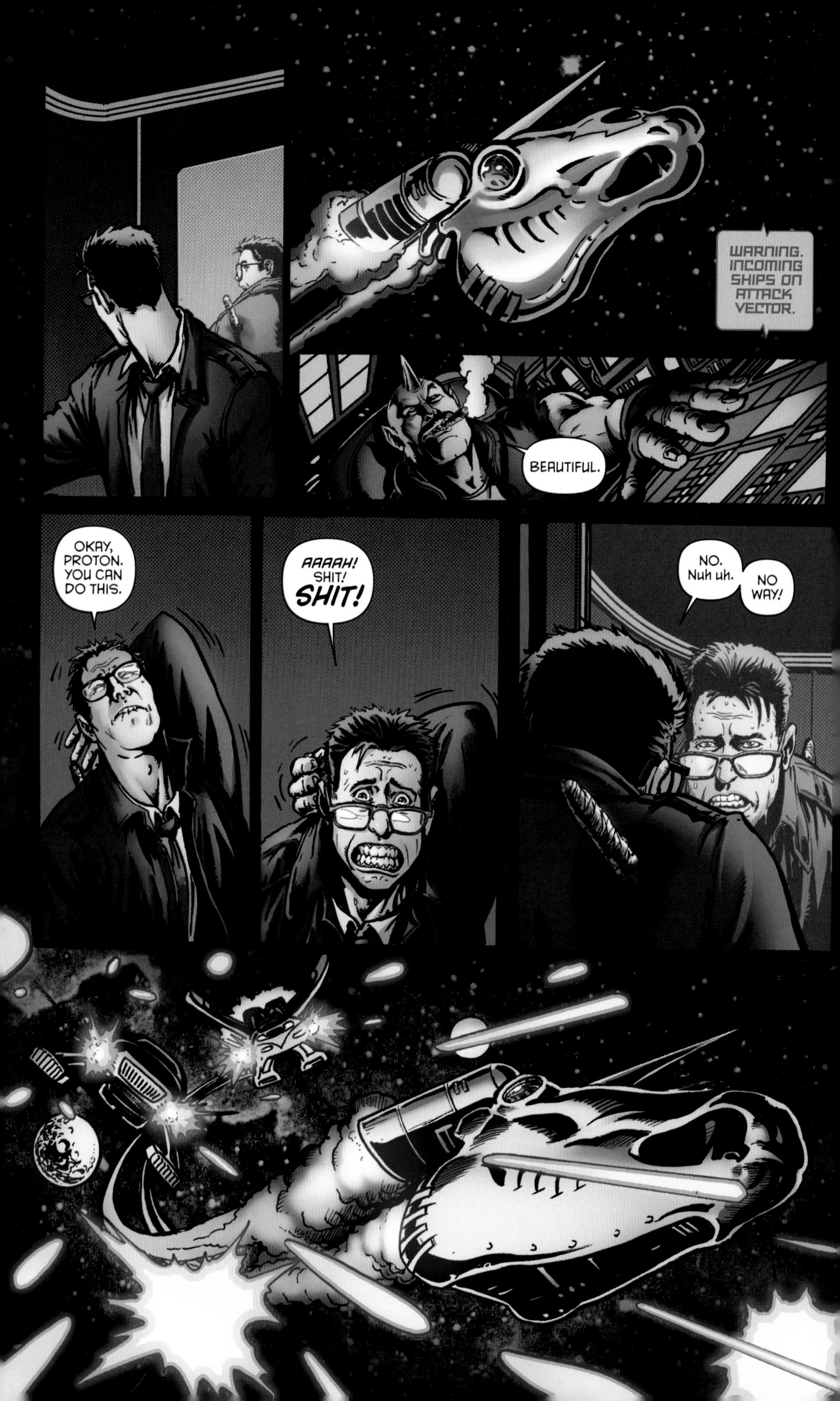
WARNING. INCOMING SHIPS ON ATTACK VECTOR.
BEAUTIFUL.
OKAY, PROTON. YOU CAN DO THIS.
AAAAH! SHIT! SHIT!
NO. Nuh uh.
NO WAY!

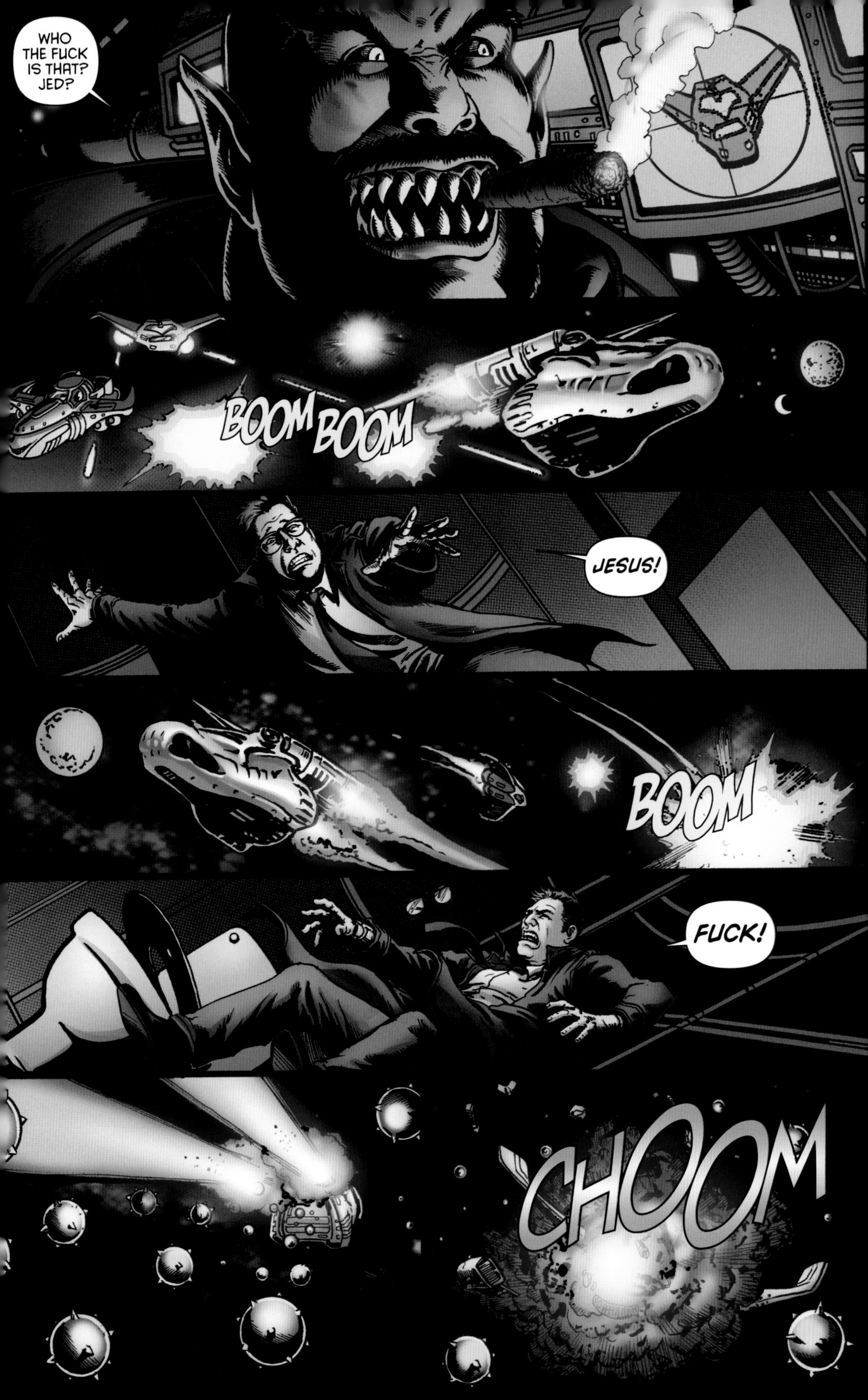
WHO THE FUCK IS THAT? JED?
BOOM BOOM
JESUS!
BOOM
FUCK!
CHOOM

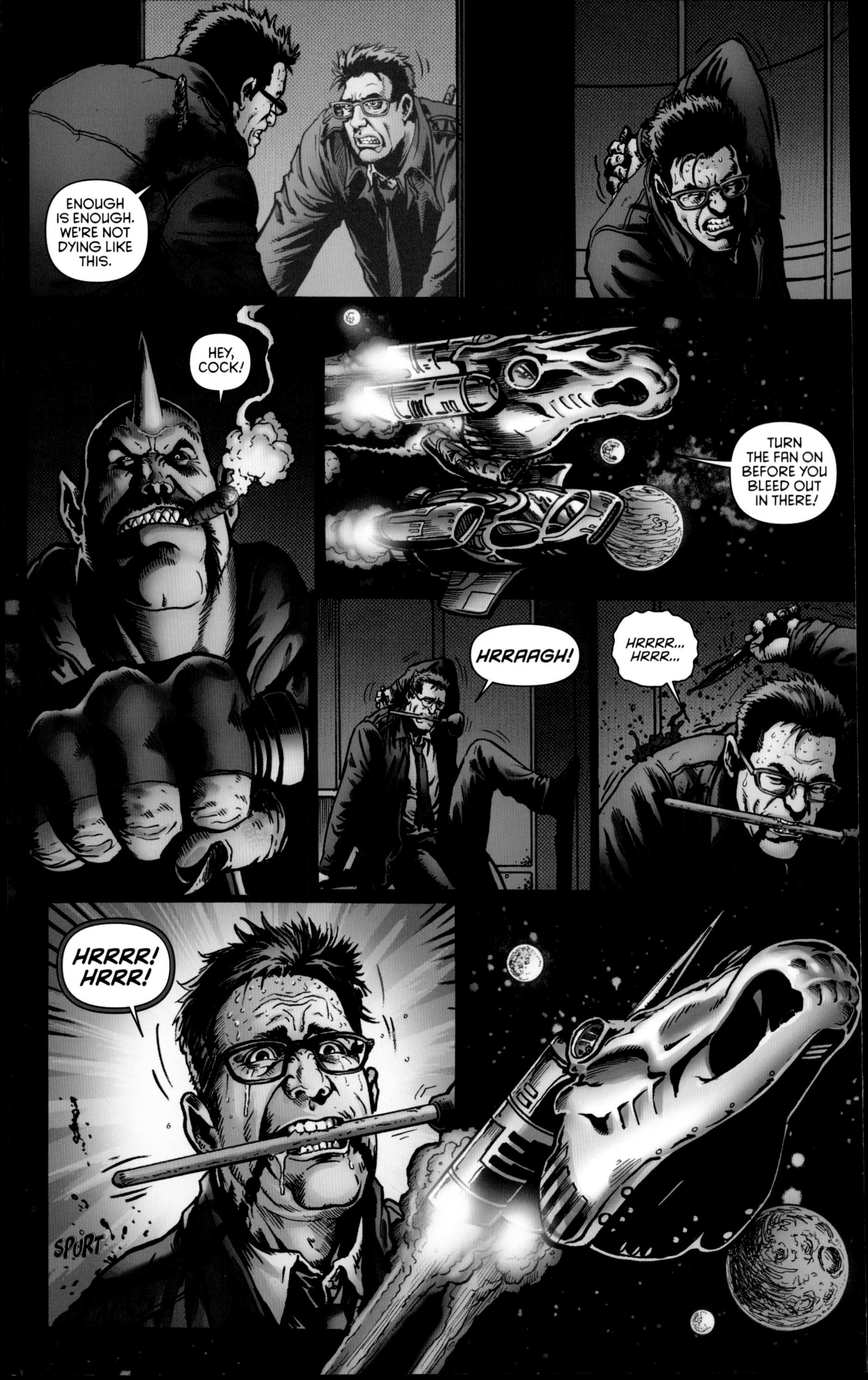
ENOUGH IS ENOUGH. WE'RE NOT DYING LIKE THIS.
HEY, COCK!
TURN THE FAN ON BEFORE YOU BLEED OUT IN THERE!
HRRAAGH!
HRRRR... HRRR...
HRRRR! HRRR!
SPURT

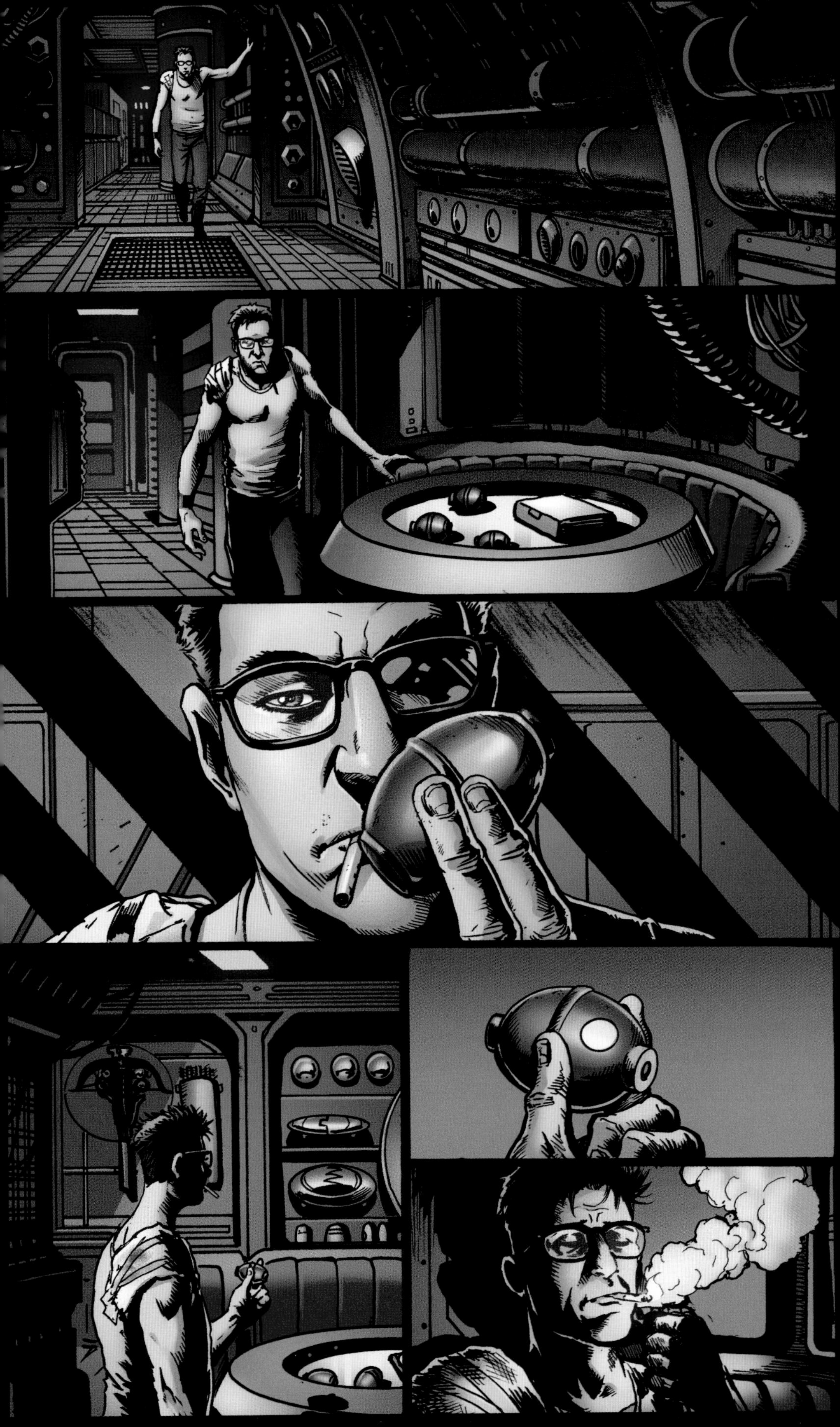

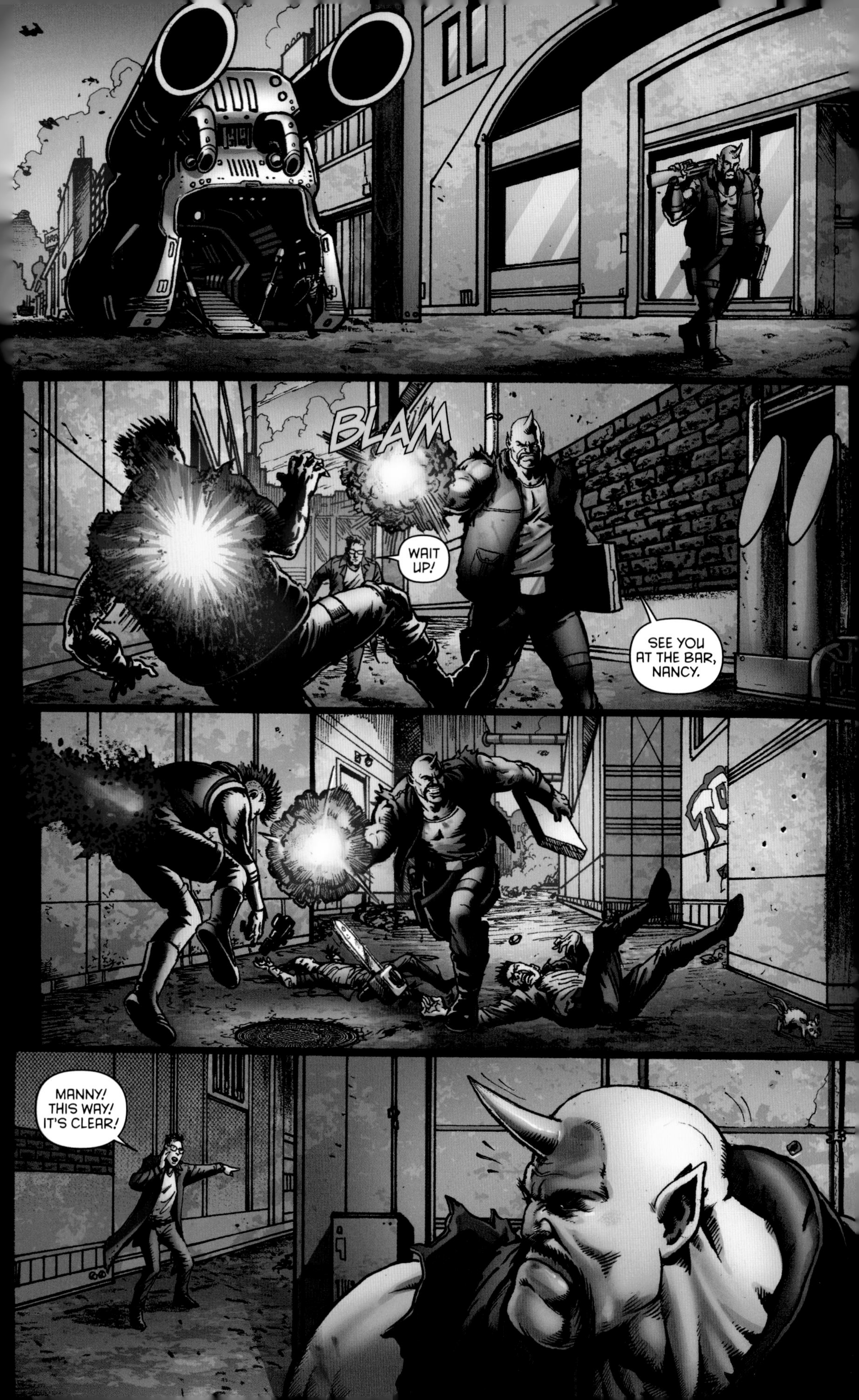
BLAM
WAIT UP!
SEE YOU AT THE BAR, NANCY.
MANNY! THIS WAY! IT'S CLEAR!

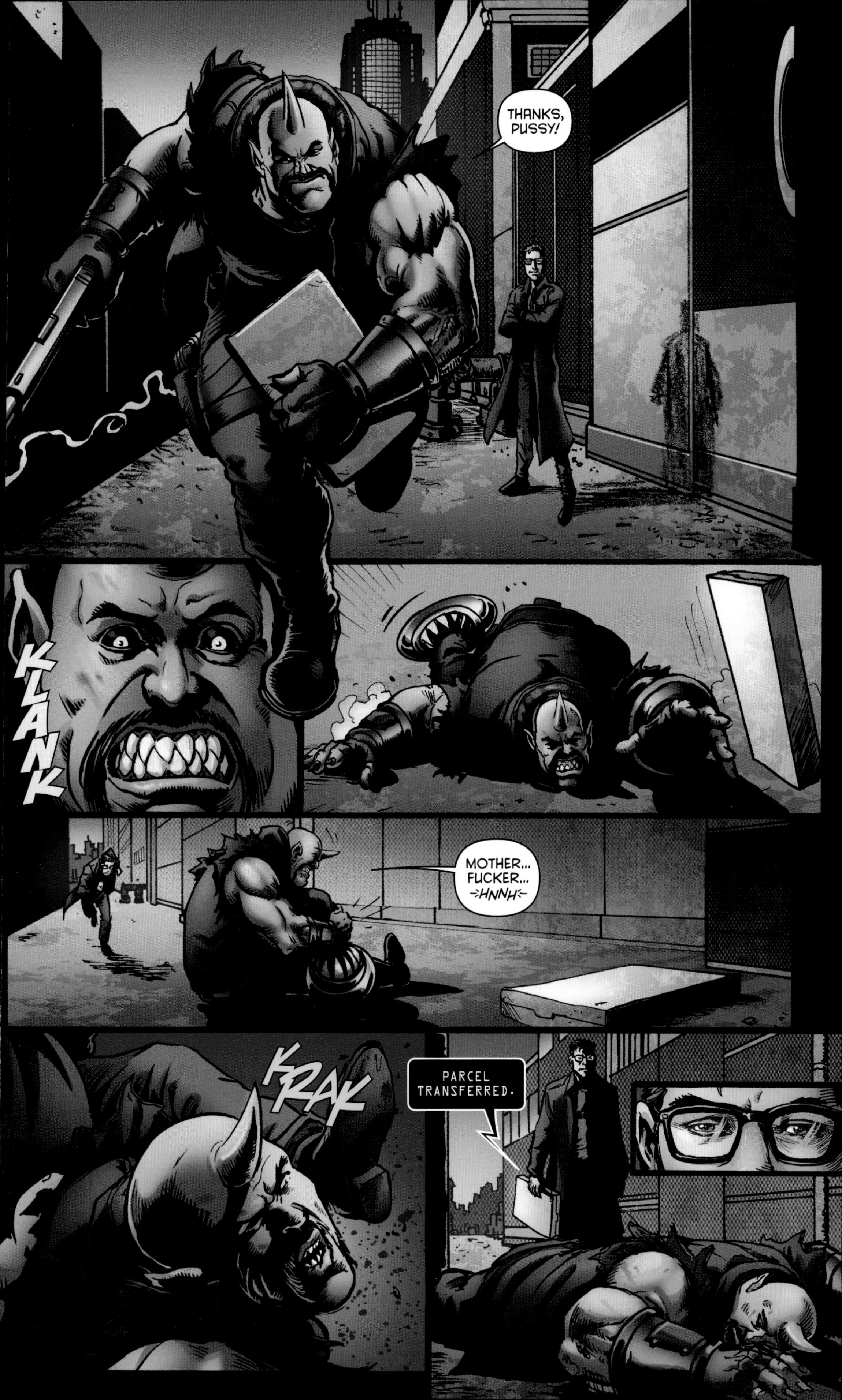
THANKS, PUSSY!
KLANK
MOTHER... FUCKER... -HNNH-
KRAK
PARCEL TRANSFERRED.

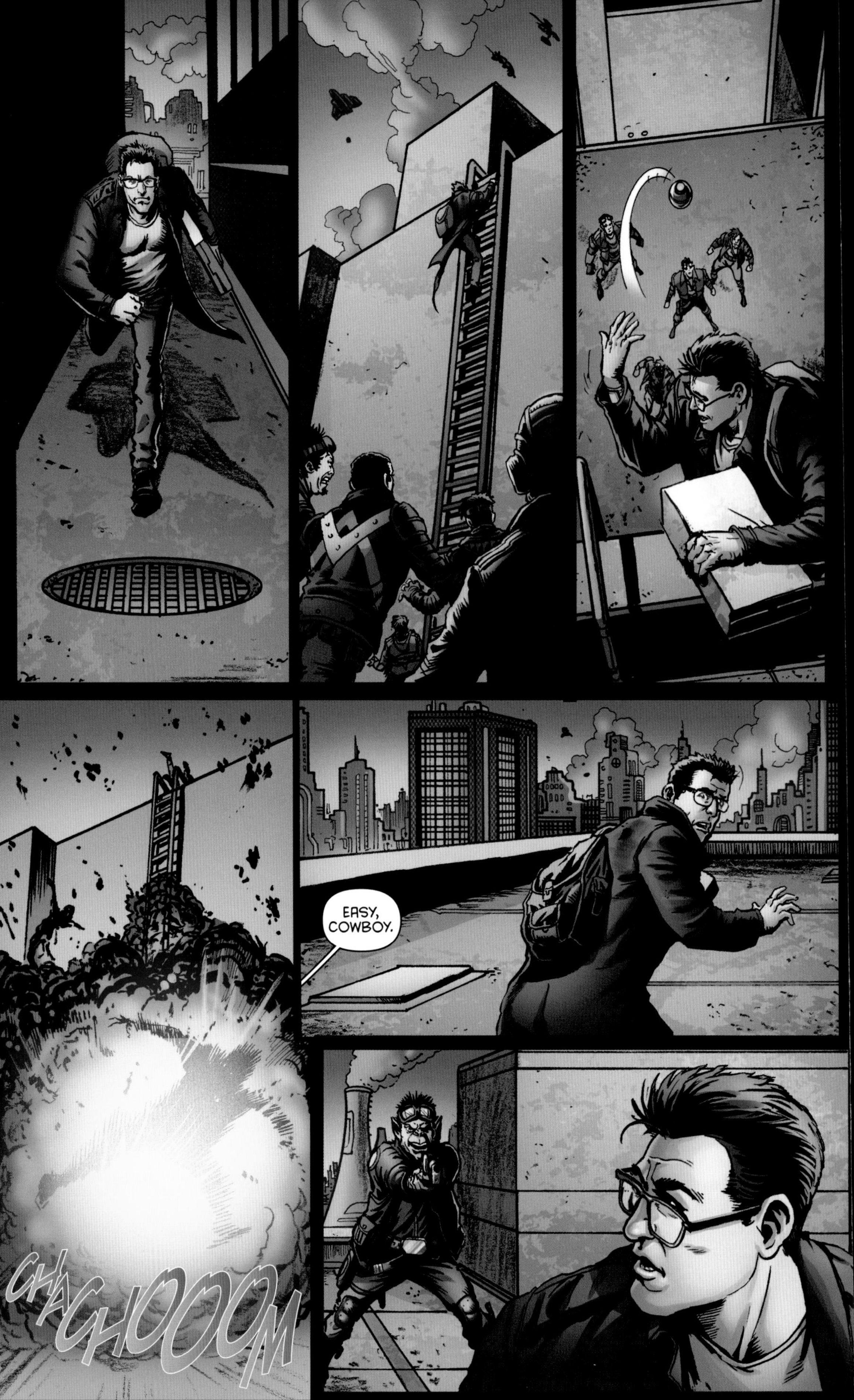
EASY, COWBOY.
CHA-CHOOOM

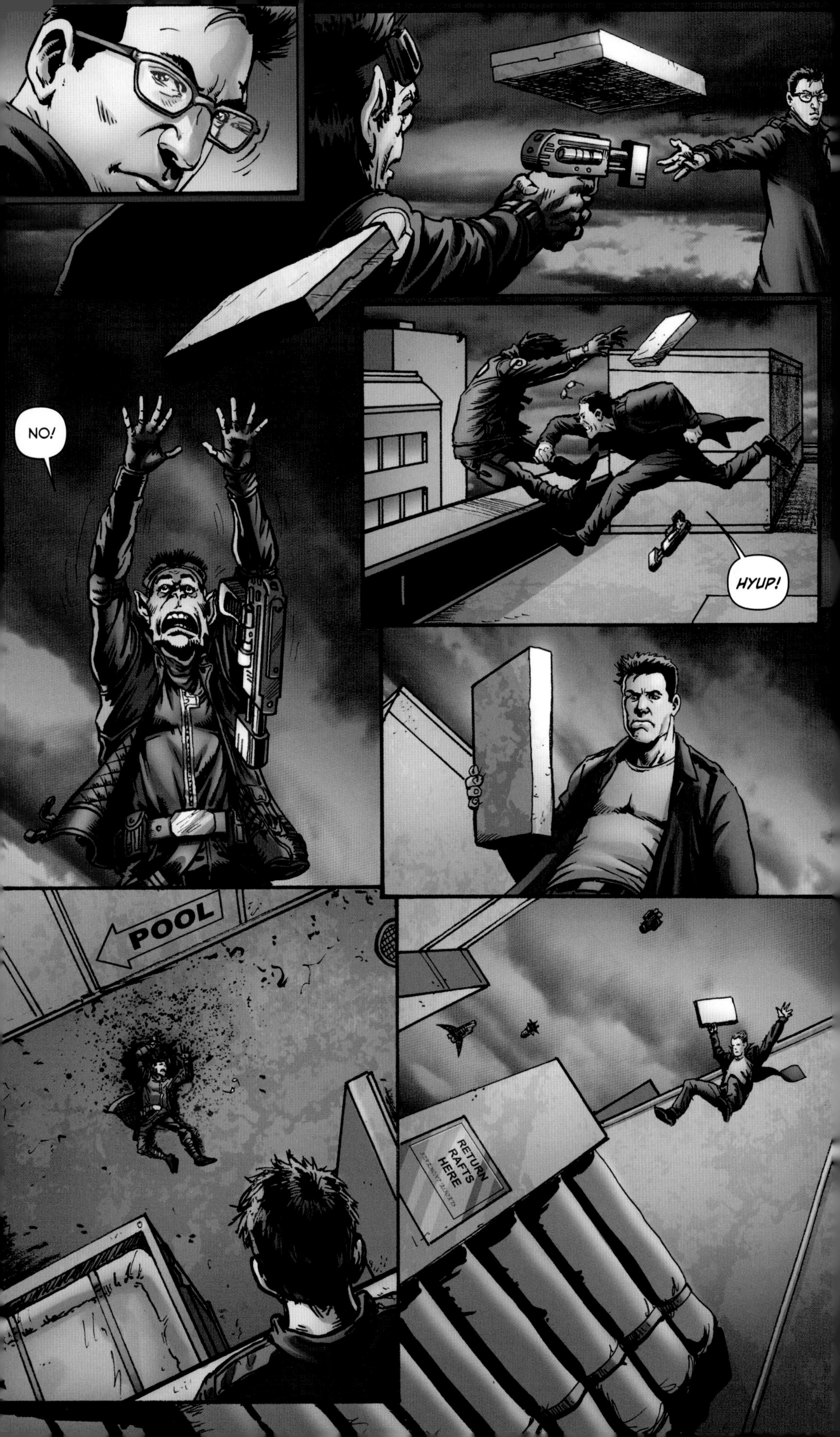
NO!
HYUP!
POOL
RETURN
RAFTS
HERE

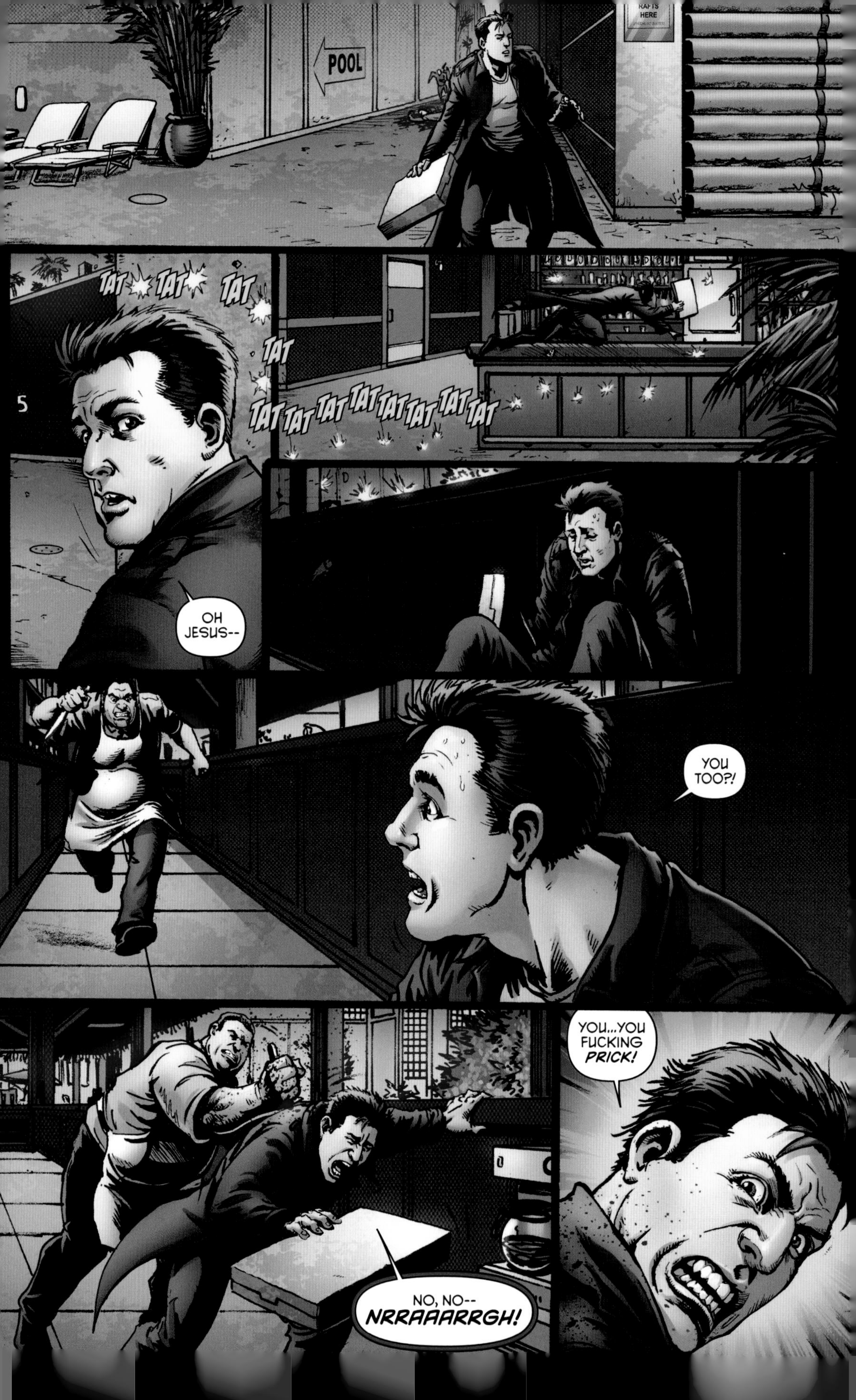
POOL
TAT TAT TAT
TAT
TAT TAT TAT TAT TAT TAT TAT TAT
OH JESUS--
YOU TOO?!
NO, NO-- NRRAAARRGH!
YOU...YOU FUCKING PRICK!

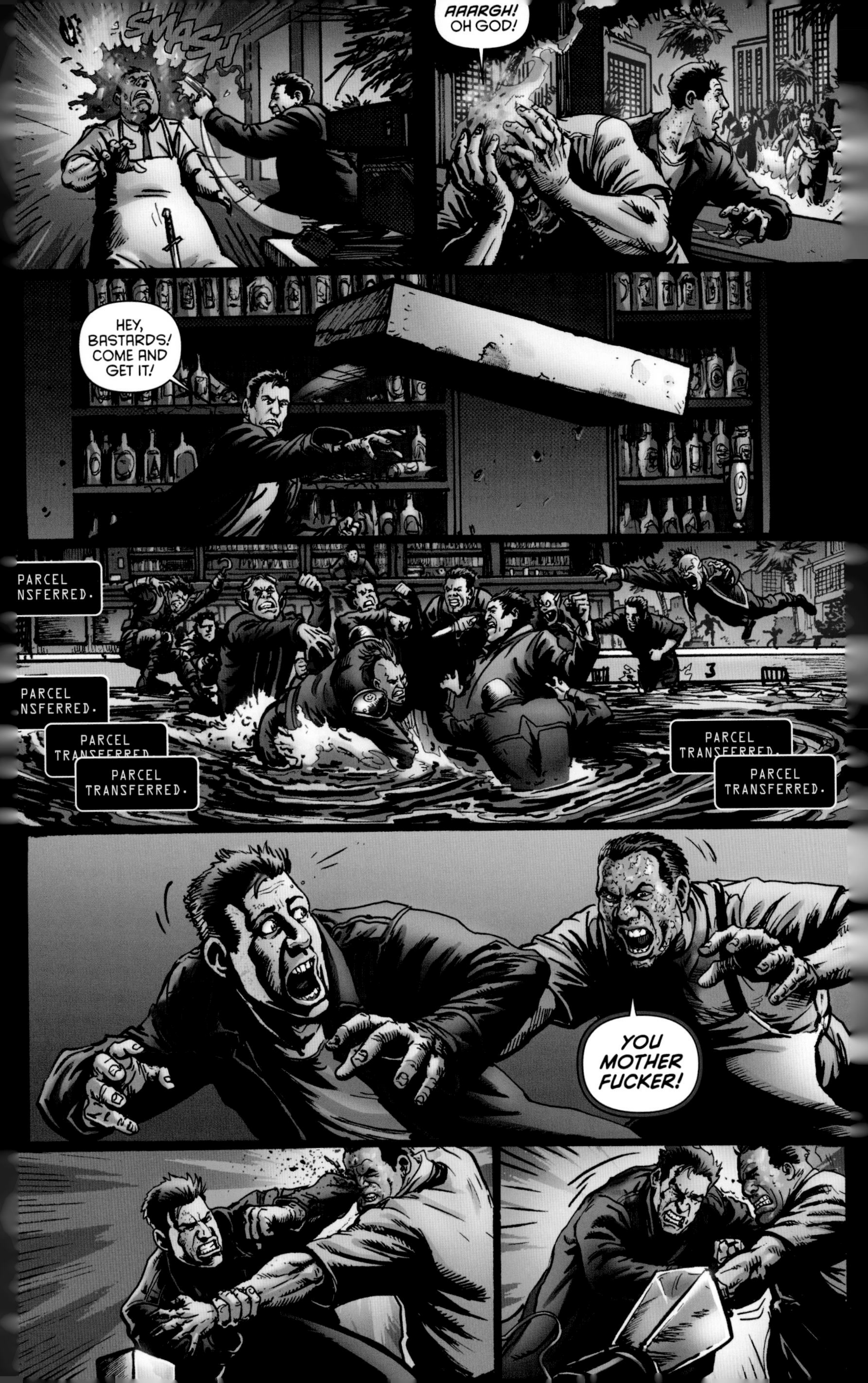
SMASH
AAARGH! OH GOD!
HEY, BASTARDS! COME AND GET IT!
PARCEL TRANSFERRED.
PARCEL TRANSFERRED.
PARCEL TRANSFERRED.
PARCEL TRANSFERRED.
PARCEL TRANSFERRED.
PARCEL TRANSFERRED.
YOU MOTHER FUCKER!

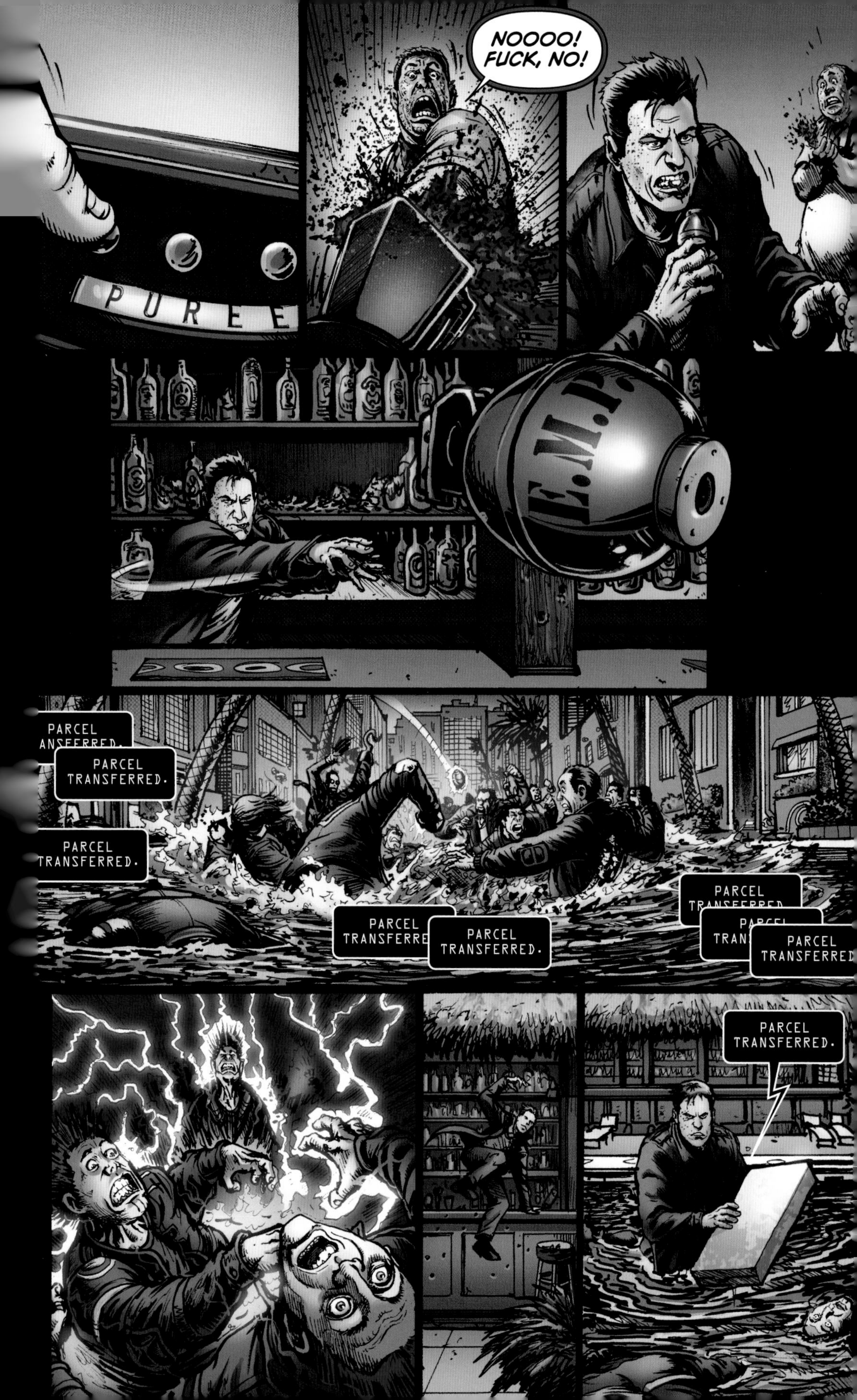
NOOOO! FUCK, NO!
PUREE
E.M.P.
PARCEL TRANSFERRED.
PARCEL TRANSFERRED.
PARCEL TRANSFERRED.
PARCEL TRANSFERRED.

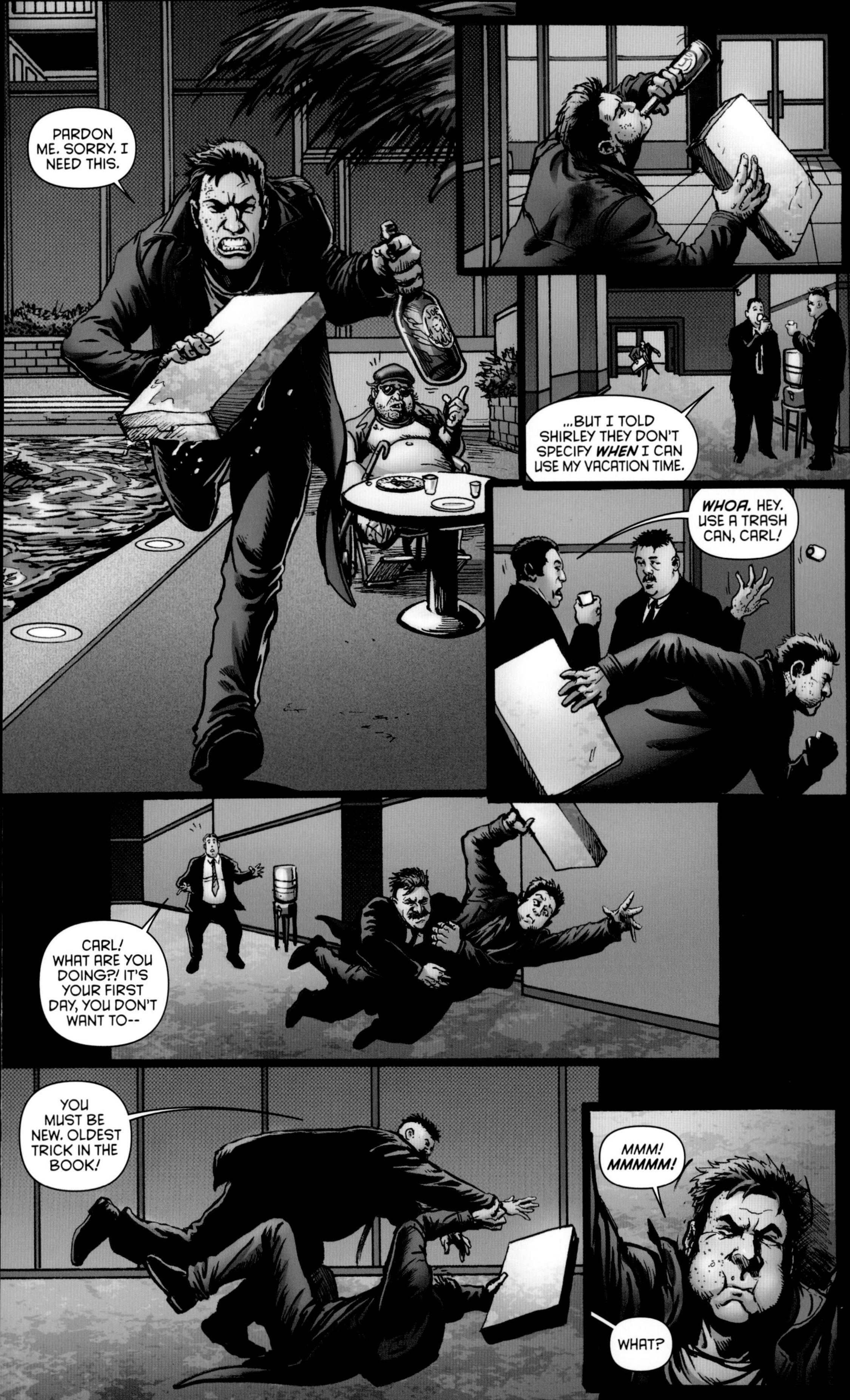
PARDON ME. SORRY. I NEED THIS.
...BUT I TOLD SHIRLEY THEY DON'T SPECIFY *WHEN* I CAN USE MY VACATION TIME.
WHOA. HEY. USE A TRASH CAN, CARL!
CARL! WHAT ARE YOU DOING?! IT'S YOUR FIRST DAY, YOU DON'T WANT TO--
YOU MUST BE NEW. OLDEST TRICK IN THE BOOK!
MMM! *MMMMM!*
WHAT?

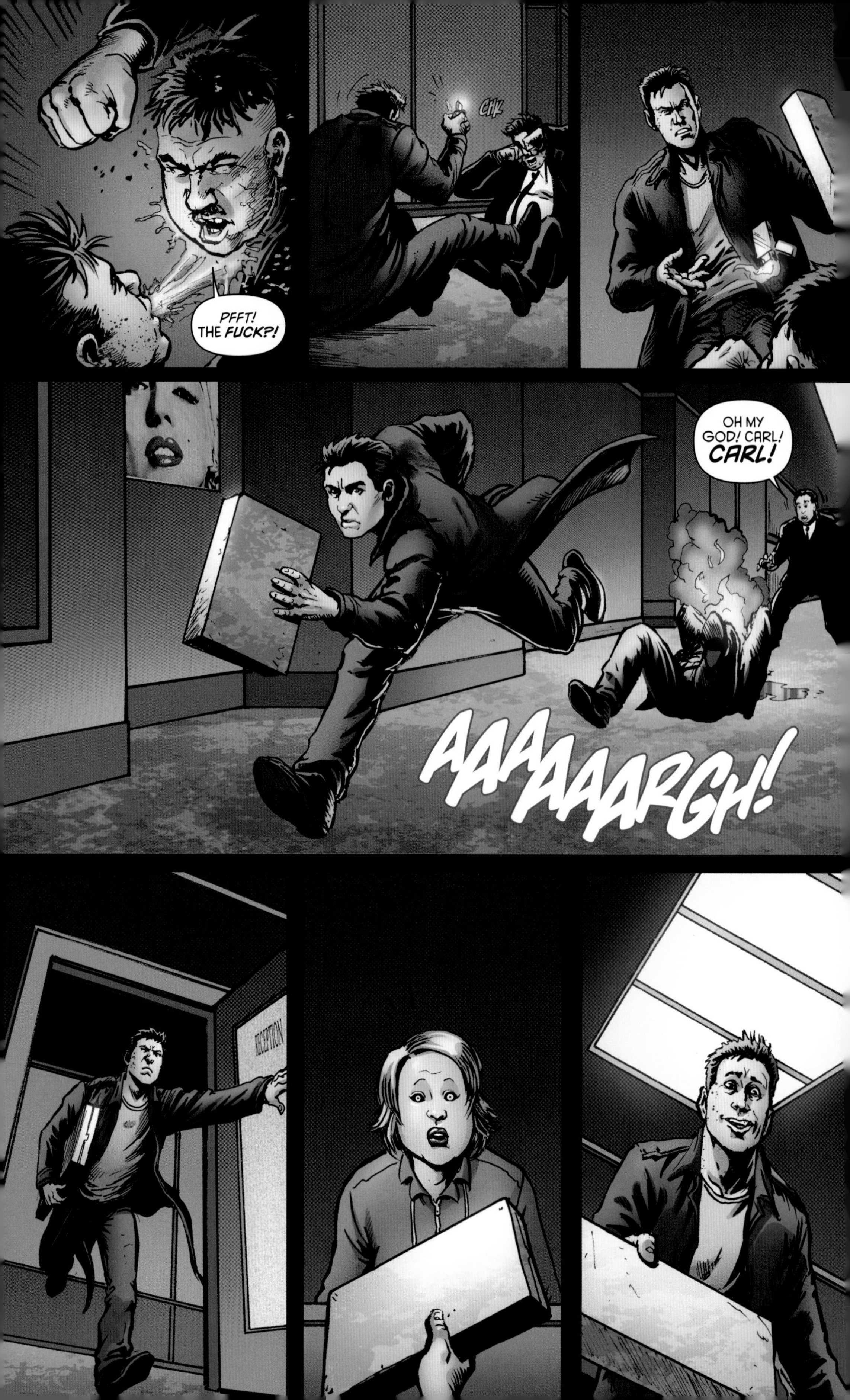
PFFT! THE FUCK?!
CHK
OH MY GOD! CARL! CARL!
AAAAAAARGH!
RECEPTION

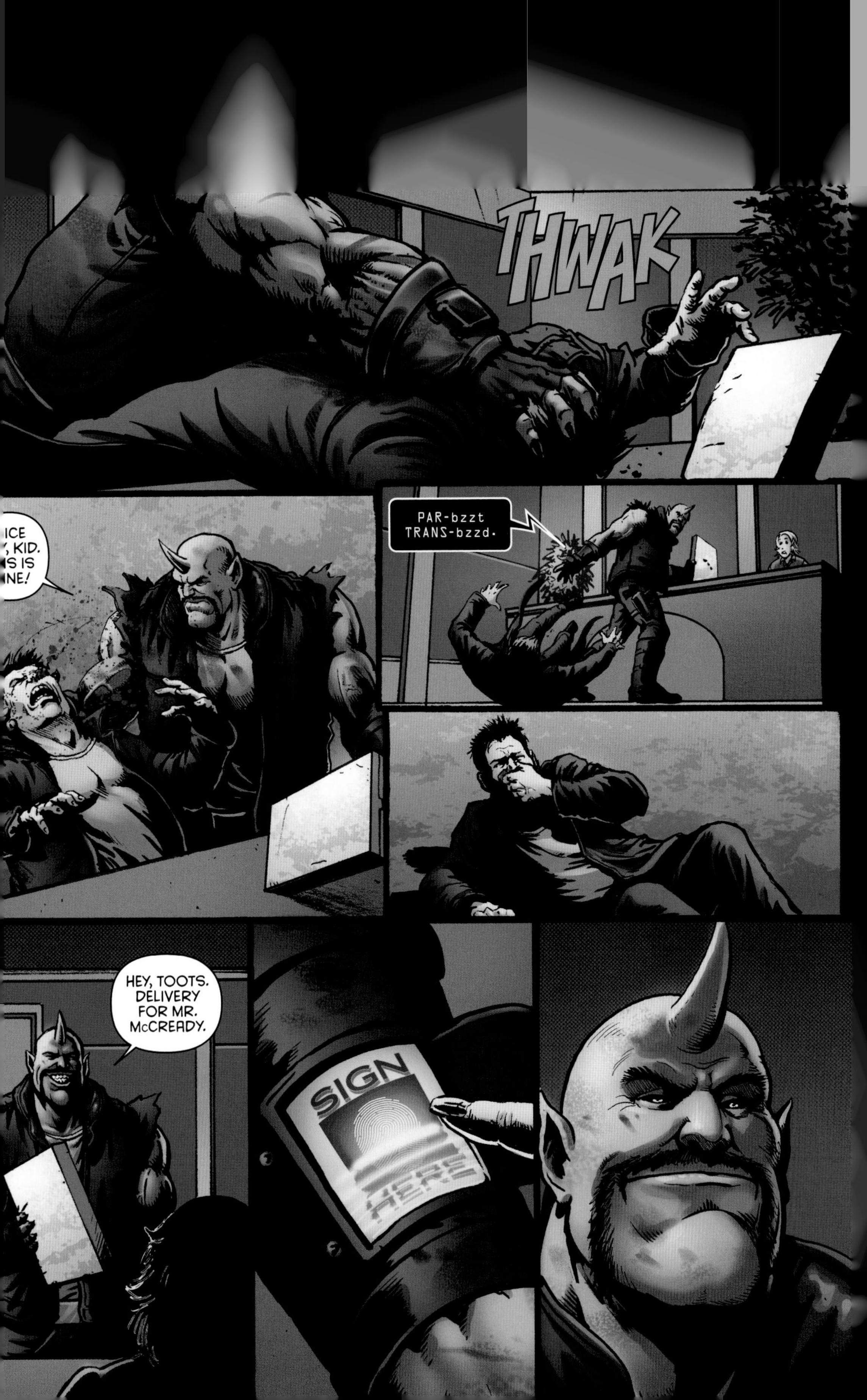
THWAK
PAR-bzzt
TRANS-bzzd.
HEY, TOOTS. DELIVERY FOR MR. McCREADY.
SIGN
HERE

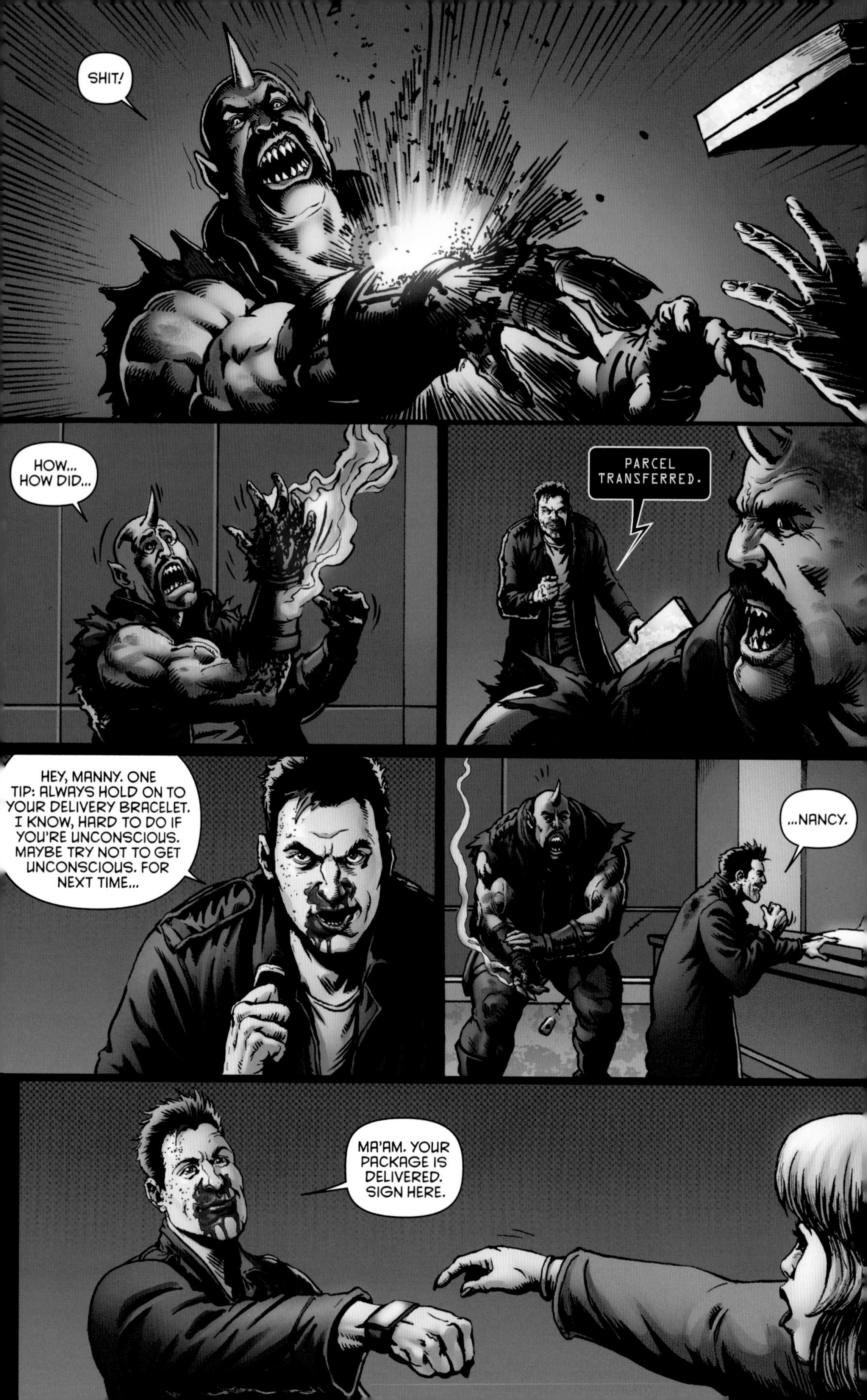
SHIT!
HOW... HOW DID...
PARCEL TRANSFERRED.
HEY, MANNY. ONE TIP: ALWAYS HOLD ON TO YOUR DELIVERY BRACELET. I KNOW, HARD TO DO IF YOU'RE UNCONSCIOUS. MAYBE TRY NOT TO GET UNCONSCIOUS. FOR NEXT TIME...
...NANCY.
MA'AM. YOUR PACKAGE IS DELIVERED. SIGN HERE.

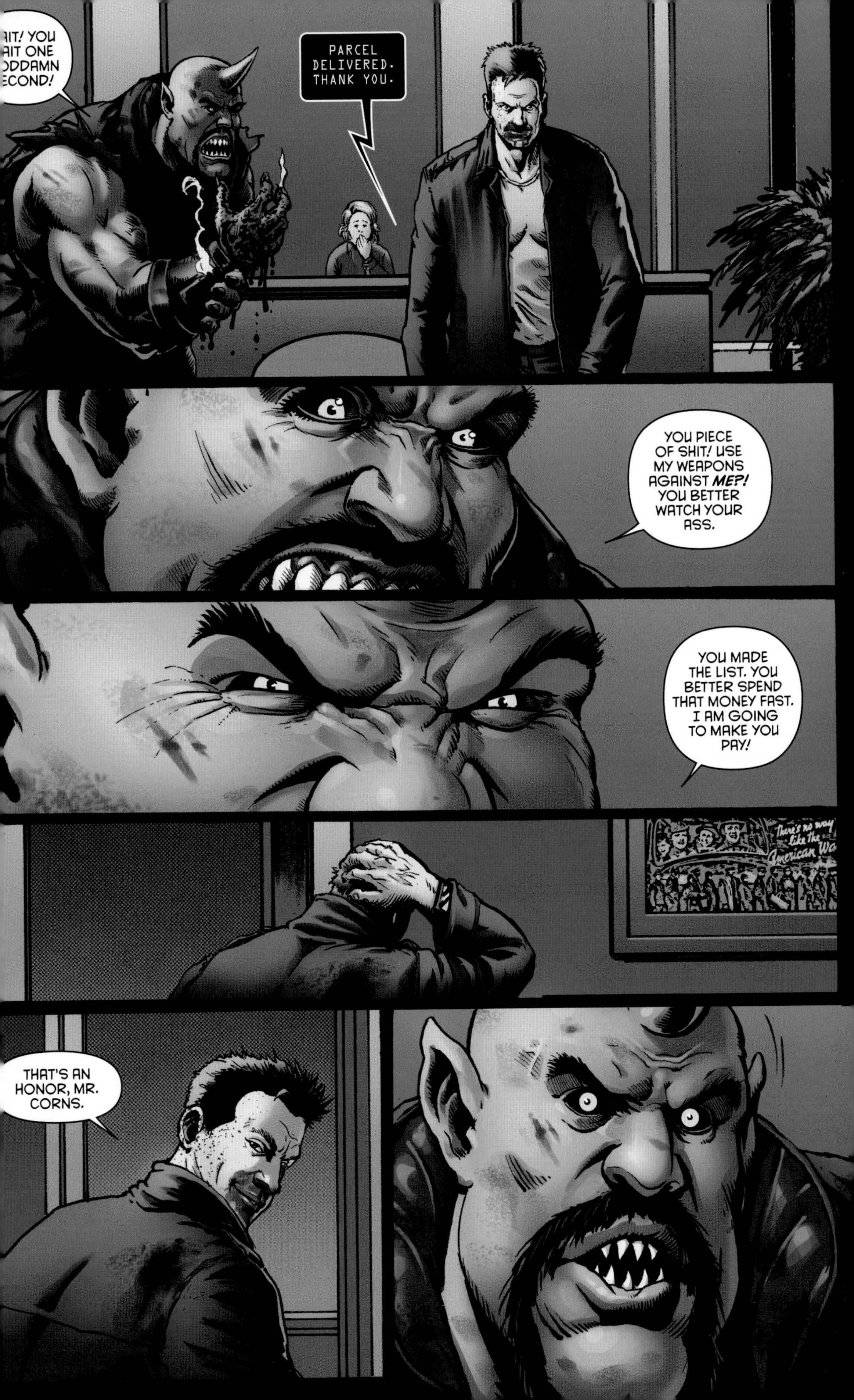
AIT! YOU AIT ONE ODDAMN ECOND!
PARCEL DELIVERED. THANK YOU.
YOU PIECE OF SHIT! USE MY WEAPONS AGAINST **ME?!** YOU BETTER WATCH YOUR ASS.
YOU MADE THE LIST. YOU BETTER SPEND THAT MONEY FAST. I AM GOING TO MAKE YOU PAY!
There's no way like the American Wa
THAT'S AN HONOR, MR. CORNS.

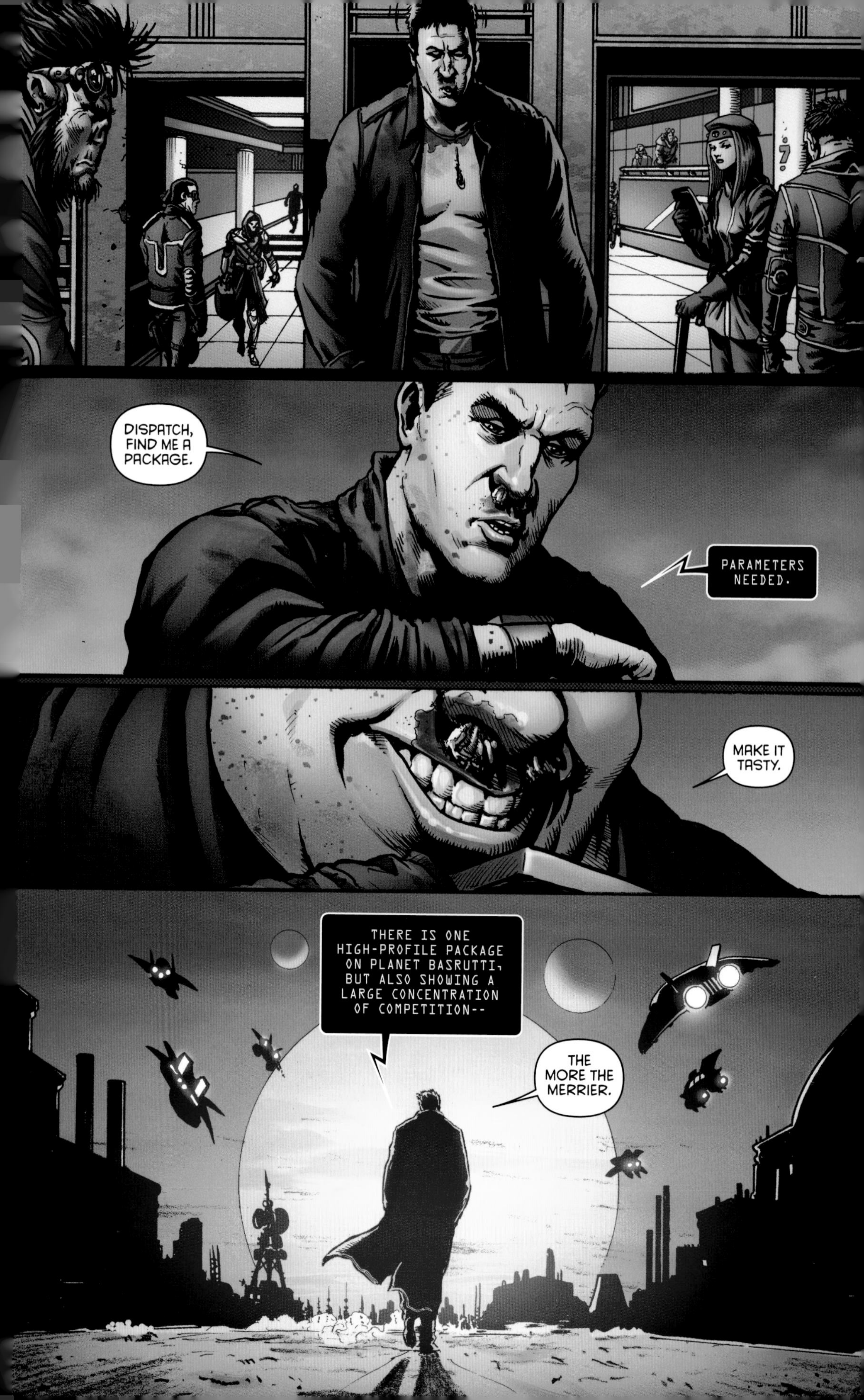
DISPATCH, FIND ME A PACKAGE.
PARAMETERS NEEDED.
MAKE IT TASTY.
THERE IS ONE HIGH-PROFILE PACKAGE ON PLANET BASRUTTI, BUT ALSO SHOWING A LARGE CONCENTRATION OF COMPETITION--
THE MORE THE MERRIER.

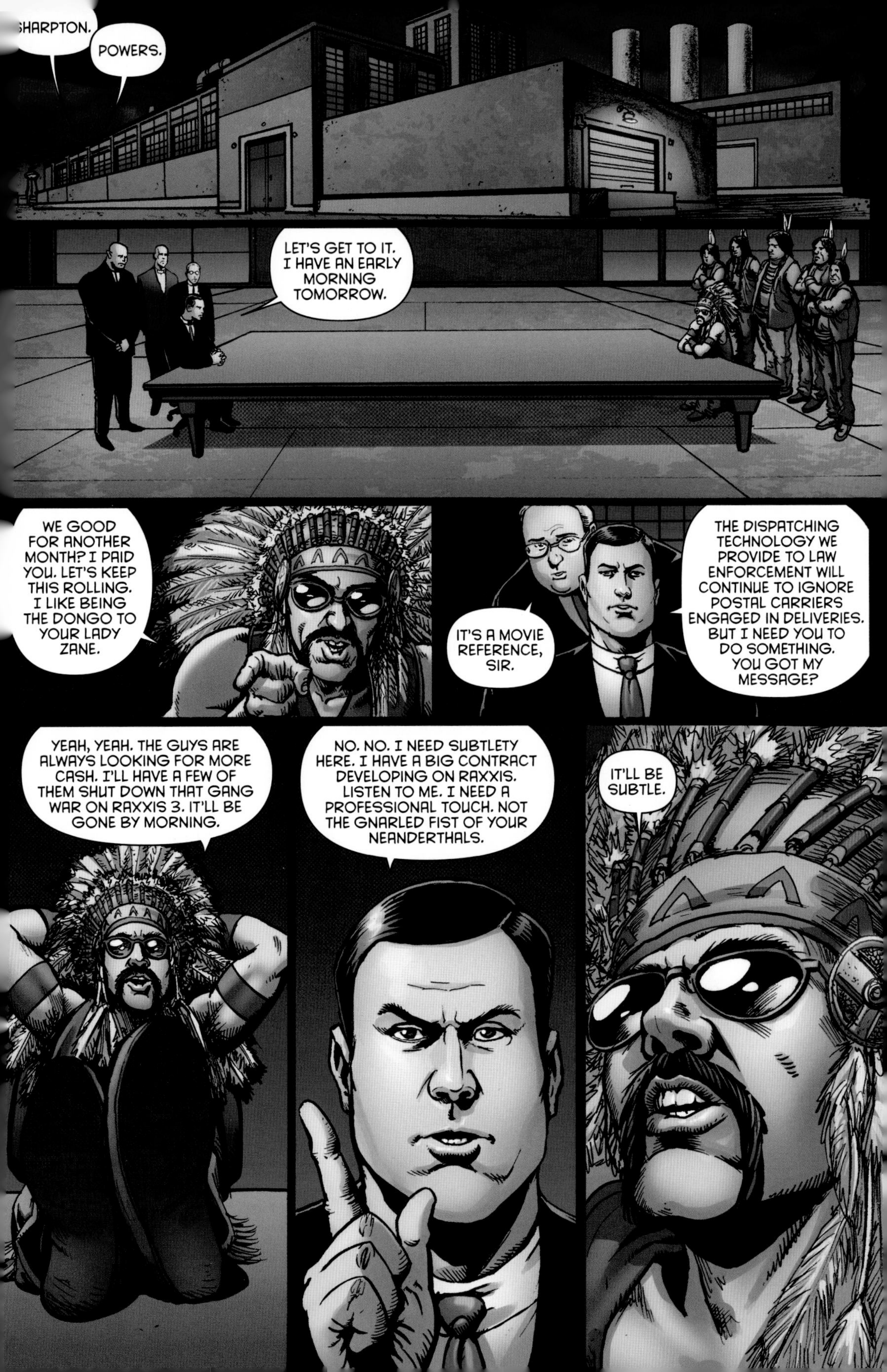
SHARPTON.
POWERS.
LET'S GET TO IT. I HAVE AN EARLY MORNING TOMORROW.
WE GOOD FOR ANOTHER MONTH? I PAID YOU. LET'S KEEP THIS ROLLING. I LIKE BEING THE DONGO TO YOUR LADY ZANE.
IT'S A MOVIE REFERENCE, SIR.
THE DISPATCHING TECHNOLOGY WE PROVIDE TO LAW ENFORCEMENT WILL CONTINUE TO IGNORE POSTAL CARRIERS ENGAGED IN DELIVERIES. BUT I NEED YOU TO DO SOMETHING. YOU GOT MY MESSAGE?
YEAH, YEAH. THE GUYS ARE ALWAYS LOOKING FOR MORE CASH. I'LL HAVE A FEW OF THEM SHUT DOWN THAT GANG WAR ON RAXXIS 3. IT'LL BE GONE BY MORNING.
NO. NO. I NEED SUBTLETY HERE. I HAVE A BIG CONTRACT DEVELOPING ON RAXXIS. LISTEN TO ME. I NEED A PROFESSIONAL TOUCH. NOT THE GNARLED FIST OF YOUR NEANDERTHALS.
IT'LL BE SUBTLE.

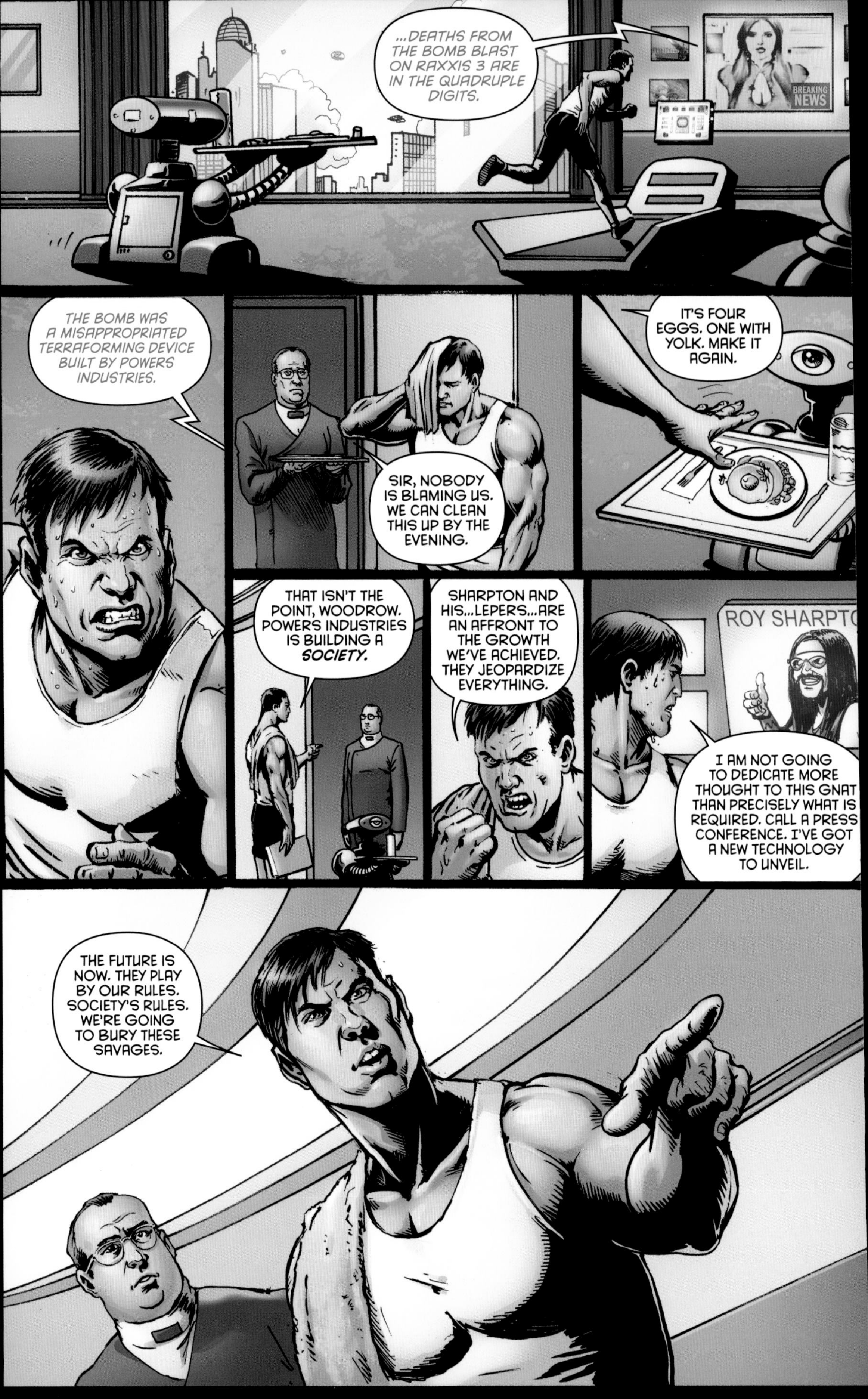
...DEATHS FROM THE BOMB BLAST ON RAXXIS 3 ARE IN THE QUADRUPLE DIGITS.
BREAKING NEWS
THE BOMB WAS A MISAPPROPRIATED TERRAFORMING DEVICE BUILT BY POWERS INDUSTRIES.
SIR, NOBODY IS BLAMING US. WE CAN CLEAN THIS UP BY THE EVENING.
IT'S FOUR EGGS. ONE WITH YOLK. MAKE IT AGAIN.
THAT ISN'T THE POINT, WOODROW. POWERS INDUSTRIES IS BUILDING A SOCIETY.
SHARPTON AND HIS...LEPERS...ARE AN AFFRONT TO THE GROWTH WE'VE ACHIEVED. THEY JEOPARDIZE EVERYTHING.
I AM NOT GOING TO DEDICATE MORE THOUGHT TO THIS GNAT THAN PRECISELY WHAT IS REQUIRED. CALL A PRESS CONFERENCE. I'VE GOT A NEW TECHNOLOGY TO UNVEIL.
THE FUTURE IS NOW. THEY PLAY BY OUR RULES. SOCIETY'S RULES. WE'RE GOING TO BURY THESE SAVAGES.

EPISODE 2

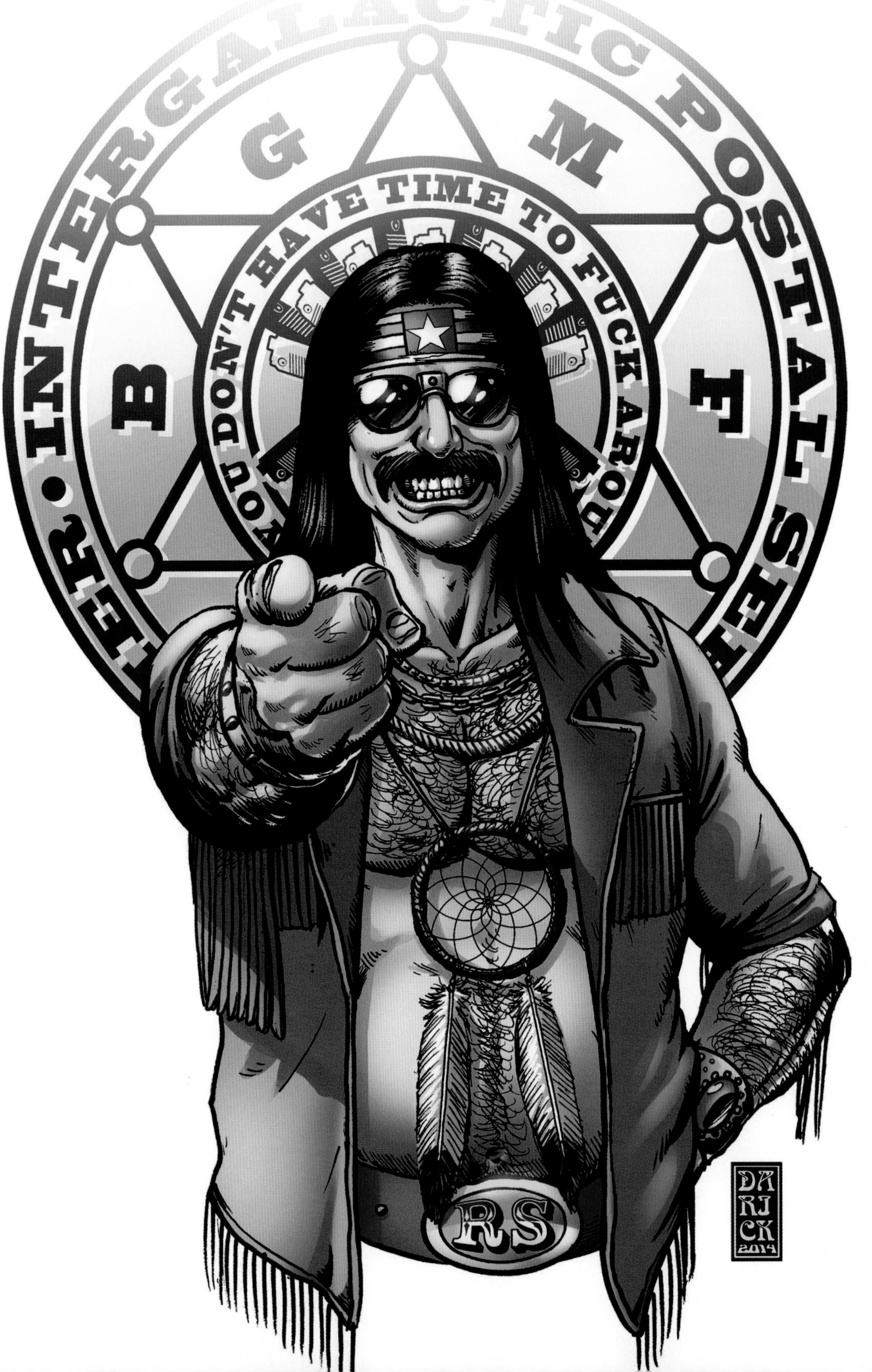
INTERGALACTIC POSTAL
B G M F
YOU DON'T HAVE TIME TO FUCK
RS
DARICK 2014

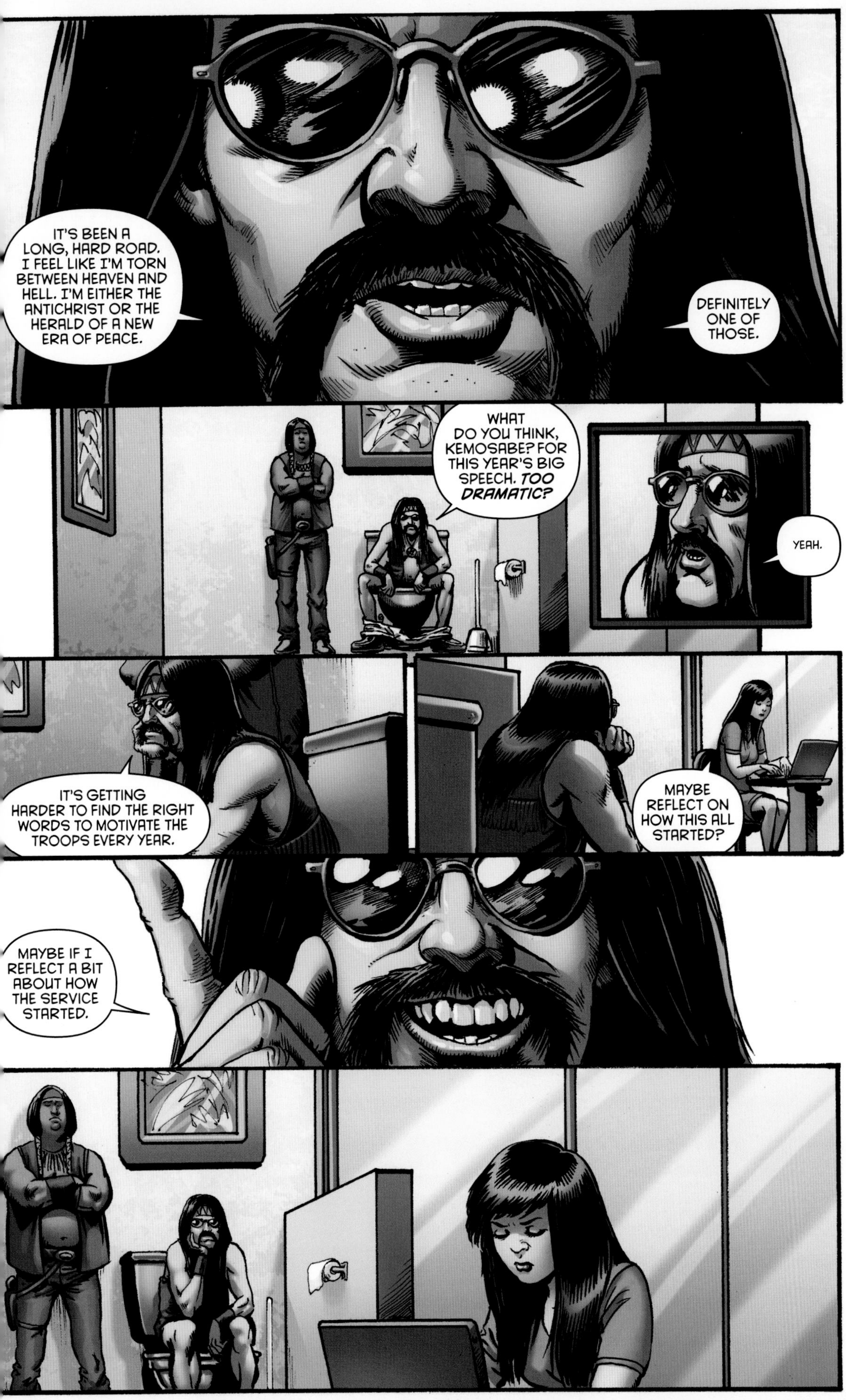
IT'S BEEN A LONG, HARD ROAD. I FEEL LIKE I'M TORN BETWEEN HEAVEN AND HELL. I'M EITHER THE ANTICHRIST OR THE HERALD OF A NEW ERA OF PEACE.
DEFINITELY ONE OF THOSE.
WHAT DO YOU THINK, KEMOSABE? FOR THIS YEAR'S BIG SPEECH. *TOO DRAMATIC?*
YEAH.
IT'S GETTING HARDER TO FIND THE RIGHT WORDS TO MOTIVATE THE TROOPS EVERY YEAR.
MAYBE REFLECT ON HOW THIS ALL STARTED?
MAYBE IF I REFLECT A BIT ABOUT HOW THE SERVICE STARTED.

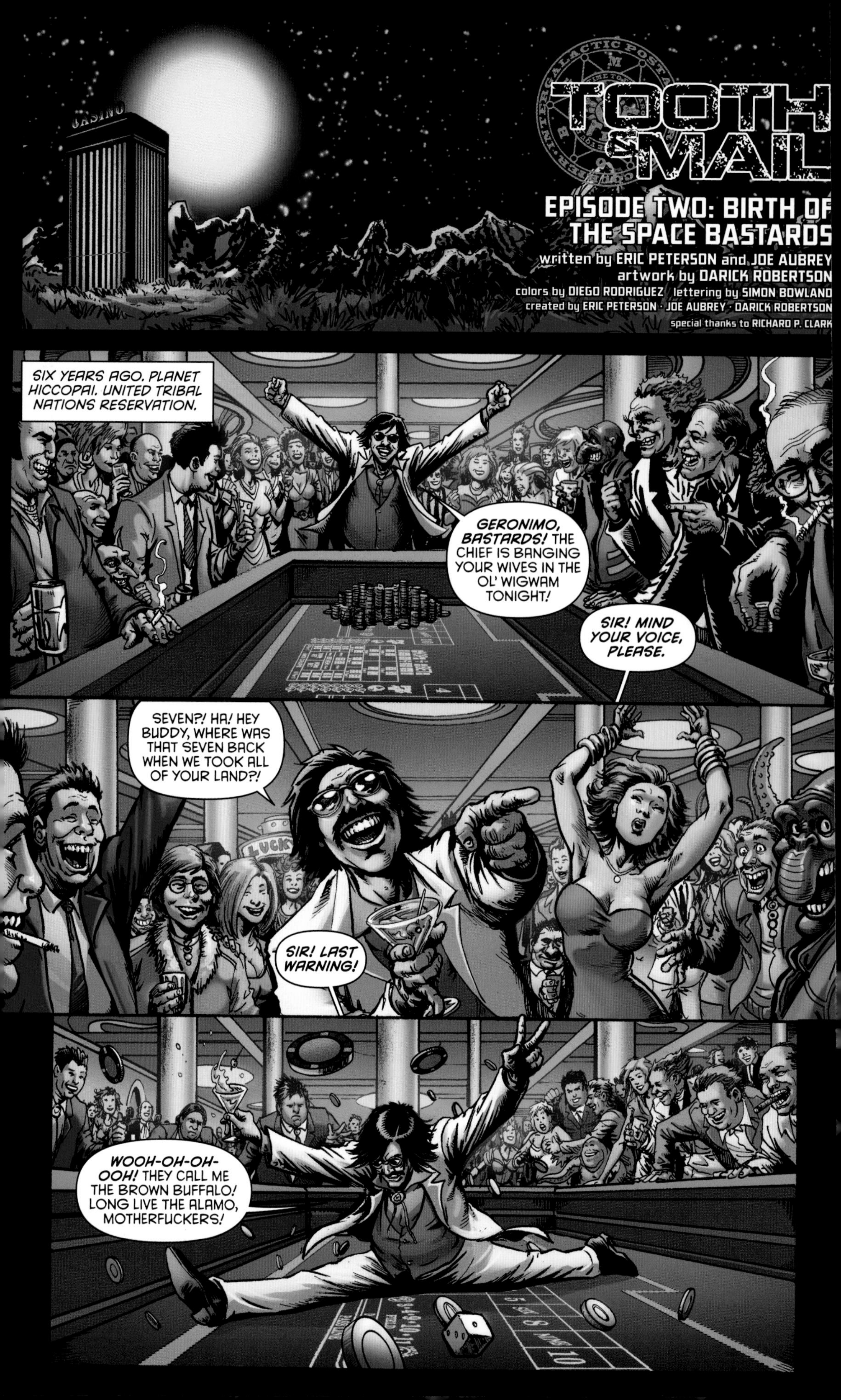

CASINO
TOOTH & MAIL
EPISODE TWO: BIRTH OF THE SPACE BASTARDS
written by ERIC PETERSON and JOE AUBREY
artwork by DARICK ROBERTSON
colors by DIEGO RODRIGUEZ lettering by SIMON BOWLAND
created by ERIC PETERSON · JOE AUBREY · DARICK ROBERTSON
special thanks to RICHARD P. CLARK
SIX YEARS AGO. PLANET HICCOPAI. UNITED TRIBAL NATIONS RESERVATION.
GERONIMO, BASTARDS! THE CHIEF IS BANGING YOUR WIVES IN THE OL' WIGWAM TONIGHT!
SIR! MIND YOUR VOICE, PLEASE.
SEVEN?! HA! HEY BUDDY, WHERE WAS THAT SEVEN BACK WHEN WE TOOK ALL OF YOUR LAND?!
SIR! LAST WARNING!
WOOH-OH-OH-OOH! THEY CALL ME THE BROWN BUFFALO! LONG LIVE THE ALAMO, MOTHERFUCKERS!

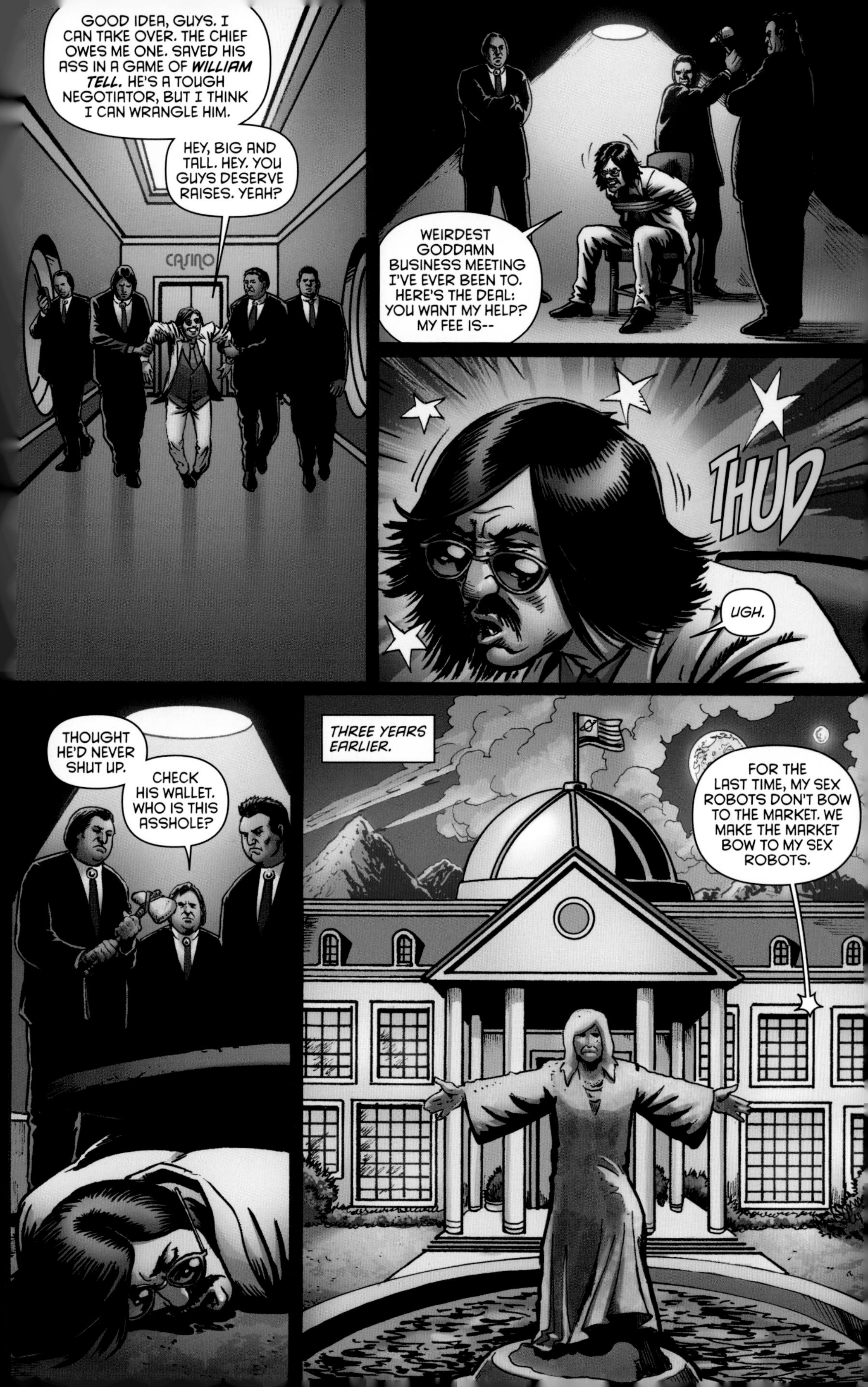
GOOD IDEA, GUYS. I CAN TAKE OVER. THE CHIEF OWES ME ONE. SAVED HIS ASS IN A GAME OF **WILLIAM TELL.** HE'S A TOUGH NEGOTIATOR, BUT I THINK I CAN WRANGLE HIM.
HEY, BIG AND TALL. HEY. YOU GUYS DESERVE RAISES. YEAH?
CASINO
WEIRDEST GODDAMN BUSINESS MEETING I'VE EVER BEEN TO. HERE'S THE DEAL: YOU WANT MY HELP? MY FEE IS--
THUD
UGH.
THOUGHT HE'D NEVER SHUT UP.
CHECK HIS WALLET. WHO IS THIS ASSHOLE?
THREE YEARS EARLIER.
FOR THE LAST TIME, MY SEX ROBOTS DON'T BOW TO THE MARKET. WE MAKE THE MARKET BOW TO MY SEX ROBOTS.

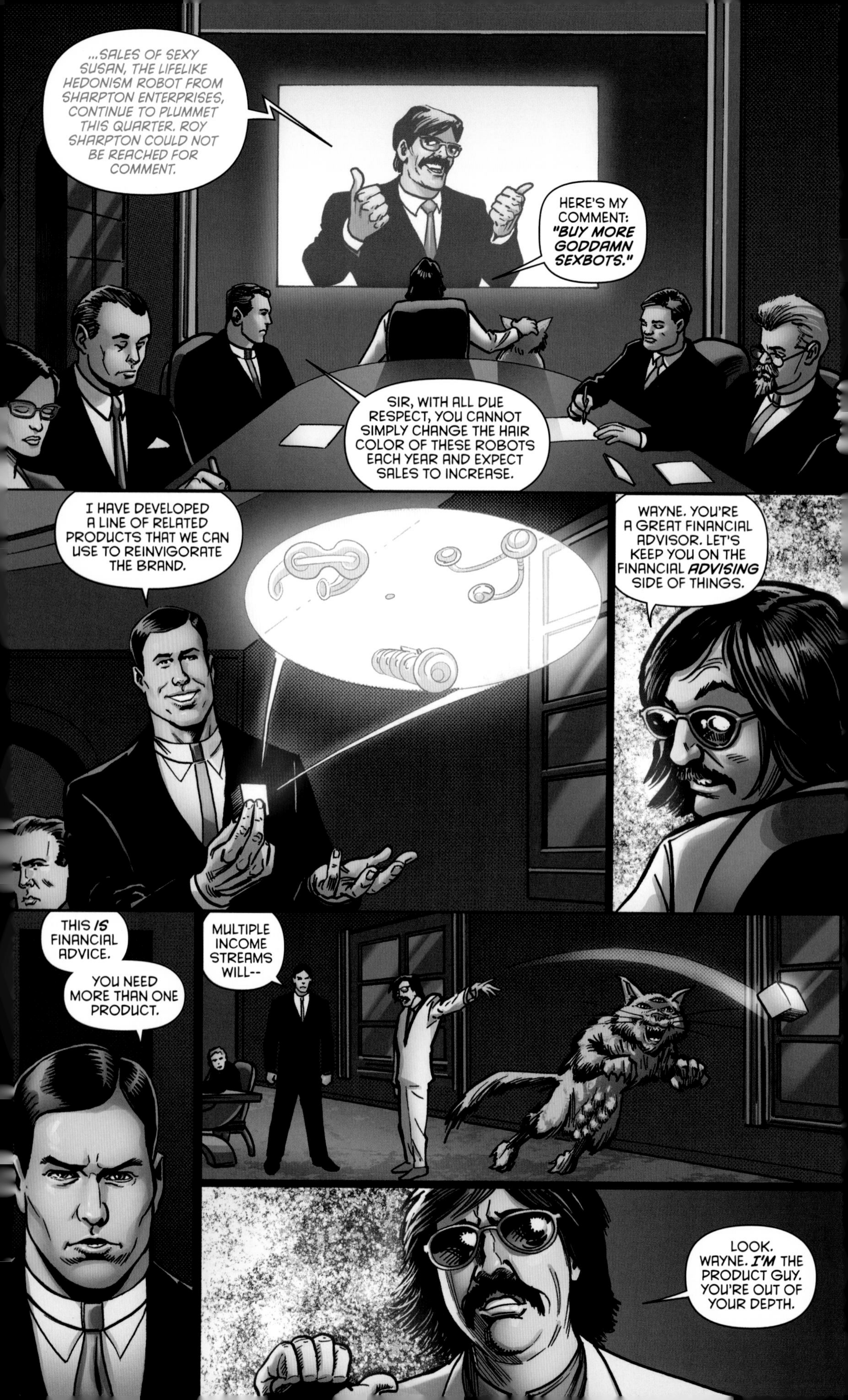
...SALES OF SEXY SUSAN, THE LIFELIKE HEDONISM ROBOT FROM SHARPTON ENTERPRISES, CONTINUE TO PLUMMET THIS QUARTER. ROY SHARPTON COULD NOT BE REACHED FOR COMMENT.
HERE'S MY COMMENT: "BUY MORE GODDAMN SEXBOTS."
SIR, WITH ALL DUE RESPECT, YOU CANNOT SIMPLY CHANGE THE HAIR COLOR OF THESE ROBOTS EACH YEAR AND EXPECT SALES TO INCREASE.
I HAVE DEVELOPED A LINE OF RELATED PRODUCTS THAT WE CAN USE TO REINVIGORATE THE BRAND.
WAYNE. YOU'RE A GREAT FINANCIAL ADVISOR. LET'S KEEP YOU ON THE FINANCIAL ADVISING SIDE OF THINGS.
THIS IS FINANCIAL ADVICE.
YOU NEED MORE THAN ONE PRODUCT.
MULTIPLE INCOME STREAMS WILL--
LOOK. WAYNE. I'M THE PRODUCT GUY. YOU'RE OUT OF YOUR DEPTH.

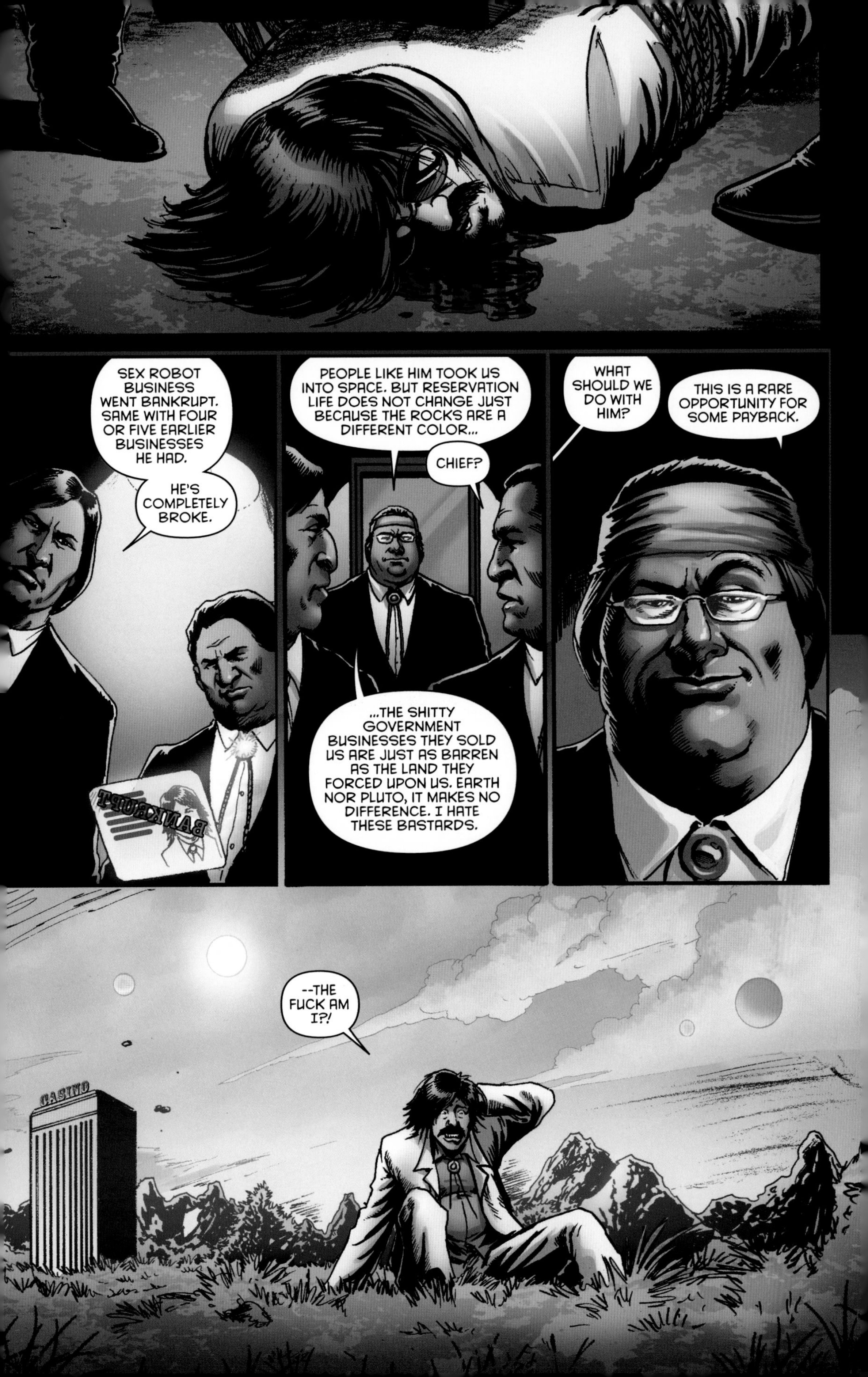
SEX ROBOT BUSINESS WENT BANKRUPT. SAME WITH FOUR OR FIVE EARLIER BUSINESSES HE HAD.
HE'S COMPLETELY BROKE.
BANKRUPT
PEOPLE LIKE HIM TOOK US INTO SPACE. BUT RESERVATION LIFE DOES NOT CHANGE JUST BECAUSE THE ROCKS ARE A DIFFERENT COLOR...
CHIEF?
...THE SHITTY GOVERNMENT BUSINESSES THEY SOLD US ARE JUST AS BARREN AS THE LAND THEY FORCED UPON US. EARTH NOR PLUTO, IT MAKES NO DIFFERENCE. I HATE THESE BASTARDS.
WHAT SHOULD WE DO WITH HIM?
THIS IS A RARE OPPORTUNITY FOR SOME PAYBACK.
--THE FUCK AM I?!
CASINO

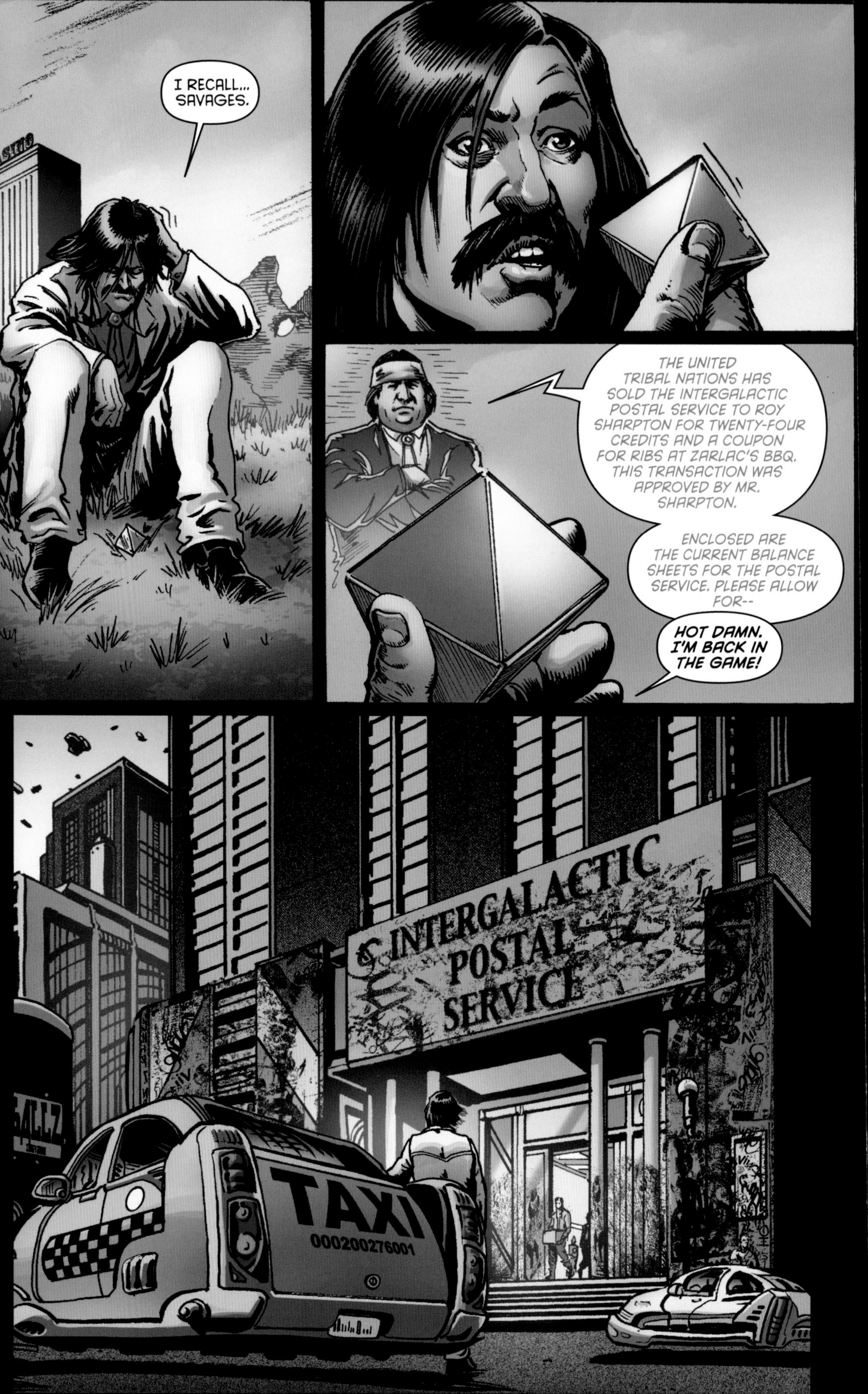
I RECALL... SAVAGES.
THE UNITED TRIBAL NATIONS HAS SOLD THE INTERGALACTIC POSTAL SERVICE TO ROY SHARPTON FOR TWENTY-FOUR CREDITS AND A COUPON FOR RIBS AT ZARLAC'S BBQ. THIS TRANSACTION WAS APPROVED BY MR. SHARPTON.
ENCLOSED ARE THE CURRENT BALANCE SHEETS FOR THE POSTAL SERVICE. PLEASE ALLOW FOR--
HOT DAMN. I'M BACK IN THE GAME!
INTERGALACTIC POSTAL SERVICE
TAXI
000200276001

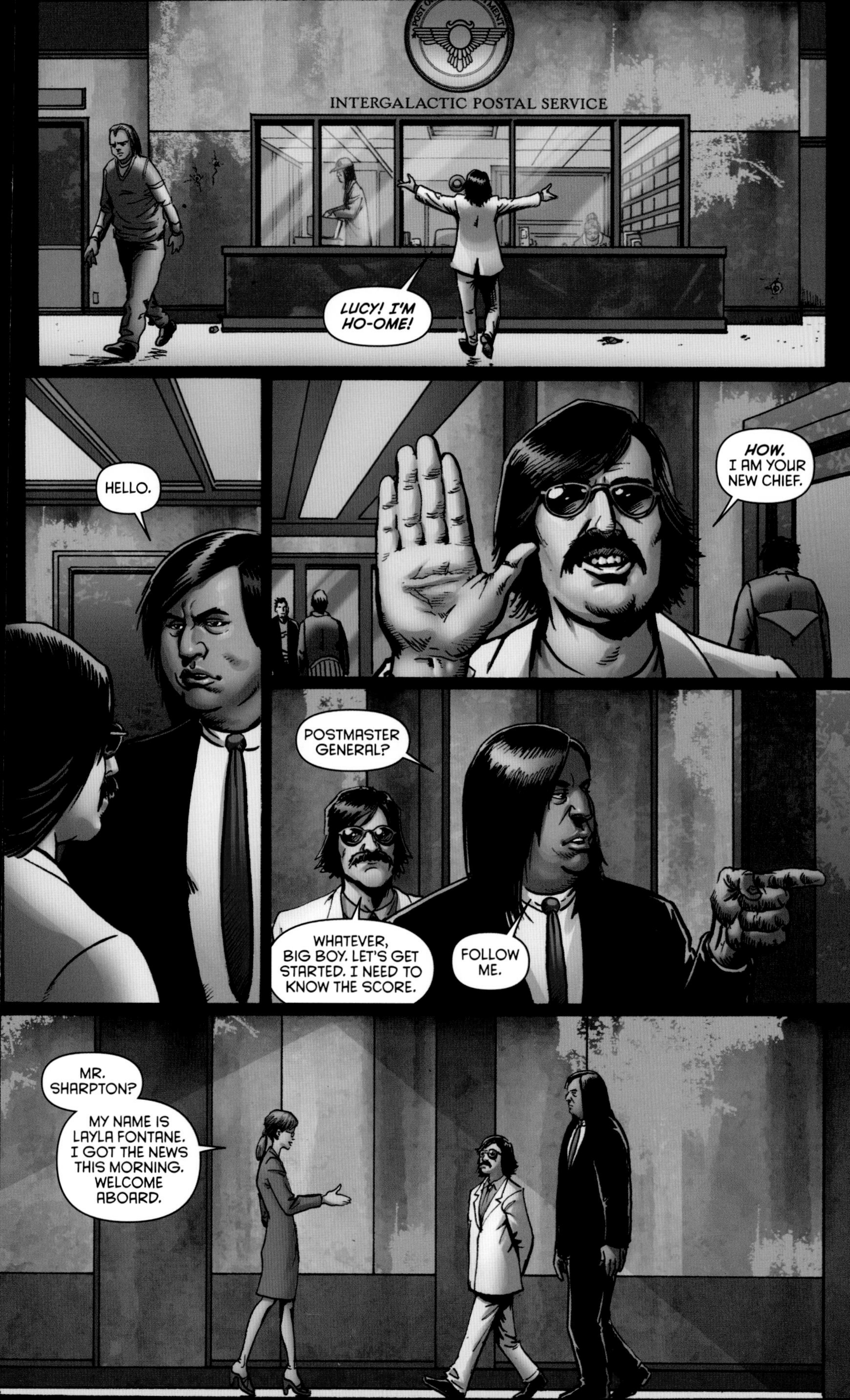
INTERGALACTIC POSTAL SERVICE
LUCY! I'M HO-OME!
HELLO.
HOW. I AM YOUR NEW CHIEF.
POSTMASTER GENERAL?
WHATEVER, BIG BOY. LET'S GET STARTED. I NEED TO KNOW THE SCORE.
FOLLOW ME.
MR. SHARPTON?
MY NAME IS LAYLA FONTANE. I GOT THE NEWS THIS MORNING. WELCOME ABOARD.

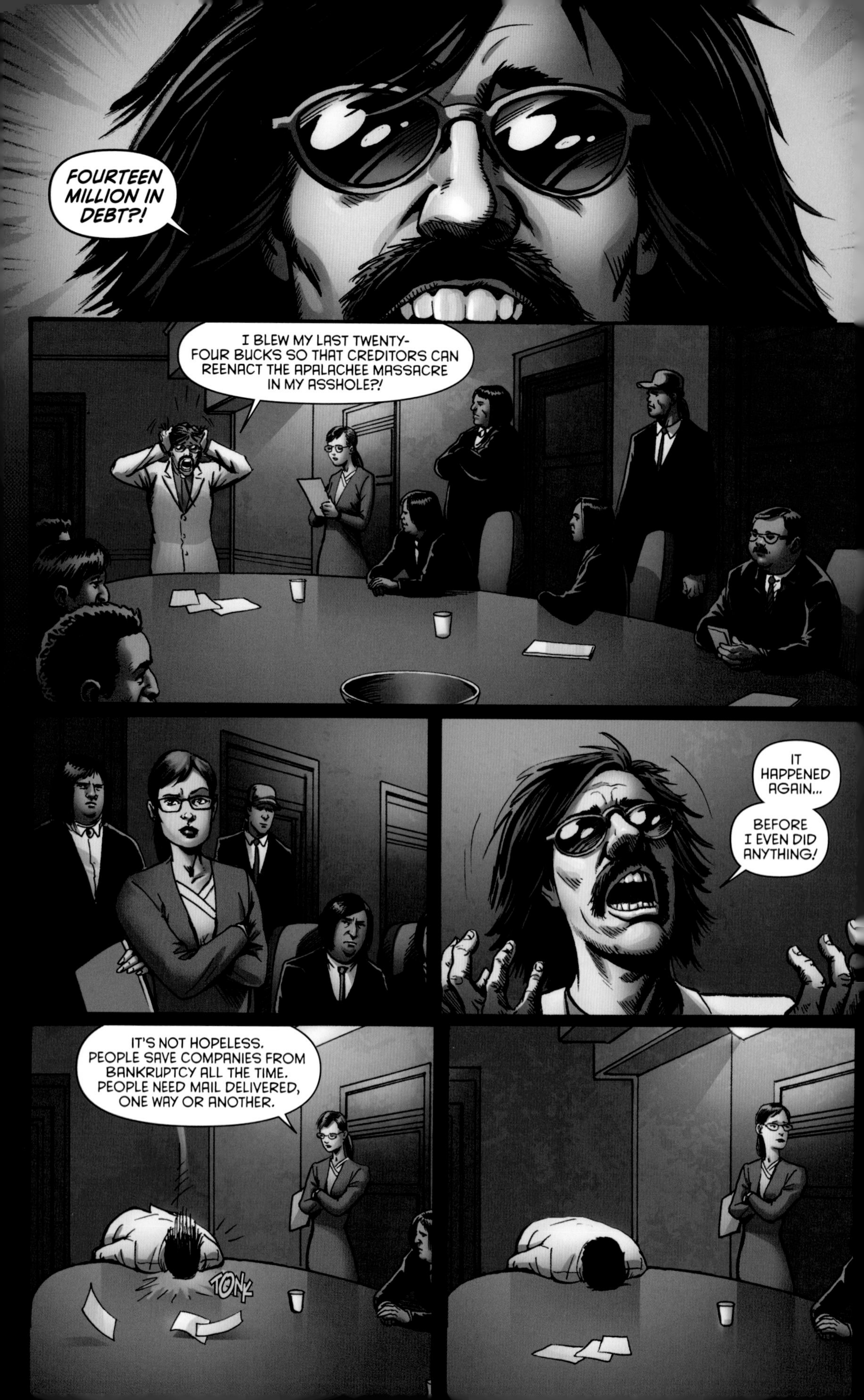
FOURTEEN MILLION IN DEBT?!
I BLEW MY LAST TWENTY-FOUR BUCKS SO THAT CREDITORS CAN REENACT THE APALACHEE MASSACRE IN MY ASSHOLE?!
IT HAPPENED AGAIN...
BEFORE I EVEN DID ANYTHING!
IT'S NOT HOPELESS. PEOPLE SAVE COMPANIES FROM BANKRUPTCY ALL THE TIME. PEOPLE NEED MAIL DELIVERED, ONE WAY OR ANOTHER.
TONK

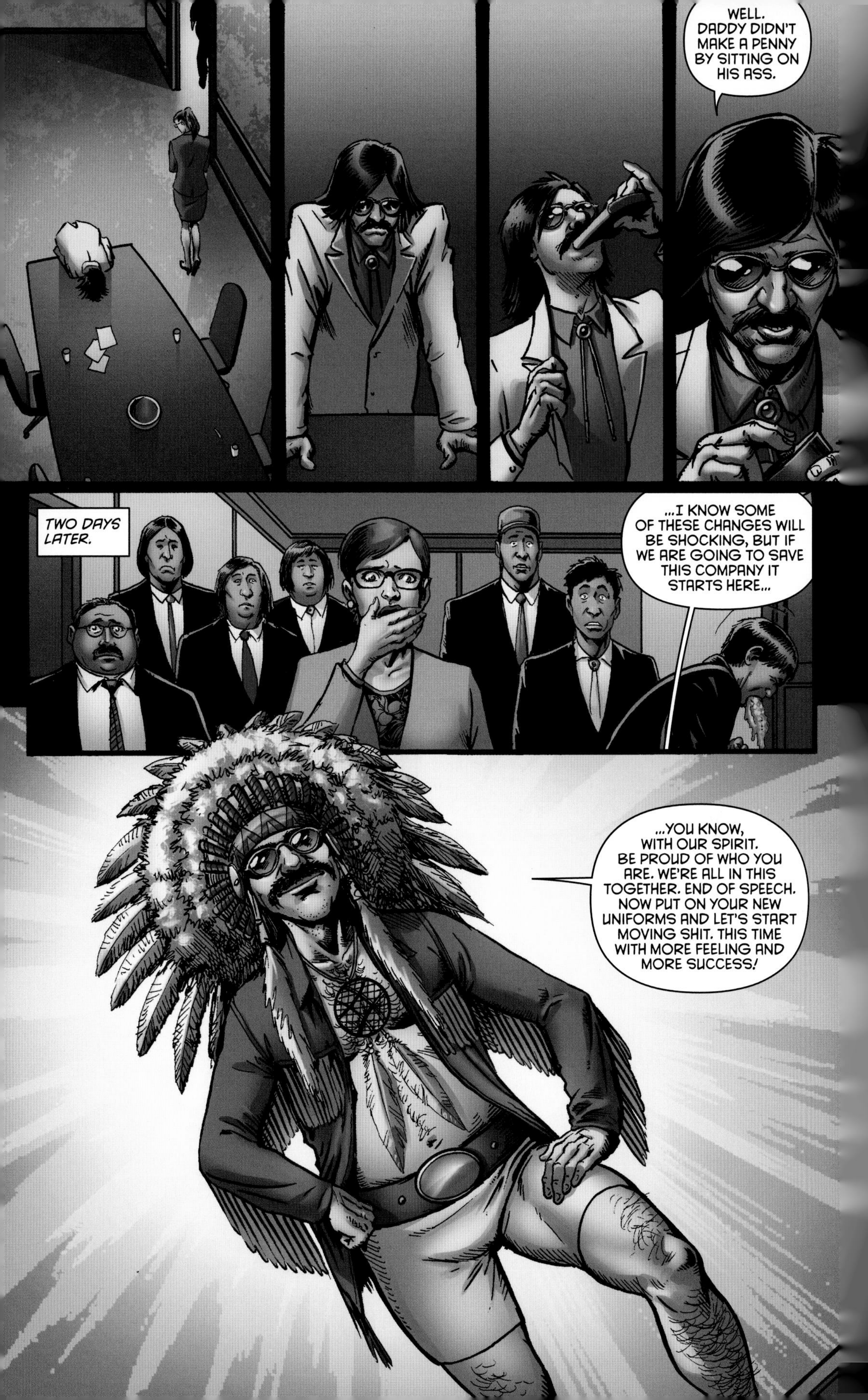
WELL. DADDY DIDN'T MAKE A PENNY BY SITTING ON HIS ASS.
TWO DAYS LATER.
...I KNOW SOME OF THESE CHANGES WILL BE SHOCKING, BUT IF WE ARE GOING TO SAVE THIS COMPANY IT STARTS HERE...
...YOU KNOW, WITH OUR SPIRIT. BE PROUD OF WHO YOU ARE. WE'RE ALL IN THIS TOGETHER. END OF SPEECH. NOW PUT ON YOUR NEW UNIFORMS AND LET'S START MOVING SHIT. THIS TIME WITH MORE FEELING AND MORE SUCCESS!

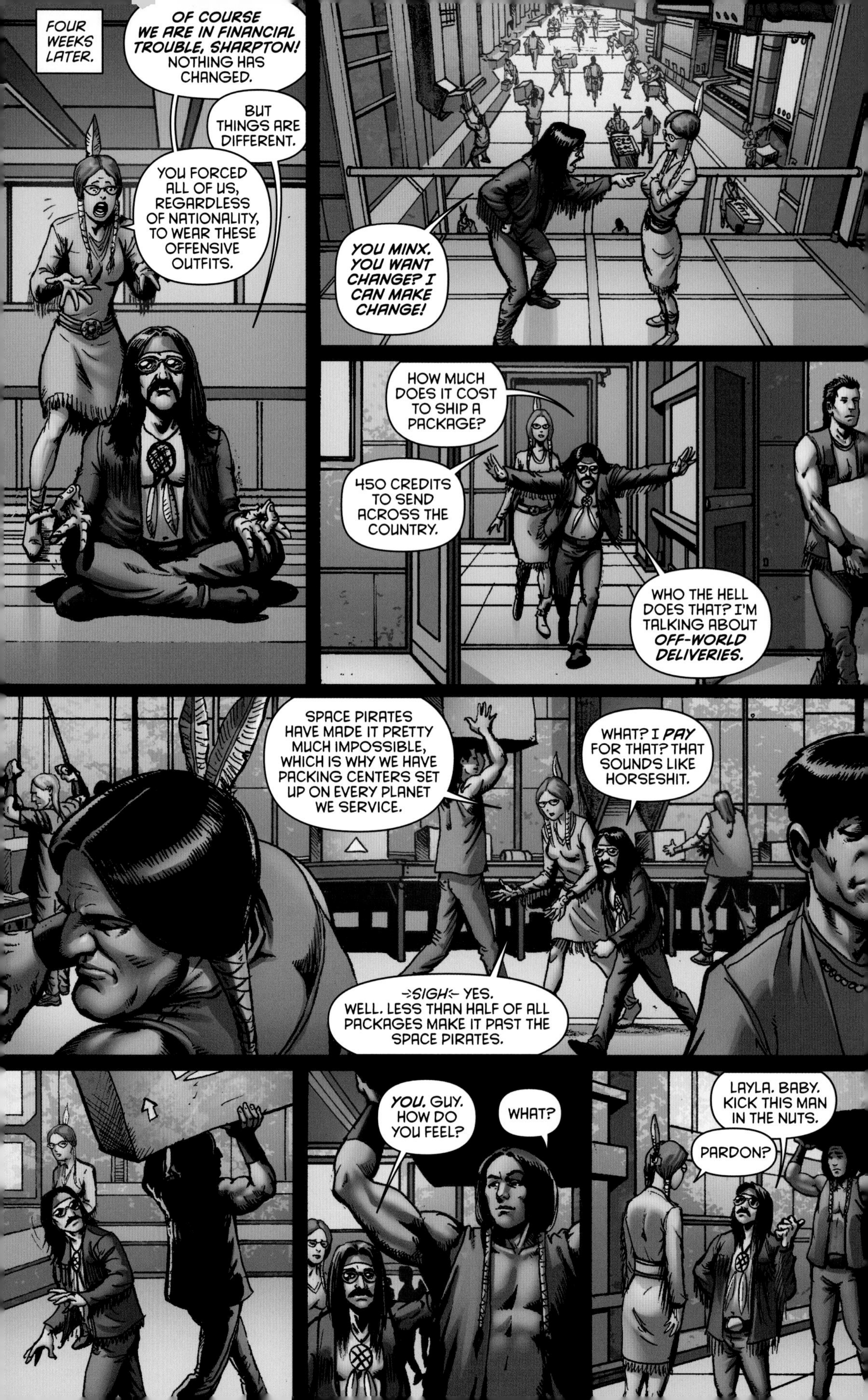
FOUR WEEKS LATER.
OF COURSE WE ARE IN FINANCIAL TROUBLE, SHARPTON! NOTHING HAS CHANGED.
BUT THINGS ARE DIFFERENT.
YOU FORCED ALL OF US, REGARDLESS OF NATIONALITY, TO WEAR THESE OFFENSIVE OUTFITS.
YOU MINX. YOU WANT CHANGE? I CAN MAKE CHANGE!
HOW MUCH DOES IT COST TO SHIP A PACKAGE?
450 CREDITS TO SEND ACROSS THE COUNTRY.
WHO THE HELL DOES THAT? I'M TALKING ABOUT OFF-WORLD DELIVERIES.
SPACE PIRATES HAVE MADE IT PRETTY MUCH IMPOSSIBLE, WHICH IS WHY WE HAVE PACKING CENTERS SET UP ON EVERY PLANET WE SERVICE.
WHAT? I PAY FOR THAT? THAT SOUNDS LIKE HORSESHIT.
⇒SIGH⇐ YES. WELL. LESS THAN HALF OF ALL PACKAGES MAKE IT PAST THE SPACE PIRATES.
YOU. GUY. HOW DO YOU FEEL?
WHAT?
LAYLA. BABY. KICK THIS MAN IN THE NUTS.
PARDON?

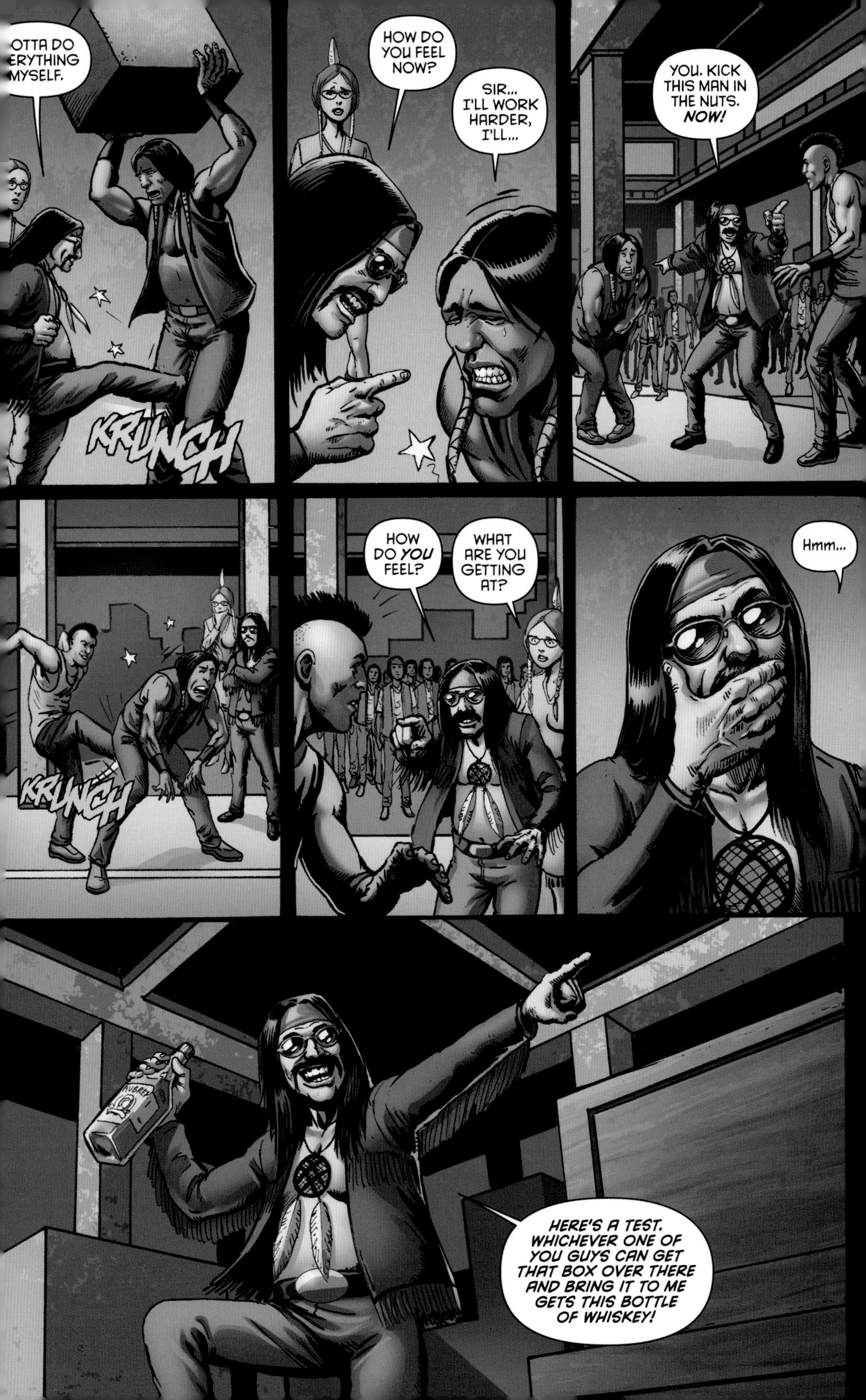
OTTA DO
ERYTHING
MYSELF.
KRUNCH
HOW DO YOU FEEL NOW?
SIR... I'LL WORK HARDER, I'LL...
YOU. KICK THIS MAN IN THE NUTS. NOW!
KRUNCH
HOW DO YOU FEEL?
WHAT ARE YOU GETTING AT?
Hmm...
HERE'S A TEST. WHICHEVER ONE OF YOU GUYS CAN GET THAT BOX OVER THERE AND BRING IT TO ME GETS THIS BOTTLE OF WHISKEY!

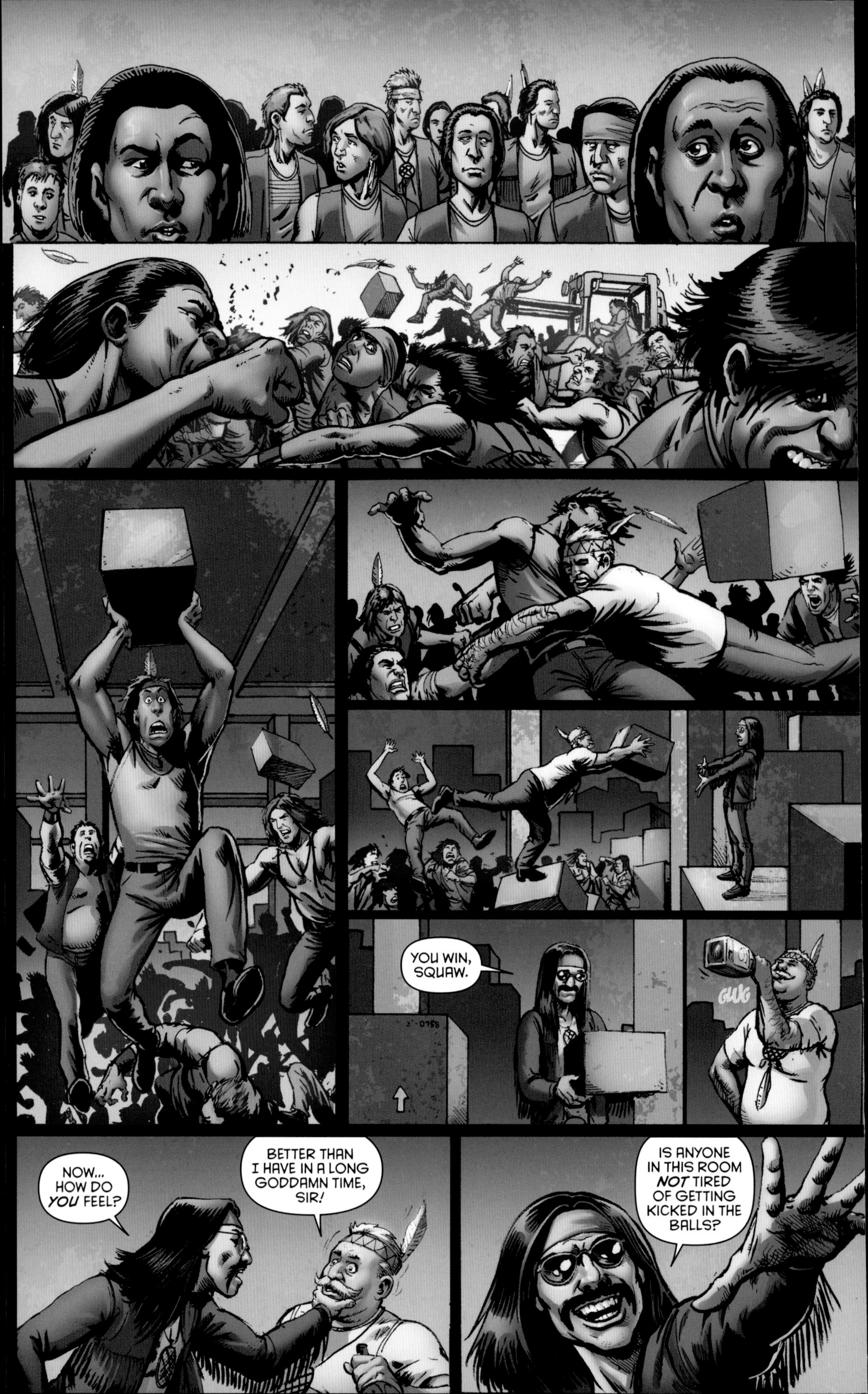
YOU WIN, SQUAW.
GLUG
NOW... HOW DO *YOU* FEEL?
BETTER THAN I HAVE IN A LONG GODDAMN TIME, SIR!
IS ANYONE IN THIS ROOM *NOT* TIRED OF GETTING KICKED IN THE BALLS?

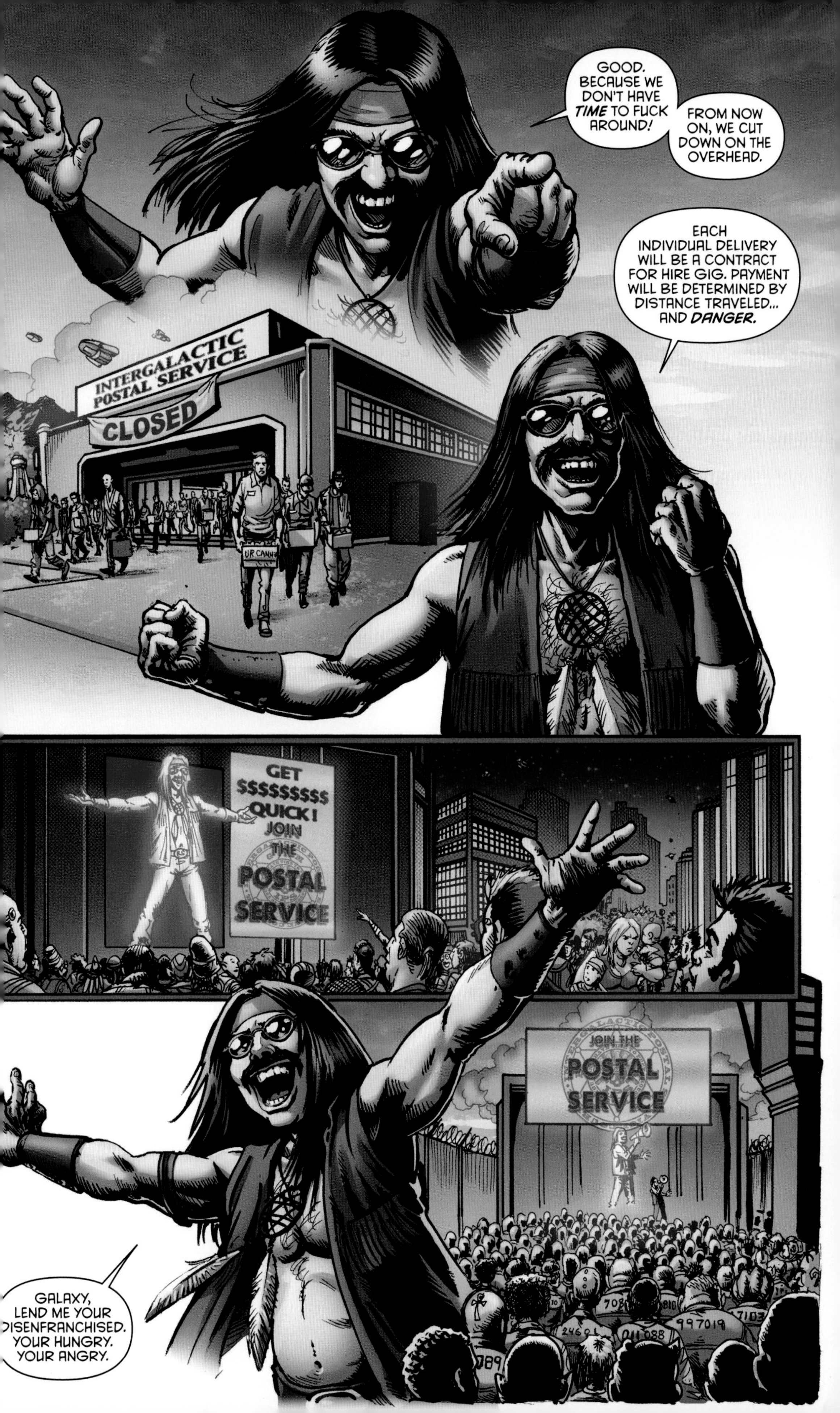
GOOD. BECAUSE WE DON'T HAVE *TIME* TO FUCK AROUND!
FROM NOW ON, WE CUT DOWN ON THE OVERHEAD.
INTERGALACTIC POSTAL SERVICE
CLOSED
EACH INDIVIDUAL DELIVERY WILL BE A CONTRACT FOR HIRE GIG. PAYMENT WILL BE DETERMINED BY DISTANCE TRAVELED... AND ***DANGER.***
GET $$$$$$$$$ QUICK! JOIN THE POSTAL SERVICE
JOIN THE POSTAL SERVICE
GALAXY, LEND ME YOUR DISENFRANCHISED. YOUR HUNGRY. YOUR ANGRY.

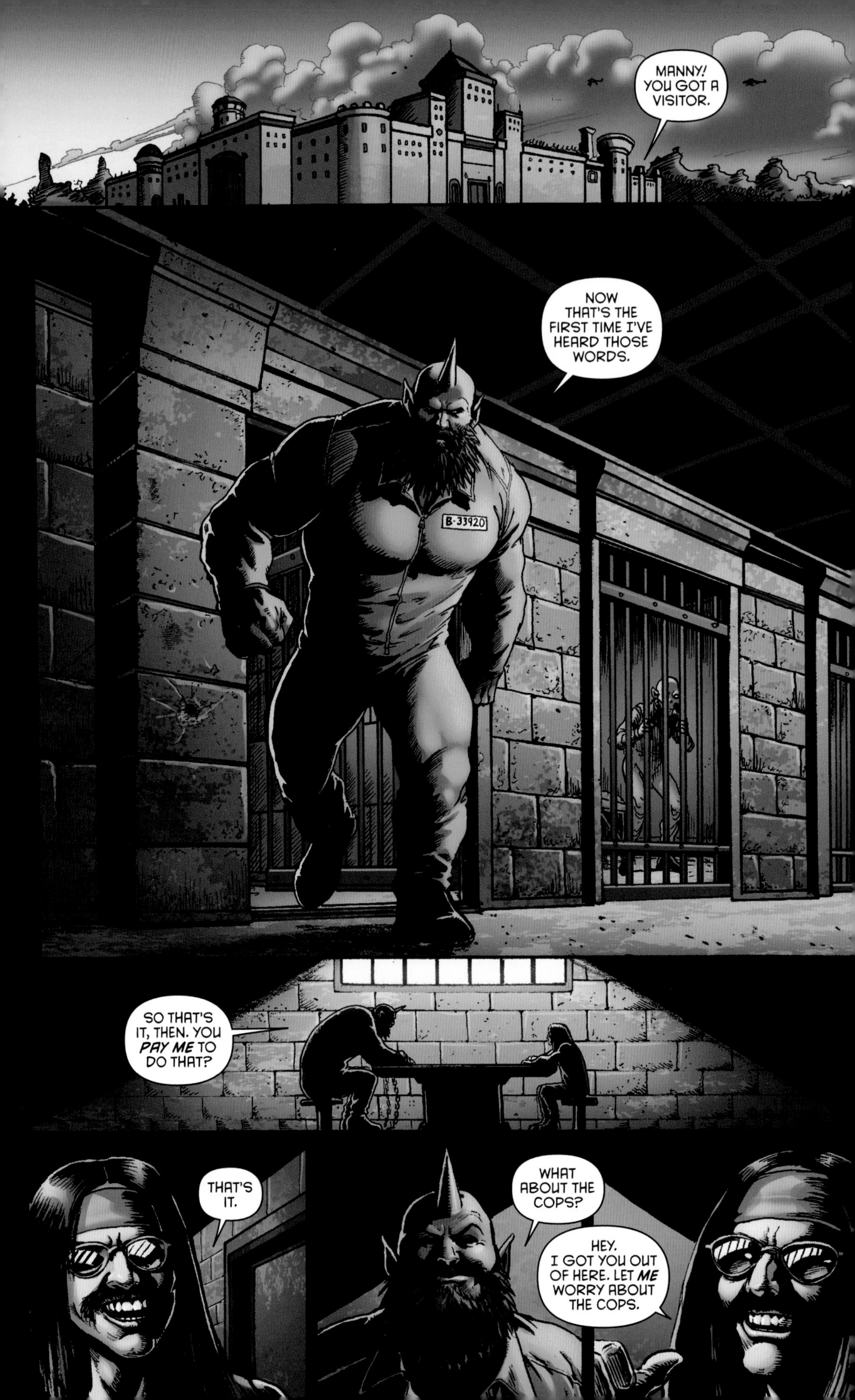

MANNY! YOU GOT A VISITOR.
NOW THAT'S THE FIRST TIME I'VE HEARD THOSE WORDS.
B-33920
SO THAT'S IT, THEN. YOU *PAY ME* TO DO THAT?
THAT'S IT.
WHAT ABOUT THE COPS?
HEY. I GOT YOU OUT OF HERE. LET *ME* WORRY ABOUT THE COPS.

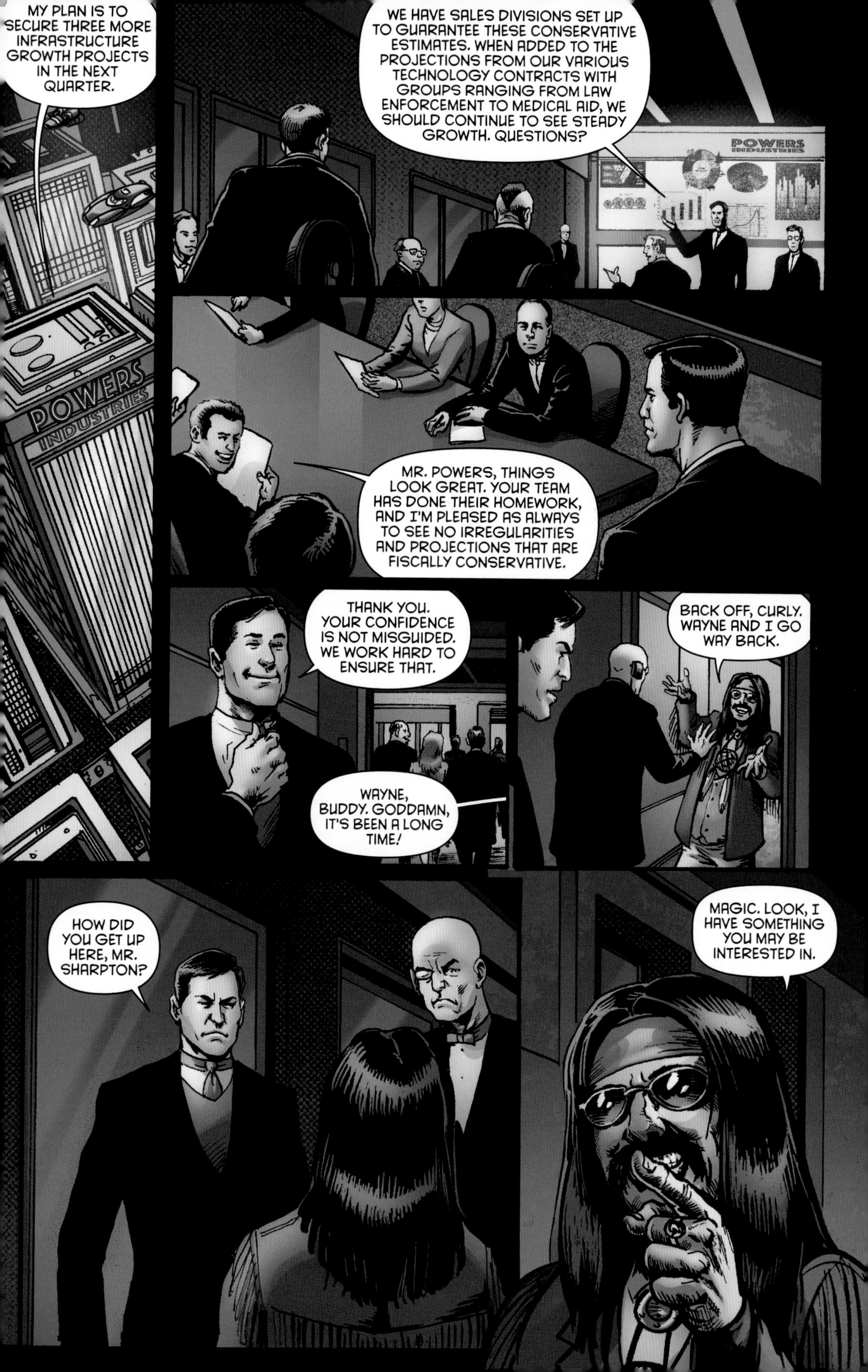
MY PLAN IS TO SECURE THREE MORE INFRASTRUCTURE GROWTH PROJECTS IN THE NEXT QUARTER.
WE HAVE SALES DIVISIONS SET UP TO GUARANTEE THESE CONSERVATIVE ESTIMATES. WHEN ADDED TO THE PROJECTIONS FROM OUR VARIOUS TECHNOLOGY CONTRACTS WITH GROUPS RANGING FROM LAW ENFORCEMENT TO MEDICAL AID, WE SHOULD CONTINUE TO SEE STEADY GROWTH. QUESTIONS?
POWERS INDUSTRIES
POWERS INDUSTRIES
MR. POWERS, THINGS LOOK GREAT. YOUR TEAM HAS DONE THEIR HOMEWORK, AND I'M PLEASED AS ALWAYS TO SEE NO IRREGULARITIES AND PROJECTIONS THAT ARE FISCALLY CONSERVATIVE.
THANK YOU. YOUR CONFIDENCE IS NOT MISGUIDED. WE WORK HARD TO ENSURE THAT.
WAYNE, BUDDY. GODDAMN, IT'S BEEN A LONG TIME!
BACK OFF, CURLY. WAYNE AND I GO WAY BACK.
HOW DID YOU GET UP HERE, MR. SHARPTON?
MAGIC. LOOK, I HAVE SOMETHING YOU MAY BE INTERESTED IN.

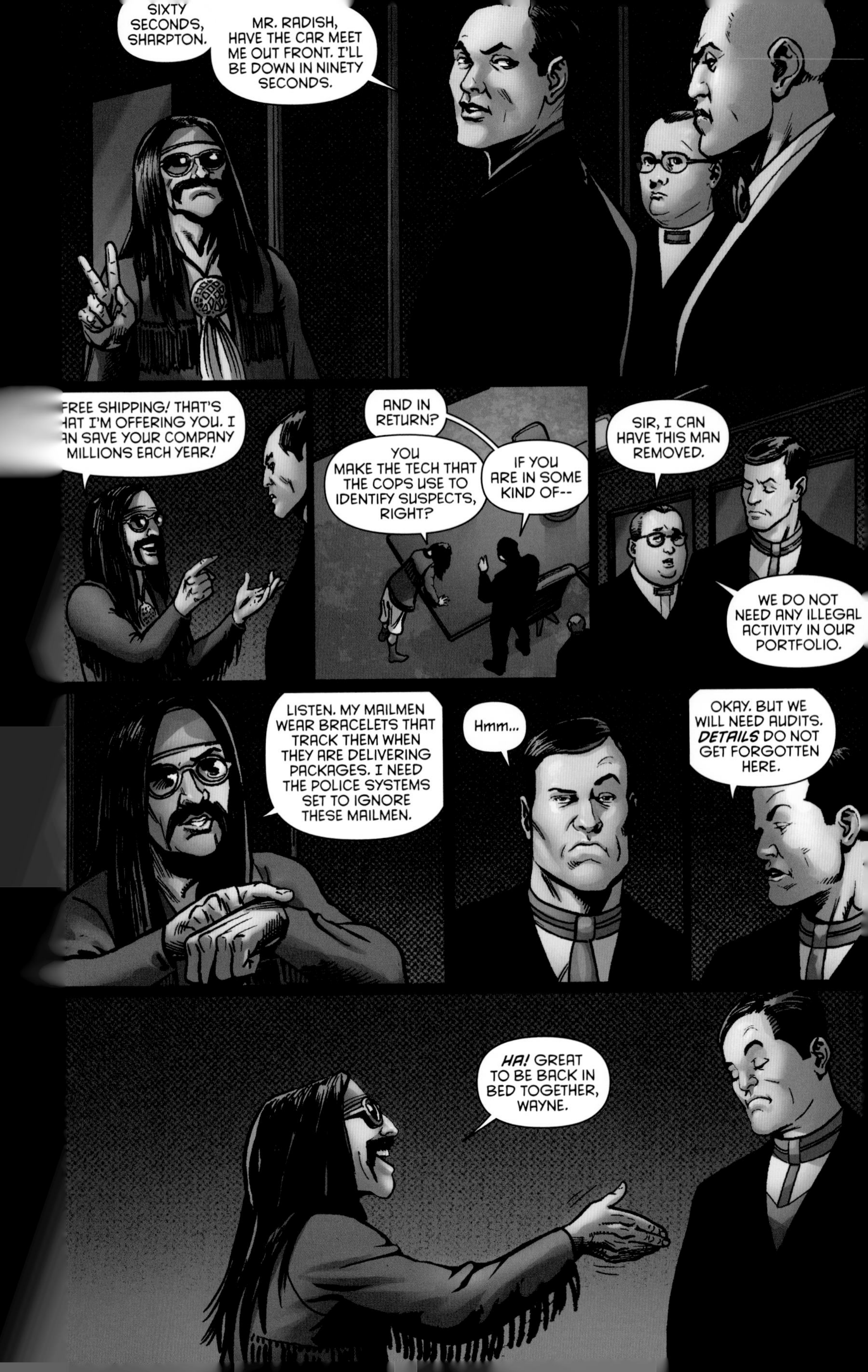
SIXTY SECONDS, SHARPTON.
MR. RADISH, HAVE THE CAR MEET ME OUT FRONT. I'LL BE DOWN IN NINETY SECONDS.
FREE SHIPPING! THAT'S HAT I'M OFFERING YOU. I AN SAVE YOUR COMPANY MILLIONS EACH YEAR!
AND IN RETURN?
YOU MAKE THE TECH THAT THE COPS USE TO IDENTIFY SUSPECTS, RIGHT?
IF YOU ARE IN SOME KIND OF--
SIR, I CAN HAVE THIS MAN REMOVED.
WE DO NOT NEED ANY ILLEGAL ACTIVITY IN OUR PORTFOLIO.
LISTEN. MY MAILMEN WEAR BRACELETS THAT TRACK THEM WHEN THEY ARE DELIVERING PACKAGES. I NEED THE POLICE SYSTEMS SET TO IGNORE THESE MAILMEN.
Hmm...
OKAY. BUT WE WILL NEED AUDITS. *DETAILS* DO NOT GET FORGOTTEN HERE.
HA! GREAT TO BE BACK IN BED TOGETHER, WAYNE.

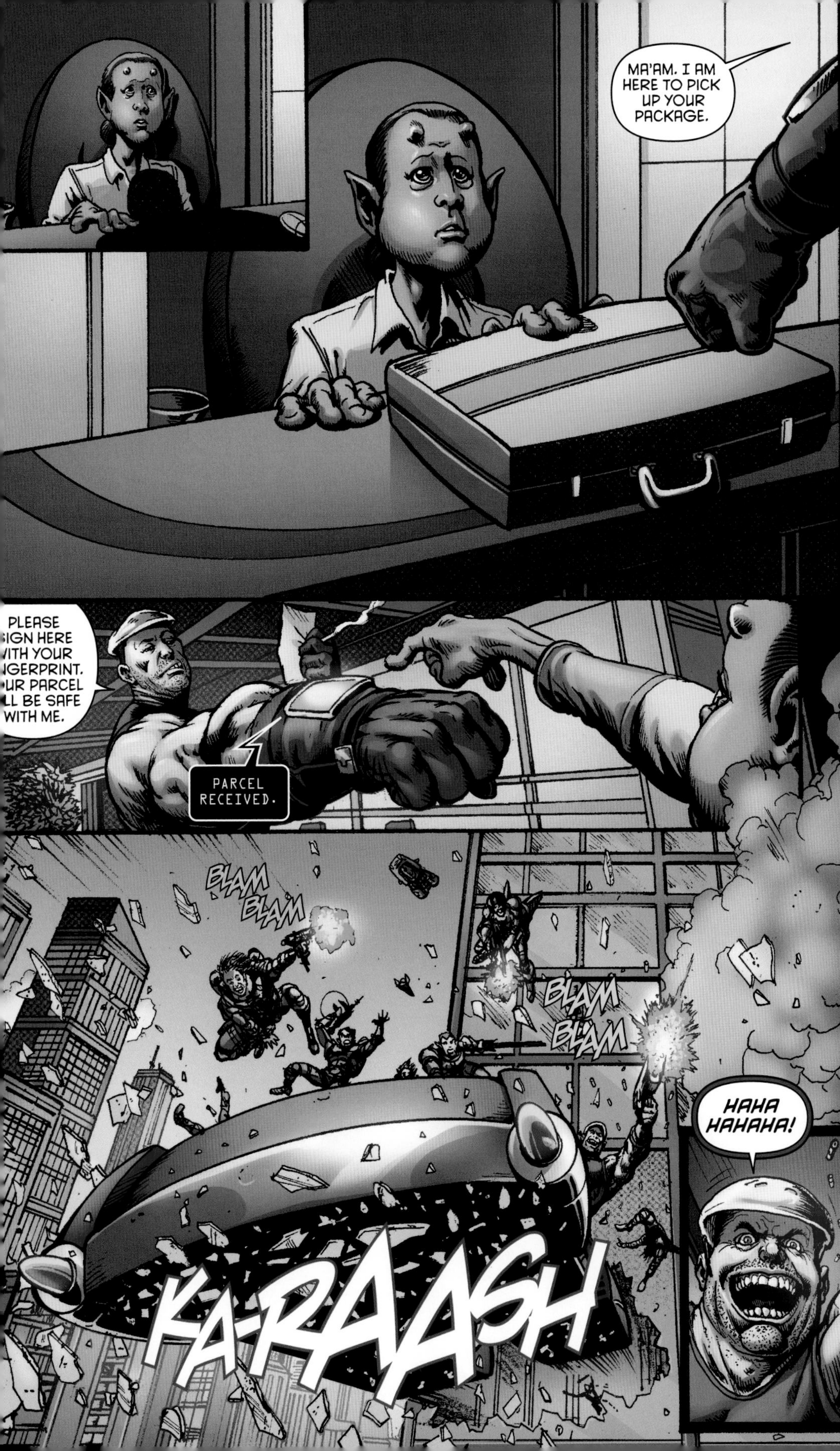
MA'AM. I AM HERE TO PICK UP YOUR PACKAGE.
PLEASE
IGN HERE
ITH YOUR
IGERPRINT.
UR PARCEL
LL BE SAFE
WITH ME.
PARCEL RECEIVED.
BLAM BLAM
BLAM BLAM
HAHA HAHAHA!
KA-RAAASH

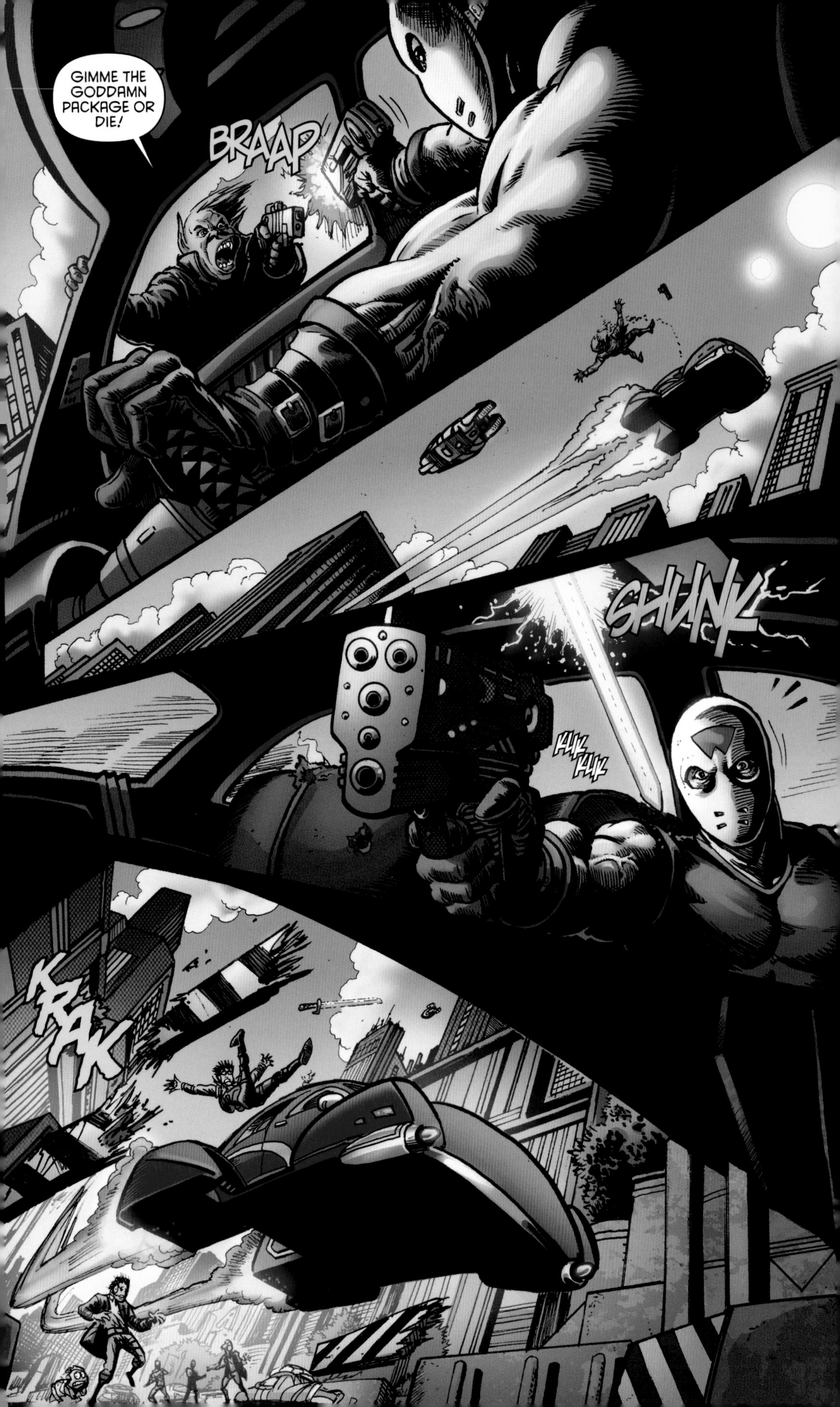

GIMME THE GODDAMN PACKAGE OR DIE!
BRAAP
SHUNK
KLIK KLIK
KRAK

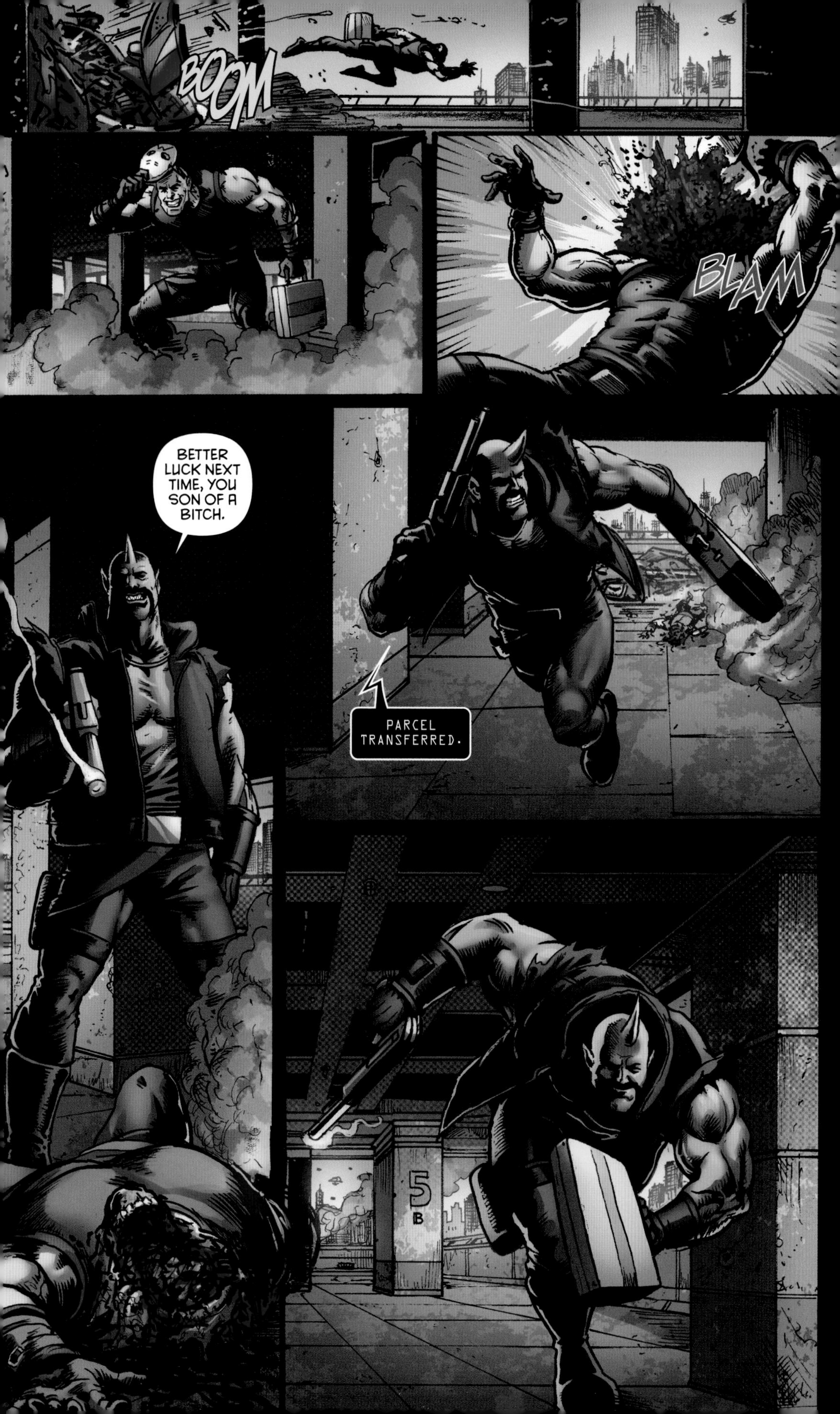
BOOM
BLAM
BETTER LUCK NEXT TIME, YOU SON OF A BITCH.
PARCEL TRANSFERRED.
5
B

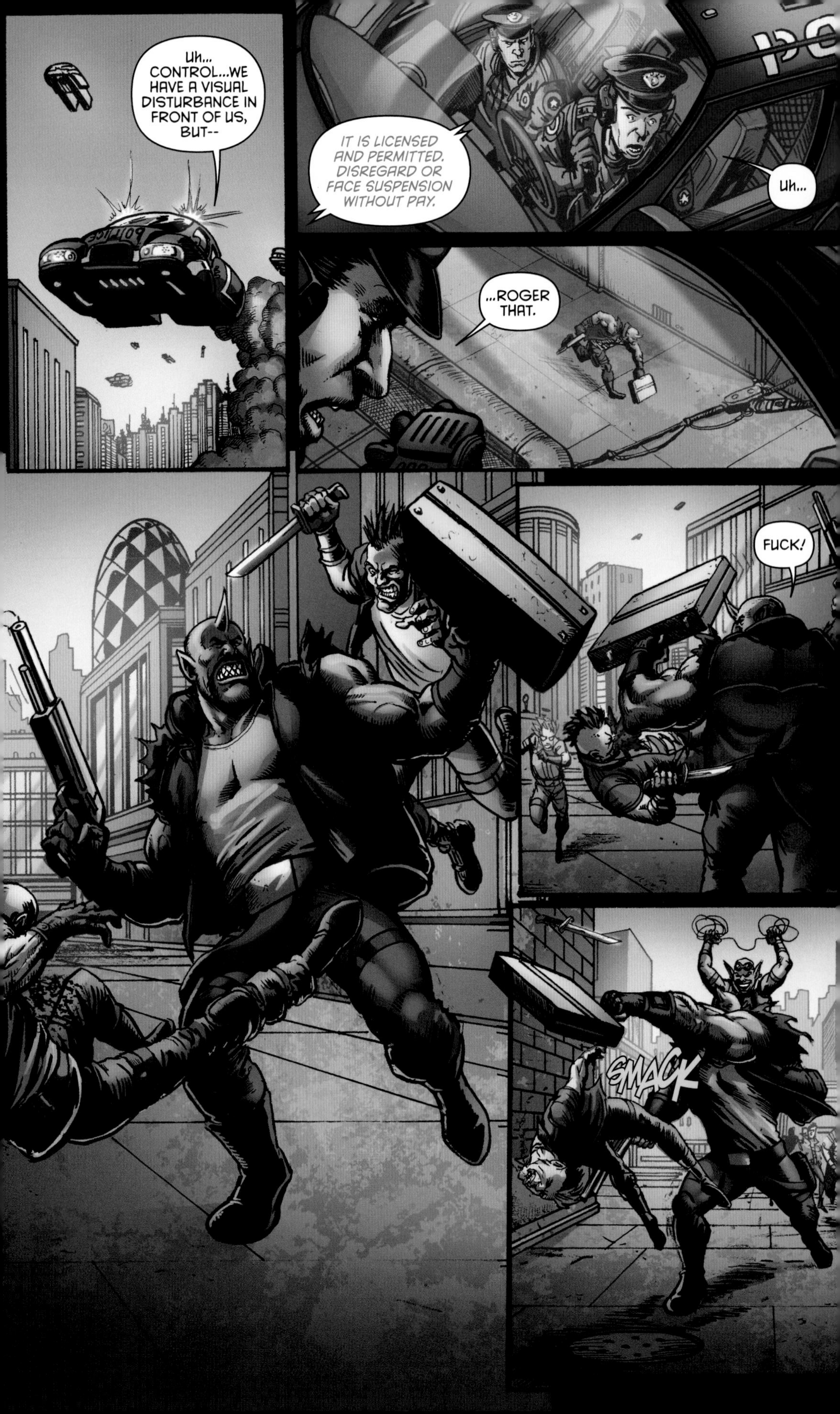
UH... CONTROL...WE HAVE A VISUAL DISTURBANCE IN FRONT OF US, BUT--
IT IS LICENSED AND PERMITTED. DISREGARD OR FACE SUSPENSION WITHOUT PAY.
UH...
...ROGER THAT.
FUCK!
SMACK

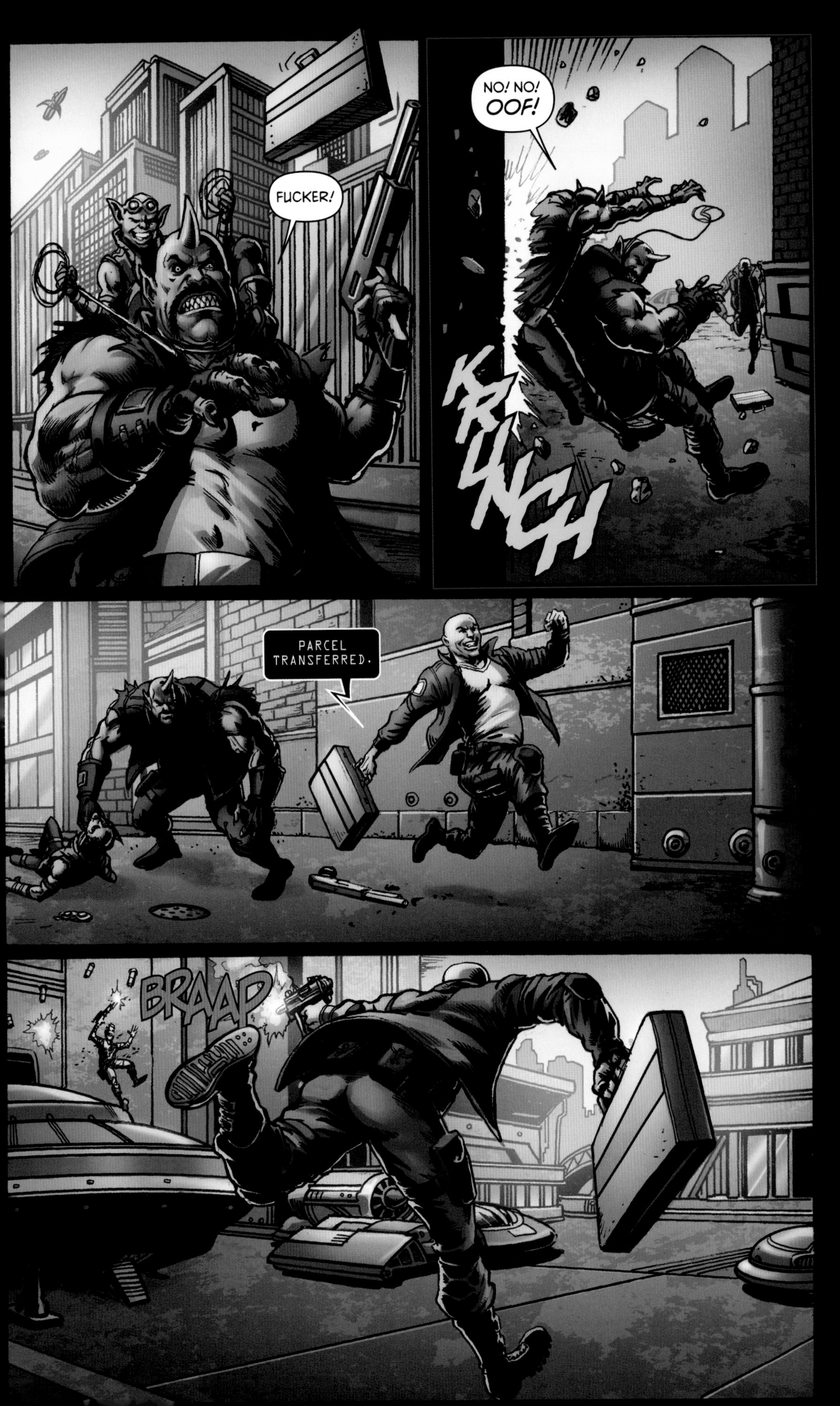
FUCKER!
NO! NO! OOF!
KRUNCH
PARCEL TRANSFERRED.
BRAAP

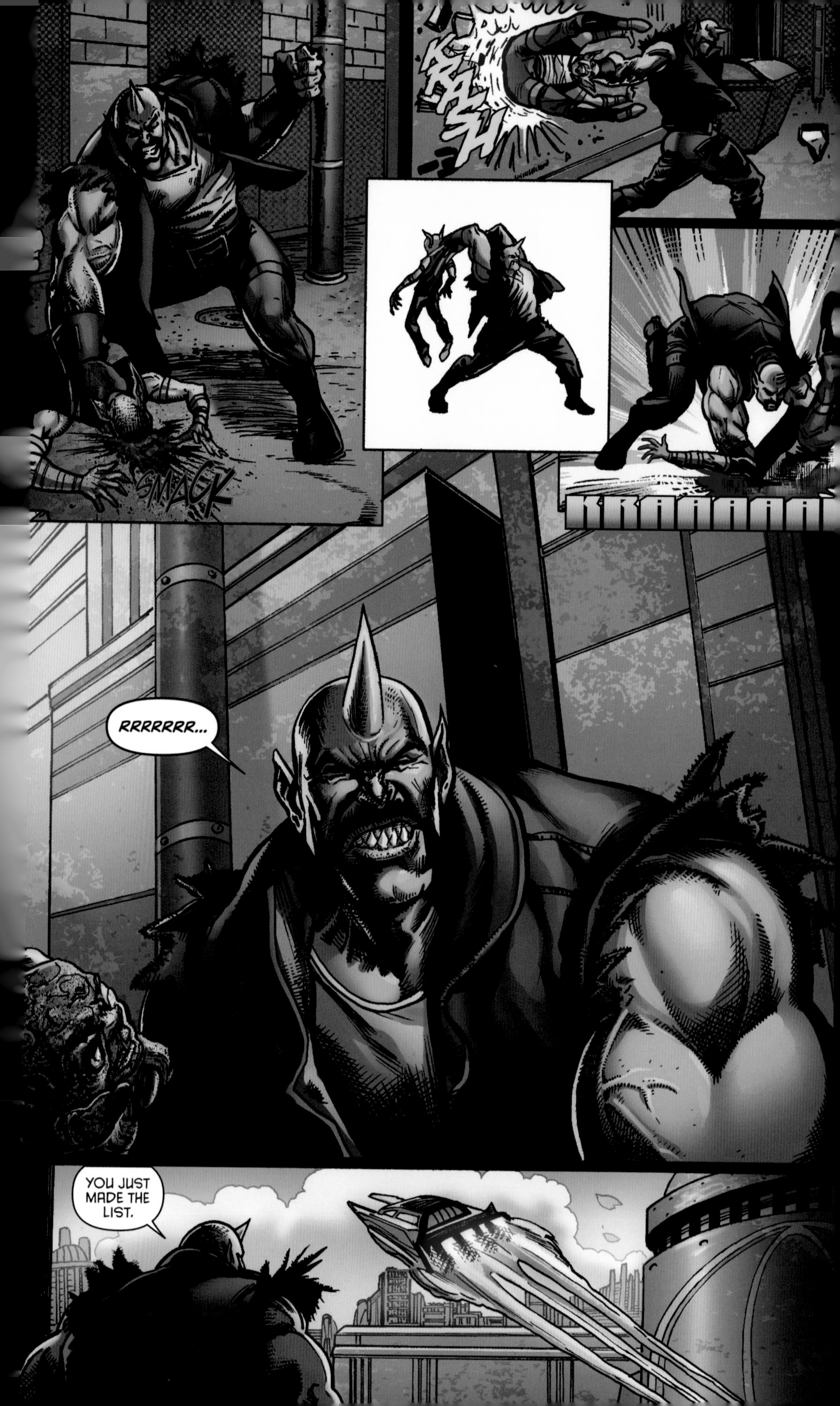
KRASH
SMACK
KRAAAAAA
RRRRRRR...
YOU JUST MADE THE LIST.

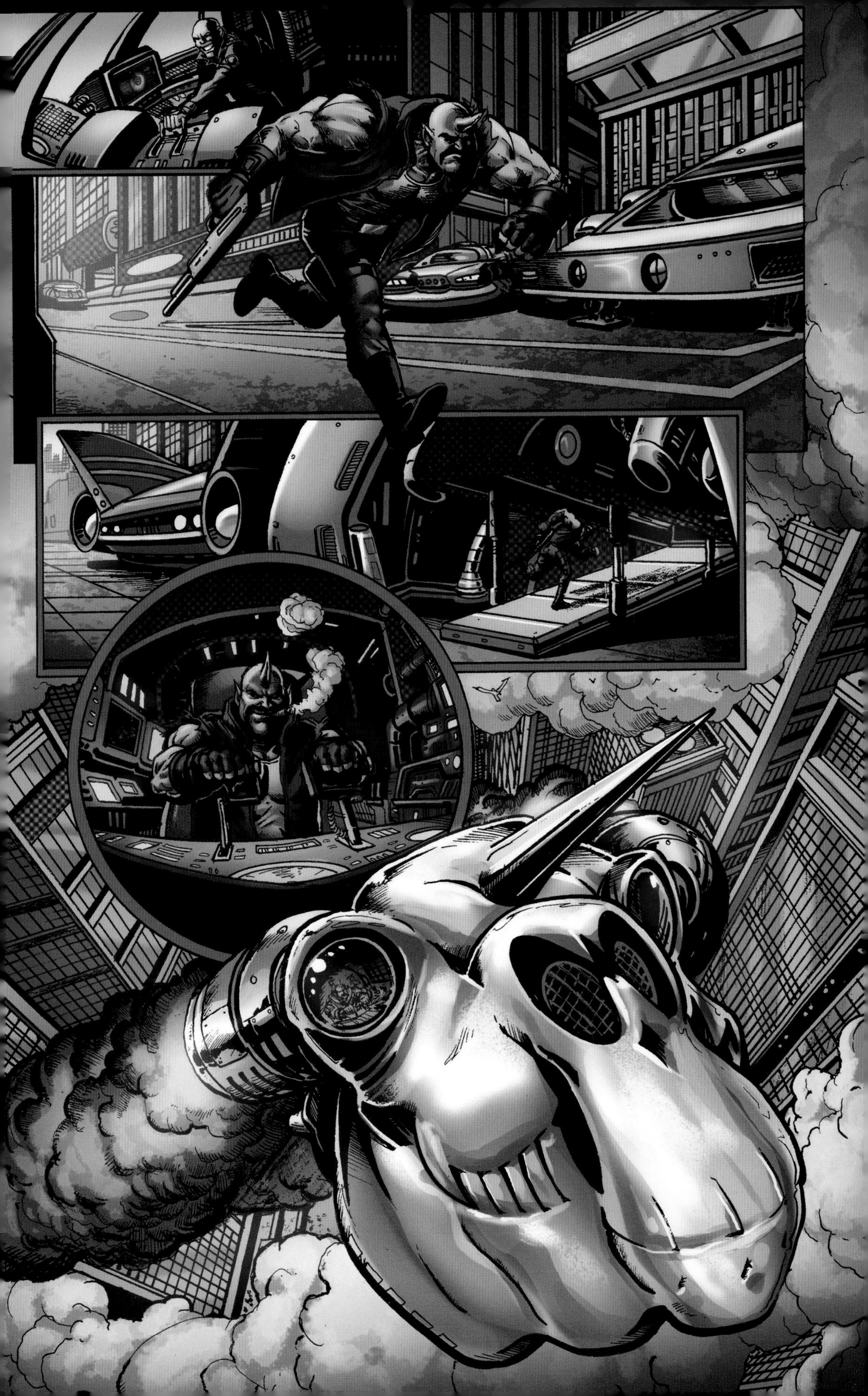

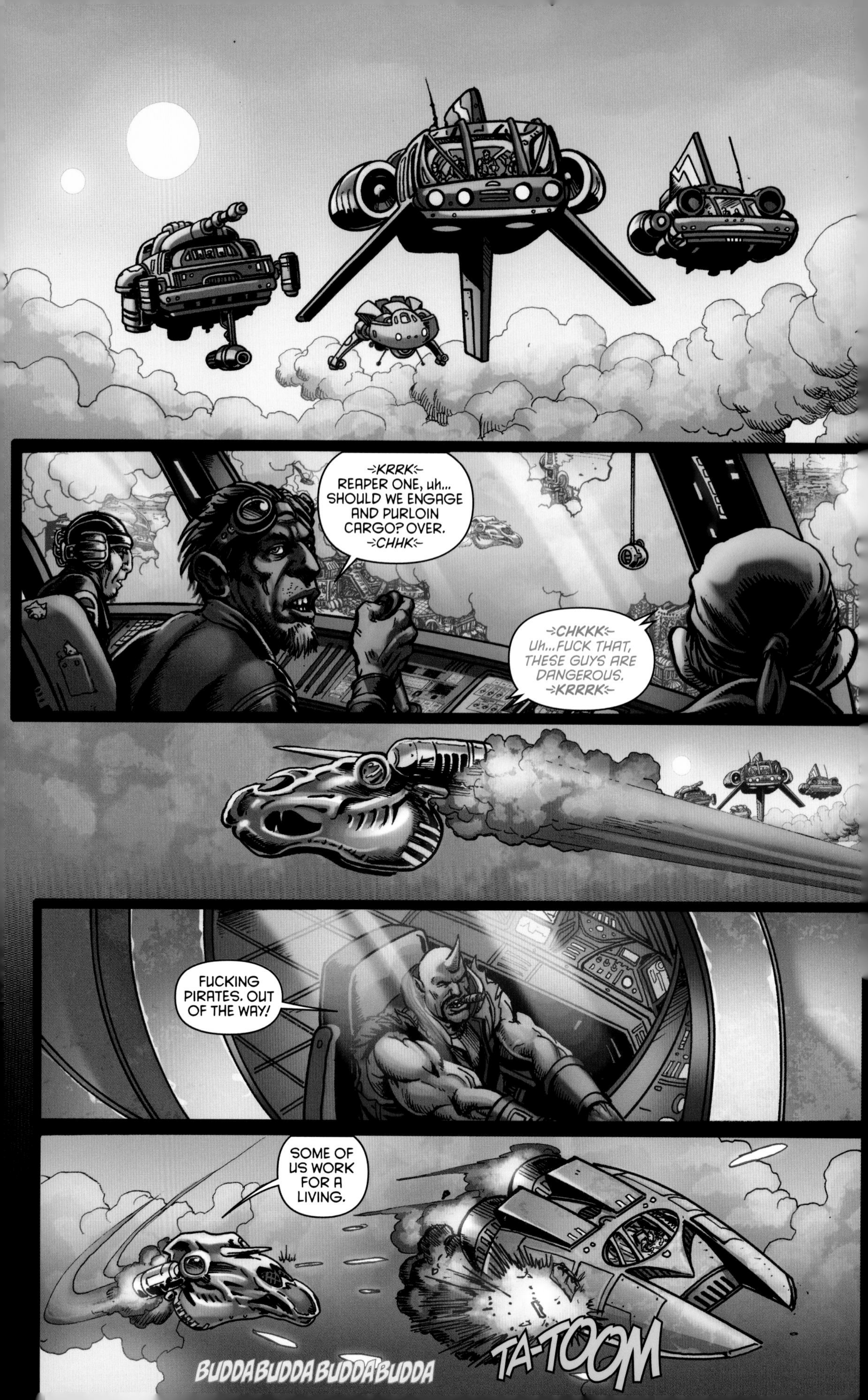

-KRRK- REAPER ONE, uh... SHOULD WE ENGAGE AND PURLOIN CARGO? OVER. -CHHK-
-CHKKK- Uh...FUCK THAT, THESE GUYS ARE DANGEROUS. -KRRRK-
FUCKING PIRATES. OUT OF THE WAY!
SOME OF US WORK FOR A LIVING.
BUDDA BUDDA BUDDA BUDDA
TA-TOOM

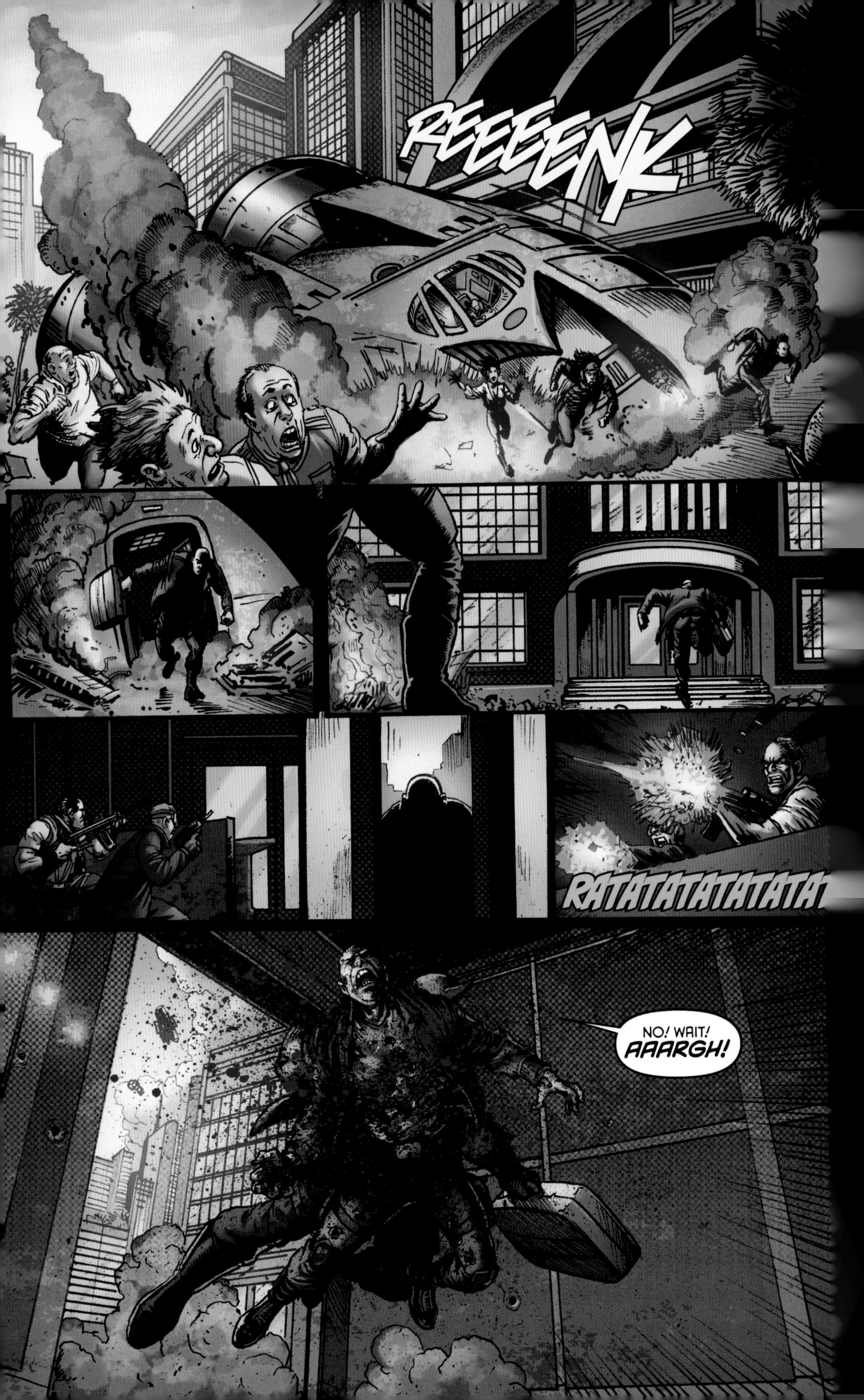
REEEENK
RATATATATATATATAT
NO! WAIT!
AAARGH!

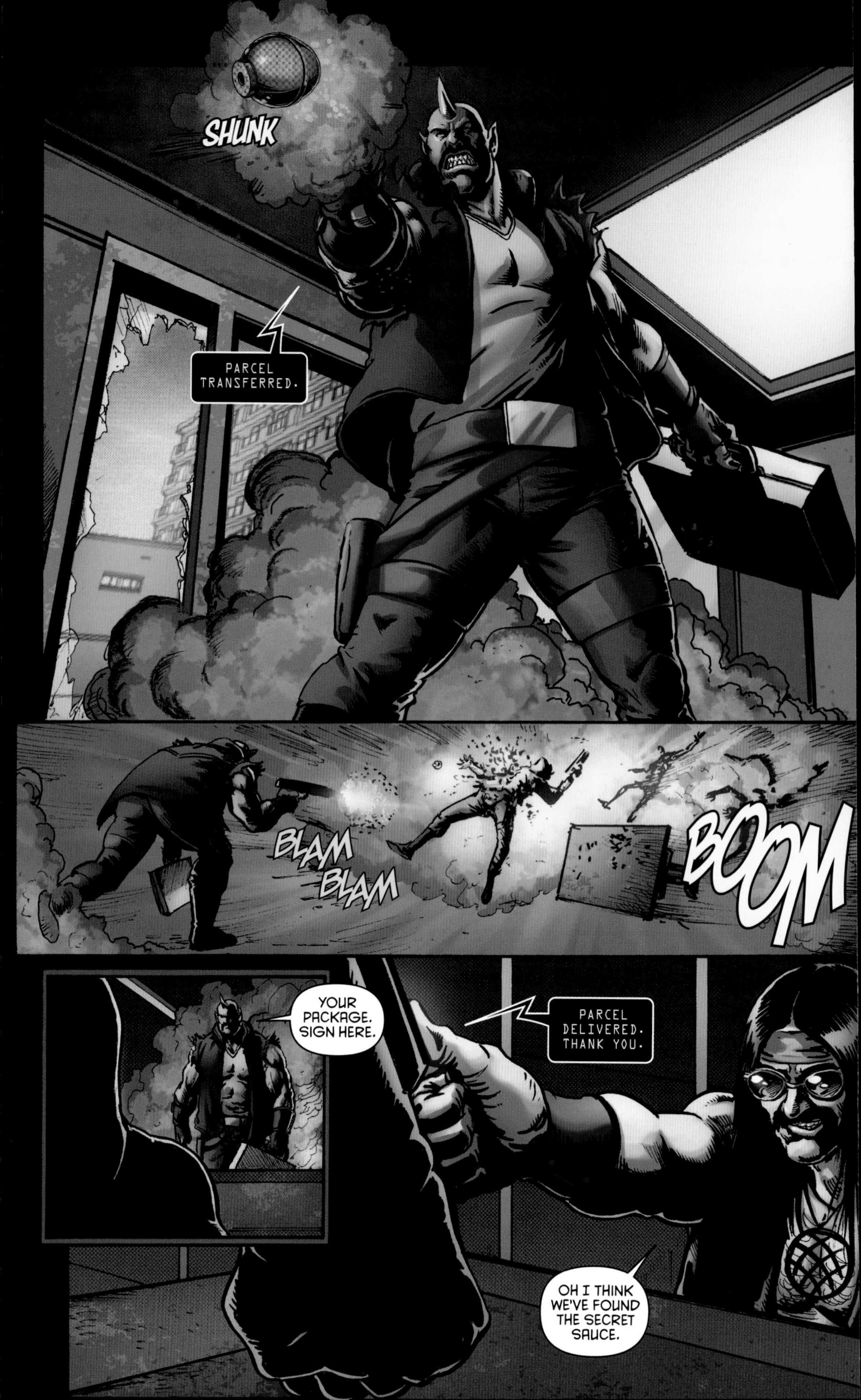
SHUNK
PARCEL TRANSFERRED.
BLAM BLAM
BOOM
YOUR PACKAGE. SIGN HERE.
PARCEL DELIVERED. THANK YOU.
OH I THINK WE'VE FOUND THE SECRET SAUCE.

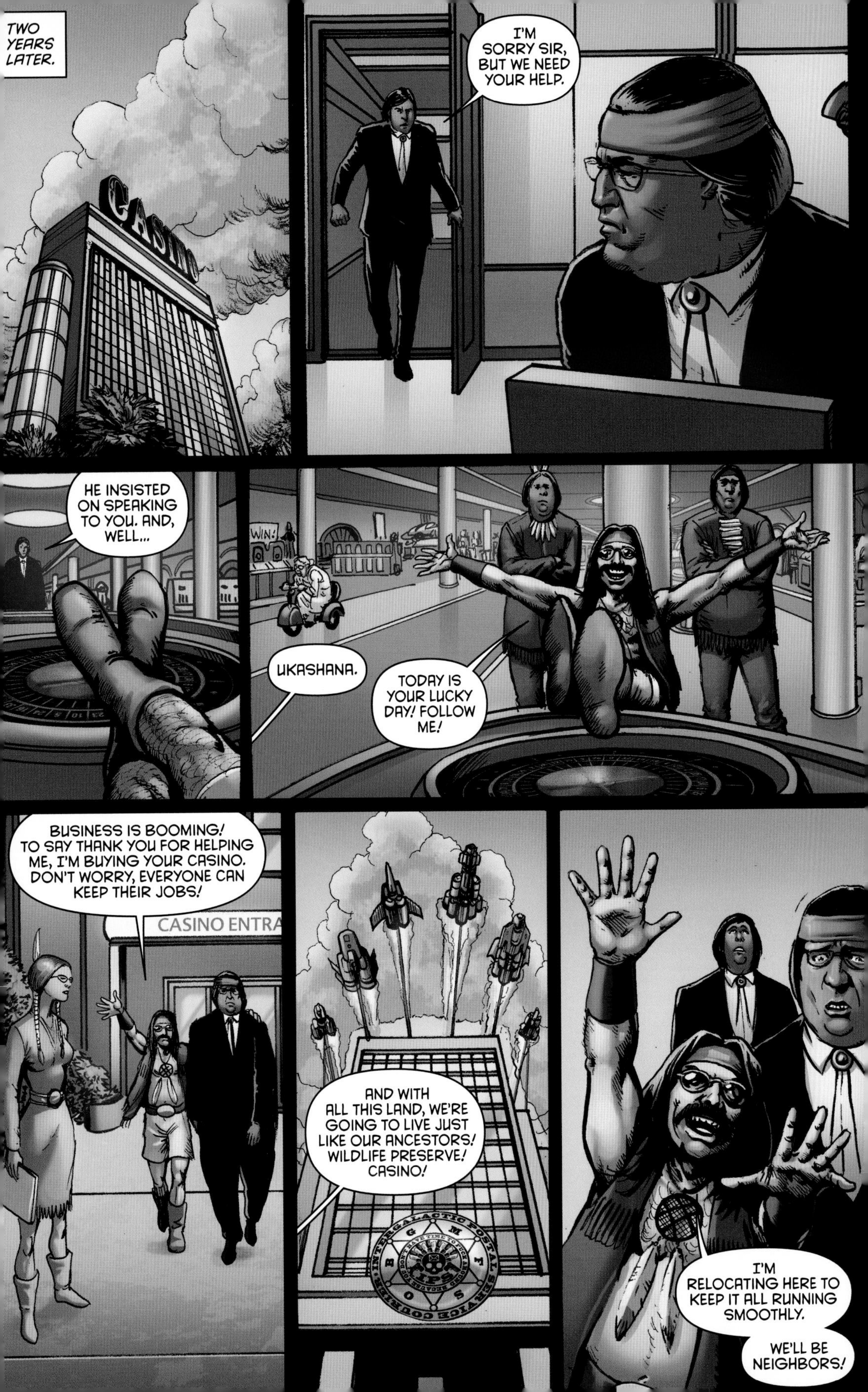
TWO YEARS LATER.
I'M SORRY SIR, BUT WE NEED YOUR HELP.
HE INSISTED ON SPEAKING TO YOU. AND, WELL...
WIN!
UKASHANA.
TODAY IS YOUR LUCKY DAY! FOLLOW ME!
BUSINESS IS BOOMING! TO SAY THANK YOU FOR HELPING ME, I'M BUYING YOUR CASINO. DON'T WORRY, EVERYONE CAN KEEP THEIR JOBS!
CASINO ENTRA
AND WITH ALL THIS LAND, WE'RE GOING TO LIVE JUST LIKE OUR ANCESTORS! WILDLIFE PRESERVE! CASINO!
INTERGALACTIC POSTAL SERVICE COURIER
IPS
I'M RELOCATING HERE TO KEEP IT ALL RUNNING SMOOTHLY.
WE'LL BE NEIGHBORS!

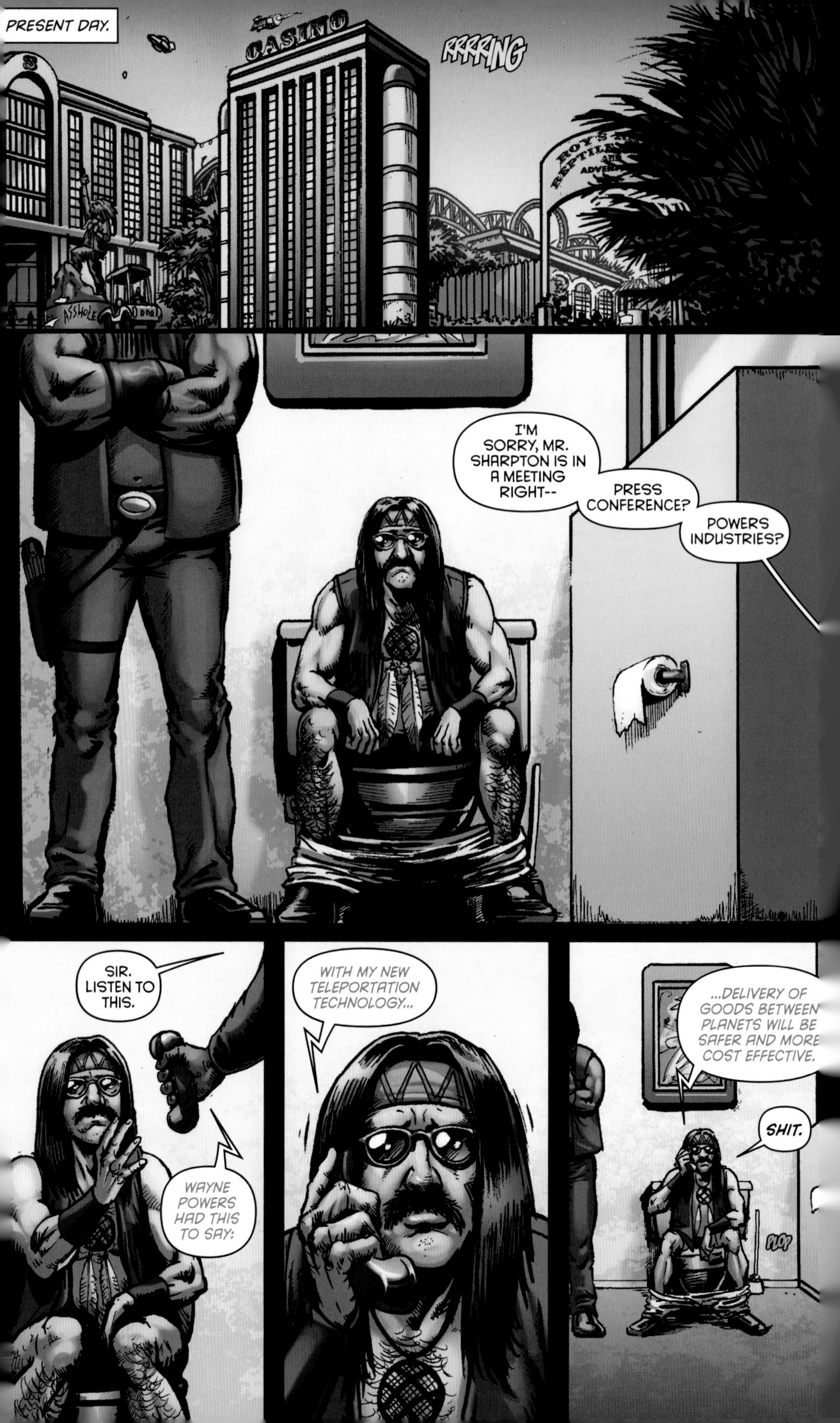
PRESENT DAY.
CASINO
RRRRING
ASSHOLE
I'M SORRY, MR. SHARPTON IS IN A MEETING RIGHT--
PRESS CONFERENCE?
POWERS INDUSTRIES?
SIR. LISTEN TO THIS.
WAYNE POWERS HAD THIS TO SAY:
WITH MY NEW TELEPORTATION TECHNOLOGY...
...DELIVERY OF GOODS BETWEEN PLANETS WILL BE SAFER AND MORE COST EFFECTIVE.
SHIT.
PLOP

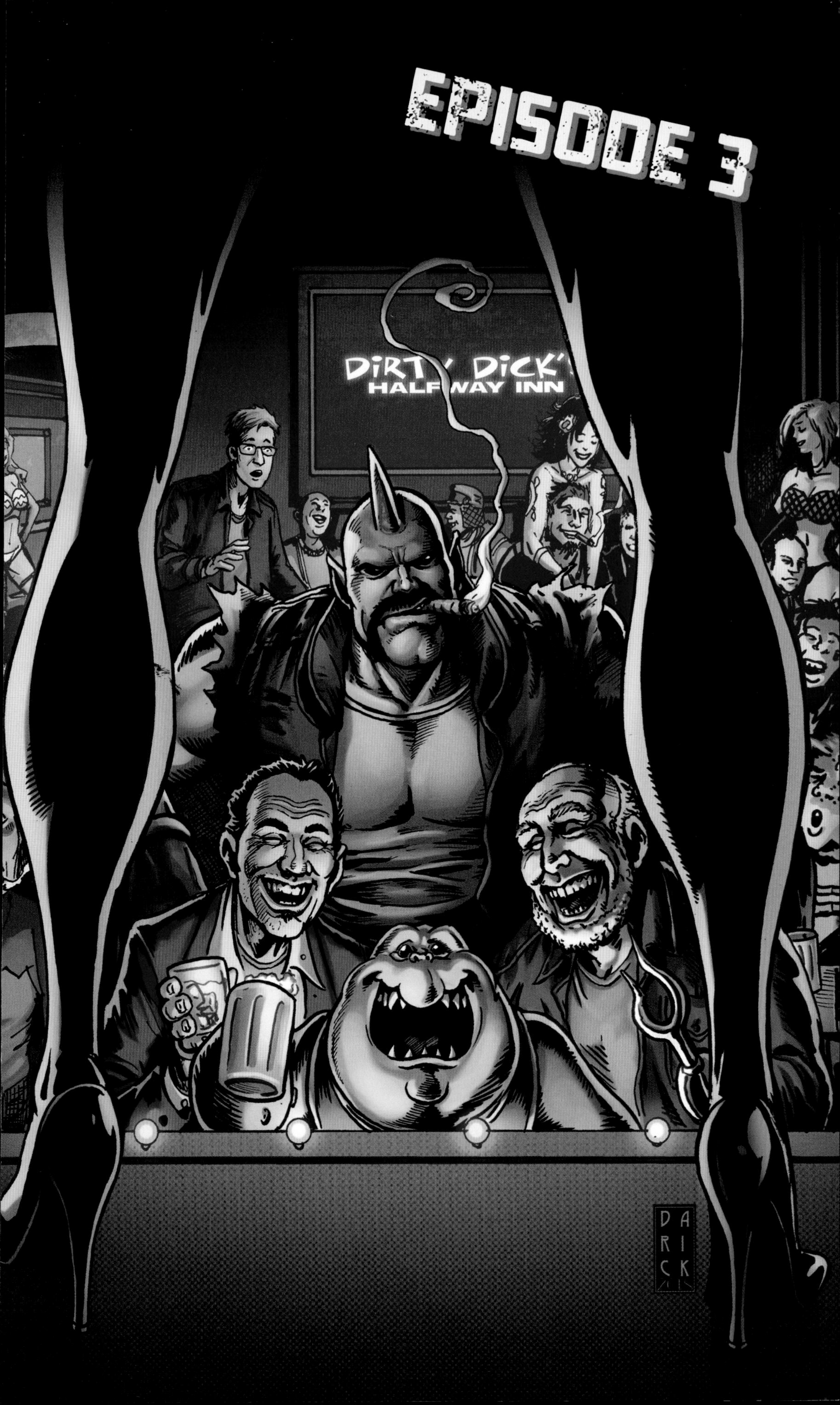

EPISODE 3

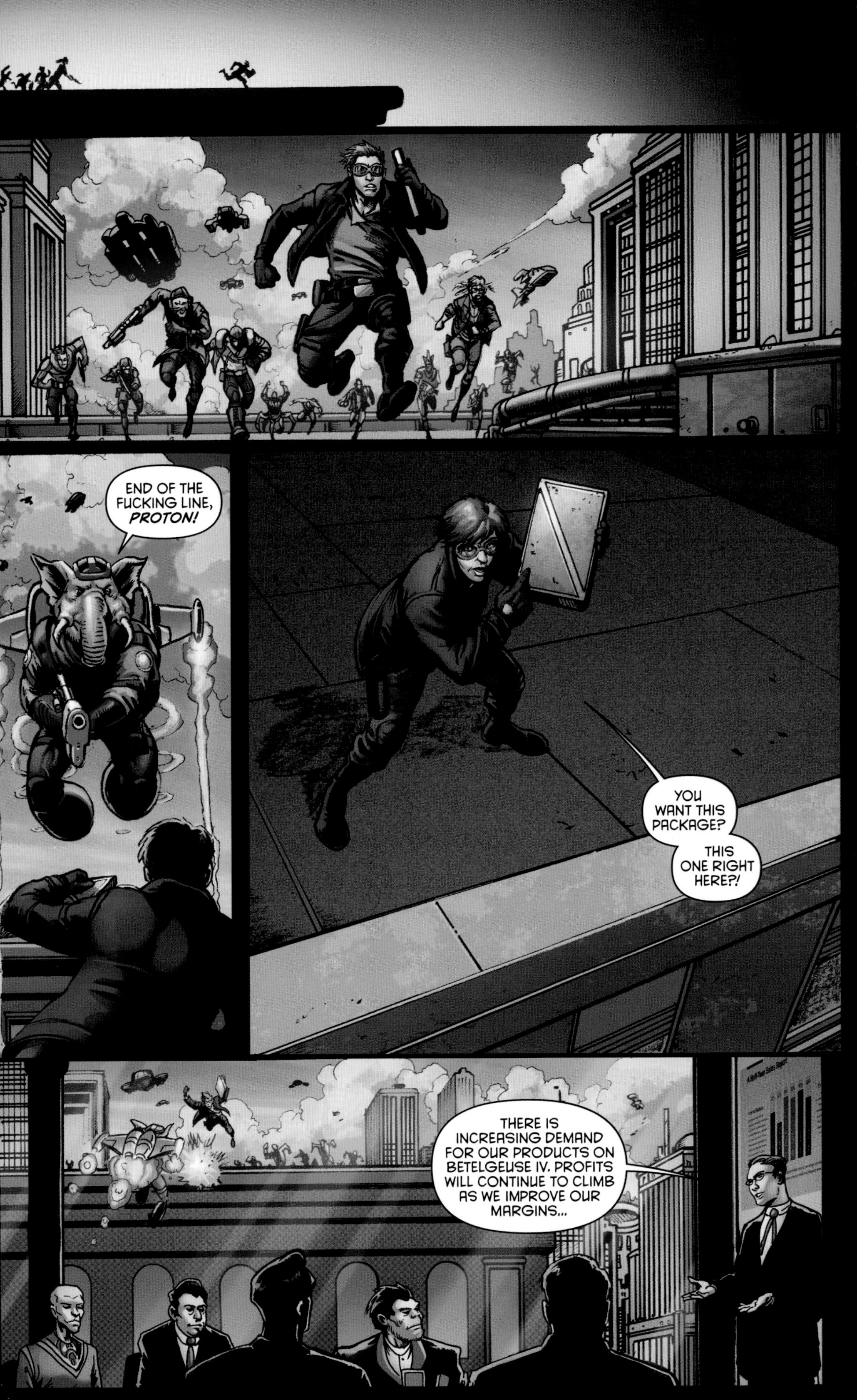

END OF THE FUCKING LINE, PROTON!
YOU WANT THIS PACKAGE?
THIS ONE RIGHT HERE?!
THERE IS INCREASING DEMAND FOR OUR PRODUCTS ON BETELGEUSE IV. PROFITS WILL CONTINUE TO CLIMB AS WE IMPROVE OUR MARGINS...

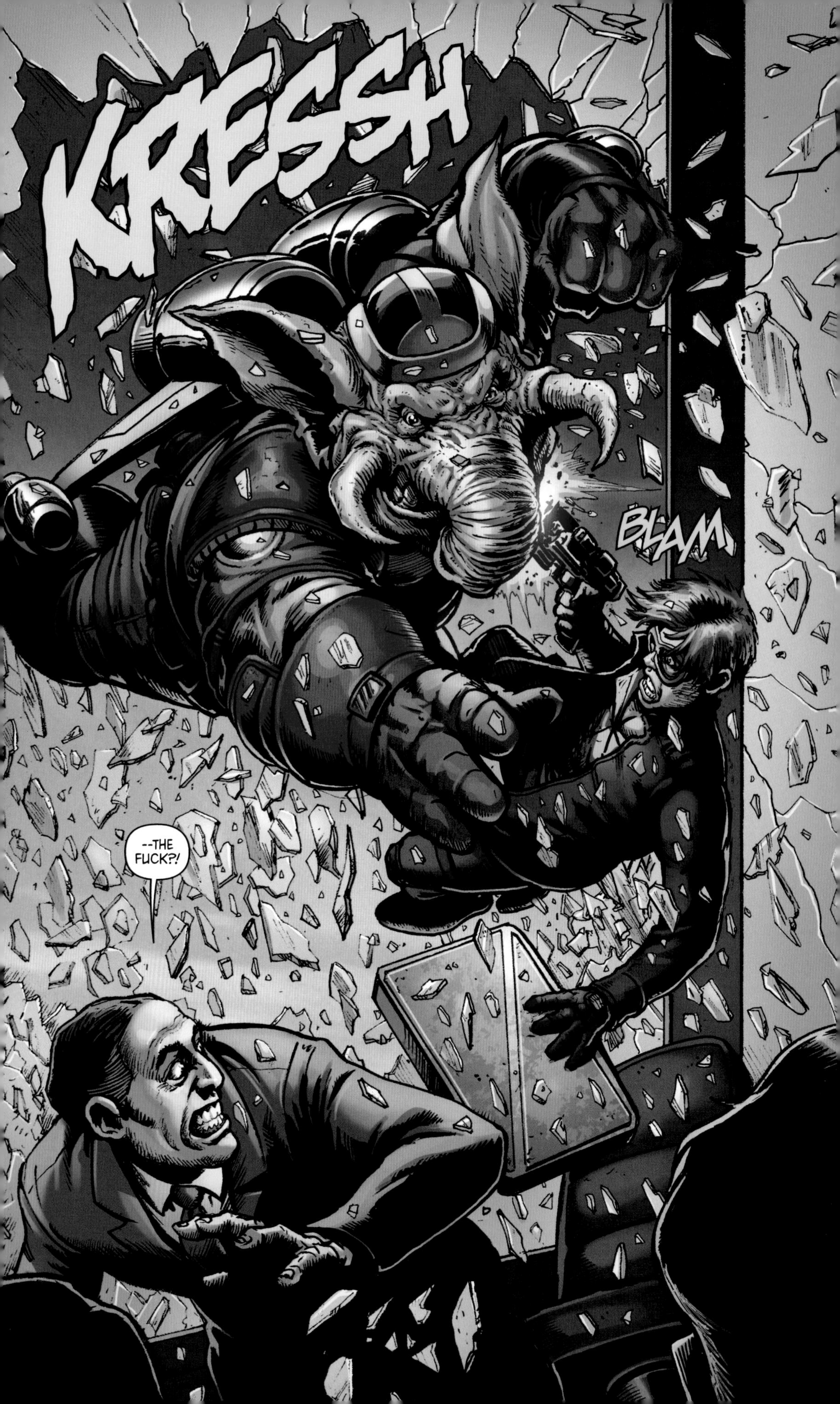
KRESSH
BLAM
--THE FUCK?!

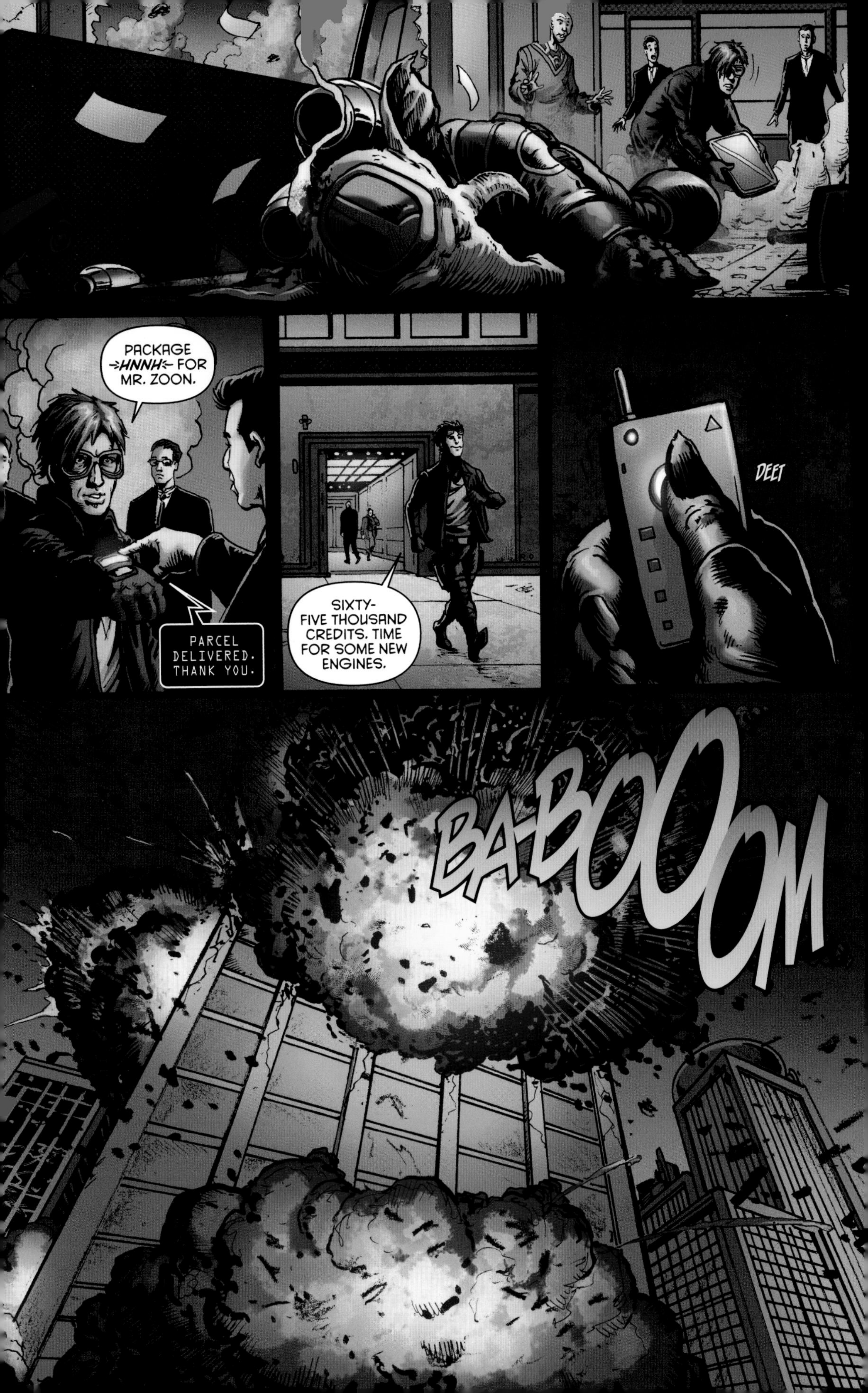

PACKAGE -HNNH- FOR MR. ZOON.
PARCEL DELIVERED. THANK YOU.
SIXTY-FIVE THOUSAND CREDITS. TIME FOR SOME NEW ENGINES.
DEET
BA-BOOOM

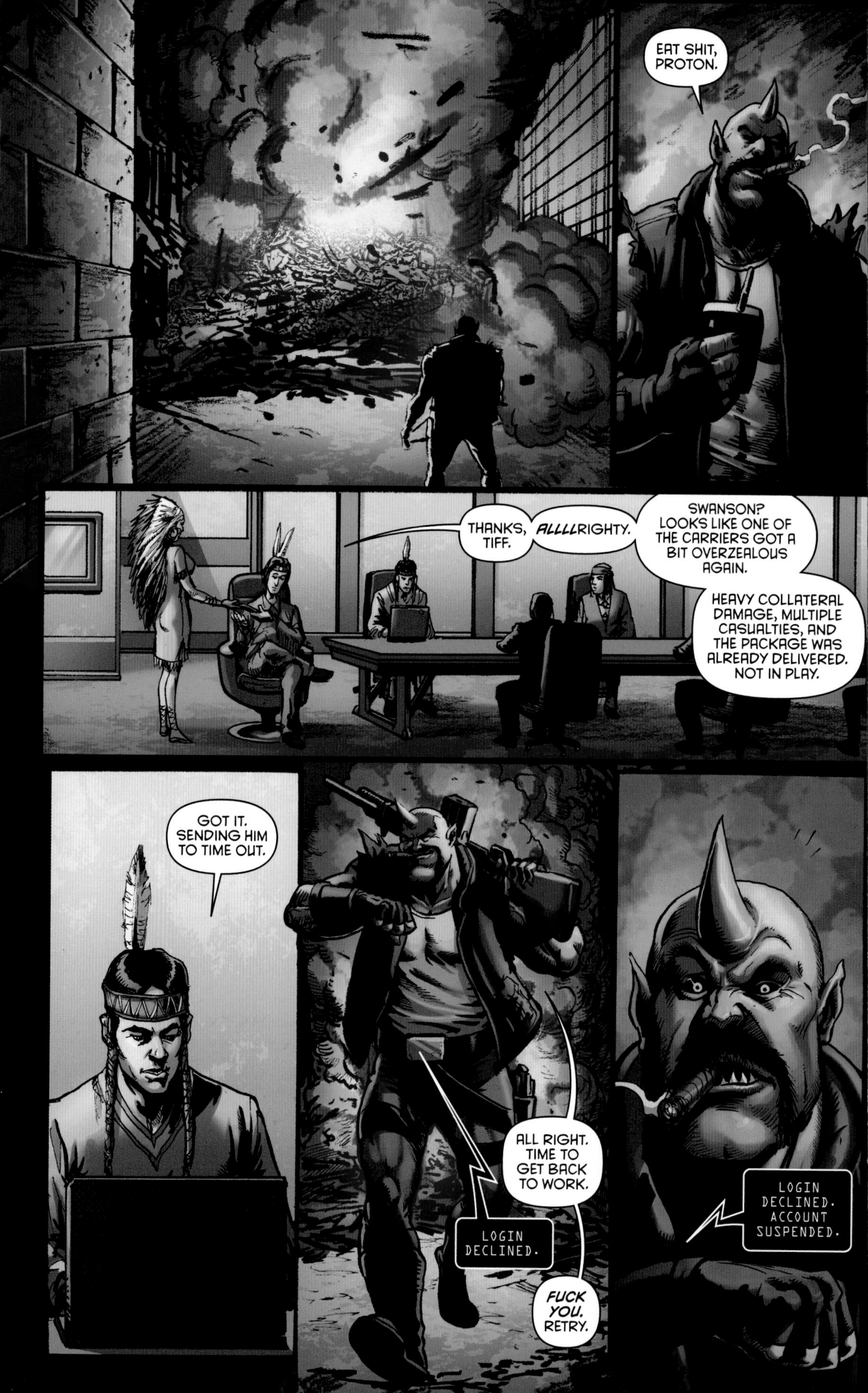
EAT SHIT, PROTON.
THANKS, TIFF.
ALLLLRIGHTY.
SWANSON? LOOKS LIKE ONE OF THE CARRIERS GOT A BIT OVERZEALOUS AGAIN.
HEAVY COLLATERAL DAMAGE, MULTIPLE CASUALTIES, AND THE PACKAGE WAS ALREADY DELIVERED. NOT IN PLAY.
GOT IT. SENDING HIM TO TIME OUT.
ALL RIGHT. TIME TO GET BACK TO WORK.
LOGIN DECLINED.
FUCK YOU. RETRY.
LOGIN DECLINED. ACCOUNT SUSPENDED.

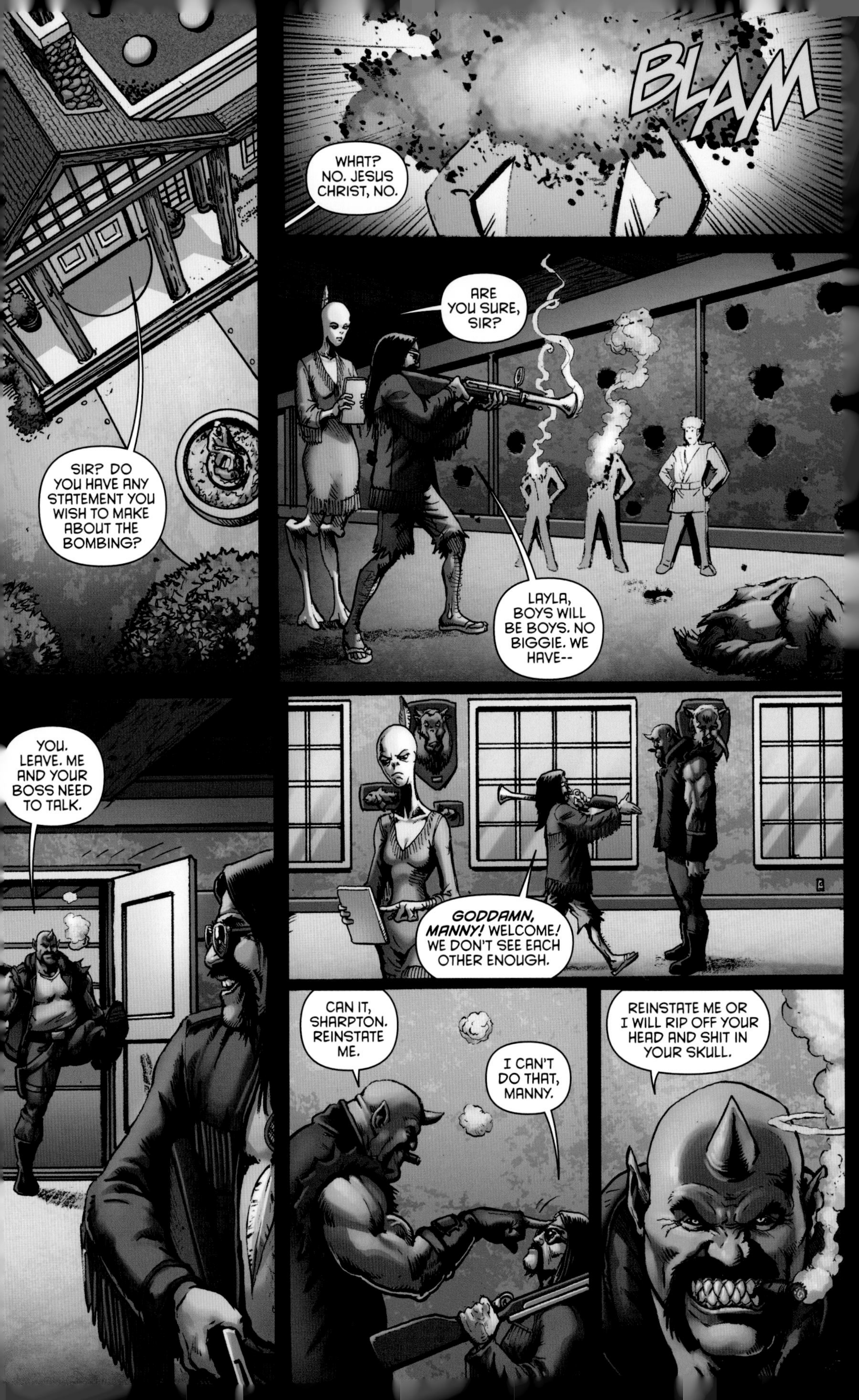
SIR? DO YOU HAVE ANY STATEMENT YOU WISH TO MAKE ABOUT THE BOMBING?
BLAM
WHAT? NO. JESUS CHRIST, NO.
ARE YOU SURE, SIR?
LAYLA, BOYS WILL BE BOYS. NO BIGGIE. WE HAVE--
YOU. LEAVE. ME AND YOUR BOSS NEED TO TALK.
GODDAMN, MANNY! WELCOME! WE DON'T SEE EACH OTHER ENOUGH.
CAN IT, SHARPTON. REINSTATE ME.
I CAN'T DO THAT, MANNY.
REINSTATE ME OR I WILL RIP OFF YOUR HEAD AND SHIT IN YOUR SKULL.

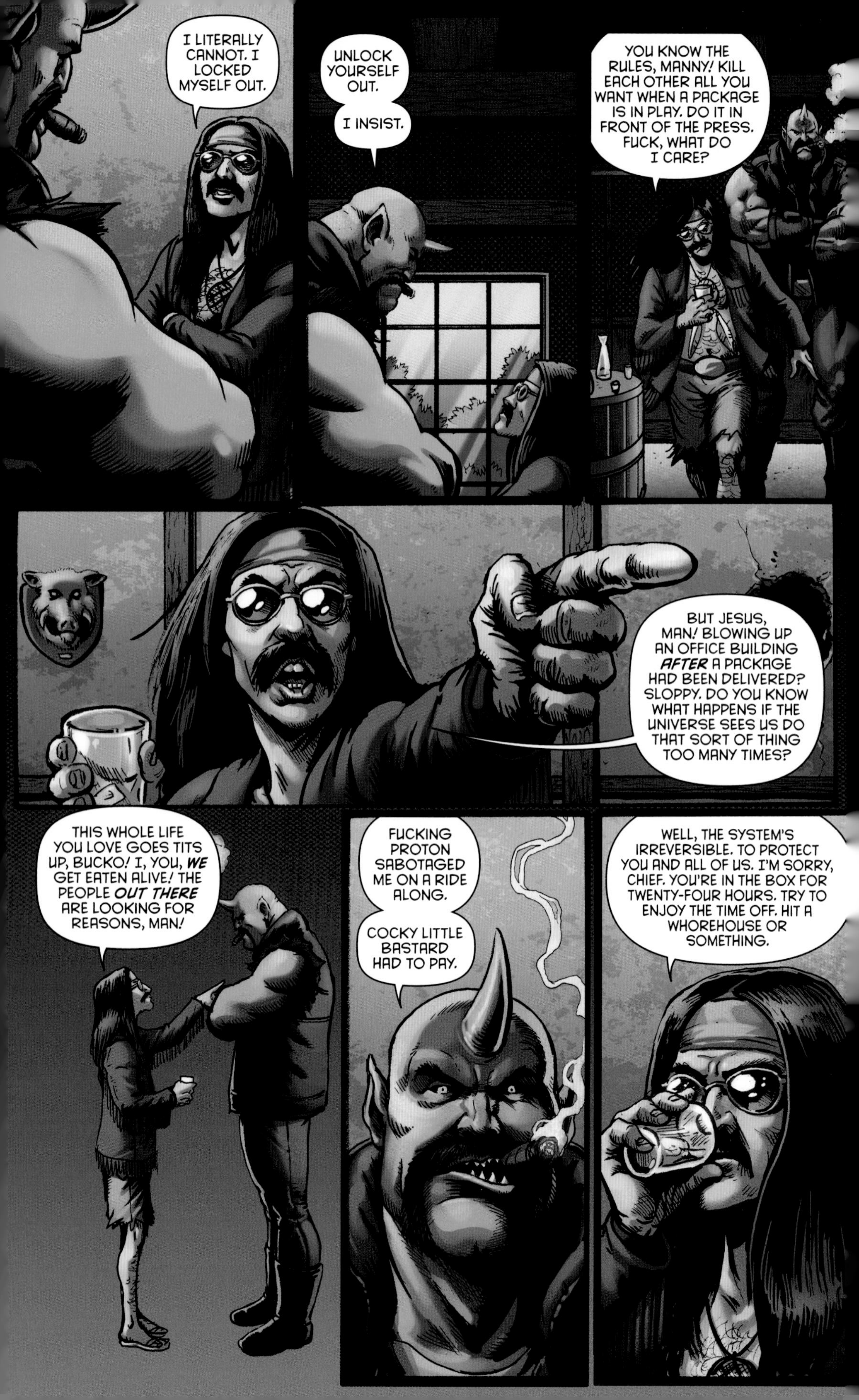
I LITERALLY CANNOT. I LOCKED MYSELF OUT.
UNLOCK YOURSELF OUT.
I INSIST.
YOU KNOW THE RULES, MANNY! KILL EACH OTHER ALL YOU WANT WHEN A PACKAGE IS IN PLAY. DO IT IN FRONT OF THE PRESS. FUCK, WHAT DO I CARE?
BUT JESUS, MAN! BLOWING UP AN OFFICE BUILDING AFTER A PACKAGE HAD BEEN DELIVERED? SLOPPY. DO YOU KNOW WHAT HAPPENS IF THE UNIVERSE SEES US DO THAT SORT OF THING TOO MANY TIMES?
THIS WHOLE LIFE YOU LOVE GOES TITS UP, BUCKO! I, YOU, WE GET EATEN ALIVE! THE PEOPLE OUT THERE ARE LOOKING FOR REASONS, MAN!
FUCKING PROTON SABOTAGED ME ON A RIDE ALONG.
COCKY LITTLE BASTARD HAD TO PAY.
WELL, THE SYSTEM'S IRREVERSIBLE. TO PROTECT YOU AND ALL OF US. I'M SORRY, CHIEF. YOU'RE IN THE BOX FOR TWENTY-FOUR HOURS. TRY TO ENJOY THE TIME OFF. HIT A WHOREHOUSE OR SOMETHING.

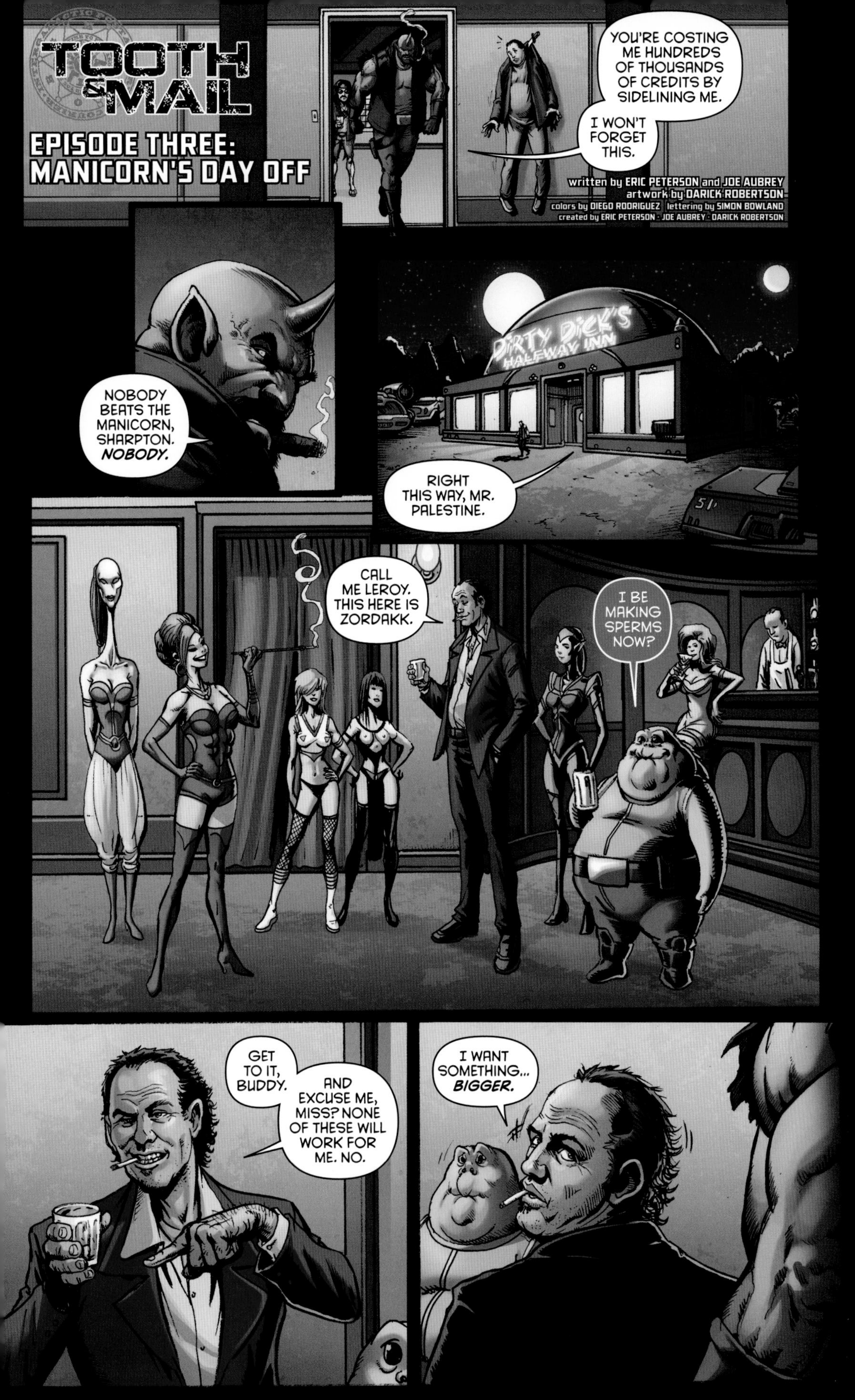
TOOTH & MAIL
EPISODE THREE: MANICORN'S DAY OFF
YOU'RE COSTING ME HUNDREDS OF THOUSANDS OF CREDITS BY SIDELINING ME.
I WON'T FORGET THIS.
written by ERIC PETERSON and JOE AUBREY
artwork by DARICK ROBERTSON
colors by DIEGO RODRIGUEZ lettering by SIMON BOWLAND
created by ERIC PETERSON · JOE AUBREY · DARICK ROBERTSON
NOBODY BEATS THE MANICORN, SHARPTON. NOBODY.
DIRTY DICK'S HALFWAY INN
RIGHT THIS WAY, MR. PALESTINE.
CALL ME LEROY. THIS HERE IS ZORDAKK.
I BE MAKING SPERMS NOW?
GET TO IT, BUDDY.
AND EXCUSE ME, MISS? NONE OF THESE WILL WORK FOR ME. NO.
I WANT SOMETHING... BIGGER.

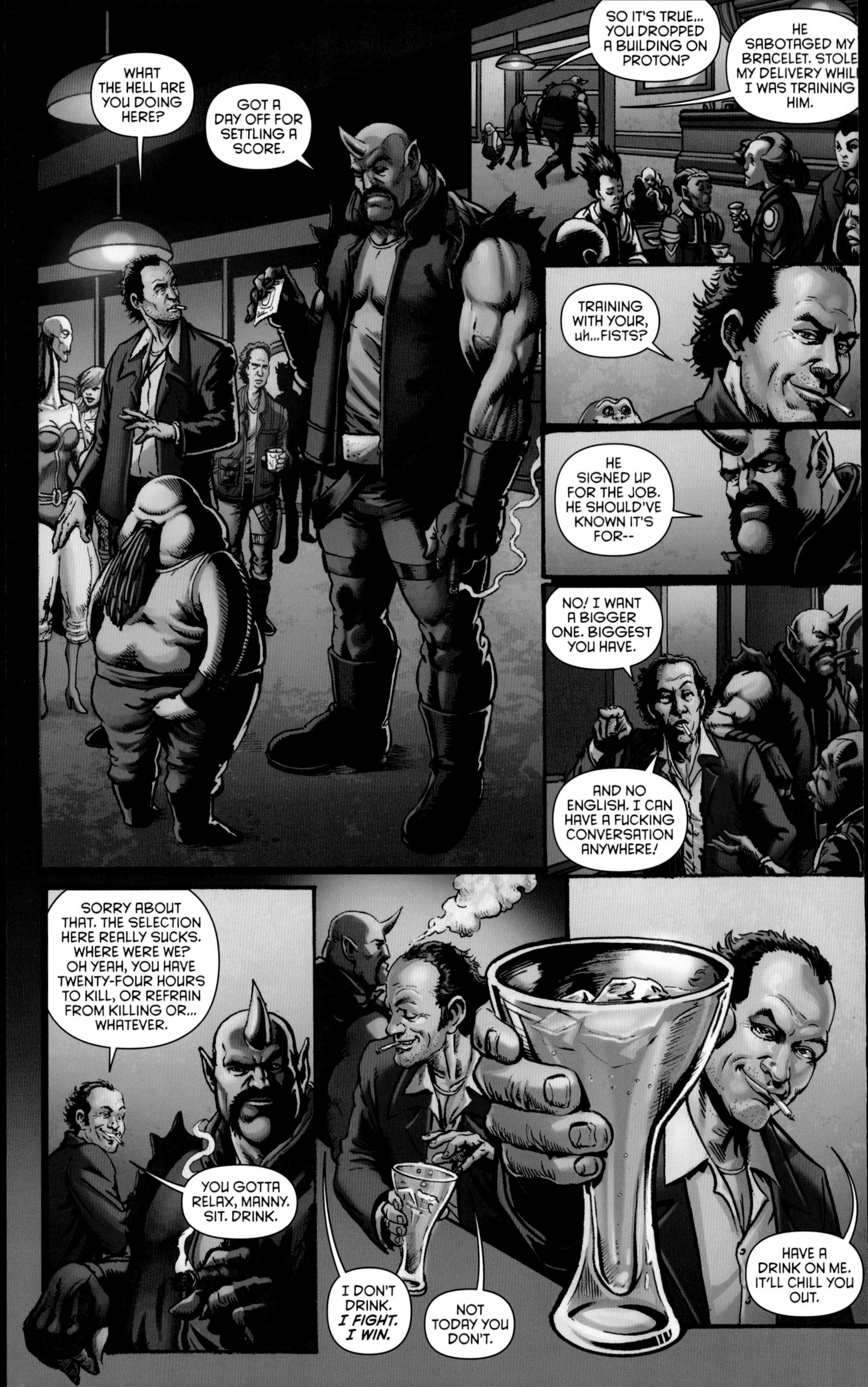
WHAT THE HELL ARE YOU DOING HERE?
GOT A DAY OFF FOR SETTLING A SCORE.
SO IT'S TRUE... YOU DROPPED A BUILDING ON PROTON?
HE SABOTAGED MY BRACELET. STOLE MY DELIVERY WHILE I WAS TRAINING HIM.
TRAINING WITH YOUR, uh...FISTS?
HE SIGNED UP FOR THE JOB. HE SHOULD'VE KNOWN IT'S FOR--
NO! I WANT A BIGGER ONE. BIGGEST YOU HAVE.
AND NO ENGLISH. I CAN HAVE A FUCKING CONVERSATION ANYWHERE!
SORRY ABOUT THAT. THE SELECTION HERE REALLY SUCKS. WHERE WERE WE? OH YEAH, YOU HAVE TWENTY-FOUR HOURS TO KILL, OR REFRAIN FROM KILLING OR... WHATEVER.
YOU GOTTA RELAX, MANNY. SIT. DRINK.
I DON'T DRINK. *I FIGHT. I WIN.*
NOT TODAY YOU DON'T.
HAVE A DRINK ON ME. IT'LL CHILL YOU OUT.

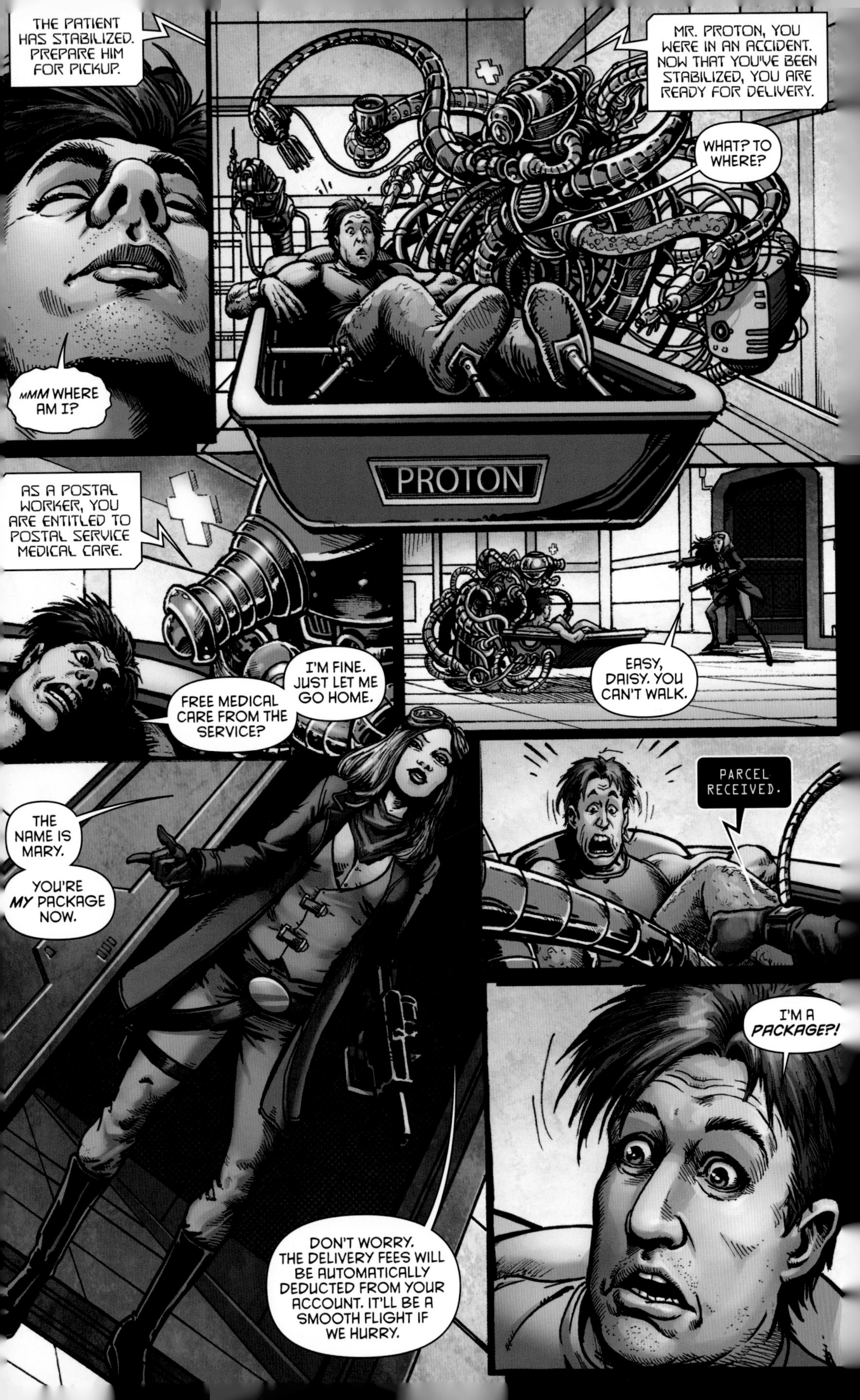
THE PATIENT HAS STABILIZED. PREPARE HIM FOR PICKUP.
MMM WHERE AM I?
MR. PROTON, YOU WERE IN AN ACCIDENT. NOW THAT YOU'VE BEEN STABILIZED, YOU ARE READY FOR DELIVERY.
WHAT? TO WHERE?
PROTON
AS A POSTAL WORKER, YOU ARE ENTITLED TO POSTAL SERVICE MEDICAL CARE.
FREE MEDICAL CARE FROM THE SERVICE?
I'M FINE. JUST LET ME GO HOME.
EASY, DAISY. YOU CAN'T WALK.
THE NAME IS MARY.
YOU'RE *MY* PACKAGE NOW.
PARCEL RECEIVED.
DON'T WORRY. THE DELIVERY FEES WILL BE AUTOMATICALLY DEDUCTED FROM YOUR ACCOUNT. IT'LL BE A SMOOTH FLIGHT IF WE HURRY.
I'M A *PACKAGE?!*

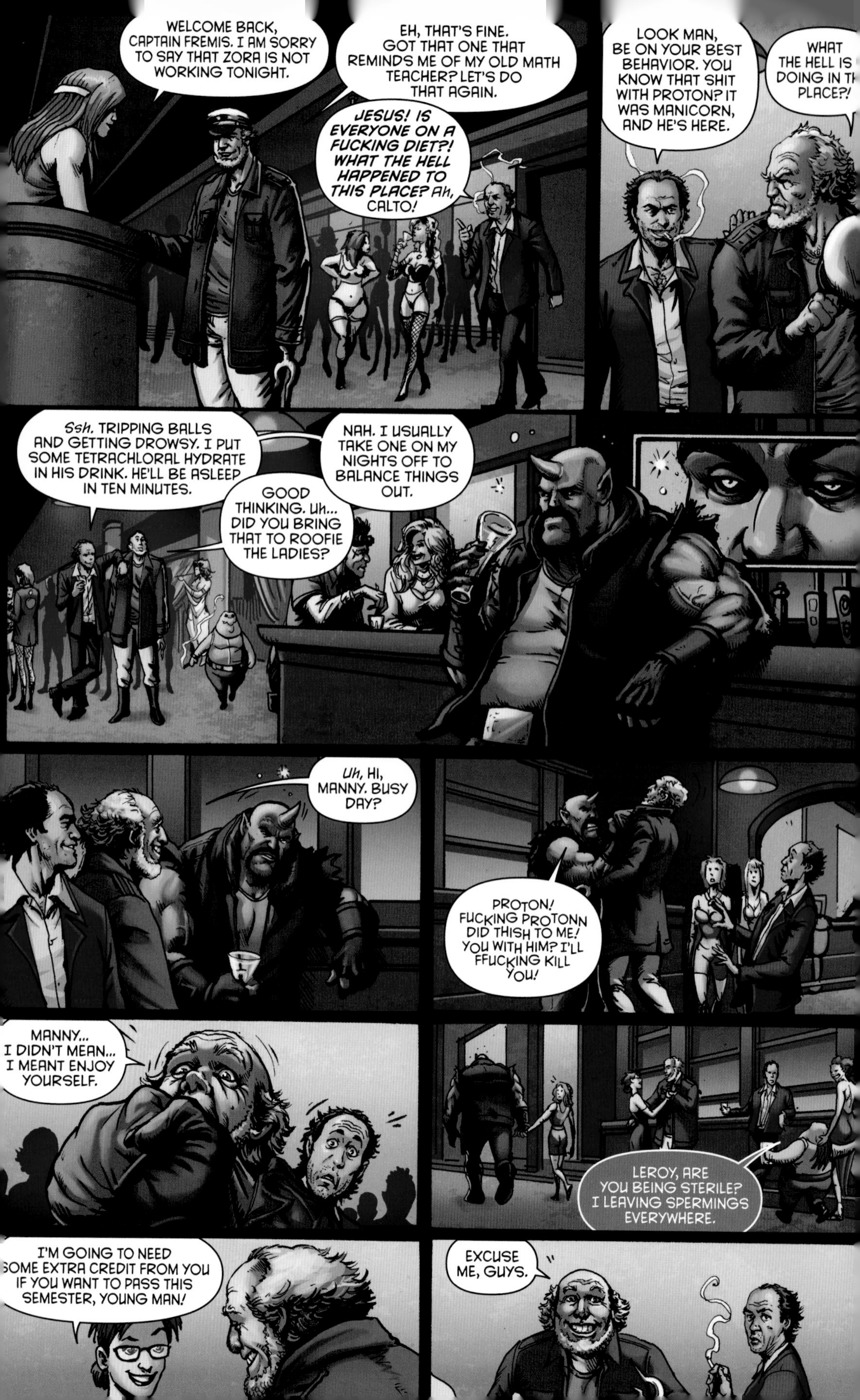
WELCOME BACK, CAPTAIN FREMIS. I AM SORRY TO SAY THAT ZORA IS NOT WORKING TONIGHT.
EH, THAT'S FINE. GOT THAT ONE THAT REMINDS ME OF MY OLD MATH TEACHER? LET'S DO THAT AGAIN.
JESUS! IS EVERYONE ON A FUCKING DIET?! WHAT THE HELL HAPPENED TO THIS PLACE? Ah, CALTO!
LOOK MAN, BE ON YOUR BEST BEHAVIOR. YOU KNOW THAT SHIT WITH PROTON? IT WAS MANICORN, AND HE'S HERE.
WHAT THE HELL IS DOING IN T PLACE?!
Ssh. TRIPPING BALLS AND GETTING DROWSY. I PUT SOME TETRACHLORAL HYDRATE IN HIS DRINK. HE'LL BE ASLEEP IN TEN MINUTES.
GOOD THINKING. Uh... DID YOU BRING THAT TO ROOFIE THE LADIES?
NAH. I USUALLY TAKE ONE ON MY NIGHTS OFF TO BALANCE THINGS OUT.
Uh, HI, MANNY. BUSY DAY?
PROTON! FUCKING PROTONN DID THISH TO ME! YOU WITH HIM? I'LL FFUCKING KILL YOU!
MANNY... I DIDN'T MEAN... I MEANT ENJOY YOURSELF.
LEROY, ARE YOU BEING STERILE? I LEAVING SPERMINGS EVERYWHERE.
I'M GOING TO NEED SOME EXTRA CREDIT FROM YOU IF YOU WANT TO PASS THIS SEMESTER, YOUNG MAN!
EXCUSE ME, GUYS.

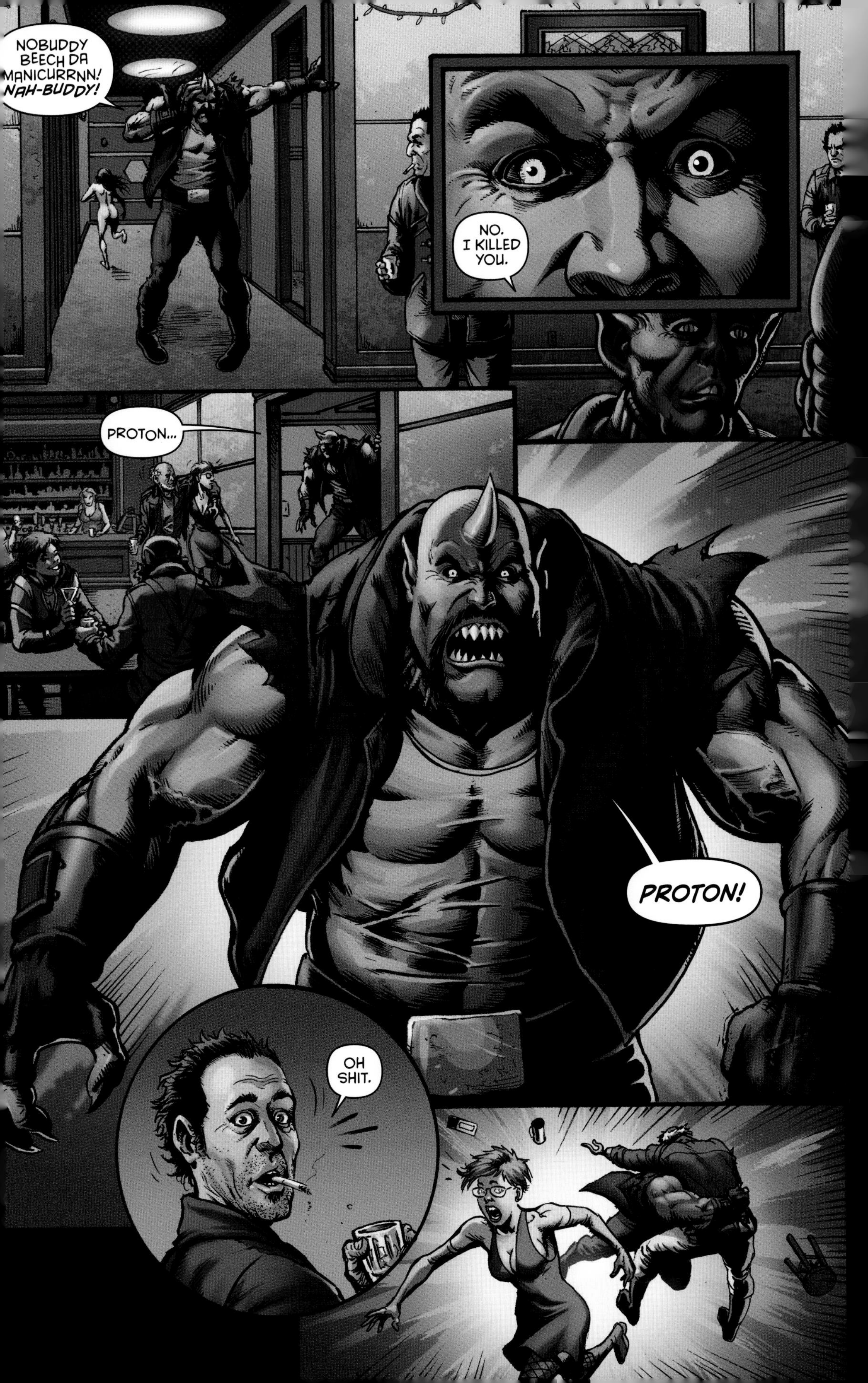
NOBUDDY BEECH DA MANICURRNN! NAH-BUDDY!
NO. I KILLED YOU.
PROTON...
PROTON!
OH SHIT.

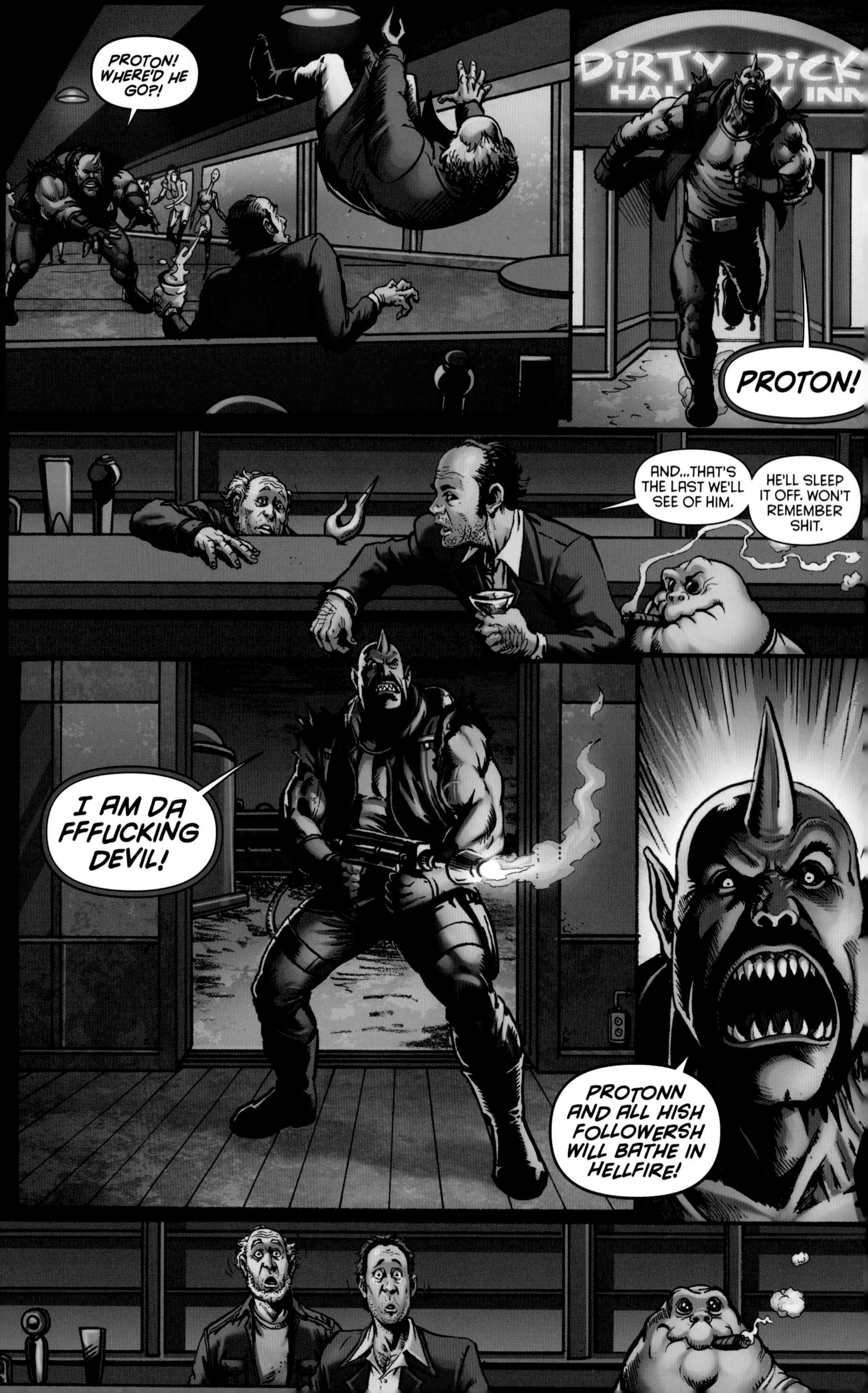
PROTON! WHERE'D HE GO?!
DIRTY DICK
HAL Y INN
PROTON!
AND...THAT'S THE LAST WE'LL SEE OF HIM.
HE'LL SLEEP IT OFF. WON'T REMEMBER SHIT.
I AM DA FFFUCKING DEVIL!
PROTONN AND ALL HISH FOLLOWERSH WILL BATHE IN HELLFIRE!

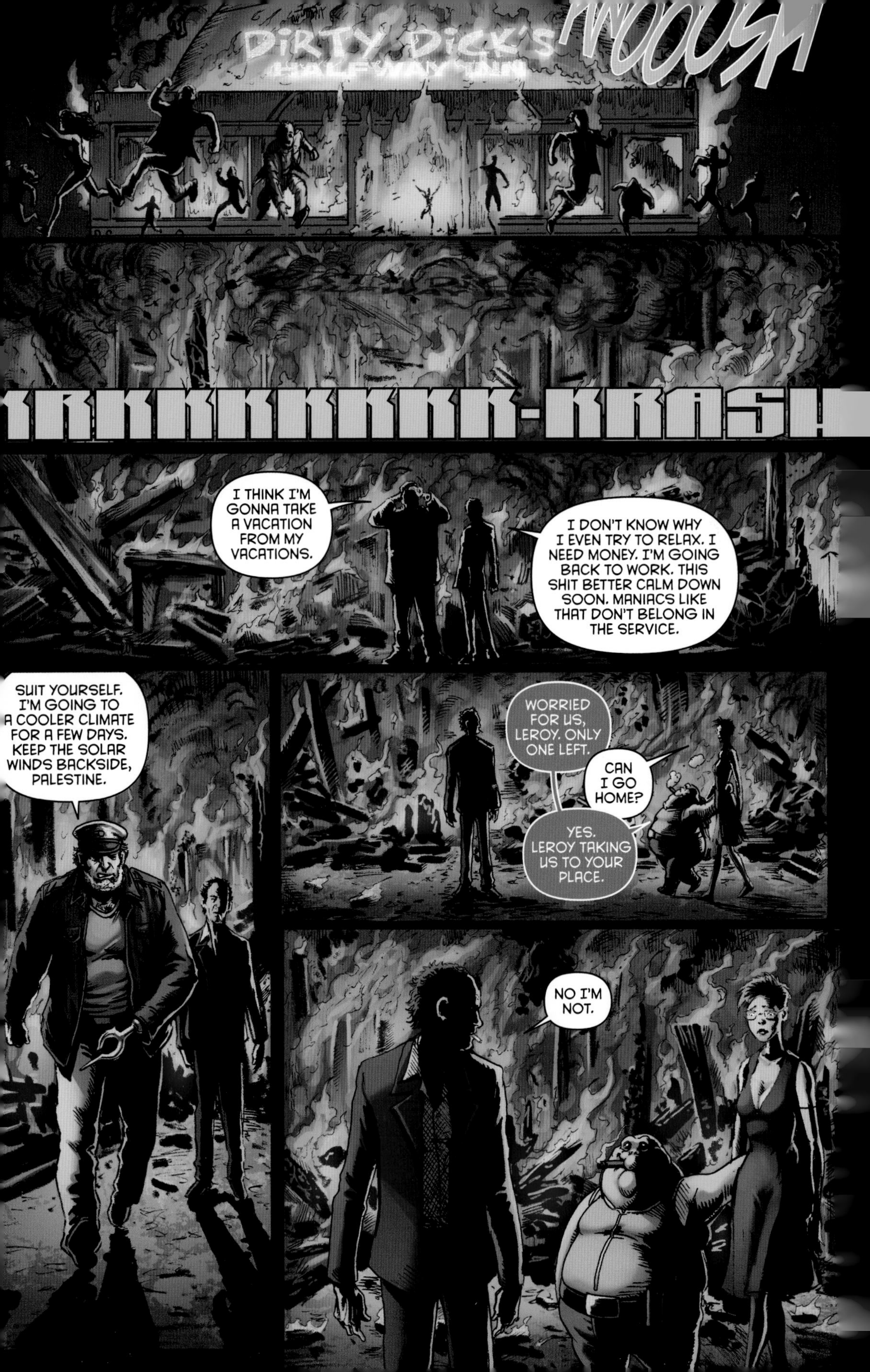

DIRTY DICK'S HALFWAY INN
WOOOSH
KRKKKKKKK-KRASH
I THINK I'M GONNA TAKE A VACATION FROM MY VACATIONS.
I DON'T KNOW WHY I EVEN TRY TO RELAX. I NEED MONEY. I'M GOING BACK TO WORK. THIS SHIT BETTER CALM DOWN SOON. MANIACS LIKE THAT DON'T BELONG IN THE SERVICE.
SUIT YOURSELF. I'M GOING TO A COOLER CLIMATE FOR A FEW DAYS. KEEP THE SOLAR WINDS BACKSIDE, PALESTINE.
WORRIED FOR US, LEROY. ONLY ONE LEFT.
CAN I GO HOME?
YES. LEROY TAKING US TO YOUR PLACE.
NO I'M NOT.

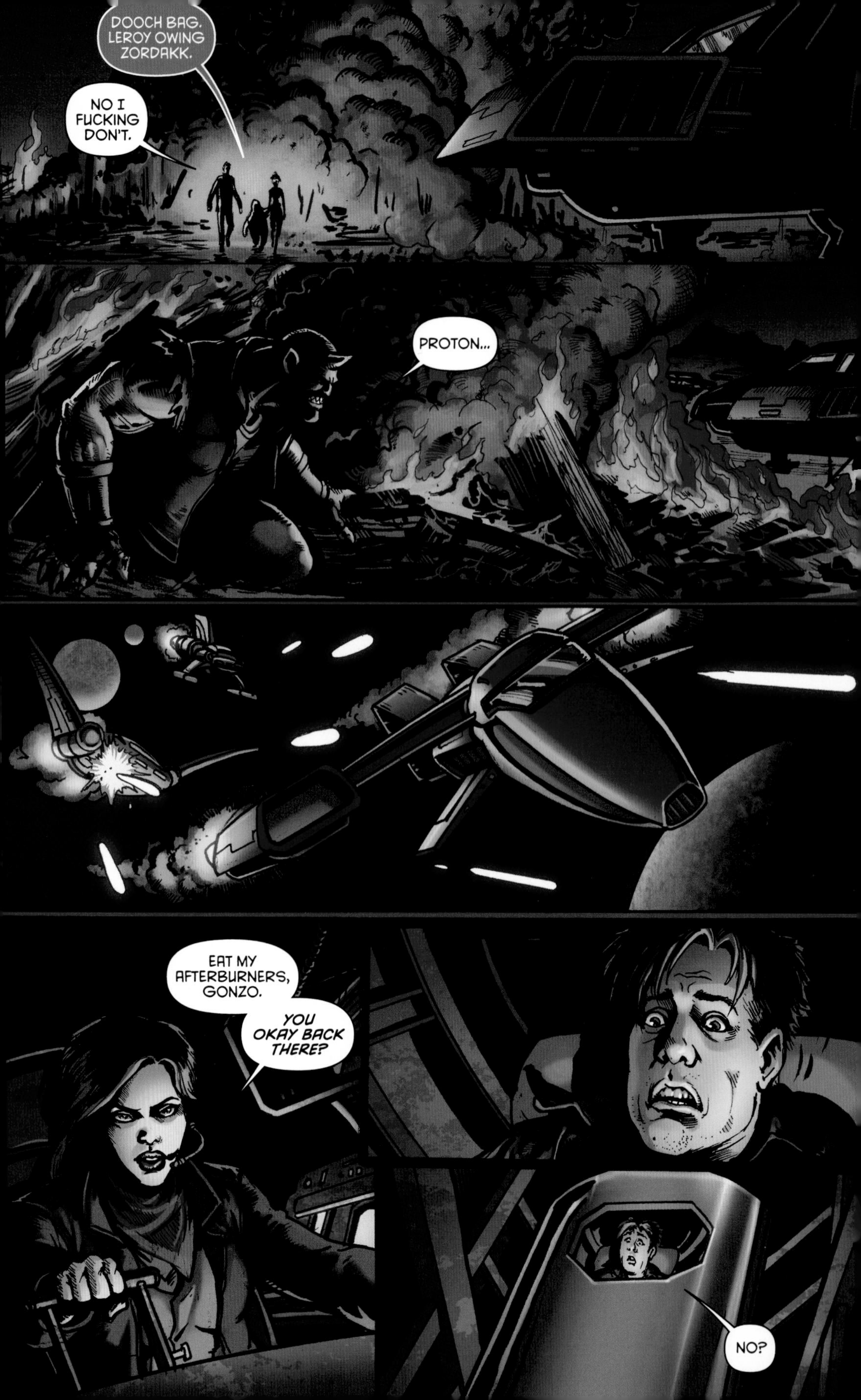
DOOCH BAG. LEROY OWING ZORDAKK.
NO I FUCKING DON'T.
PROTON...
EAT MY AFTERBURNERS, GONZO.
YOU OKAY BACK THERE?
NO?

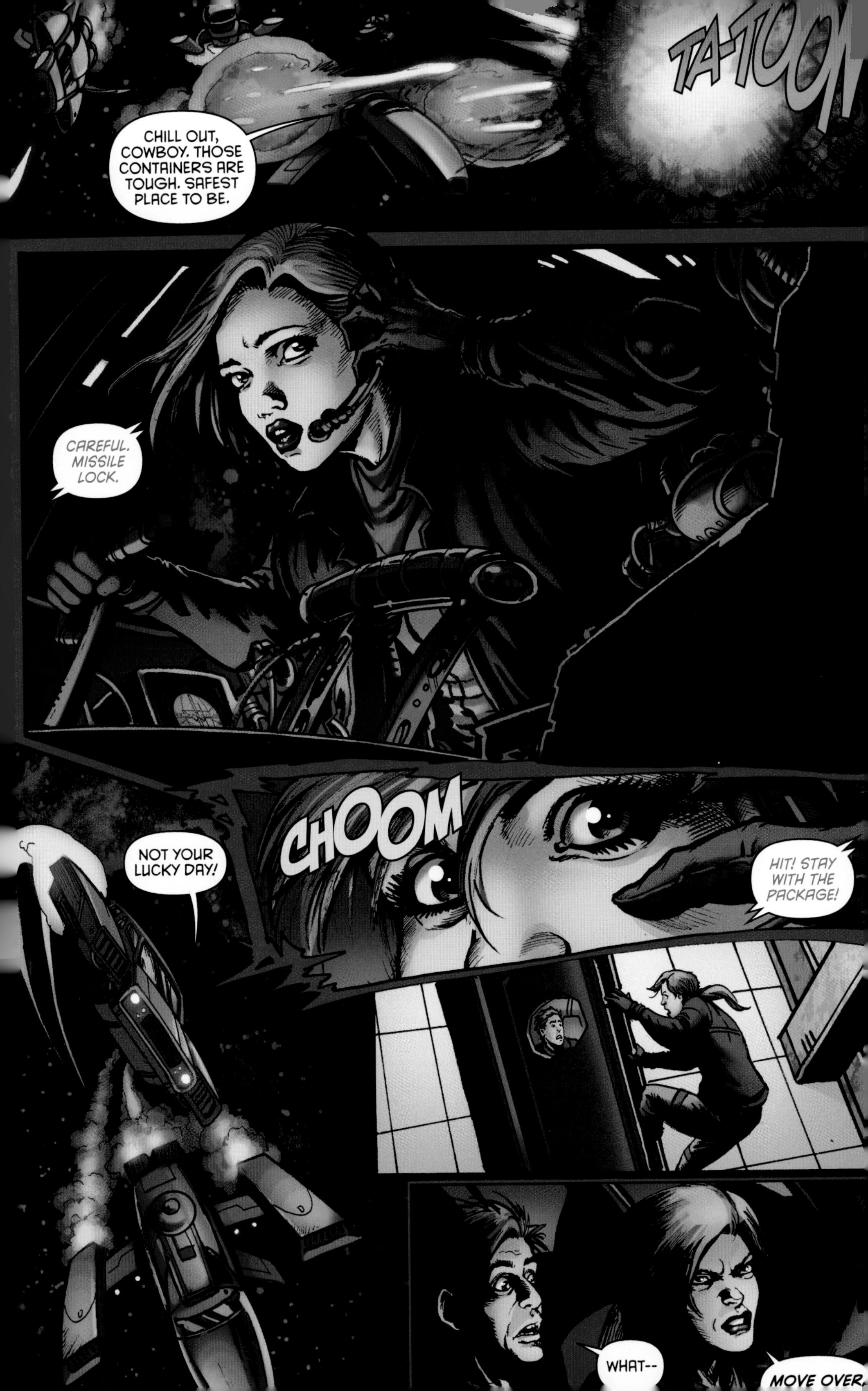
TA-TOOM
CHILL OUT, COWBOY. THOSE CONTAINERS ARE TOUGH. SAFEST PLACE TO BE.
CAREFUL. MISSILE LOCK.
NOT YOUR LUCKY DAY!
CHOOM
HIT! STAY WITH THE PACKAGE!
WHAT--
MOVE OVER.

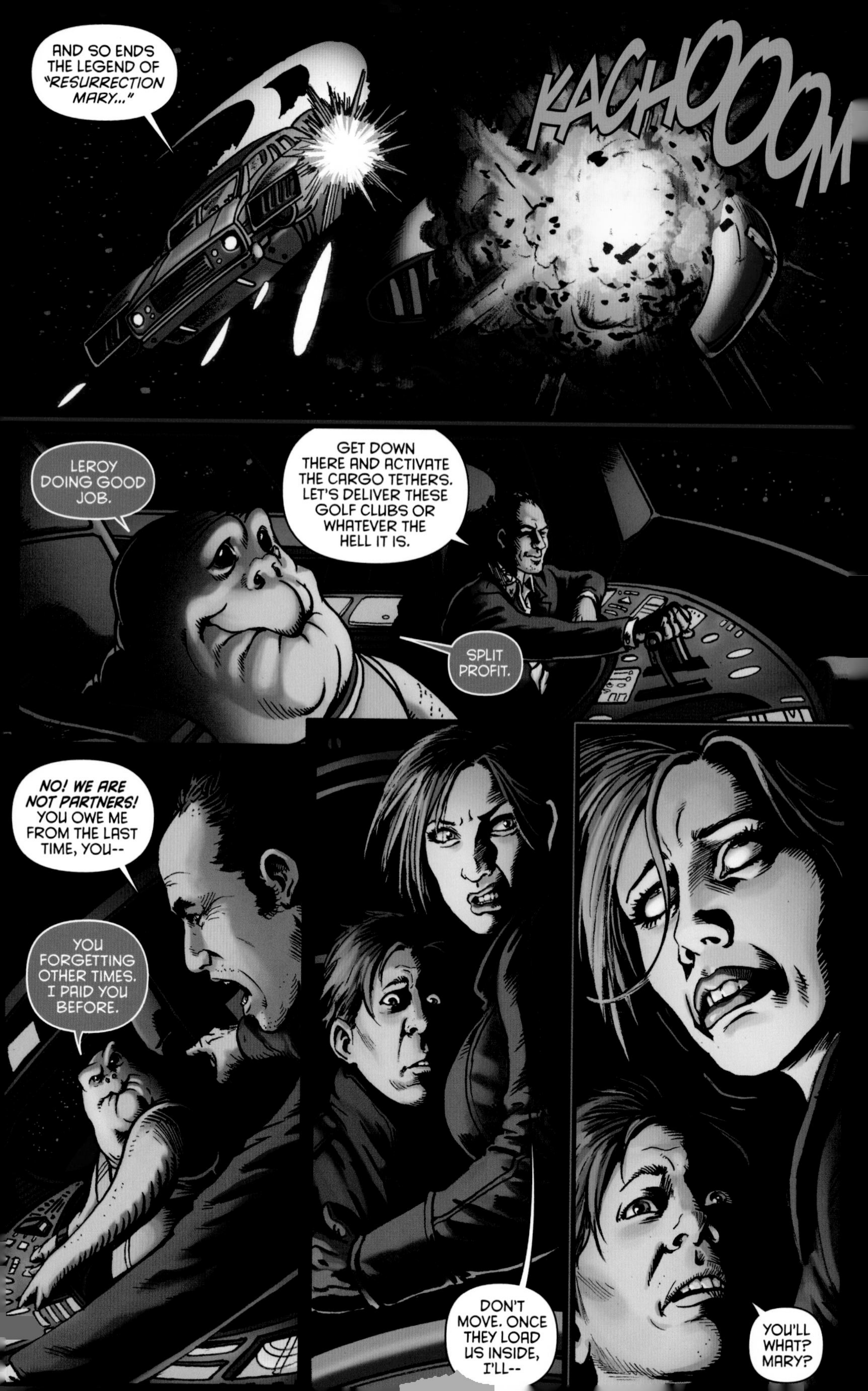
AND SO ENDS THE LEGEND OF "RESURRECTION MARY..."
KACHOOOOM
LEROY DOING GOOD JOB.
GET DOWN THERE AND ACTIVATE THE CARGO TETHERS. LET'S DELIVER THESE GOLF CLUBS OR WHATEVER THE HELL IT IS.
SPLIT PROFIT.
NO! WE ARE NOT PARTNERS! YOU OWE ME FROM THE LAST TIME, YOU--
YOU FORGETTING OTHER TIMES. I PAID YOU BEFORE.
DON'T MOVE. ONCE THEY LOAD US INSIDE, I'LL--
YOU'LL WHAT? MARY?

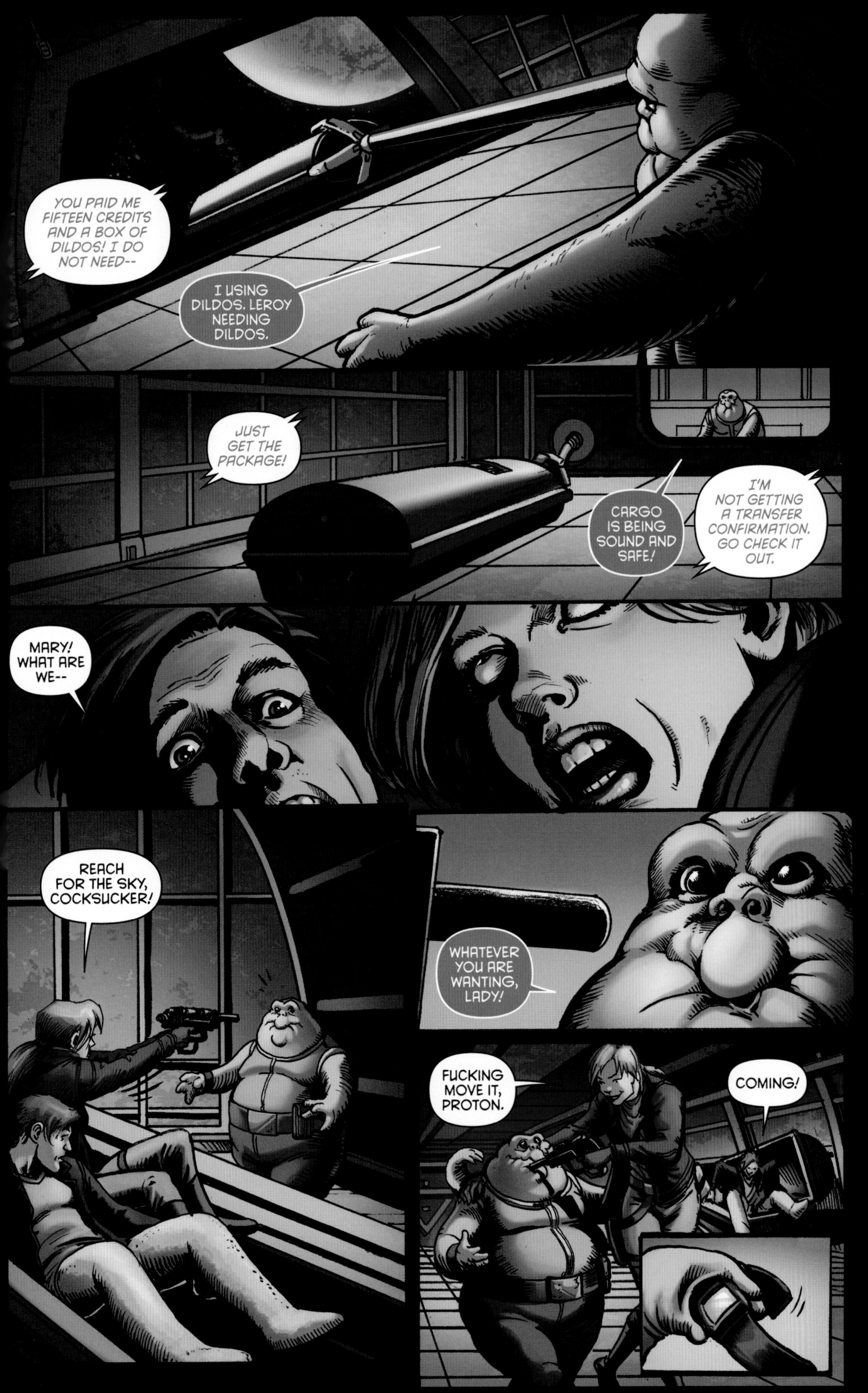
YOU PAID ME FIFTEEN CREDITS AND A BOX OF DILDOS! I DO NOT NEED--
I USING DILDOS. LEROY NEEDING DILDOS.
JUST GET THE PACKAGE!
CARGO IS BEING SOUND AND SAFE!
I'M NOT GETTING A TRANSFER CONFIRMATION. GO CHECK IT OUT.
MARY! WHAT ARE WE--
REACH FOR THE SKY, COCKSUCKER!
WHATEVER YOU ARE WANTING, LADY!
FUCKING MOVE IT, PROTON.
COMING!

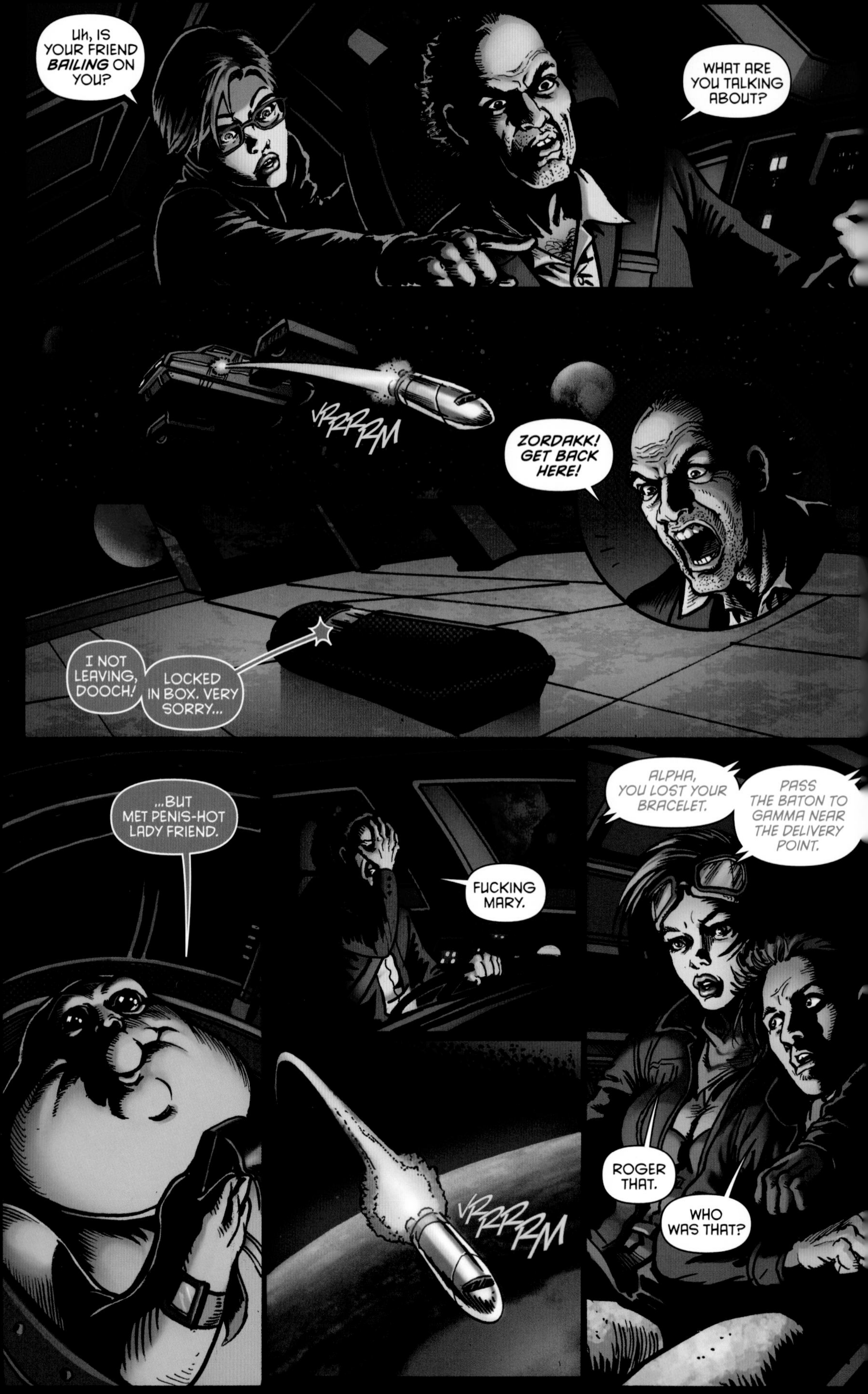

UH, IS YOUR FRIEND BAILING ON YOU?
WHAT ARE YOU TALKING ABOUT?
VRRRRM
ZORDAKK! GET BACK HERE!
I NOT LEAVING, DOOCH!
LOCKED IN BOX. VERY SORRY...
...BUT MET PENIS-HOT LADY FRIEND.
FUCKING MARY.
VRRRRM
ALPHA, YOU LOST YOUR BRACELET.
PASS THE BATON TO GAMMA NEAR THE DELIVERY POINT.
ROGER THAT.
WHO WAS THAT?

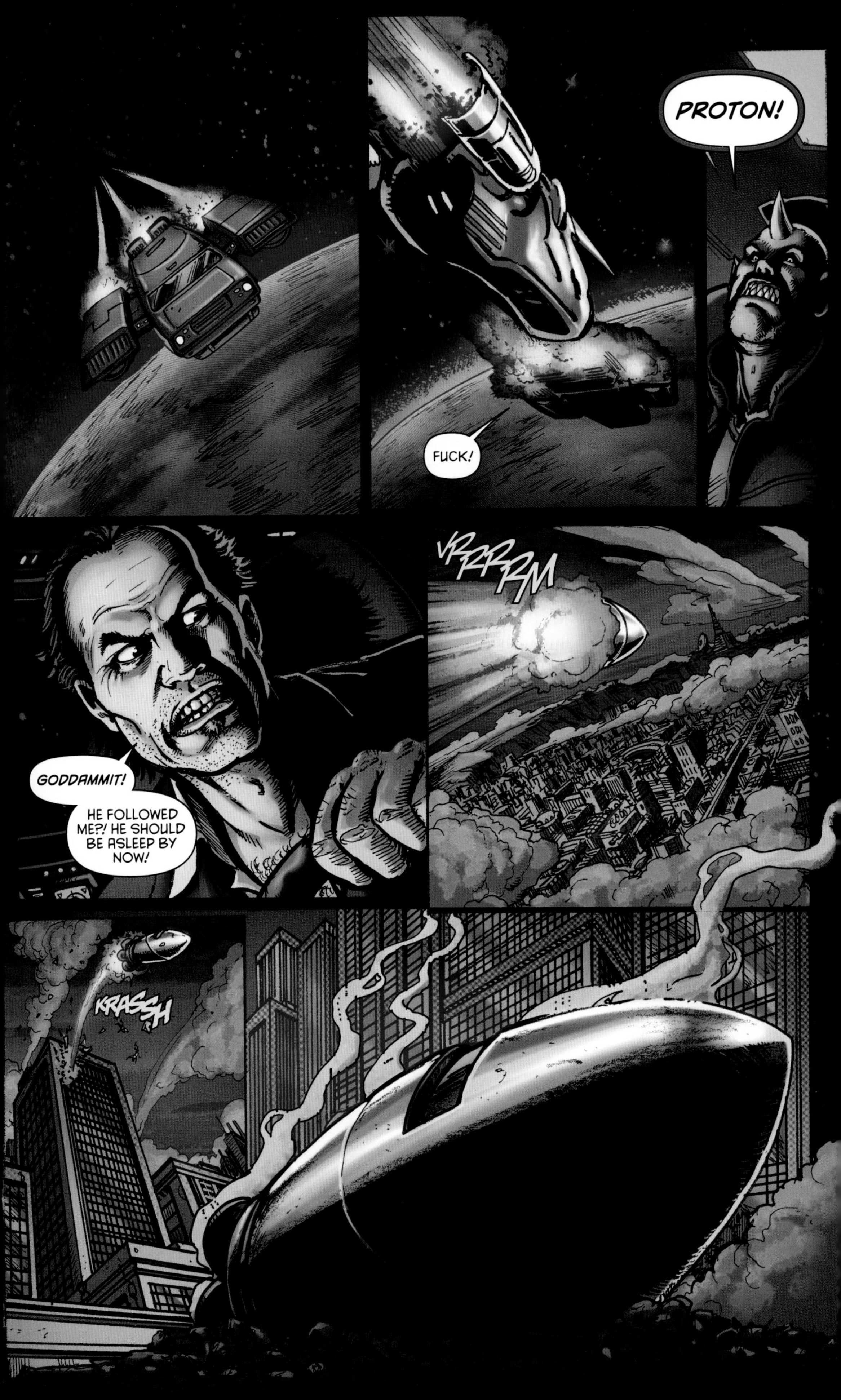
PROTON!
FUCK!
GODDAMMIT!
HE FOLLOWED ME?! HE SHOULD BE ASLEEP BY NOW!
VRRRRM
KRASSH

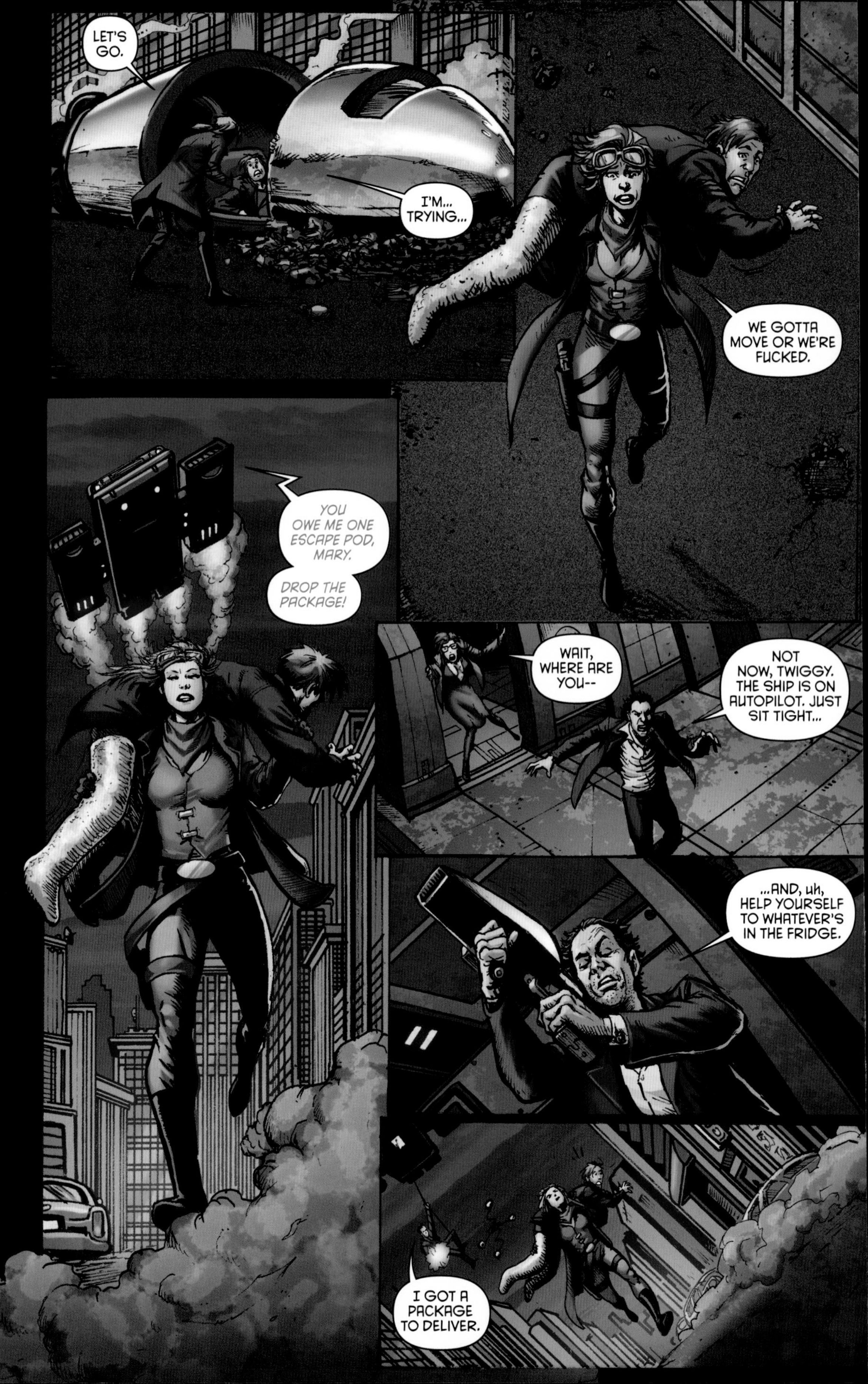
LET'S GO.
I'M... TRYING...
WE GOTTA MOVE OR WE'RE FUCKED.
YOU OWE ME ONE ESCAPE POD, MARY.
DROP THE PACKAGE!
WAIT, WHERE ARE YOU--
NOT NOW, TWIGGY. THE SHIP IS ON AUTOPILOT. JUST SIT TIGHT...
...AND, uh, HELP YOURSELF TO WHATEVER'S IN THE FRIDGE.
I GOT A PACKAGE TO DELIVER.

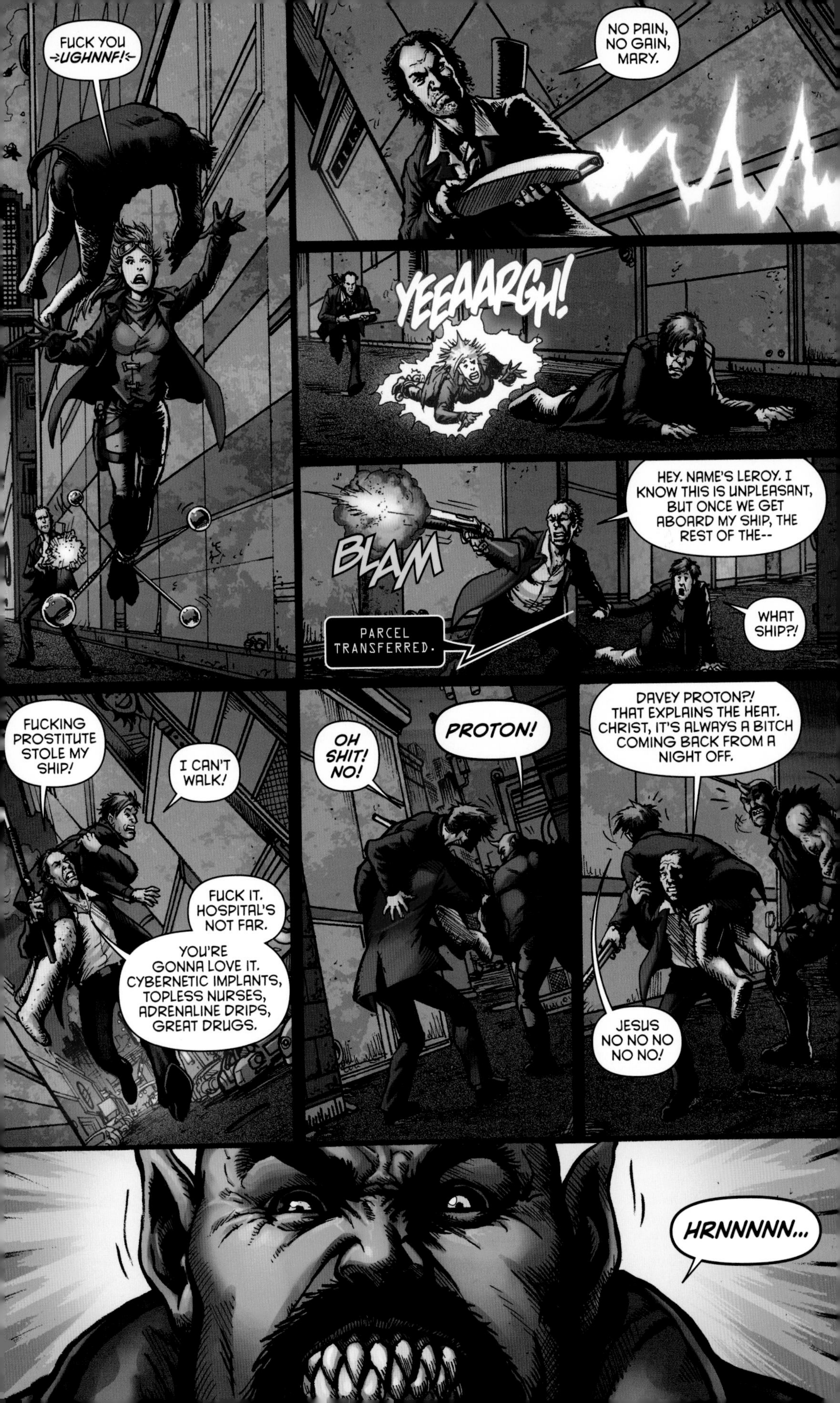
FUCK YOU
-UGHNNF!-
NO PAIN, NO GAIN, MARY.
YEEAARGH!
BLAM
HEY. NAME'S LEROY. I KNOW THIS IS UNPLEASANT, BUT ONCE WE GET ABOARD MY SHIP, THE REST OF THE--
WHAT SHIP?!
PARCEL TRANSFERRED.
FUCKING PROSTITUTE STOLE MY SHIP!
I CAN'T WALK!
FUCK IT. HOSPITAL'S NOT FAR.
YOU'RE GONNA LOVE IT. CYBERNETIC IMPLANTS, TOPLESS NURSES, ADRENALINE DRIPS, GREAT DRUGS.
OH SHIT! NO!
PROTON!
DAVEY PROTON?! THAT EXPLAINS THE HEAT. CHRIST, IT'S ALWAYS A BITCH COMING BACK FROM A NIGHT OFF.
JESUS NO NO NO NO NO!
HRNNNNN...

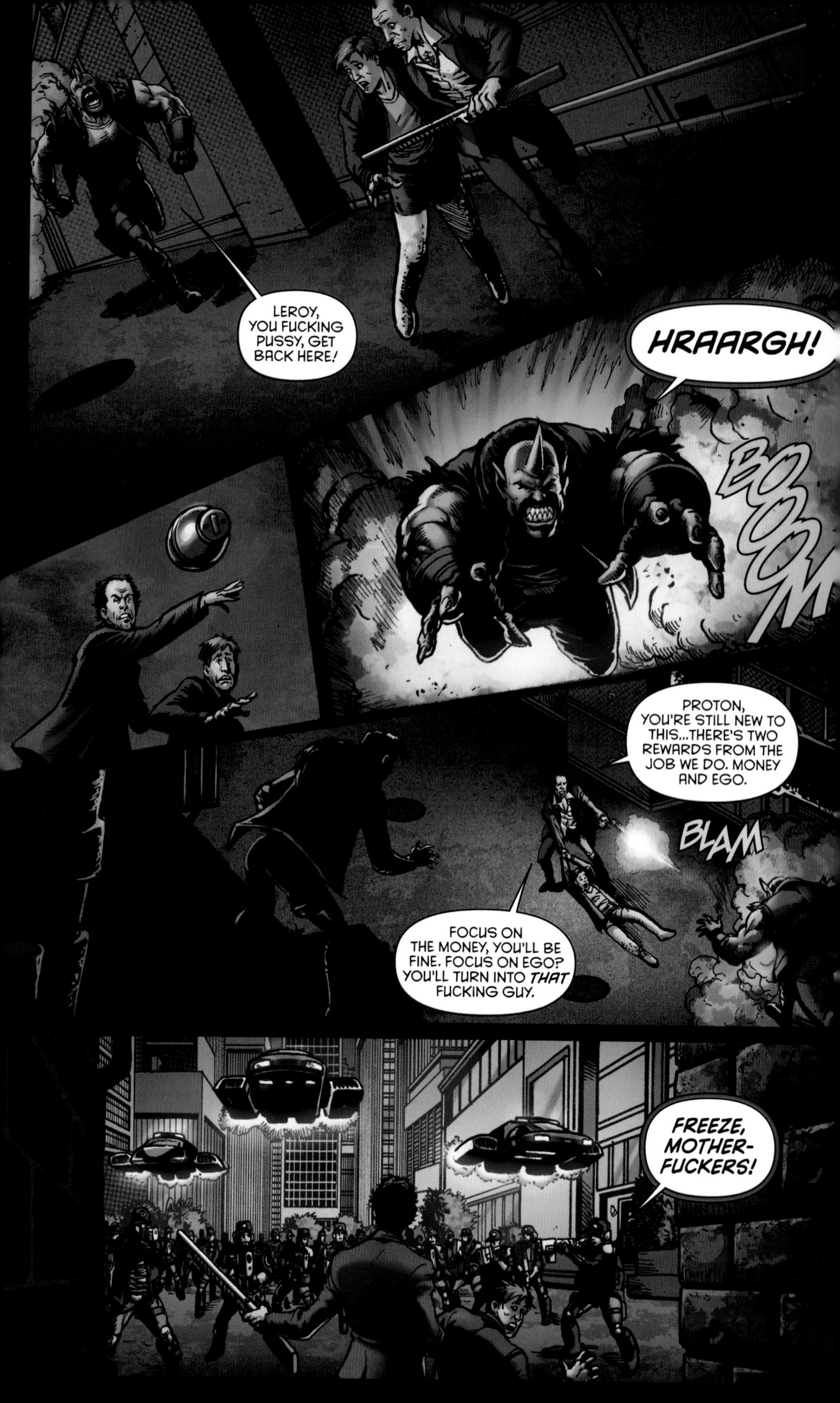

LEROY, YOU FUCKING PUSSY, GET BACK HERE!
HRAARGH!
BOOOOM
PROTON, YOU'RE STILL NEW TO THIS...THERE'S TWO REWARDS FROM THE JOB WE DO. MONEY AND EGO.
BLAM
FOCUS ON THE MONEY, YOU'LL BE FINE. FOCUS ON EGO? YOU'LL TURN INTO *THAT* FUCKING GUY.
FREEZE, MOTHER-FUCKERS!

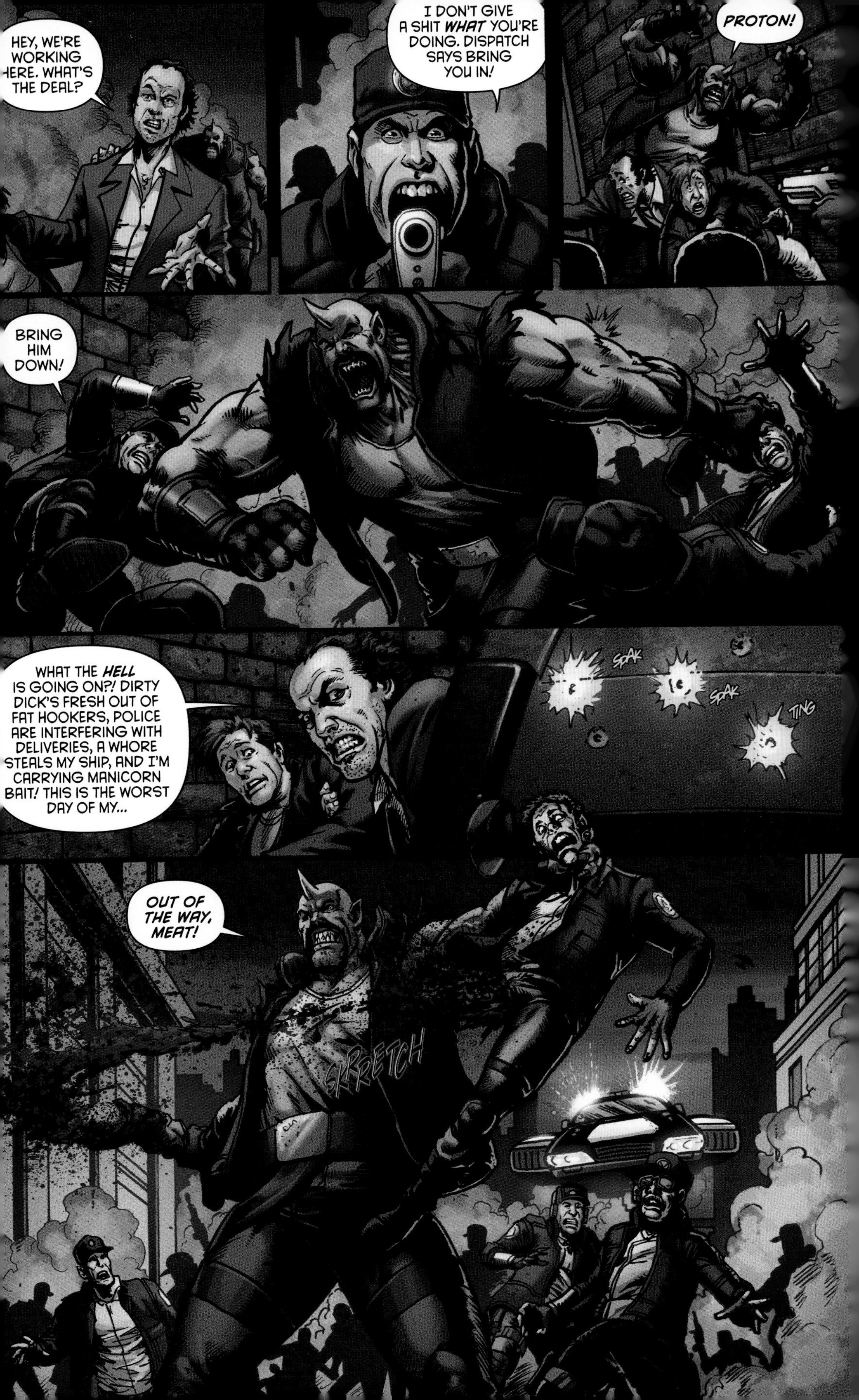

HEY, WE'RE WORKING HERE. WHAT'S THE DEAL?
I DON'T GIVE A SHIT *WHAT* YOU'RE DOING. DISPATCH SAYS BRING YOU IN!
PROTON!
BRING HIM DOWN!
WHAT THE *HELL* IS GOING ON?! DIRTY DICK'S FRESH OUT OF FAT HOOKERS, POLICE ARE INTERFERING WITH DELIVERIES, A WHORE STEALS MY SHIP, AND I'M CARRYING MANICORN BAIT! THIS IS THE WORST DAY OF MY...
SPAK
SPAK
TING
OUT OF THE WAY, MEAT!
SKRRETCH

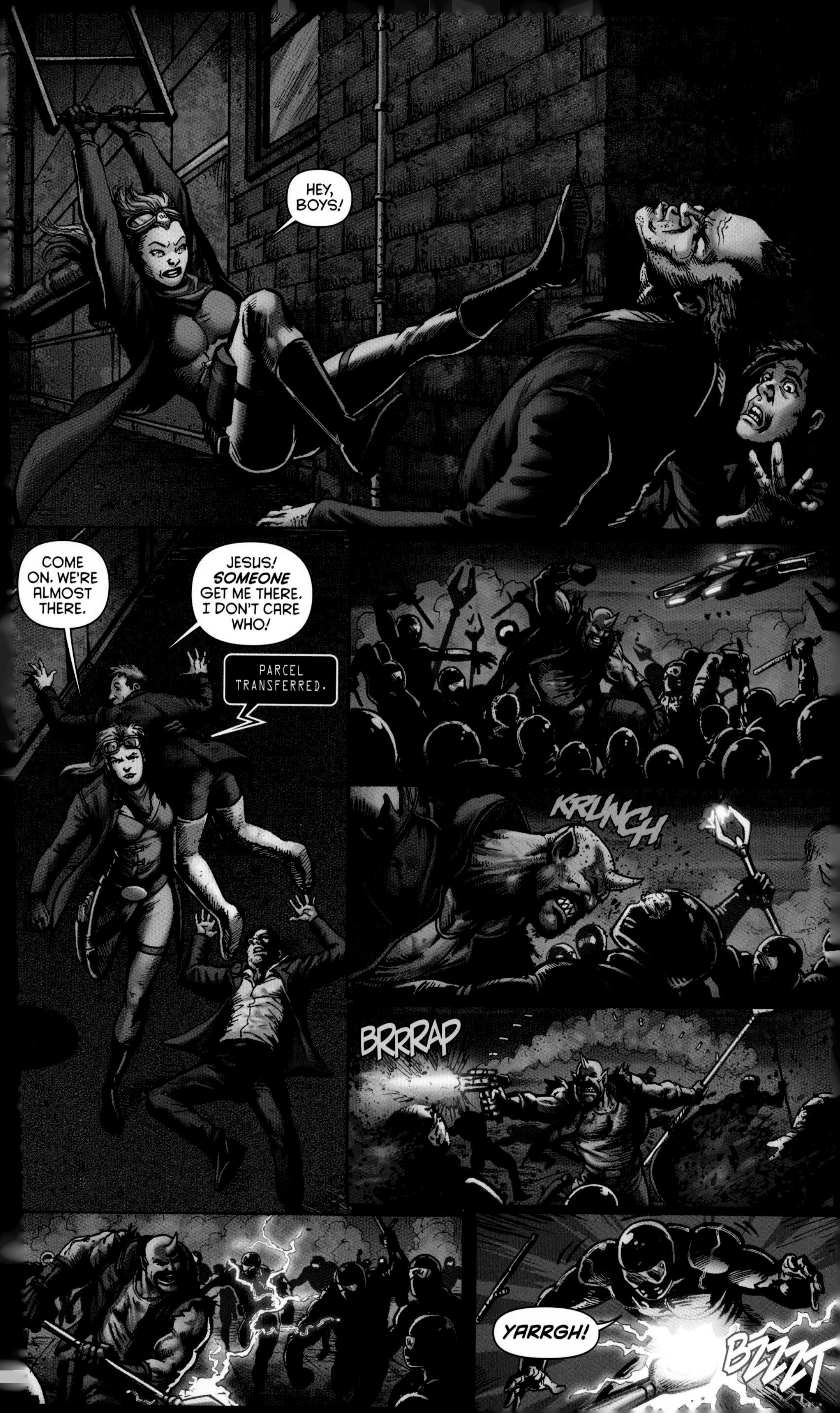
HEY, BOYS!
COME ON. WE'RE ALMOST THERE.
JESUS! SOMEONE GET ME THERE. I DON'T CARE WHO!
PARCEL TRANSFERRED.
KRUNCH
BRRRAP
YARRGH!
BZZZT

SHUNK

KRRASSH

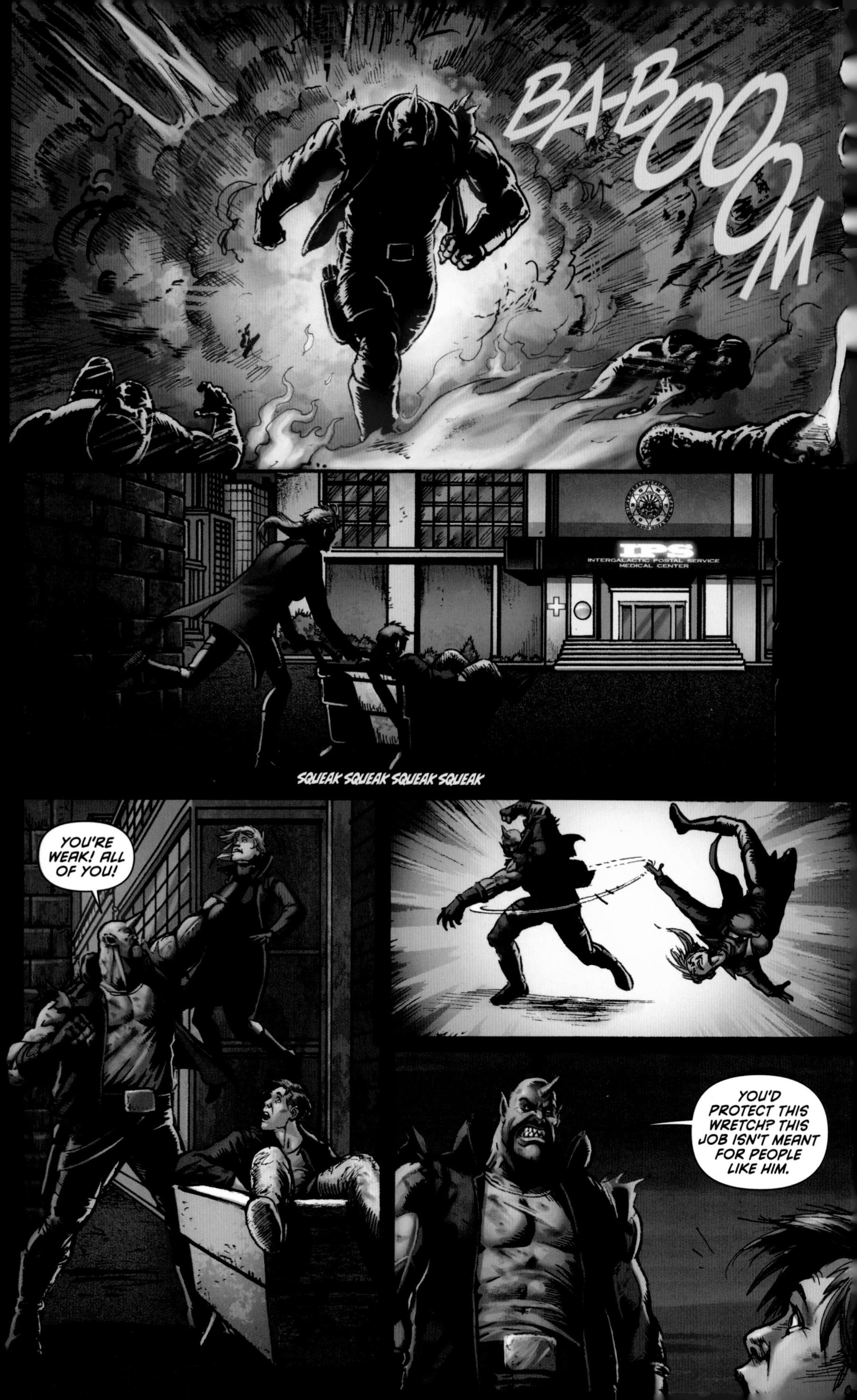
BA-BOOOOM
IPS
INTERGALACTIC POSTAL SERVICE
MEDICAL CENTER
SQUEAK SQUEAK SQUEAK SQUEAK
YOU'RE WEAK! ALL OF YOU!
YOU'D PROTECT THIS WRETCH? THIS JOB ISN'T MEANT FOR PEOPLE LIKE HIM.

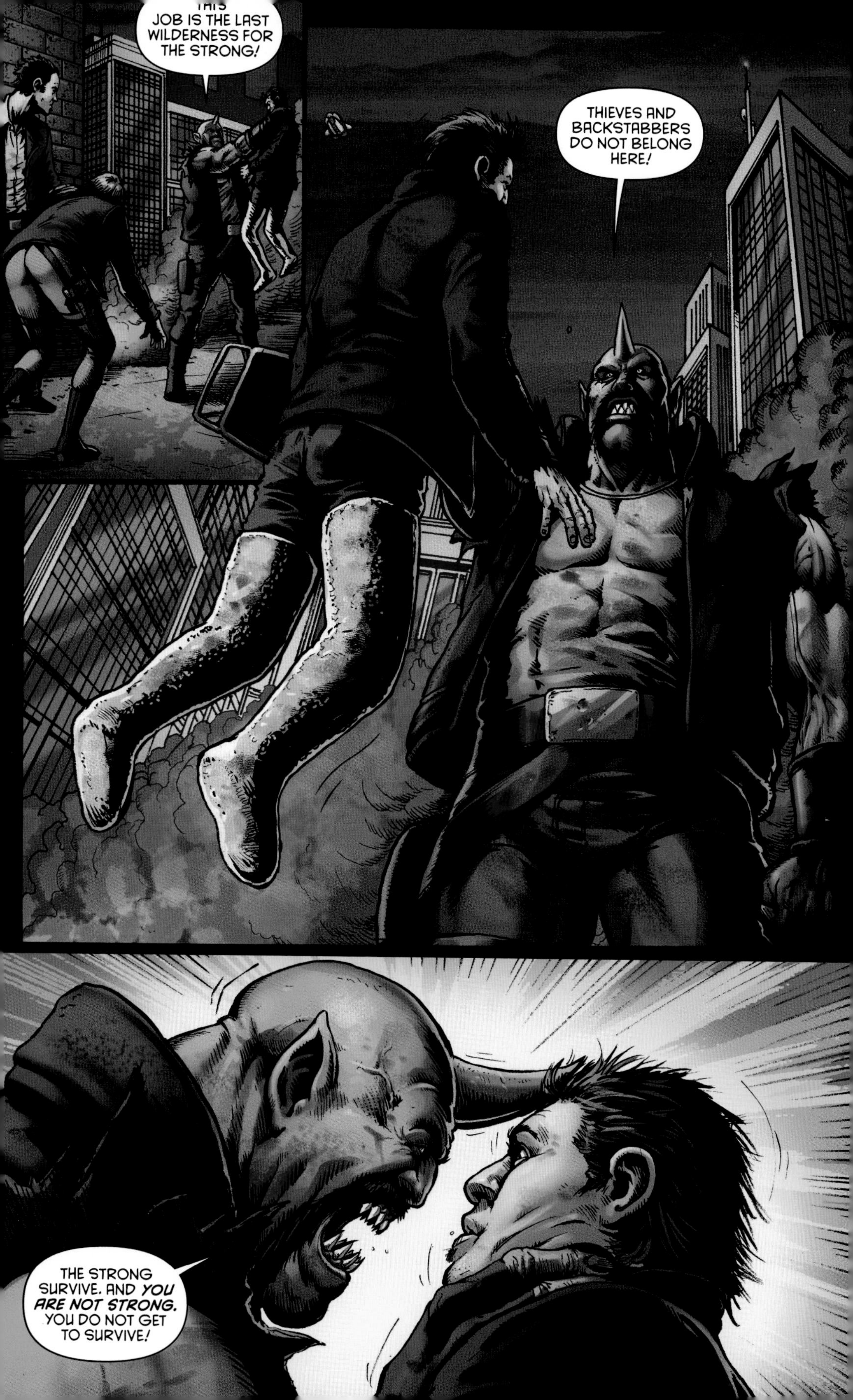
THIS JOB IS THE LAST WILDERNESS FOR THE STRONG!
THIEVES AND BACKSTABBERS DO NOT BELONG HERE!
THE STRONG SURVIVE. AND *YOU ARE NOT STRONG.* YOU DO NOT GET TO SURVIVE!

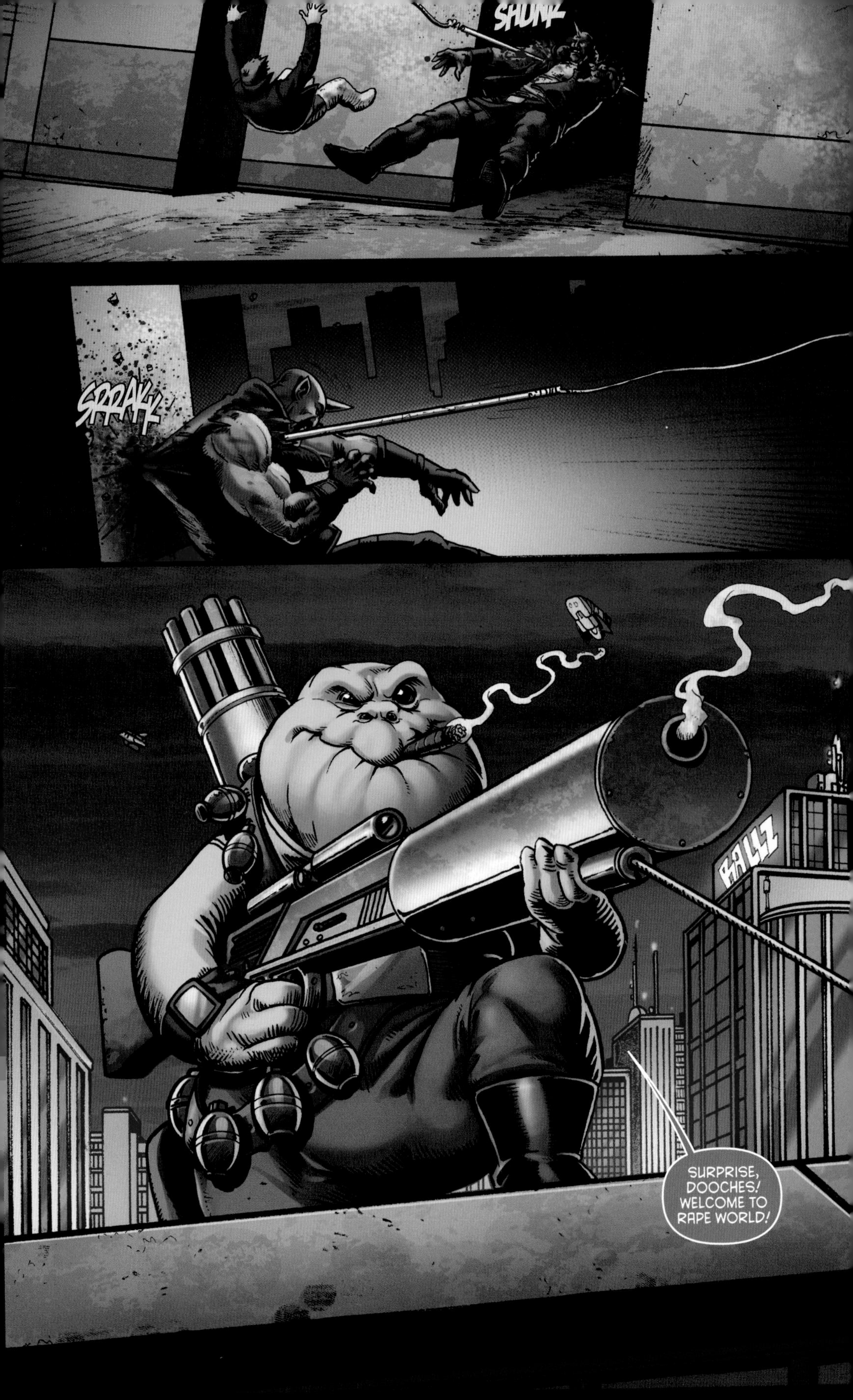
SHUNK
SRRAKK
SURPRISE, DOOCHES! WELCOME TO RAPE WORLD!
BALLZ

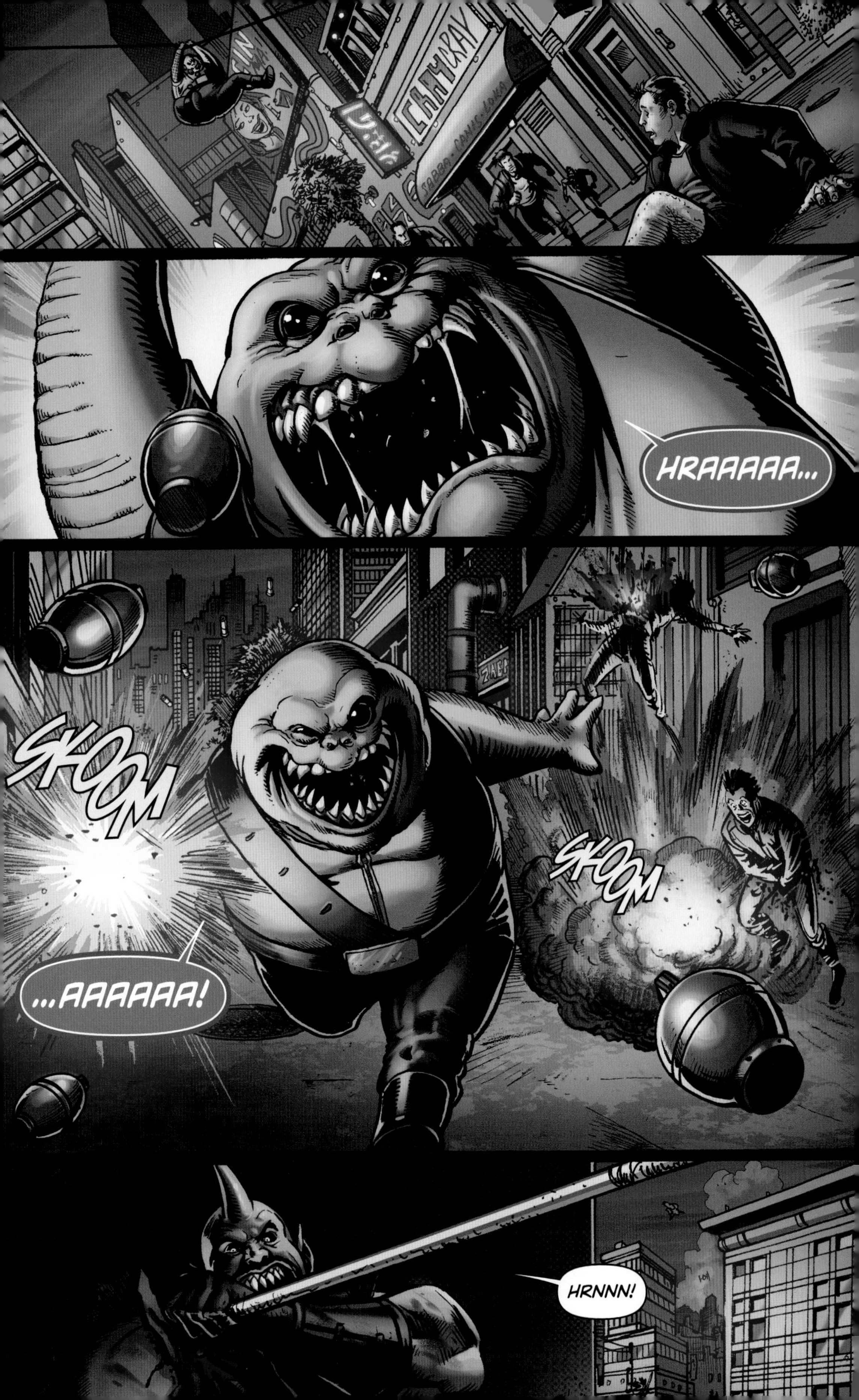
HRAAAAAA...
SKOOM
SKOOM
...AAAAAA!
HRNNN!

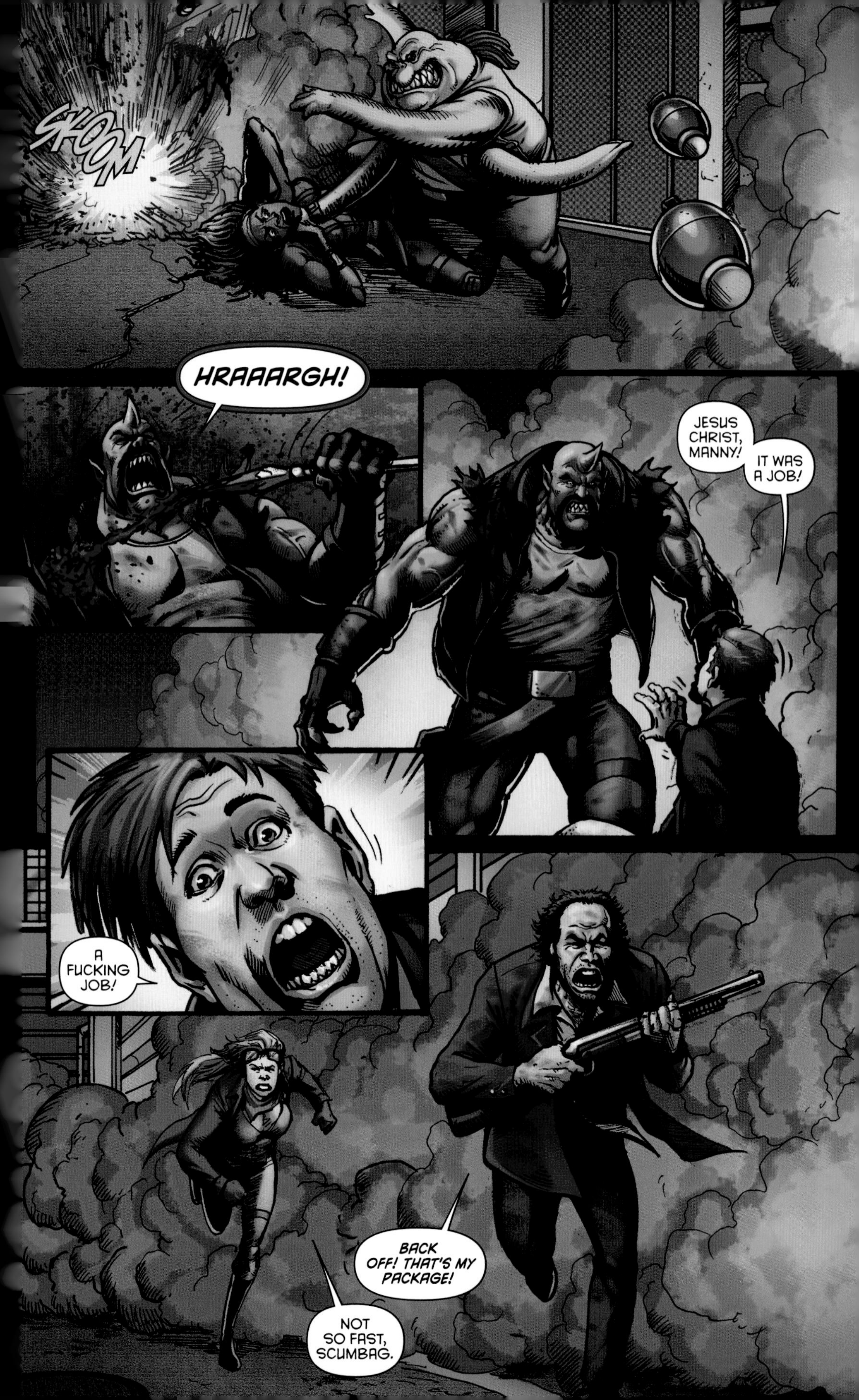
SKOOM
HRAAARGH!
JESUS CHRIST, MANNY!
IT WAS A JOB!
A FUCKING JOB!
BACK OFF! THAT'S MY PACKAGE!
NOT SO FAST, SCUMBAG.

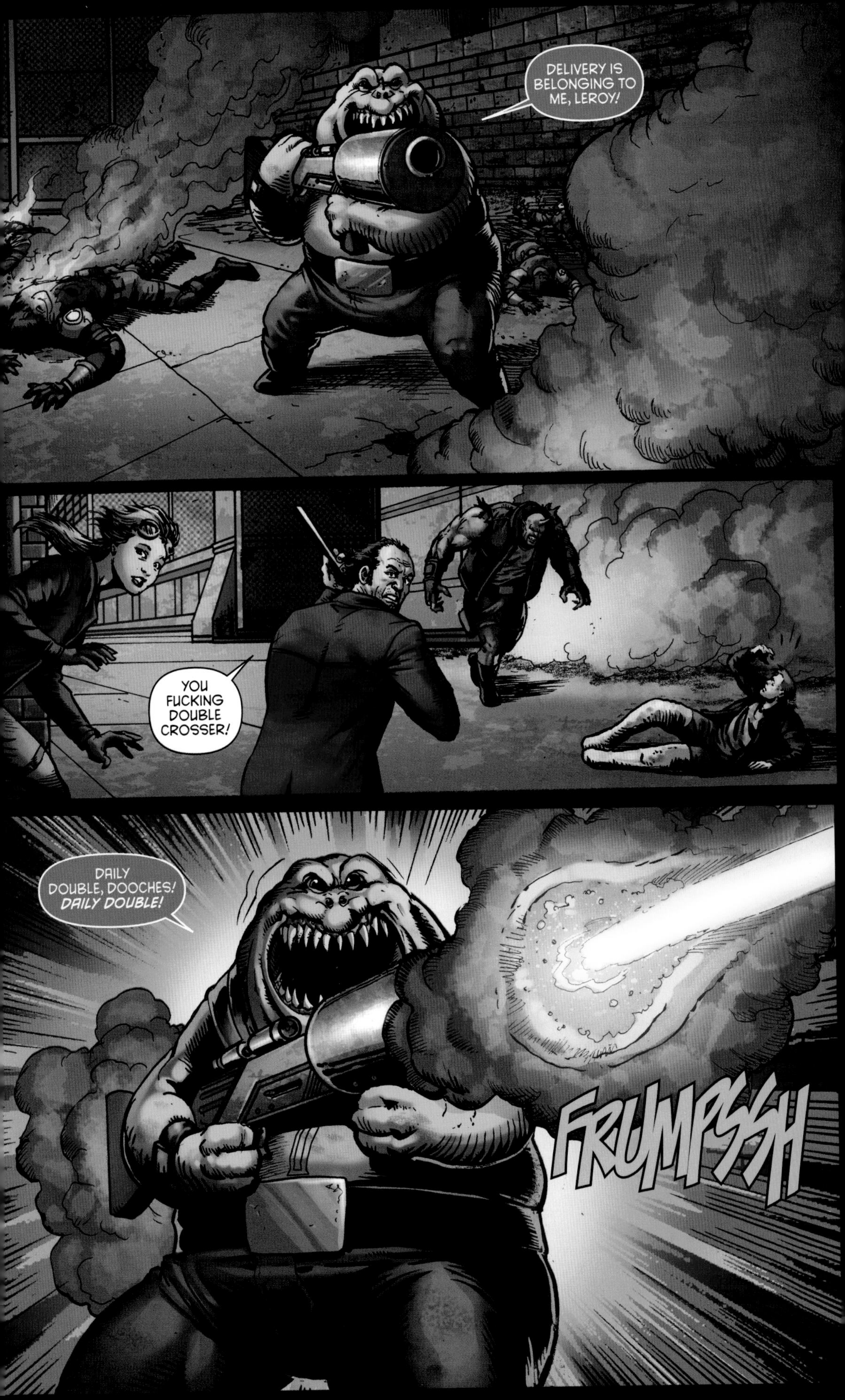
DELIVERY IS BELONGING TO ME, LEROY!
YOU FUCKING DOUBLE CROSSER!
DAILY DOUBLE, DOOCHES! *DAILY DOUBLE!*
FRUMPSSH

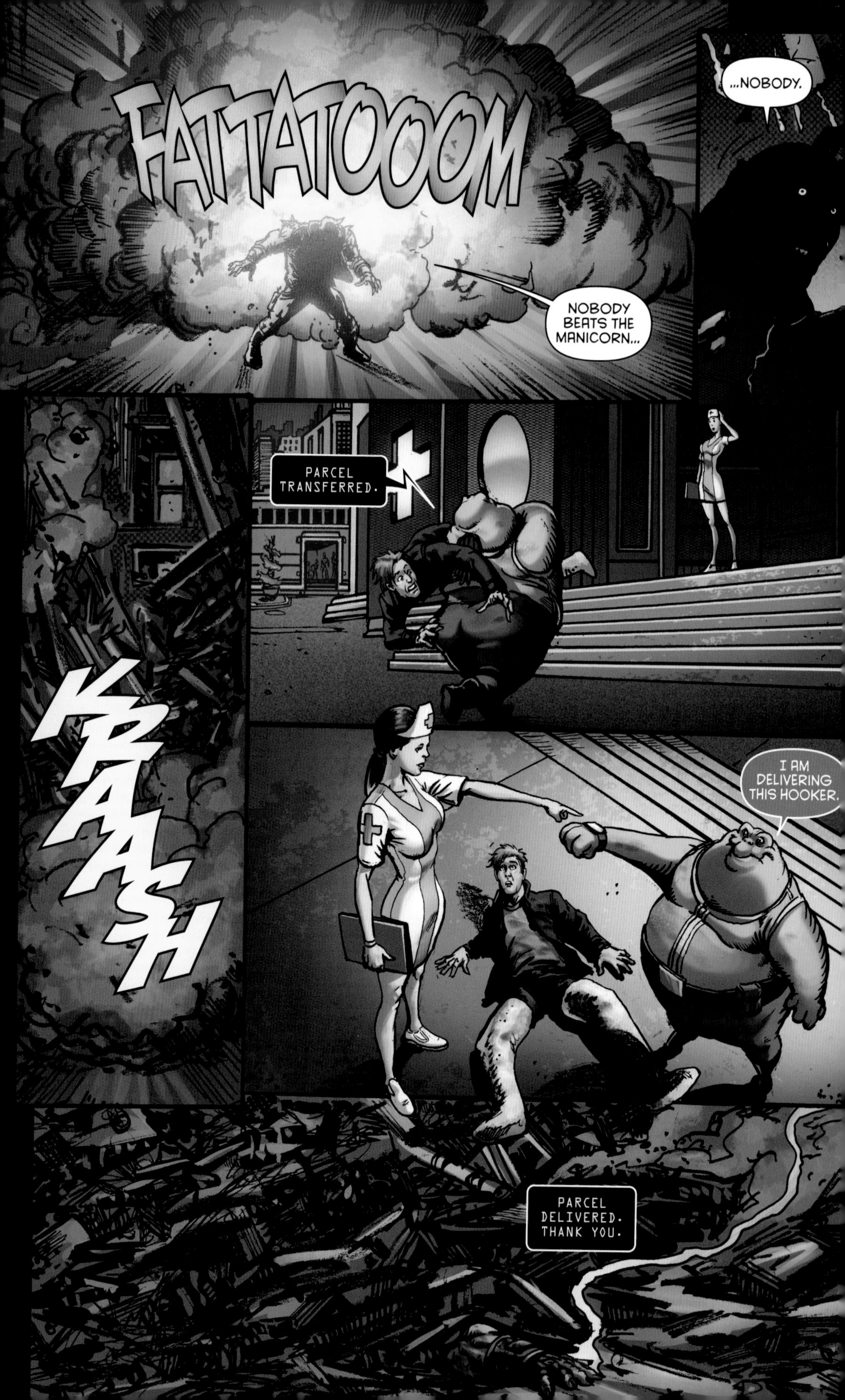
FATTATOOOM
NOBODY BEATS THE MANICORN...
...NOBODY.
KRAASH
PARCEL TRANSFERRED.
I AM DELIVERING THIS HOOKER.
PARCEL DELIVERED. THANK YOU.

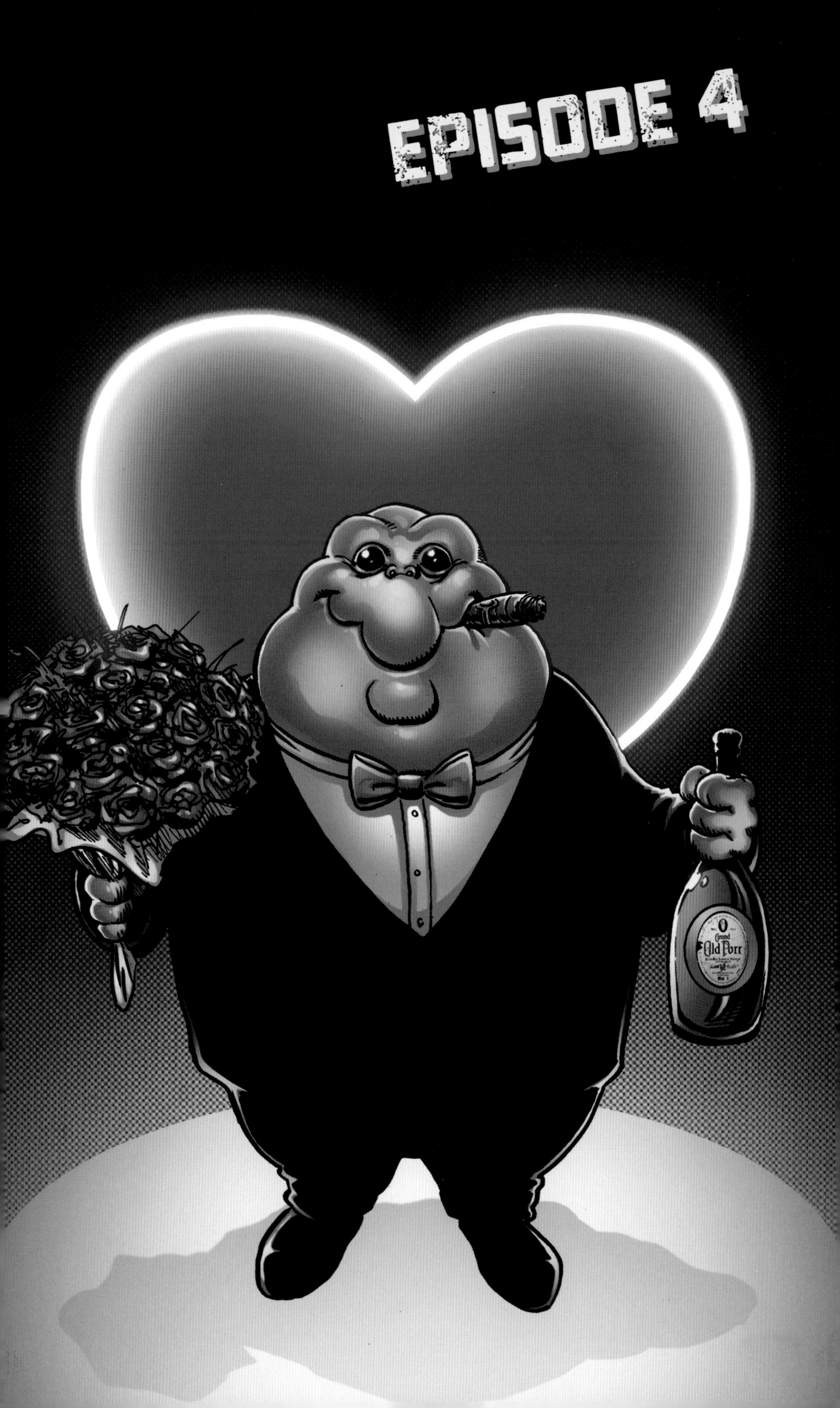
EPISODE 4
Grand
Old Porr

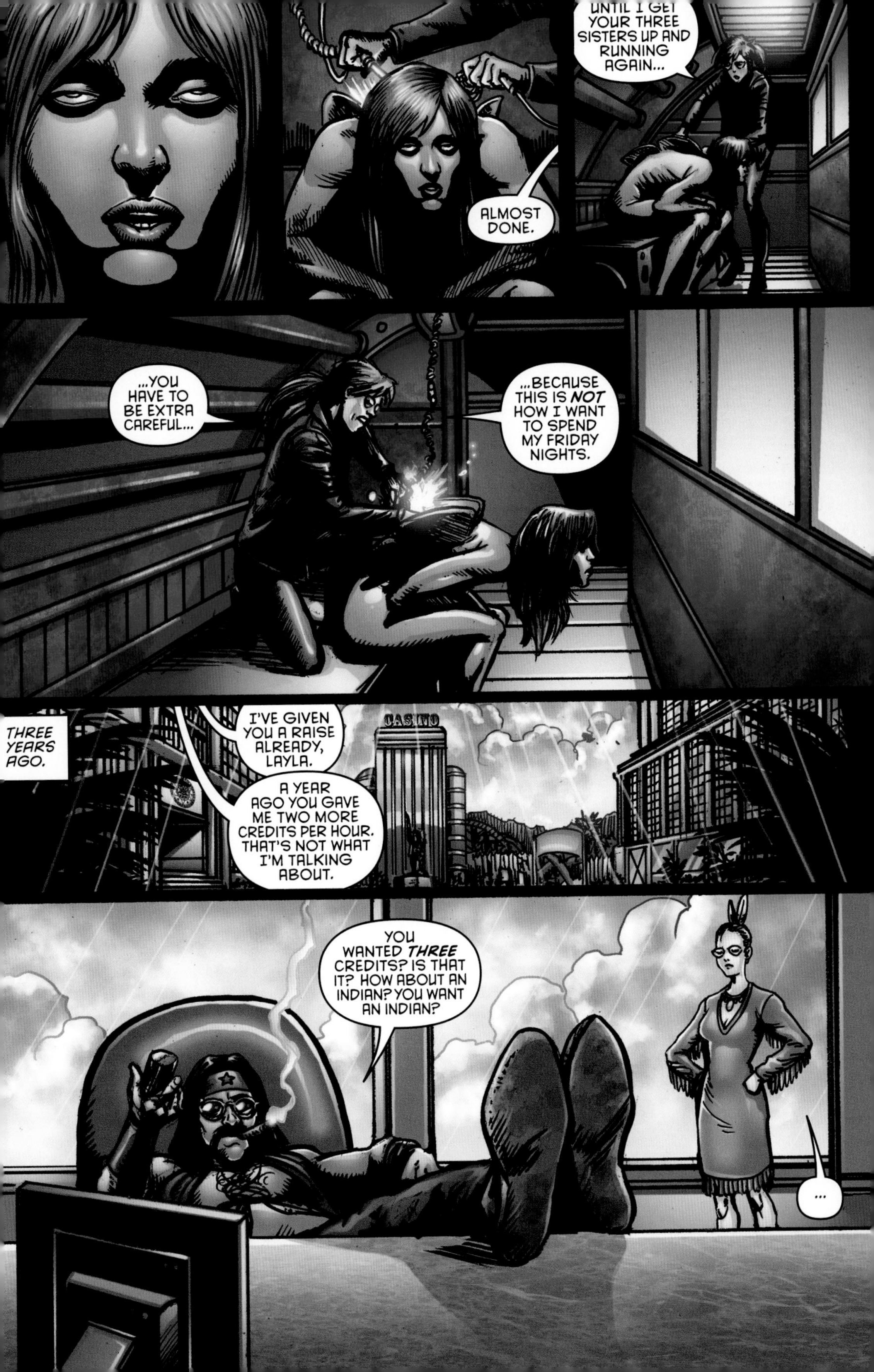

UNTIL I GET YOUR THREE SISTERS UP AND RUNNING AGAIN...
ALMOST DONE.
...YOU HAVE TO BE EXTRA CAREFUL...
...BECAUSE THIS IS *NOT* HOW I WANT TO SPEND MY FRIDAY NIGHTS.
THREE YEARS AGO.
CASINO
I'VE GIVEN YOU A RAISE ALREADY, LAYLA.
A YEAR AGO YOU GAVE ME TWO MORE CREDITS PER HOUR. THAT'S NOT WHAT I'M TALKING ABOUT.
YOU WANTED ***THREE*** CREDITS? IS THAT IT? HOW ABOUT AN INDIAN? YOU WANT AN INDIAN?
...

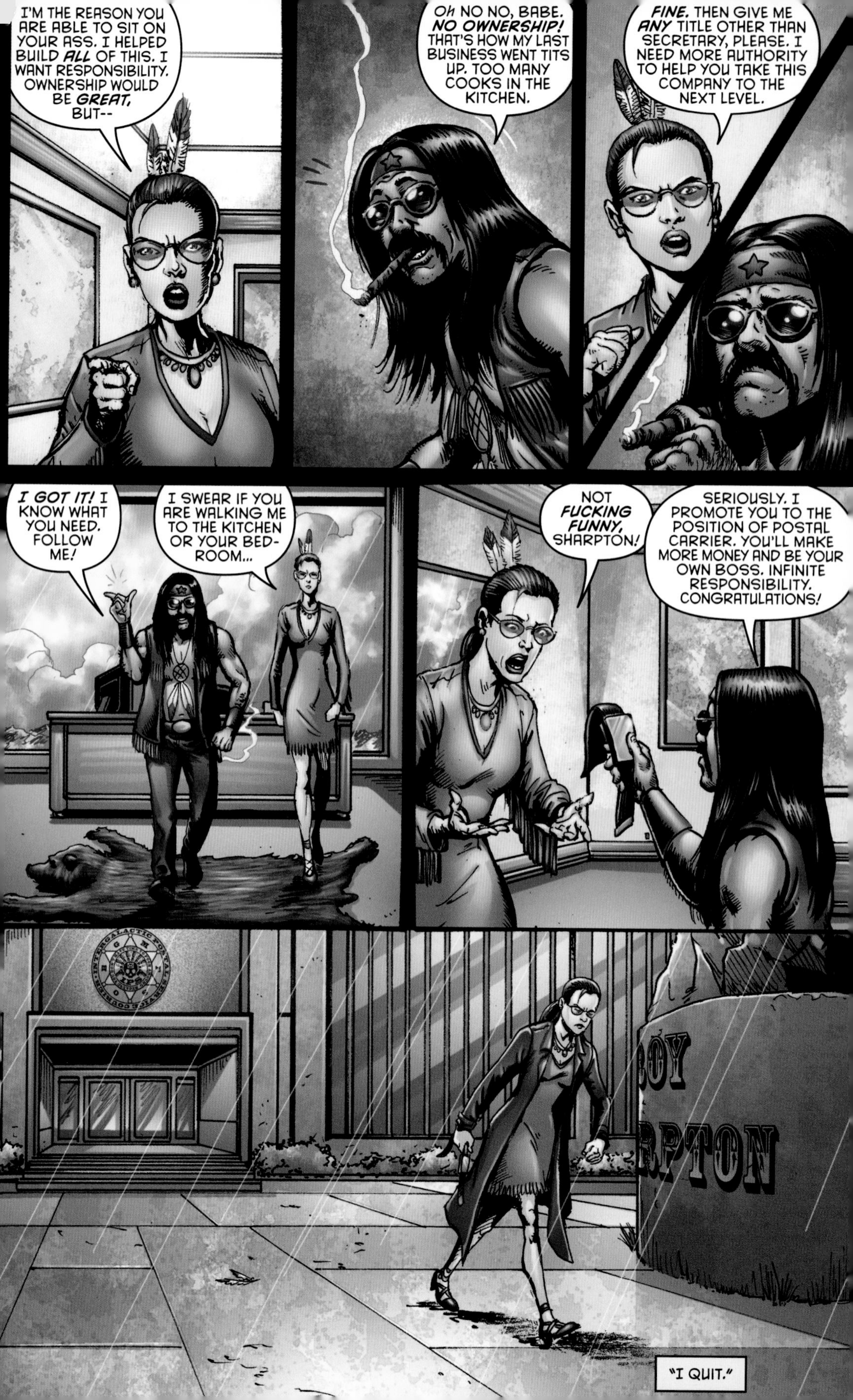
I'M THE REASON YOU ARE ABLE TO SIT ON YOUR ASS. I HELPED BUILD ALL OF THIS. I WANT RESPONSIBILITY. OWNERSHIP WOULD BE GREAT, BUT--
Oh NO NO, BABE. NO OWNERSHIP! THAT'S HOW MY LAST BUSINESS WENT TITS UP. TOO MANY COOKS IN THE KITCHEN.
FINE. THEN GIVE ME ANY TITLE OTHER THAN SECRETARY, PLEASE. I NEED MORE AUTHORITY TO HELP YOU TAKE THIS COMPANY TO THE NEXT LEVEL.
I GOT IT! I KNOW WHAT YOU NEED. FOLLOW ME!
I SWEAR IF YOU ARE WALKING ME TO THE KITCHEN OR YOUR BED-ROOM...
NOT FUCKING FUNNY, SHARPTON!
SERIOUSLY. I PROMOTE YOU TO THE POSITION OF POSTAL CARRIER. YOU'LL MAKE MORE MONEY AND BE YOUR OWN BOSS. INFINITE RESPONSIBILITY. CONGRATULATIONS!
INTERGALACTIC POSTAL SERVICE
COY
RPTON
"I QUIT."

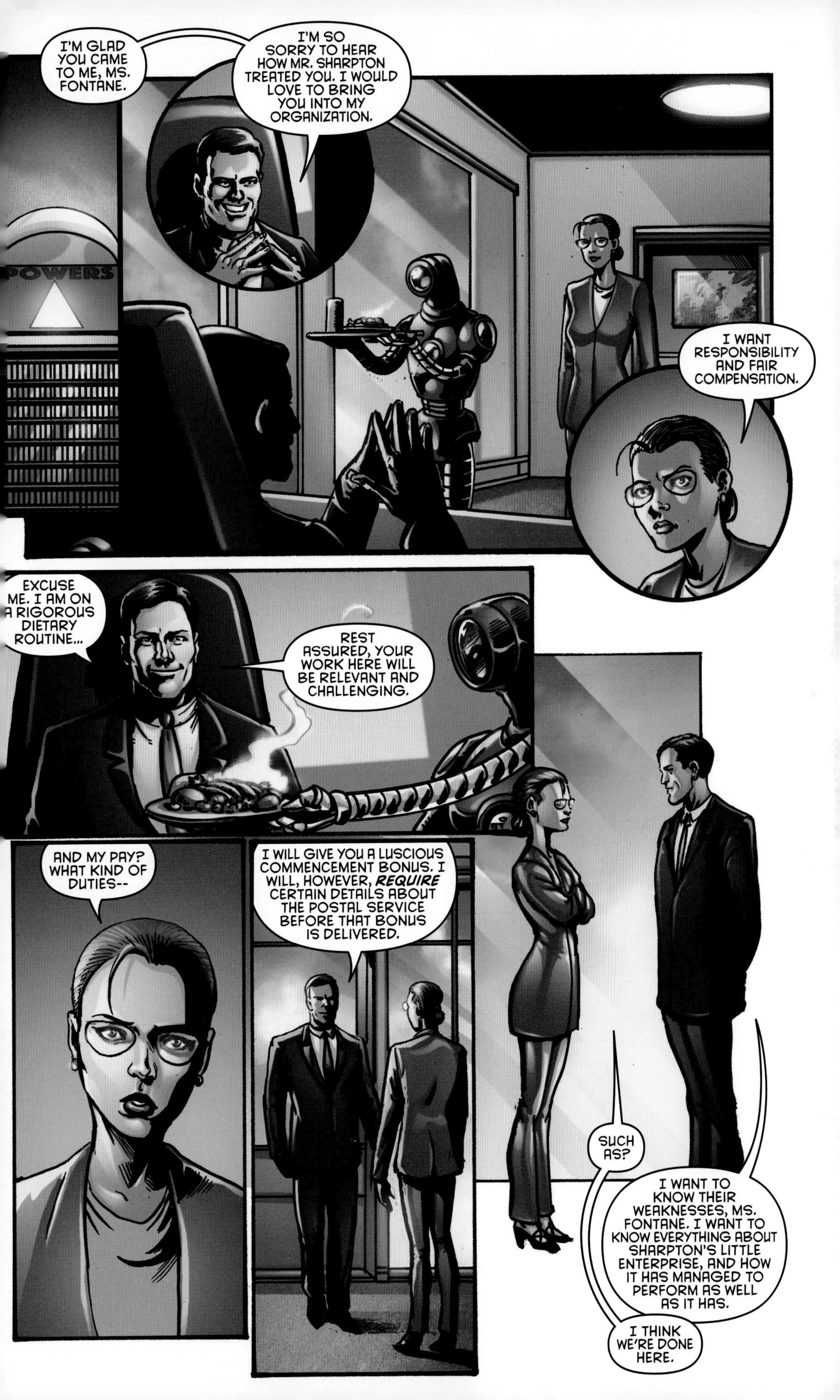
I'M GLAD YOU CAME TO ME, MS. FONTANE.
I'M SO SORRY TO HEAR HOW MR. SHARPTON TREATED YOU. I WOULD LOVE TO BRING YOU INTO MY ORGANIZATION.
POWERS
I WANT RESPONSIBILITY AND FAIR COMPENSATION.
EXCUSE ME. I AM ON A RIGOROUS DIETARY ROUTINE...
REST ASSURED, YOUR WORK HERE WILL BE RELEVANT AND CHALLENGING.
AND MY PAY? WHAT KIND OF DUTIES--
I WILL GIVE YOU A LUSCIOUS COMMENCEMENT BONUS. I WILL, HOWEVER, *REQUIRE* CERTAIN DETAILS ABOUT THE POSTAL SERVICE BEFORE THAT BONUS IS DELIVERED.
SUCH AS?
I WANT TO KNOW THEIR WEAKNESSES, MS. FONTANE. I WANT TO KNOW EVERYTHING ABOUT SHARPTON'S LITTLE ENTERPRISE, AND HOW IT HAS MANAGED TO PERFORM AS WELL AS IT HAS.
I THINK WE'RE DONE HERE.

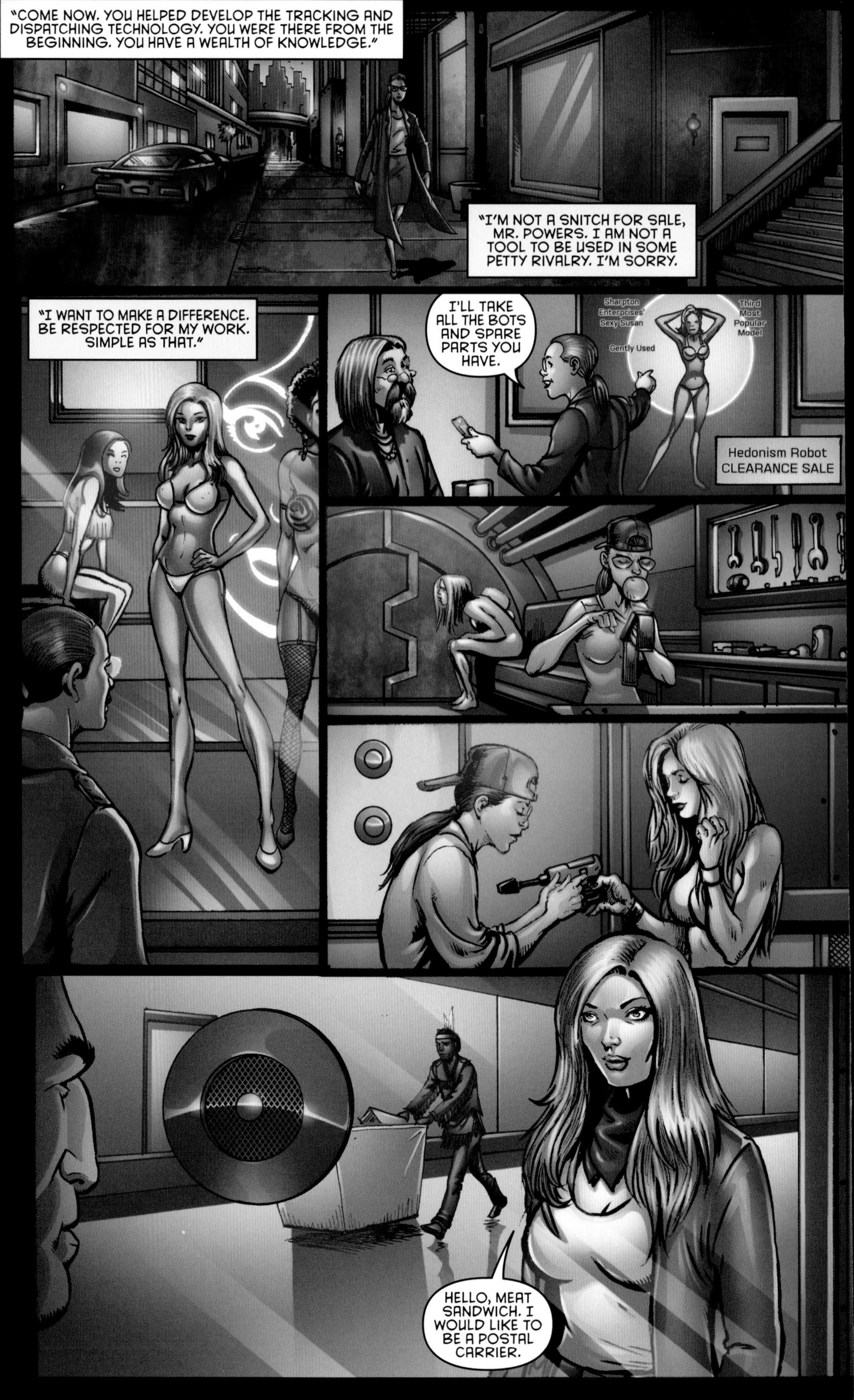

"COME NOW. YOU HELPED DEVELOP THE TRACKING AND DISPATCHING TECHNOLOGY. YOU WERE THERE FROM THE BEGINNING. YOU HAVE A WEALTH OF KNOWLEDGE."
"I'M NOT A SNITCH FOR SALE, MR. POWERS. I AM NOT A TOOL TO BE USED IN SOME PETTY RIVALRY. I'M SORRY.
"I WANT TO MAKE A DIFFERENCE. BE RESPECTED FOR MY WORK. SIMPLE AS THAT."
I'LL TAKE ALL THE BOTS AND SPARE PARTS YOU HAVE.
Sharpton Enterprises' Sexy Susan
Gently Used
Third Most Popular Model
Hedonism Robot CLEARANCE SALE
HELLO, MEAT SANDWICH. I WOULD LIKE TO BE A POSTAL CARRIER.

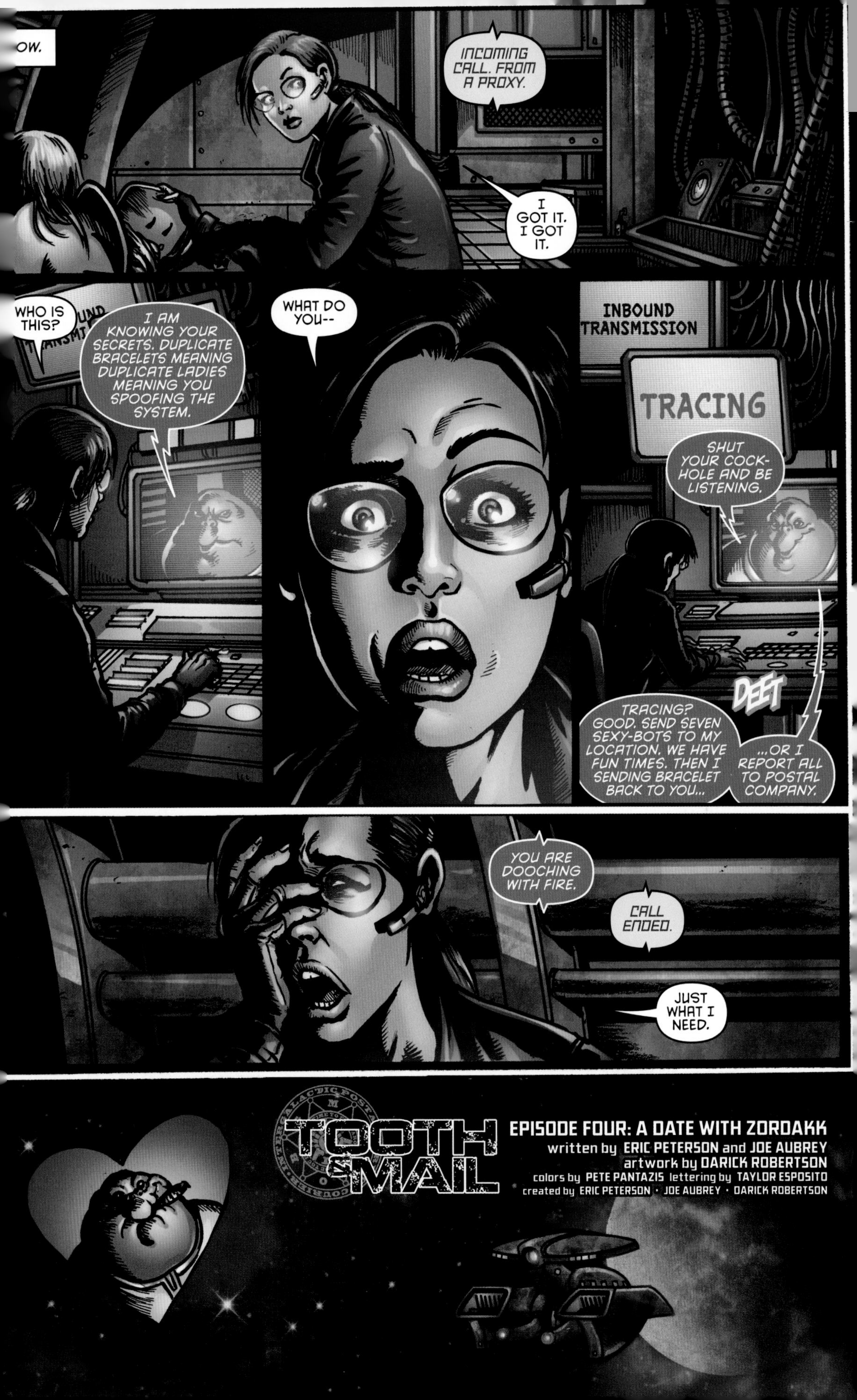

OW.
INCOMING CALL. FROM A PROXY.
I GOT IT. I GOT IT.
WHO IS THIS?
I AM KNOWING YOUR SECRETS. DUPLICATE BRACELETS MEANING DUPLICATE LADIES MEANING YOU SPOOFING THE SYSTEM.
WHAT DO YOU--
INBOUND TRANSMISSION
TRACING
SHUT YOUR COCK-HOLE AND BE LISTENING.
DEET
TRACING? GOOD. SEND SEVEN SEXY-BOTS TO MY LOCATION. WE HAVE FUN TIMES. THEN I SENDING BRACELET BACK TO YOU...
...OR I REPORT ALL TO POSTAL COMPANY.
YOU ARE DOOCHING WITH FIRE.
CALL ENDED.
JUST WHAT I NEED.
TOOTH & MAIL
EPISODE FOUR: A DATE WITH ZORDAKK
written by ERIC PETERSON and JOE AUBREY
artwork by DARICK ROBERTSON
colors by PETE PANTAZIS lettering by TAYLOR ESPOSITO
created by ERIC PETERSON · JOE AUBREY · DARICK ROBERTSON

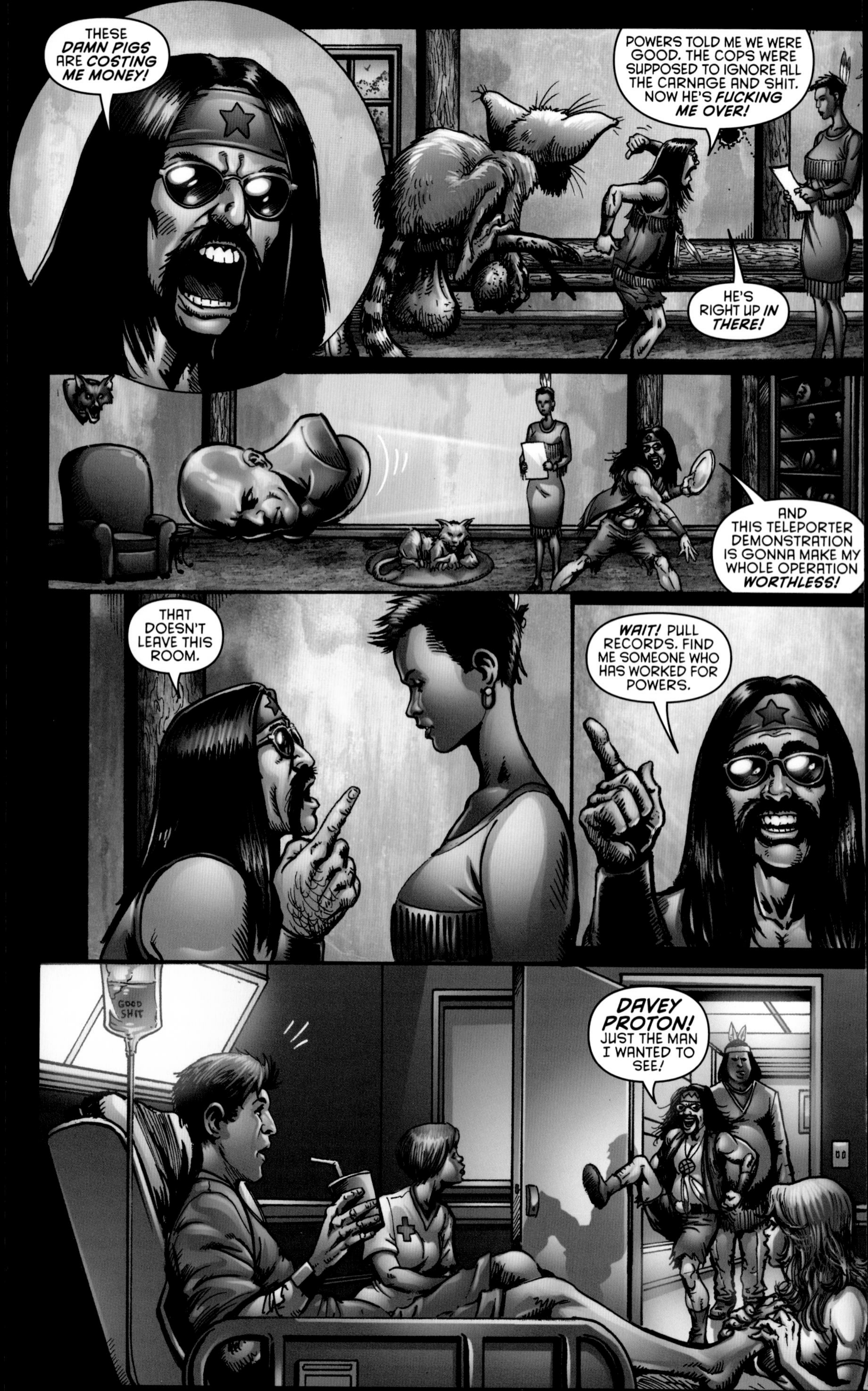
THESE DAMN PIGS ARE COSTING ME MONEY!
POWERS TOLD ME WE WERE GOOD. THE COPS WERE SUPPOSED TO IGNORE ALL THE CARNAGE AND SHIT. NOW HE'S FUCKING ME OVER!
HE'S RIGHT UP IN THERE!
AND THIS TELEPORTER DEMONSTRATION IS GONNA MAKE MY WHOLE OPERATION WORTHLESS!
THAT DOESN'T LEAVE THIS ROOM.
WAIT! PULL RECORDS. FIND ME SOMEONE WHO HAS WORKED FOR POWERS.
GOOD SHIT
DAVEY PROTON! JUST THE MAN I WANTED TO SEE!

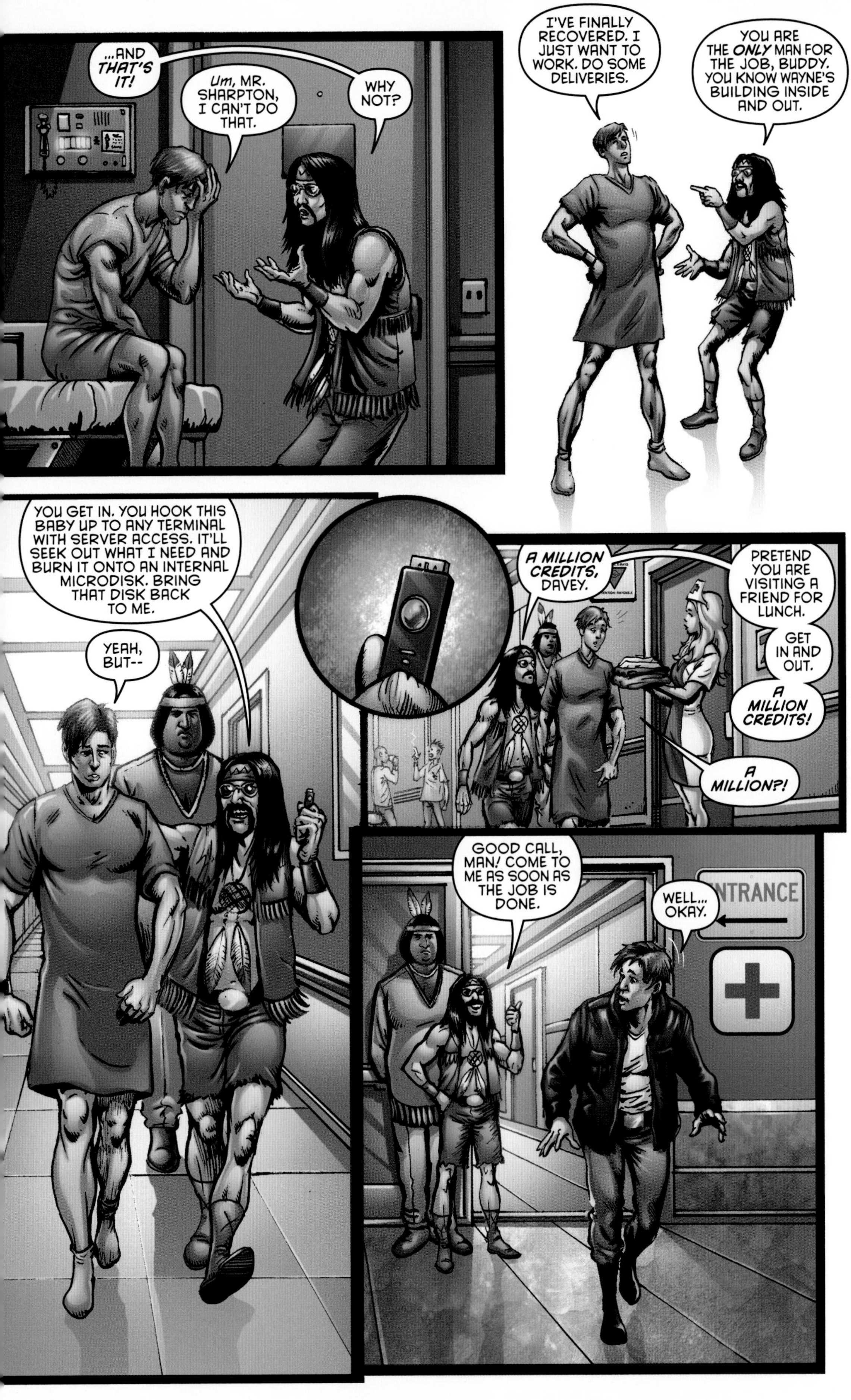

...AND THAT'S IT!
UM, MR. SHARPTON, I CAN'T DO THAT.
WHY NOT?
I'VE FINALLY RECOVERED. I JUST WANT TO WORK. DO SOME DELIVERIES.
YOU ARE THE ONLY MAN FOR THE JOB, BUDDY. YOU KNOW WAYNE'S BUILDING INSIDE AND OUT.
YOU GET IN. YOU HOOK THIS BABY UP TO ANY TERMINAL WITH SERVER ACCESS. IT'LL SEEK OUT WHAT I NEED AND BURN IT ONTO AN INTERNAL MICRODISK. BRING THAT DISK BACK TO ME.
YEAH, BUT--
A MILLION CREDITS, DAVEY.
PRETEND YOU ARE VISITING A FRIEND FOR LUNCH.
GET IN AND OUT.
A MILLION CREDITS!
A MILLION?!
GOOD CALL, MAN! COME TO ME AS SOON AS THE JOB IS DONE.
WELL... OKAY.
ENTRANCE

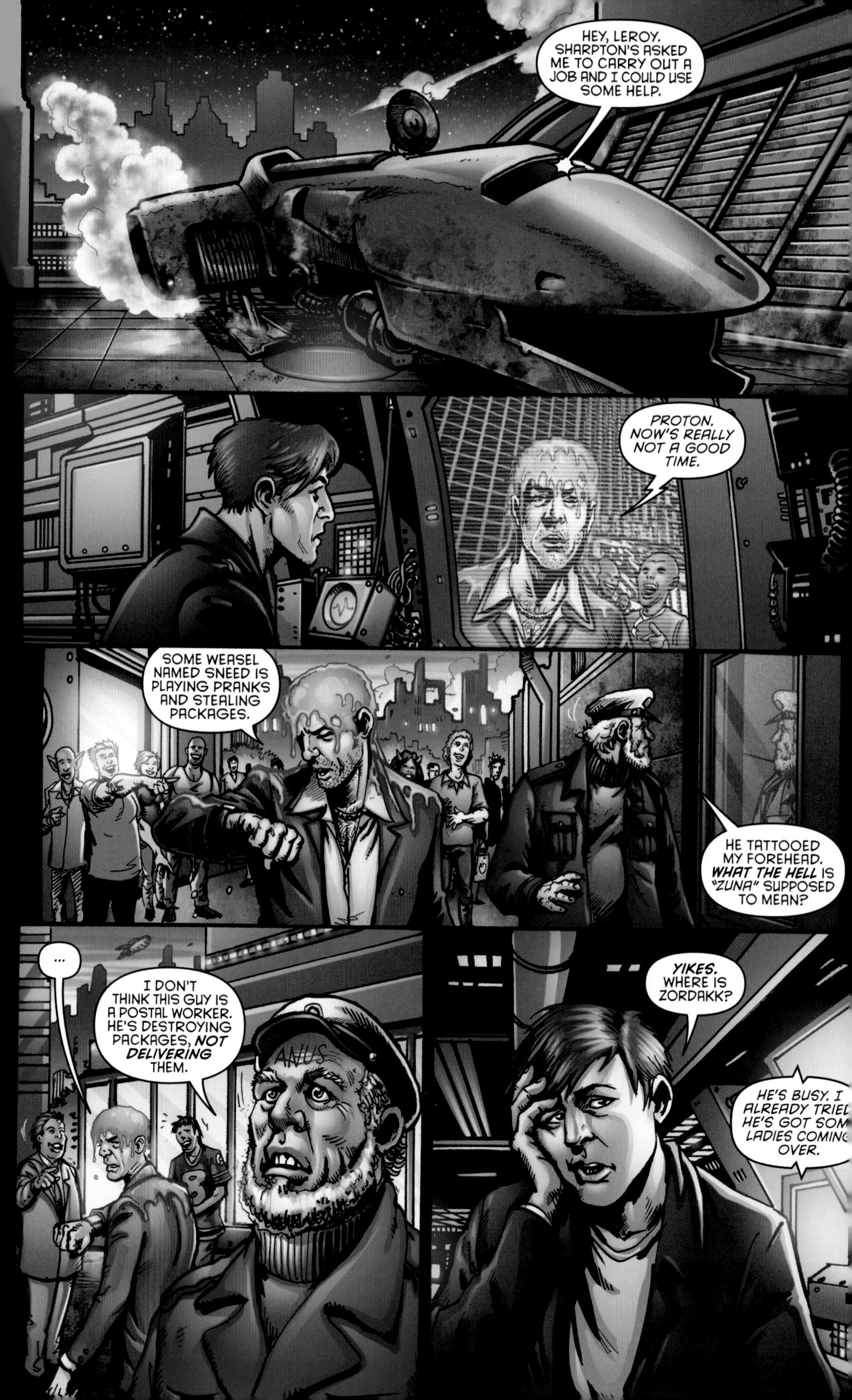
HEY, LEROY. SHARPTON'S ASKED ME TO CARRY OUT A JOB AND I COULD USE SOME HELP.
PROTON. NOW'S REALLY NOT A GOOD TIME.
SOME WEASEL NAMED SNEED IS PLAYING PRANKS AND STEALING PACKAGES.
HE TATTOOED MY FOREHEAD. WHAT THE HELL IS "ZUNA" SUPPOSED TO MEAN?
...
I DON'T THINK THIS GUY IS A POSTAL WORKER. HE'S DESTROYING PACKAGES, NOT DELIVERING THEM.
ANUS
YIKES. WHERE IS ZORDAKK?
HE'S BUSY. I ALREADY TRIED. HE'S GOT SOME LADIES COMING OVER.

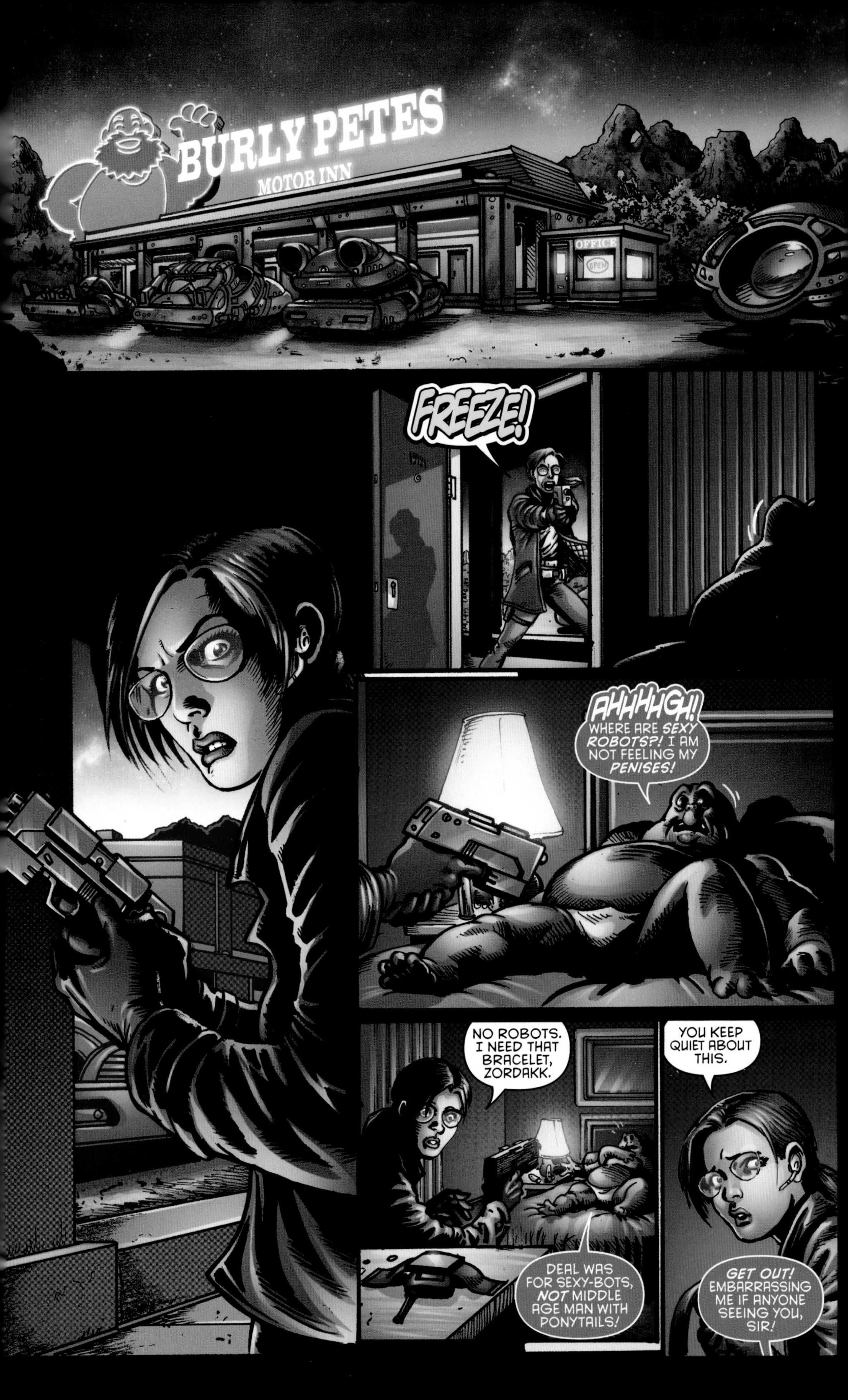
BURLY PETES
MOTOR INN
OFFICE
OPEN
FREEZE!
AHHHHGH! WHERE ARE SEXY ROBOTS?! I AM NOT FEELING MY PENISES!
NO ROBOTS. I NEED THAT BRACELET, ZORDAKK.
DEAL WAS FOR SEXY-BOTS, NOT MIDDLE AGE MAN WITH PONYTAILS!
YOU KEEP QUIET ABOUT THIS.
GET OUT! EMBARRASSING ME IF ANYONE SEEING YOU, SIR!

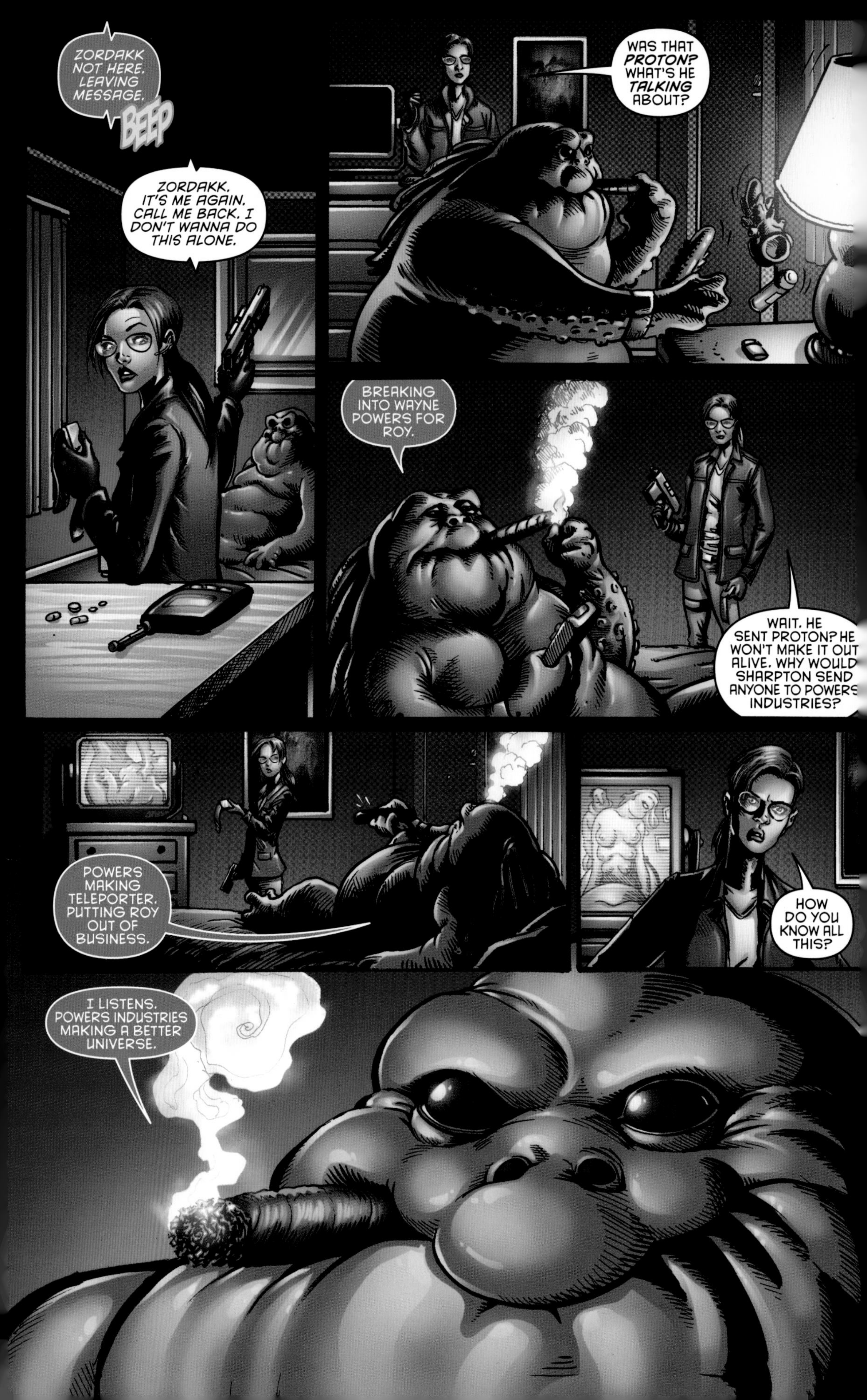
ZORDAKK NOT HERE. LEAVING MESSAGE.
BEEP
ZORDAKK. IT'S ME AGAIN. CALL ME BACK. I DON'T WANNA DO THIS ALONE.
WAS THAT PROTON? WHAT'S HE TALKING ABOUT?
BREAKING INTO WAYNE POWERS FOR ROY.
WAIT. HE SENT PROTON? HE WON'T MAKE IT OUT ALIVE. WHY WOULD SHARPTON SEND ANYONE TO POWERS INDUSTRIES?
POWERS MAKING TELEPORTER. PUTTING ROY OUT OF BUSINESS.
HOW DO YOU KNOW ALL THIS?
I LISTENS. POWERS INDUSTRIES MAKING A BETTER UNIVERSE.

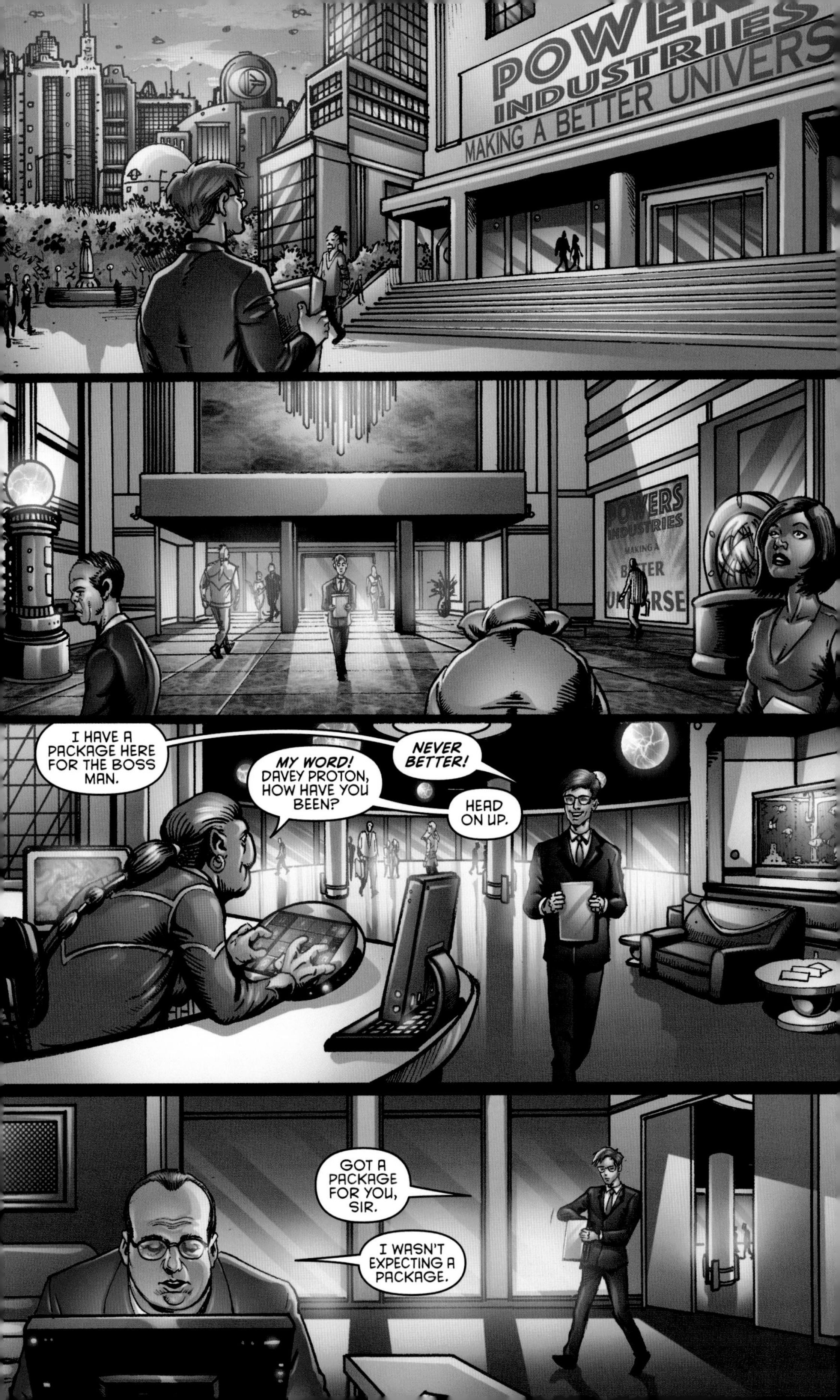
POWERS INDUSTRIES
MAKING A BETTER UNIVERS
POWERS INDUSTRIES MAKING A BETTER UNIVERSE
I HAVE A PACKAGE HERE FOR THE BOSS MAN.
MY WORD! DAVEY PROTON, HOW HAVE YOU BEEN?
NEVER BETTER!
HEAD ON UP.
GOT A PACKAGE FOR YOU, SIR.
I WASN'T EXPECTING A PACKAGE.

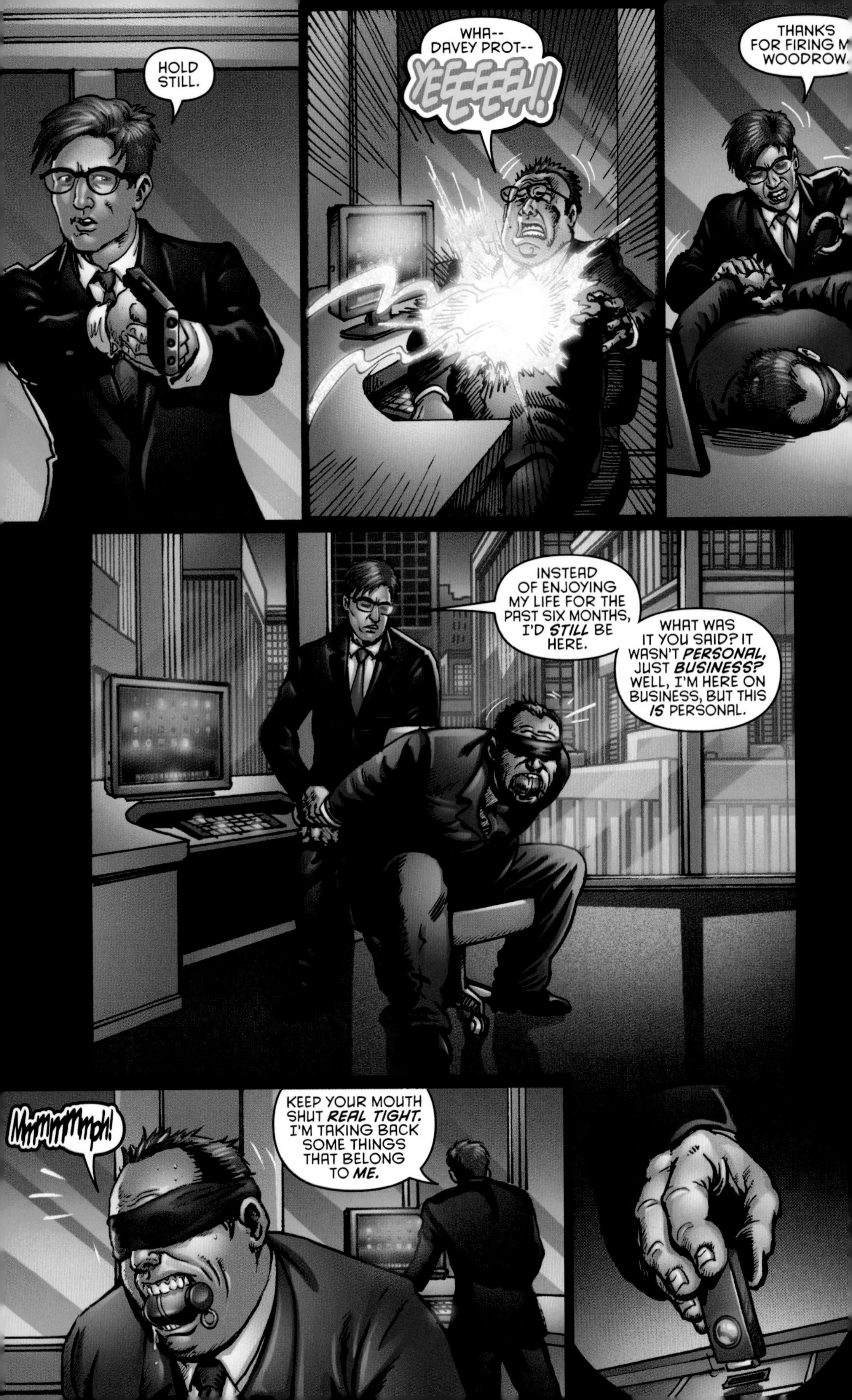
HOLD STILL.
WHA-- DAVEY PROT--
YEEEEEH!!
THANKS FOR FIRING M WOODROW.
INSTEAD OF ENJOYING MY LIFE FOR THE PAST SIX MONTHS, I'D *STILL* BE HERE.
WHAT WAS IT YOU SAID? IT WASN'T *PERSONAL,* JUST *BUSINESS?* WELL, I'M HERE ON BUSINESS, BUT THIS *IS* PERSONAL.
MmmmMmph!
KEEP YOUR MOUTH SHUT *REAL TIGHT.* I'M TAKING BACK SOME THINGS THAT BELONG TO *ME.*

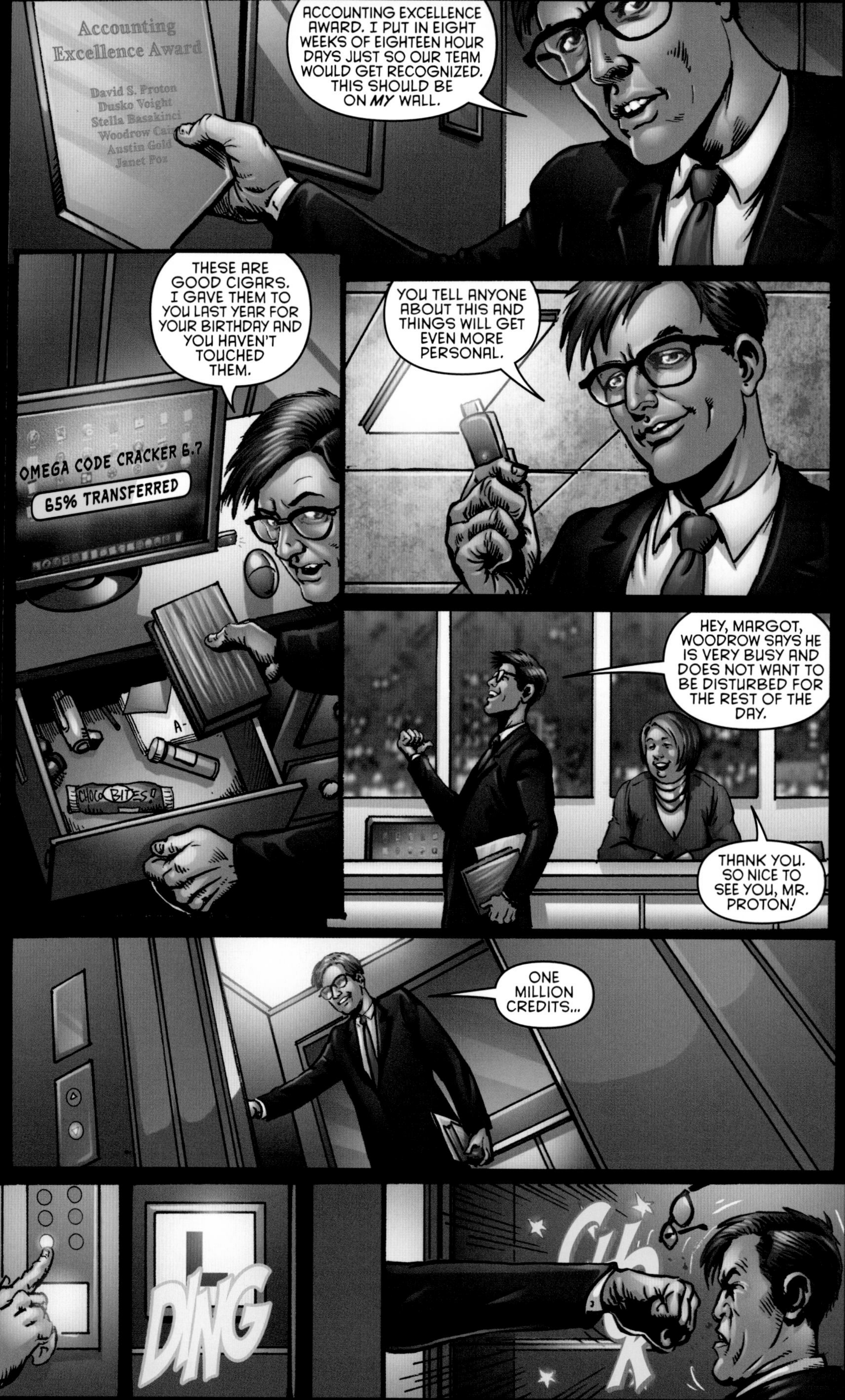
Accounting Excellence Award
David S. Proton
Dusko Voight
Stella Basakinci
Woodrow Cai
Austin Gold
Janet Poz
ACCOUNTING EXCELLENCE AWARD. I PUT IN EIGHT WEEKS OF EIGHTEEN HOUR DAYS JUST SO OUR TEAM WOULD GET RECOGNIZED. THIS SHOULD BE ON *MY* WALL.
THESE ARE GOOD CIGARS. I GAVE THEM TO YOU LAST YEAR FOR YOUR BIRTHDAY AND YOU HAVEN'T TOUCHED THEM.
OMEGA CODE CRACKER 6.7
65% TRANSFERRED
CHOCO BITES!
YOU TELL ANYONE ABOUT THIS AND THINGS WILL GET EVEN MORE PERSONAL.
HEY, MARGOT, WOODROW SAYS HE IS VERY BUSY AND DOES NOT WANT TO BE DISTURBED FOR THE REST OF THE DAY.
THANK YOU. SO NICE TO SEE YOU, MR. PROTON!
ONE MILLION CREDITS...
DING

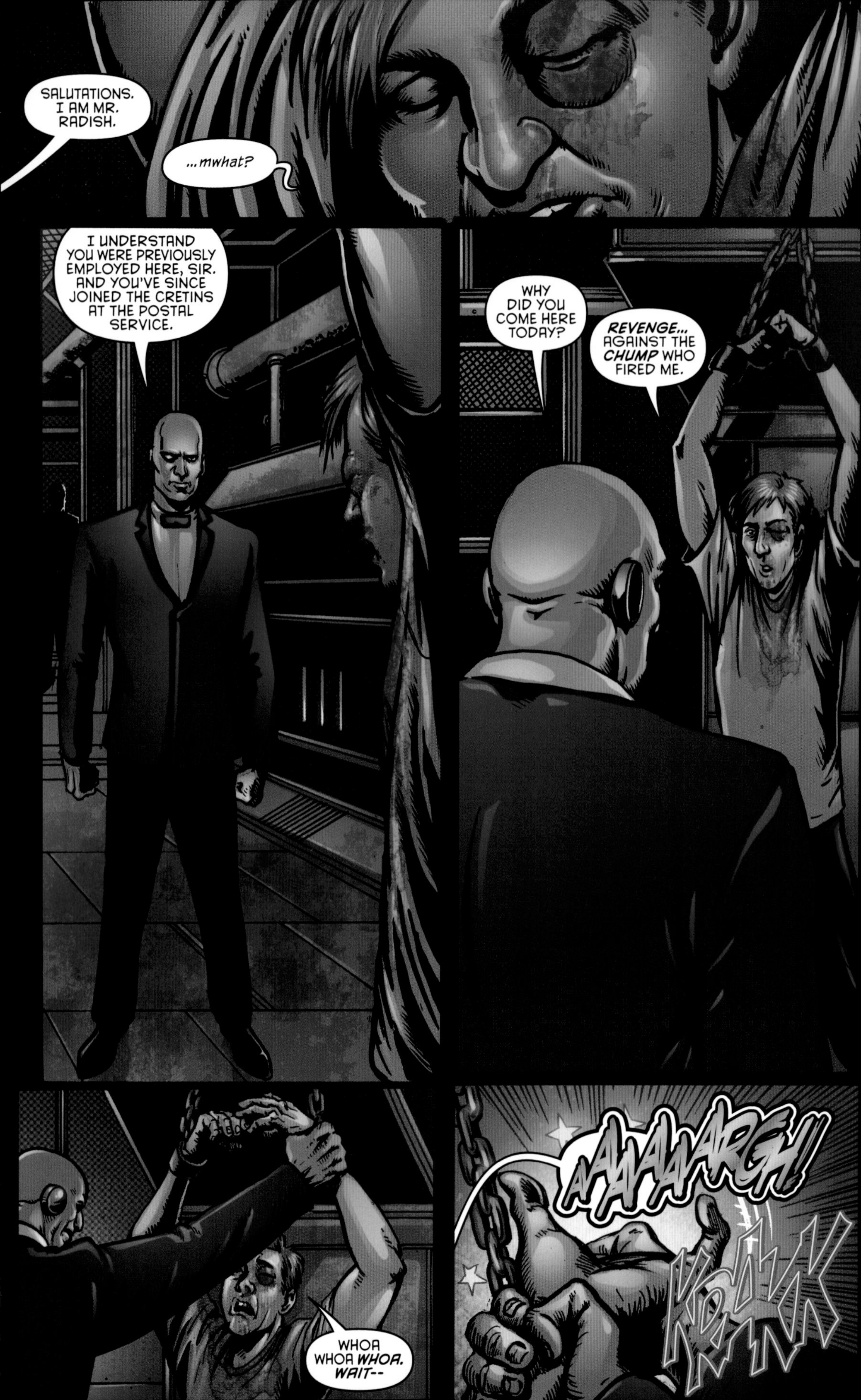
SALUTATIONS. I AM MR. RADISH.
...mwhat?
I UNDERSTAND YOU WERE PREVIOUSLY EMPLOYED HERE, SIR. AND YOU'VE SINCE JOINED THE CRETINS AT THE POSTAL SERVICE.
WHY DID YOU COME HERE TODAY?
REVENGE... AGAINST THE CHUMP WHO FIRED ME.
WHOA WHOA WHOA. WAIT--
AAAAAARGH!
KRONK

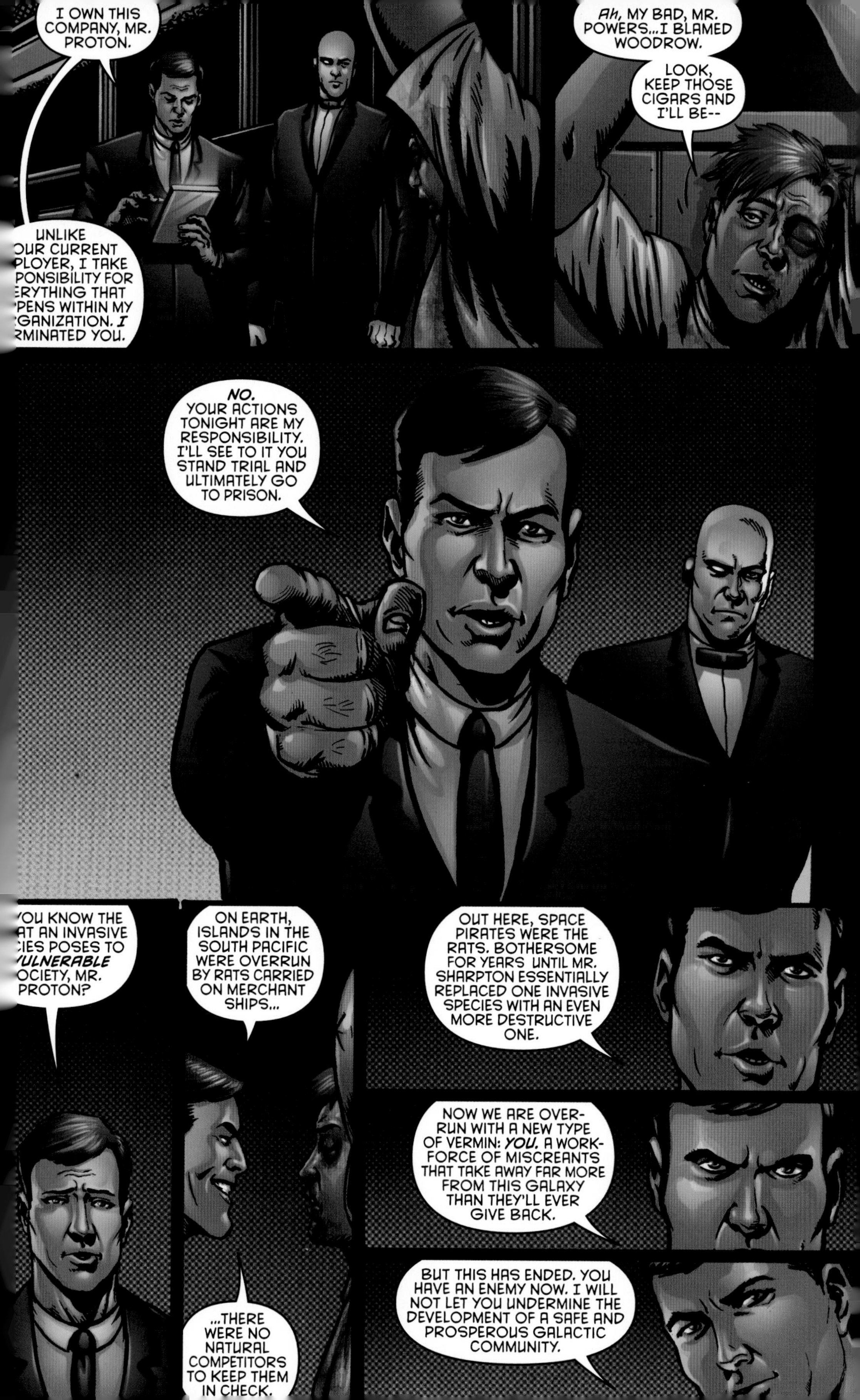
I OWN THIS COMPANY, MR. PROTON.
UNLIKE OUR CURRENT PLOYER, I TAKE PONSIBILITY FOR ERYTHING THAT PPENS WITHIN MY GANIZATION. I RMINATED YOU.
AH, MY BAD, MR. POWERS...I BLAMED WOODROW.
LOOK, KEEP THOSE CIGARS AND I'LL BE--
NO. YOUR ACTIONS TONIGHT ARE MY RESPONSIBILITY. I'LL SEE TO IT YOU STAND TRIAL AND ULTIMATELY GO TO PRISON.
YOU KNOW THE AT AN INVASIVE CIES POSES TO VULNERABLE OCIETY, MR. PROTON?
ON EARTH, ISLANDS IN THE SOUTH PACIFIC WERE OVERRUN BY RATS CARRIED ON MERCHANT SHIPS...
...THERE WERE NO NATURAL COMPETITORS TO KEEP THEM IN CHECK.
OUT HERE, SPACE PIRATES WERE THE RATS. BOTHERSOME FOR YEARS UNTIL MR. SHARPTON ESSENTIALLY REPLACED ONE INVASIVE SPECIES WITH AN EVEN MORE DESTRUCTIVE ONE.
NOW WE ARE OVER-RUN WITH A NEW TYPE OF VERMIN: YOU. A WORK-FORCE OF MISCREANTS THAT TAKE AWAY FAR MORE FROM THIS GALAXY THAN THEY'LL EVER GIVE BACK.
BUT THIS HAS ENDED. YOU HAVE AN ENEMY NOW. I WILL NOT LET YOU UNDERMINE THE DEVELOPMENT OF A SAFE AND PROSPEROUS GALACTIC COMMUNITY.

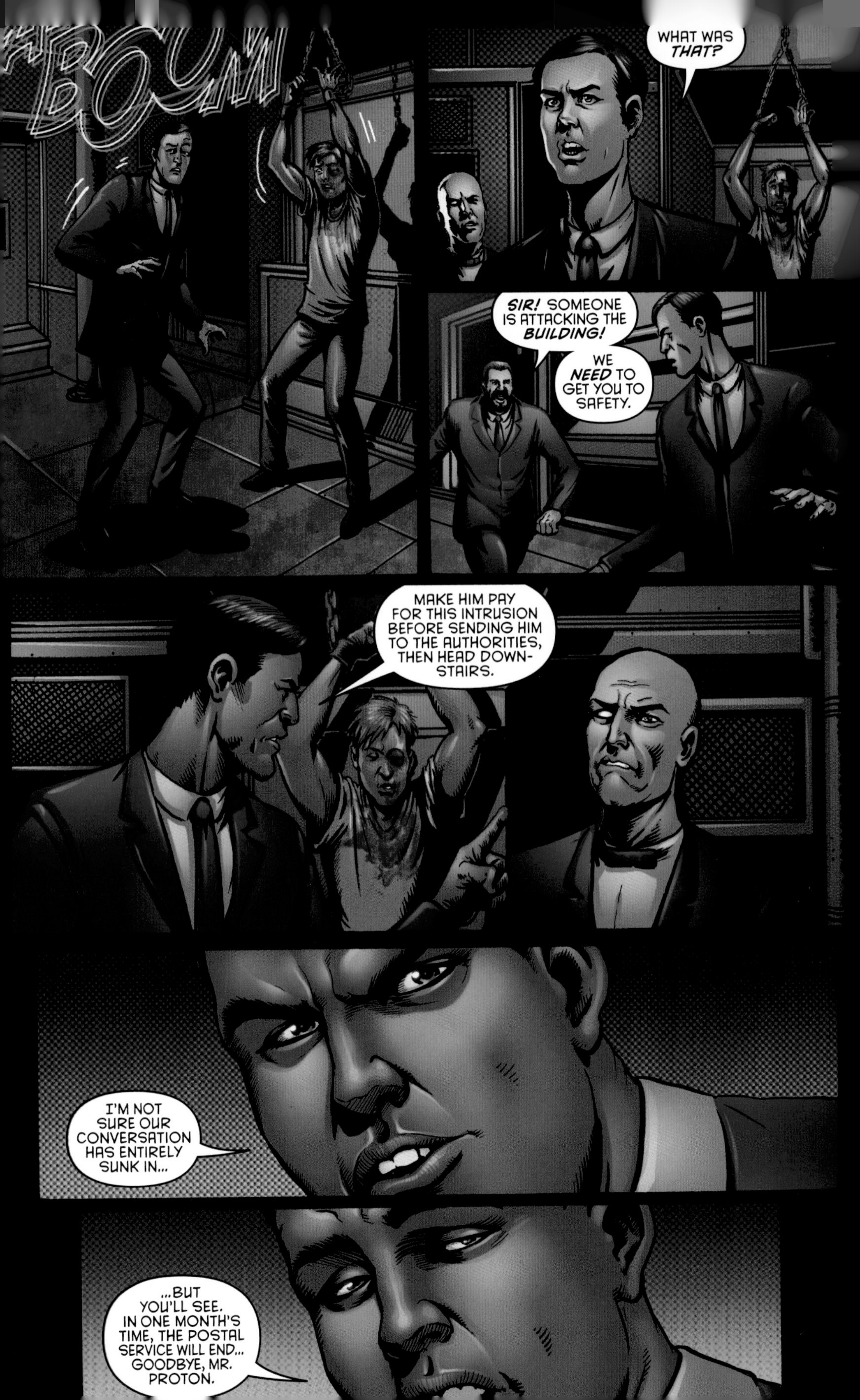
BOOM
WHAT WAS THAT?
SIR! SOMEONE IS ATTACKING THE BUILDING!
WE NEED TO GET YOU TO SAFETY.
MAKE HIM PAY FOR THIS INTRUSION BEFORE SENDING HIM TO THE AUTHORITIES, THEN HEAD DOWN-STAIRS.
I'M NOT SURE OUR CONVERSATION HAS ENTIRELY SUNK IN...
...BUT YOU'LL SEE. IN ONE MONTH'S TIME, THE POSTAL SERVICE WILL END... GOODBYE, MR. PROTON.

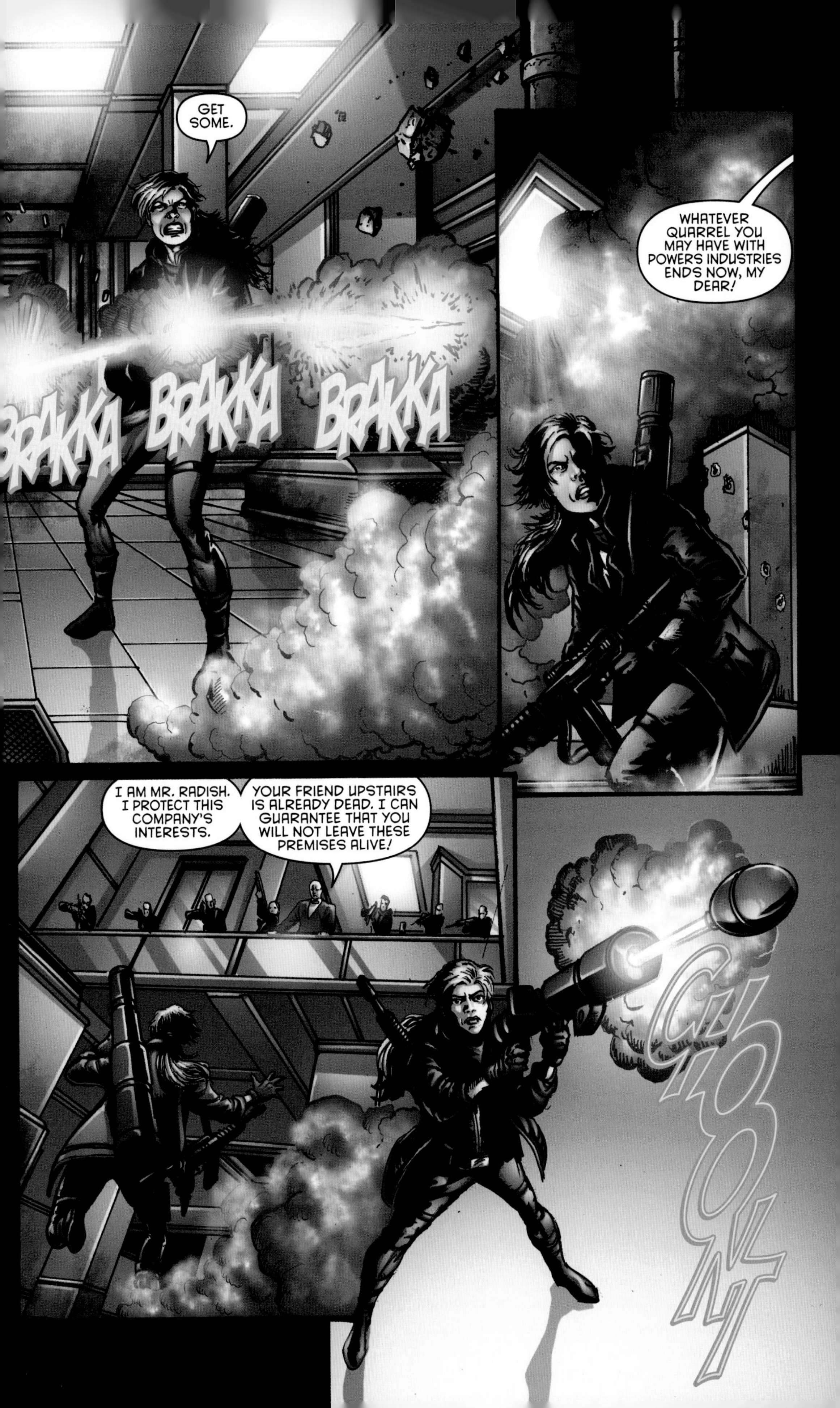
GET SOME.
BRAKKA BRAKKA BRAKKA
WHATEVER QUARREL YOU MAY HAVE WITH POWERS INDUSTRIES ENDS NOW, MY DEAR!
I AM MR. RADISH. I PROTECT THIS COMPANY'S INTERESTS.
YOUR FRIEND UPSTAIRS IS ALREADY DEAD. I CAN GUARANTEE THAT YOU WILL NOT LEAVE THESE PREMISES ALIVE!

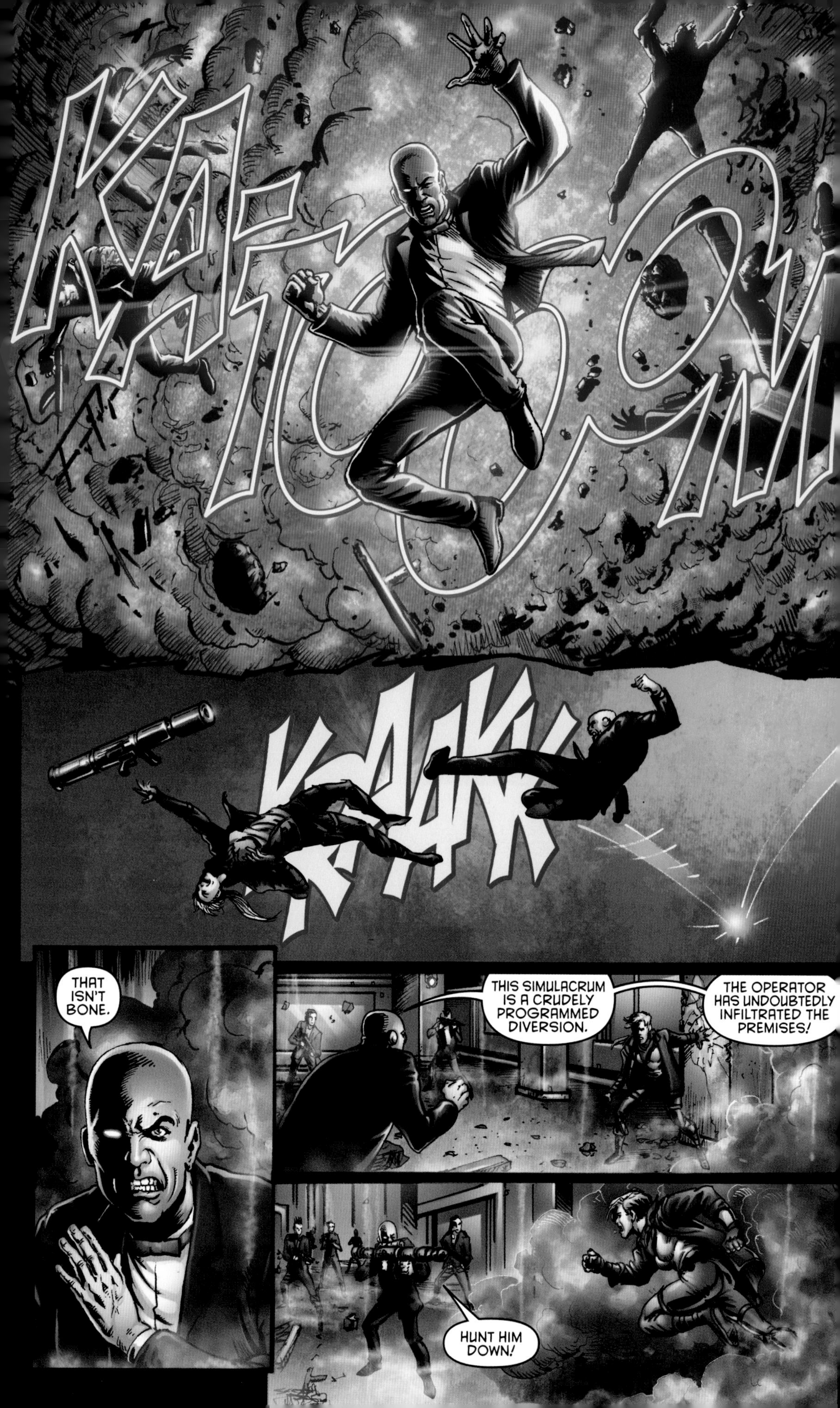
KA-TOOOM
KRAK
THAT ISN'T BONE.
THIS SIMULACRUM IS A CRUDELY PROGRAMMED DIVERSION.
THE OPERATOR HAS UNDOUBTEDLY INFILTRATED THE PREMISES!
HUNT HIM DOWN!

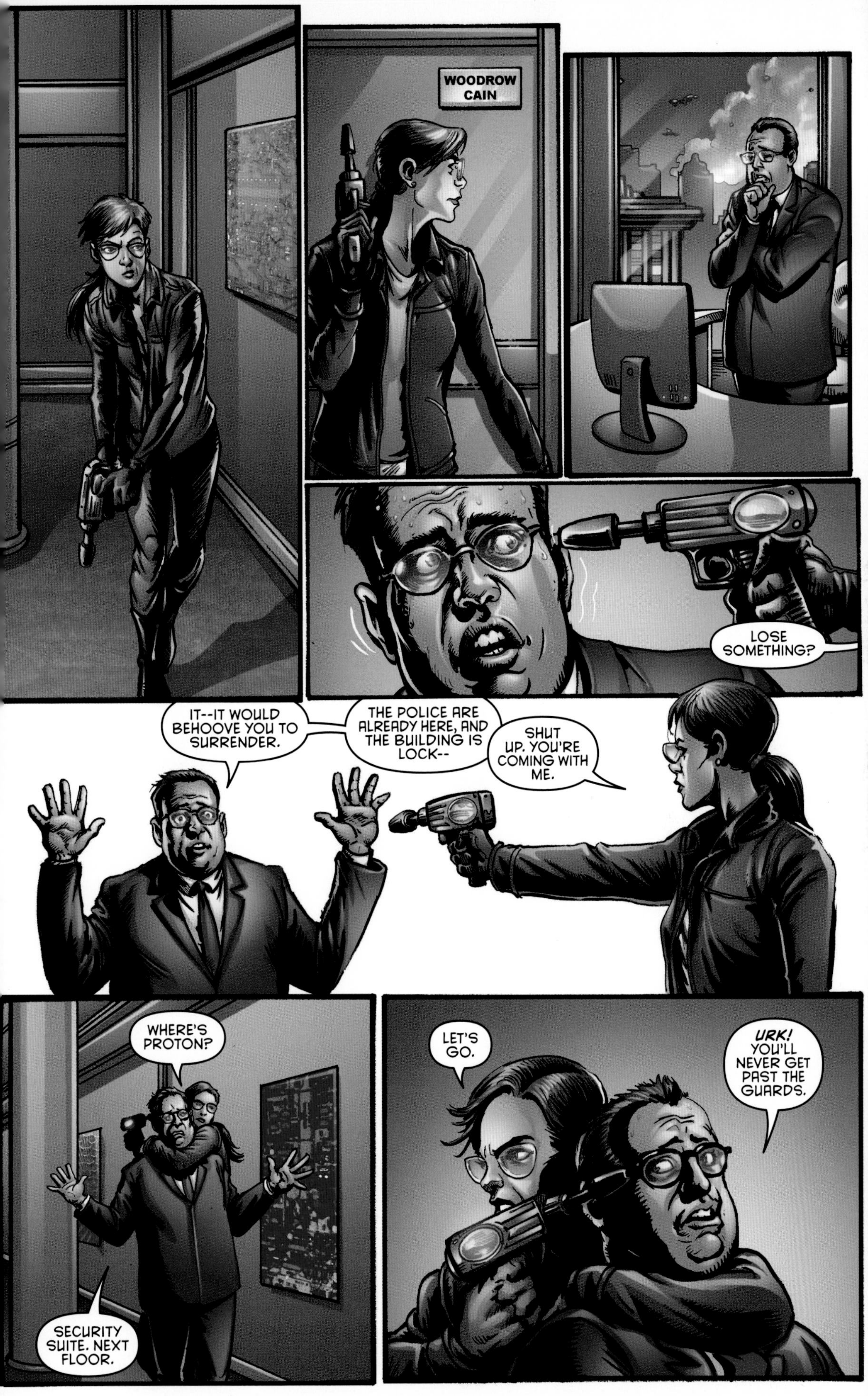
WOODROW CAIN
LOSE SOMETHING?
IT--IT WOULD BEHOOVE YOU TO SURRENDER.
THE POLICE ARE ALREADY HERE, AND THE BUILDING IS LOCK--
SHUT UP. YOU'RE COMING WITH ME.
WHERE'S PROTON?
SECURITY SUITE. NEXT FLOOR.
LET'S GO.
URK! YOU'LL NEVER GET PAST THE GUARDS.

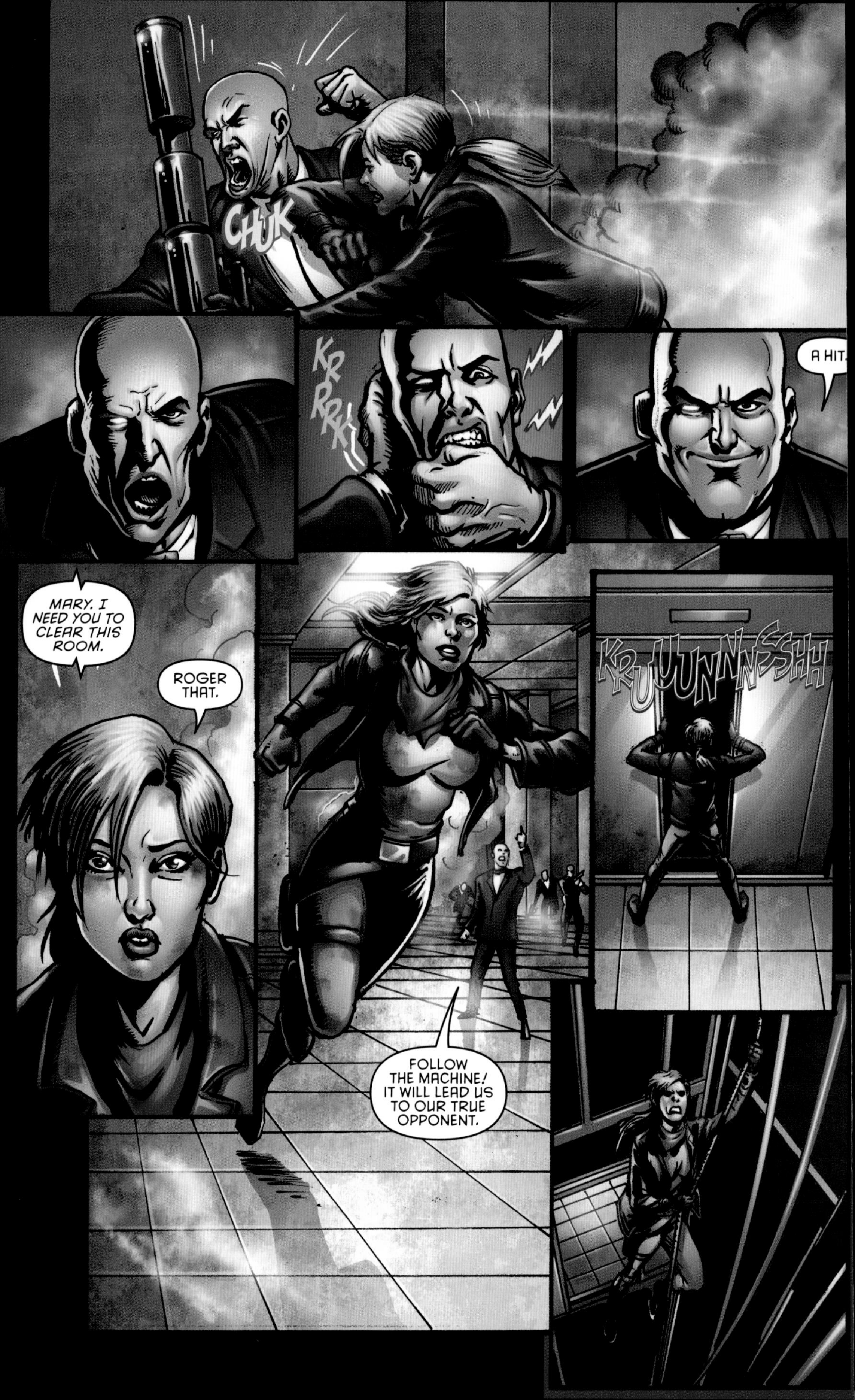
CHUK
KRRRKL
A HIT.
MARY. I NEED YOU TO CLEAR THIS ROOM.
ROGER THAT.
KRUUUNNNSSHH
FOLLOW THE MACHINE! IT WILL LEAD US TO OUR TRUE OPPONENT.

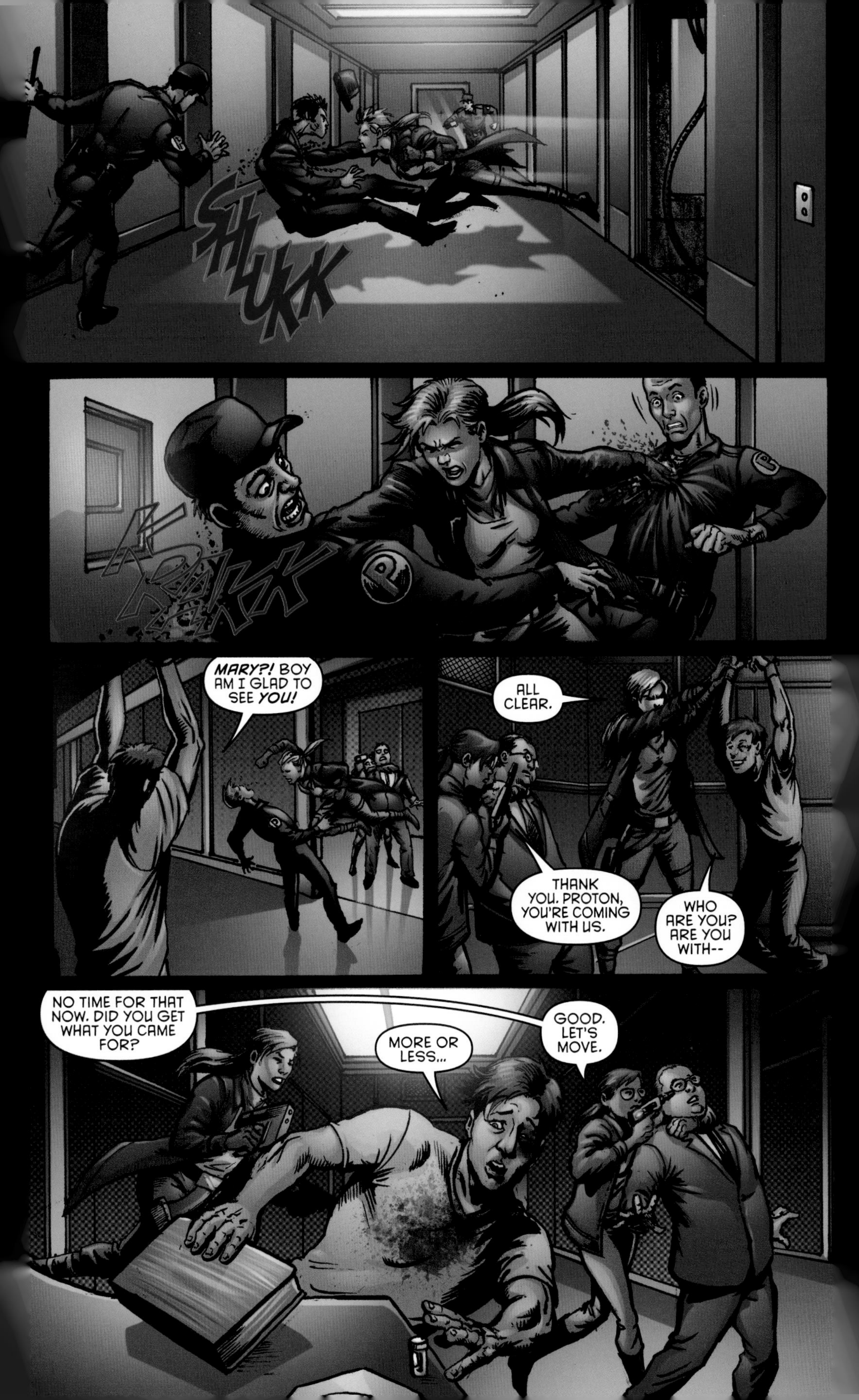

SHLUKK
MARY?! BOY AM I GLAD TO SEE YOU!
ALL CLEAR.
THANK YOU. PROTON, YOU'RE COMING WITH US.
WHO ARE YOU? ARE YOU WITH--
NO TIME FOR THAT NOW. DID YOU GET WHAT YOU CAME FOR?
MORE OR LESS...
GOOD. LET'S MOVE.

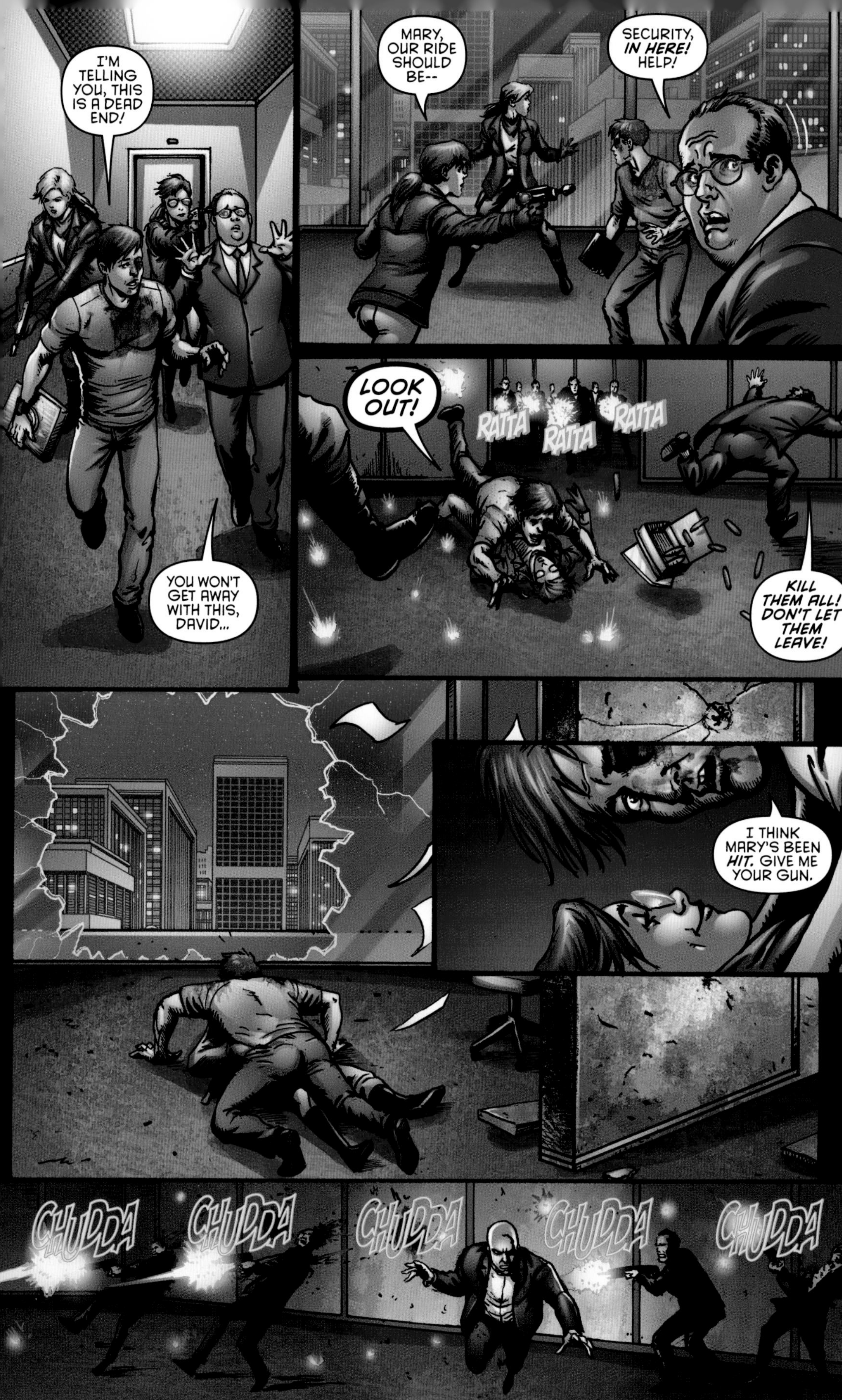
I'M TELLING YOU, THIS IS A DEAD END!
YOU WON'T GET AWAY WITH THIS, DAVID...
MARY, OUR RIDE SHOULD BE--
SECURITY, IN HERE! HELP!
LOOK OUT!
RATTA RATTA RATTA
KILL THEM ALL! DON'T LET THEM LEAVE!
I THINK MARY'S BEEN HIT. GIVE ME YOUR GUN.
CHUDDA CHUDDA CHUDDA CHUDDA CHUDDA

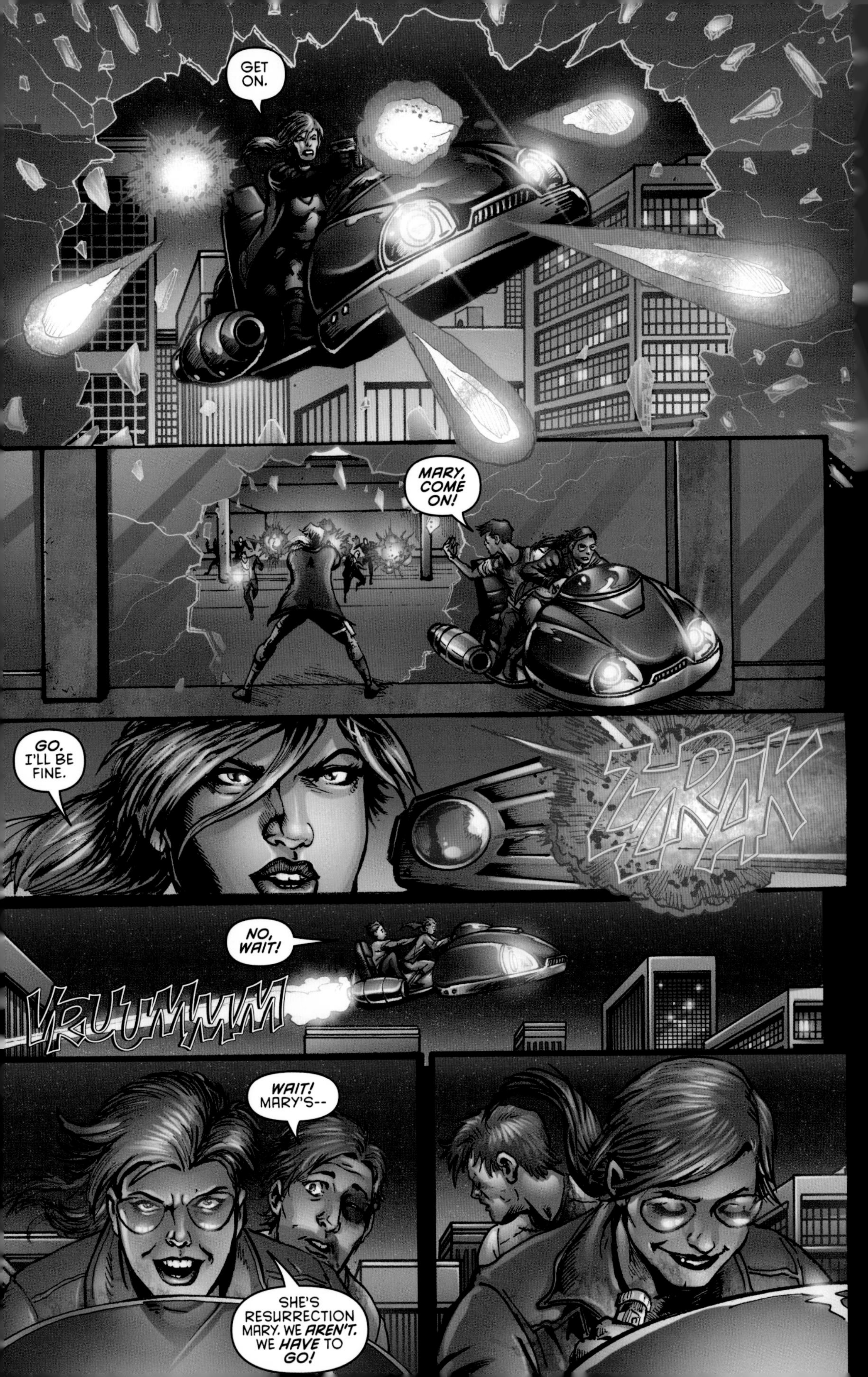
GET ON.
MARY, COME ON!
GO. I'LL BE FINE.
ZZRAK
NO, WAIT!
VRUUMMM
WAIT! MARY'S--
SHE'S RESURRECTION MARY. WE *AREN'T.* WE *HAVE* TO *GO!*

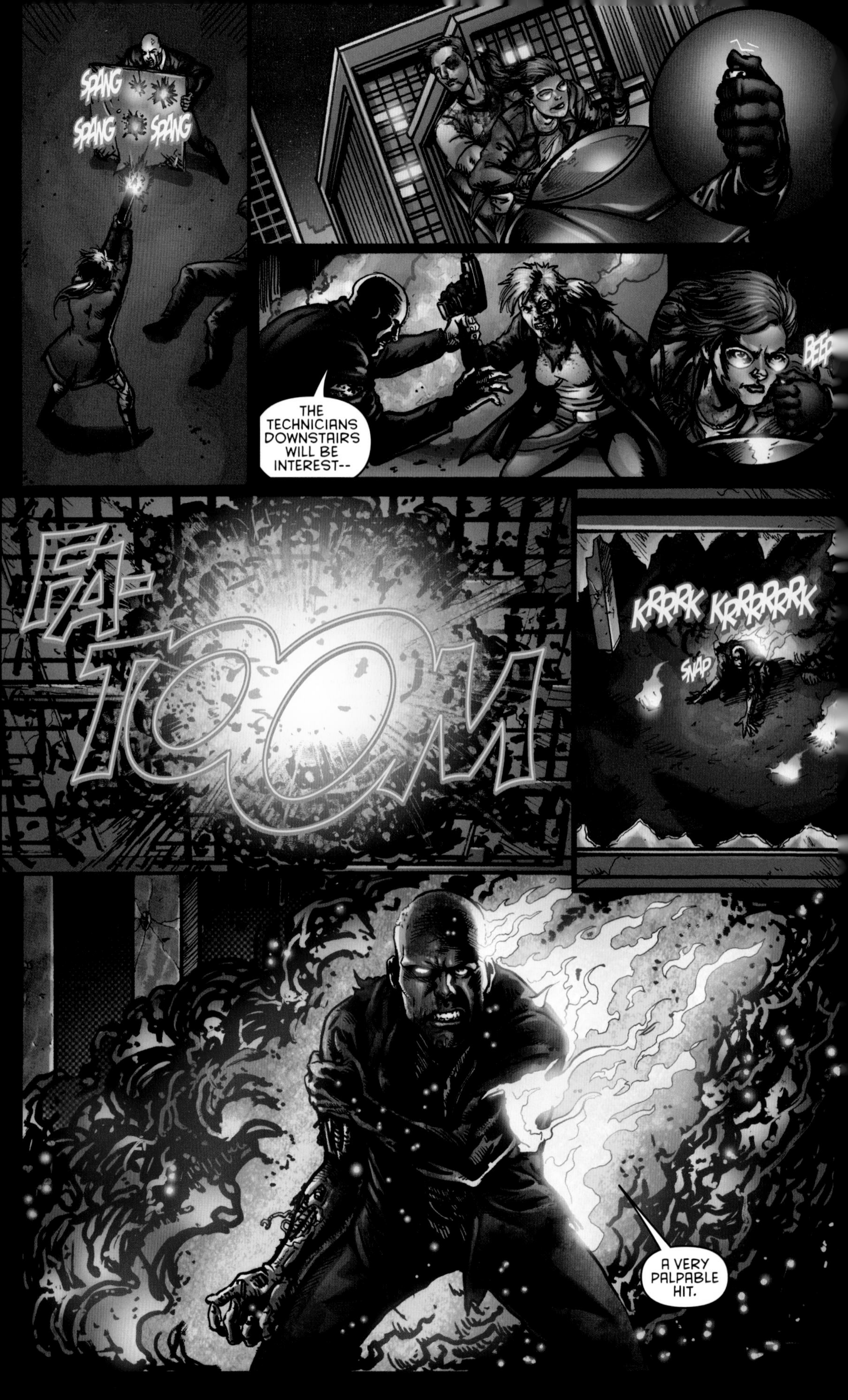
SPANG
SPANG
SPANG
SPANG
THE TECHNICIANS DOWNSTAIRS WILL BE INTEREST--
BEEP
FA-TOOM
KRRRK KRRRRRRK
SNAP
A VERY PALPABLE HIT.

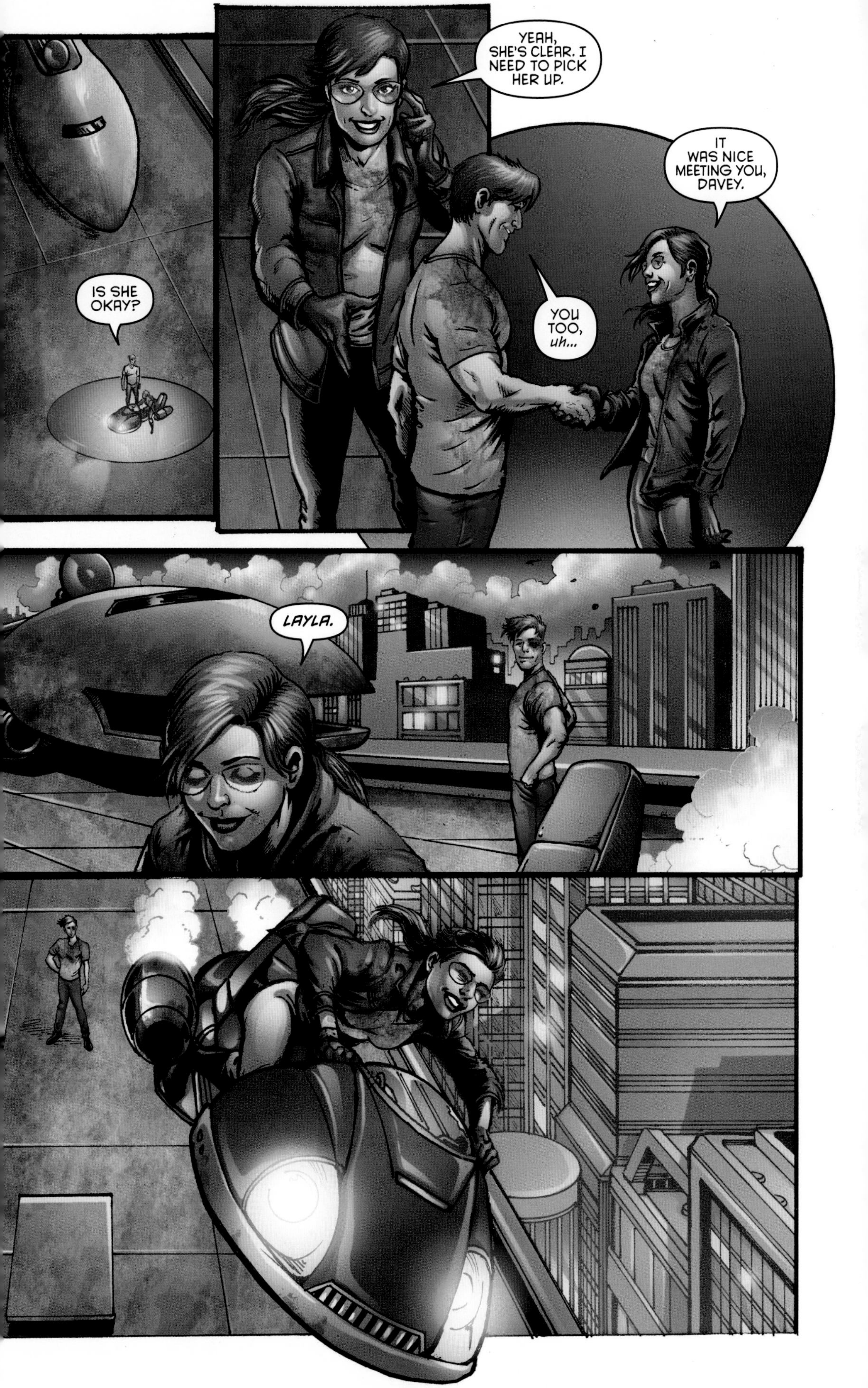
IS SHE OKAY?
YEAH, SHE'S CLEAR. I NEED TO PICK HER UP.
IT WAS NICE MEETING YOU, DAVEY.
YOU TOO, *uh...*
LAYLA.

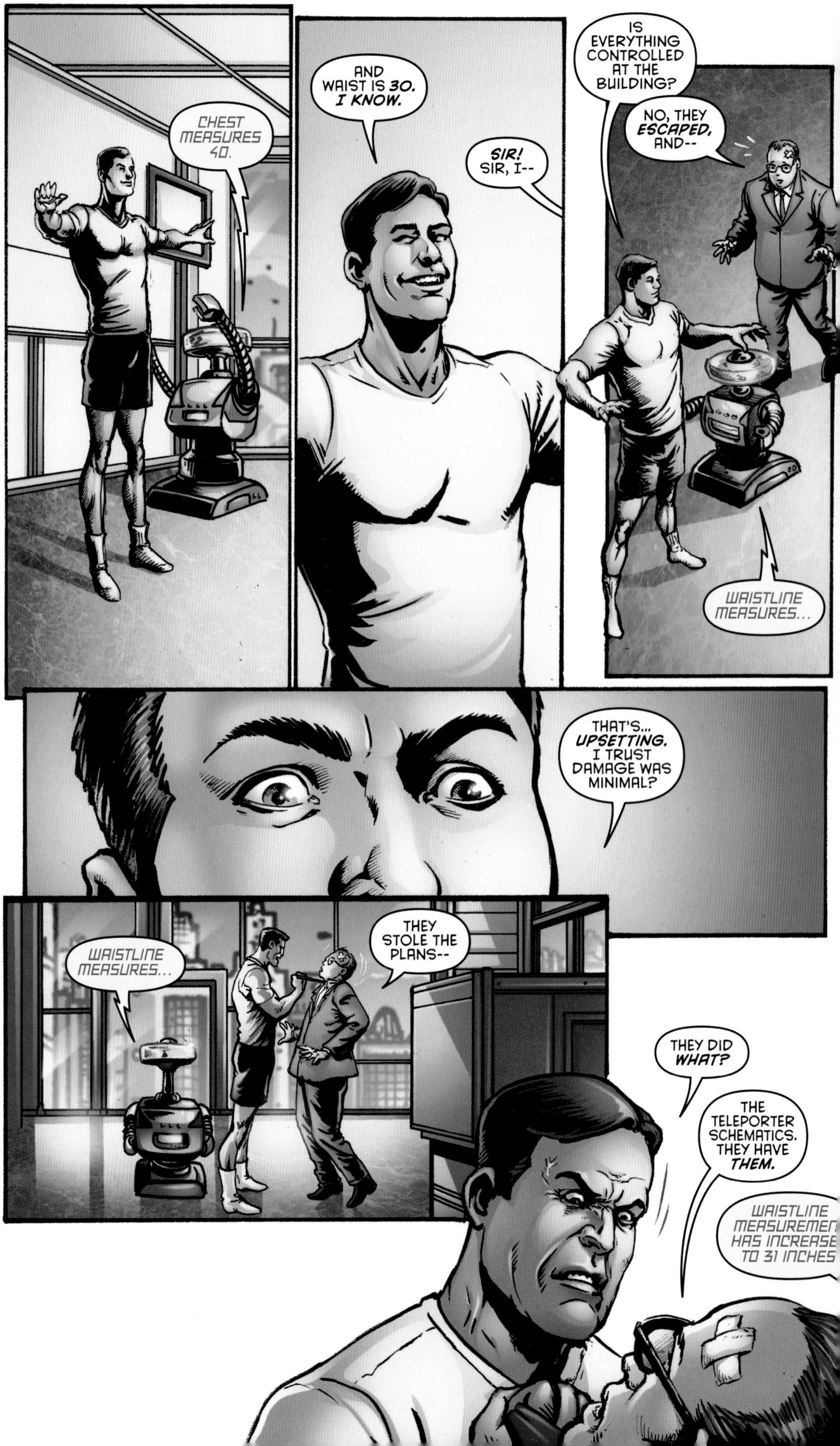
CHEST MEASURES 40.
AND WAIST IS 30. I KNOW.
SIR! SIR, I--
IS EVERYTHING CONTROLLED AT THE BUILDING?
NO, THEY ESCAPED, AND--
WAISTLINE MEASURES...
THAT'S... UPSETTING. I TRUST DAMAGE WAS MINIMAL?
WAISTLINE MEASURES...
THEY STOLE THE PLANS--
THEY DID WHAT?
THE TELEPORTER SCHEMATICS. THEY HAVE THEM.
WAISTLINE MEASUREMEN HAS INCREASE TO 31 INCHES

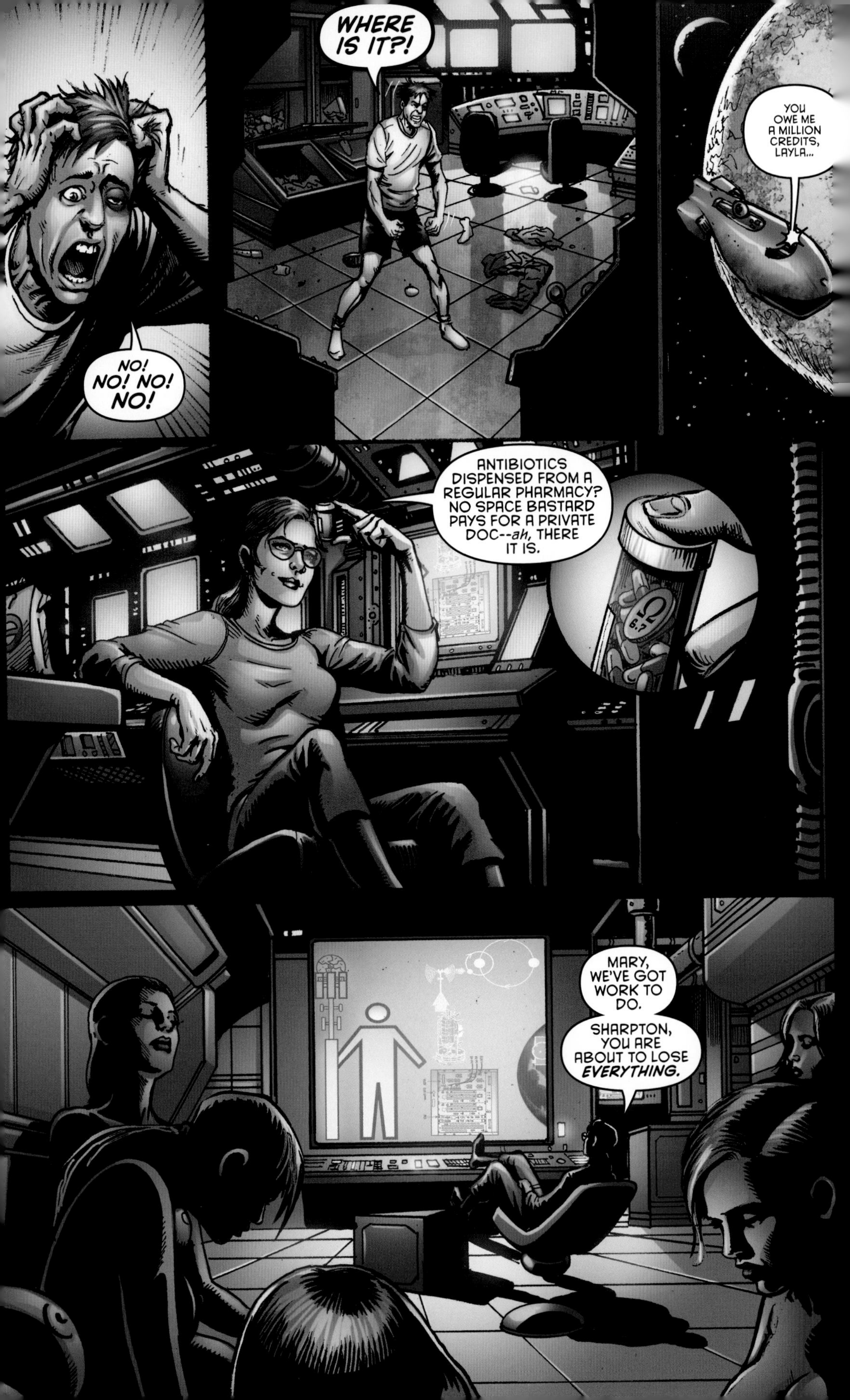
NO! NO! NO! NO!
WHERE IS IT?!
YOU OWE ME A MILLION CREDITS, LAYLA...
ANTIBIOTICS DISPENSED FROM A REGULAR PHARMACY? NO SPACE BASTARD PAYS FOR A PRIVATE DOC--*ah,* THERE IT IS.
MARY, WE'VE GOT WORK TO DO.
SHARPTON, YOU ARE ABOUT TO LOSE ***EVERYTHING.***

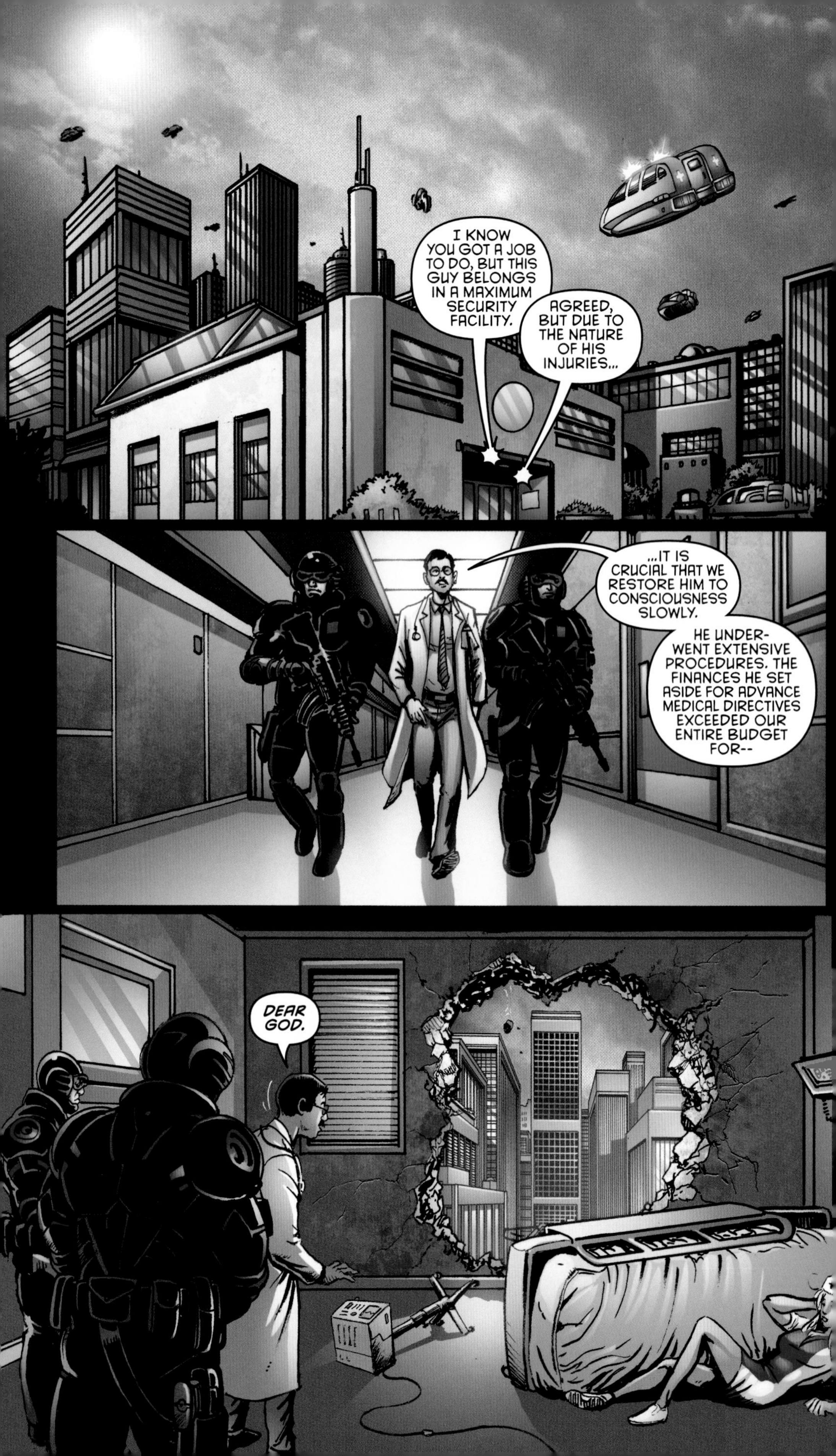
I KNOW YOU GOT A JOB TO DO, BUT THIS GUY BELONGS IN A MAXIMUM SECURITY FACILITY.
AGREED, BUT DUE TO THE NATURE OF HIS INJURIES...
...IT IS CRUCIAL THAT WE RESTORE HIM TO CONSCIOUSNESS SLOWLY.
HE UNDER-WENT EXTENSIVE PROCEDURES. THE FINANCES HE SET ASIDE FOR ADVANCE MEDICAL DIRECTIVES EXCEEDED OUR ENTIRE BUDGET FOR--
DEAR GOD.

EPISODE 5

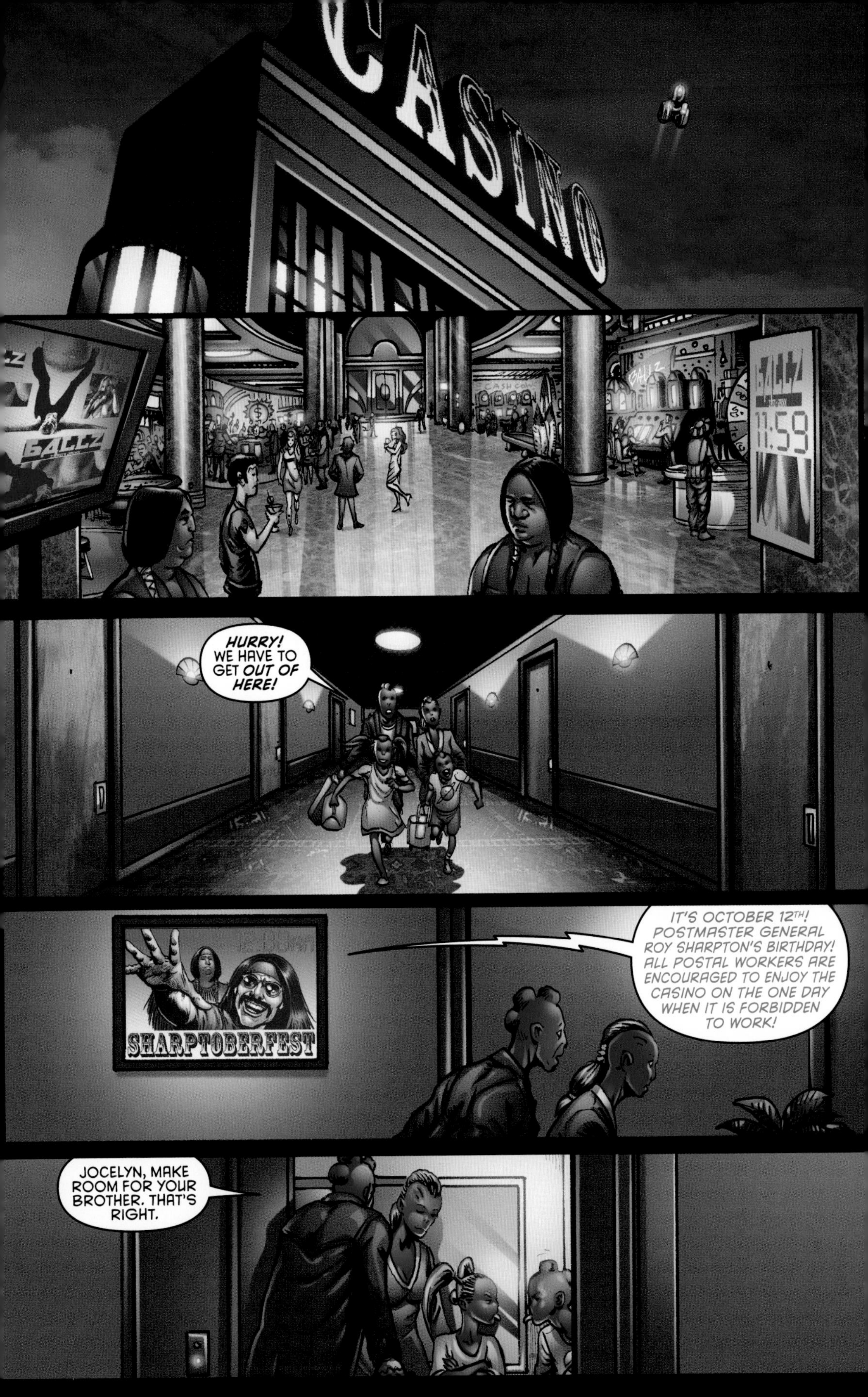
CASINO
BALLZ
BALLZ
11:59
HURRY! WE HAVE TO GET OUT OF HERE!
SHARPTOBERFEST
IT'S OCTOBER 12TH! POSTMASTER GENERAL ROY SHARPTON'S BIRTHDAY! ALL POSTAL WORKERS ARE ENCOURAGED TO ENJOY THE CASINO ON THE ONE DAY WHEN IT IS FORBIDDEN TO WORK!
JOCELYN, MAKE ROOM FOR YOUR BROTHER. THAT'S RIGHT.

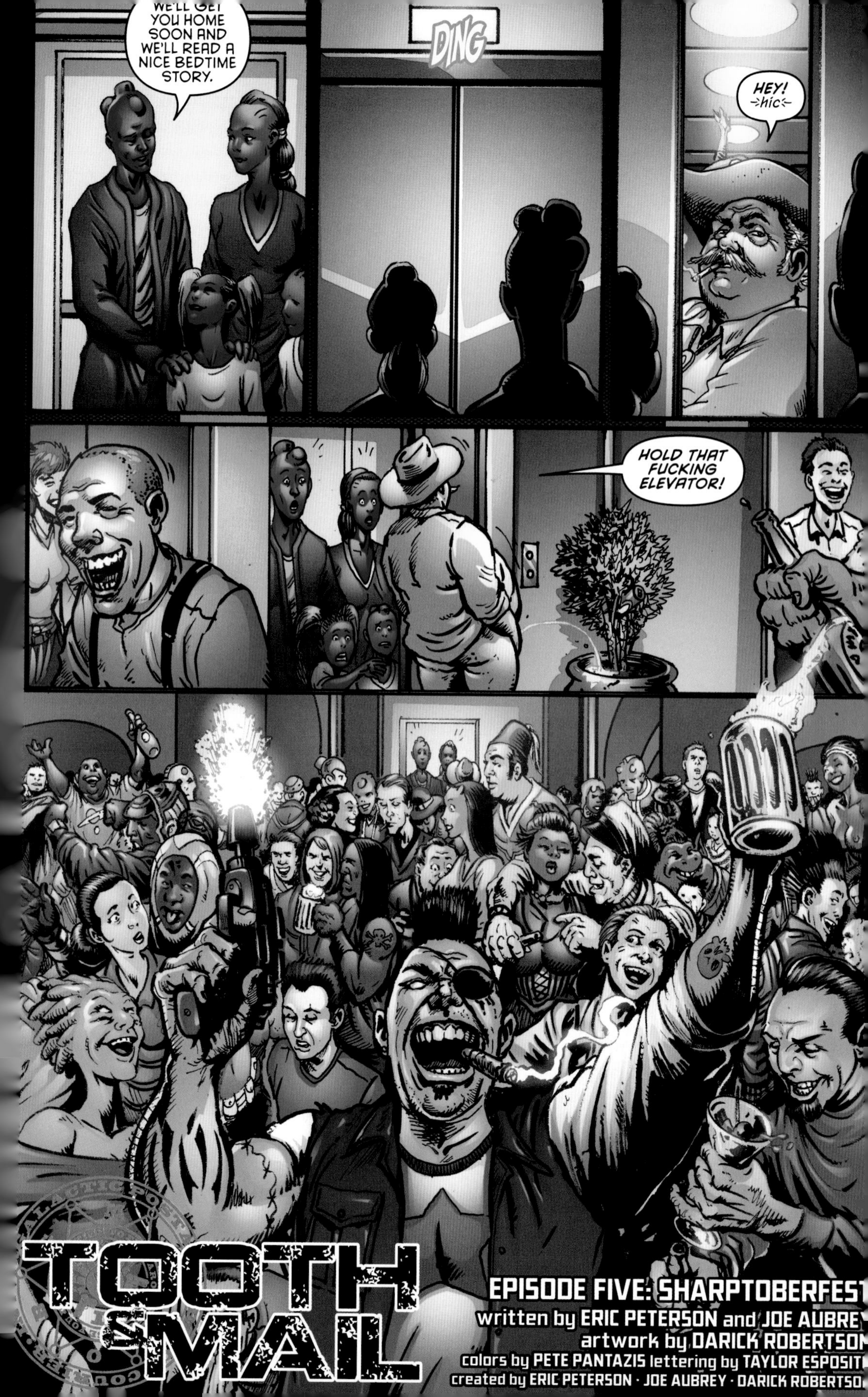

WE'LL GET YOU HOME SOON AND WE'LL READ A NICE BEDTIME STORY.
DING
HEY! -hic-
HOLD THAT FUCKING ELEVATOR!
TOOTH & NAIL
EPISODE FIVE: SHARPTOBERFEST
written by ERIC PETERSON and JOE AUBREY
artwork by DARICK ROBERTSON
colors by PETE PANTAZIS lettering by TAYLOR ESPOSITO
created by ERIC PETERSON · JOE AUBREY · DARICK ROBERTSON

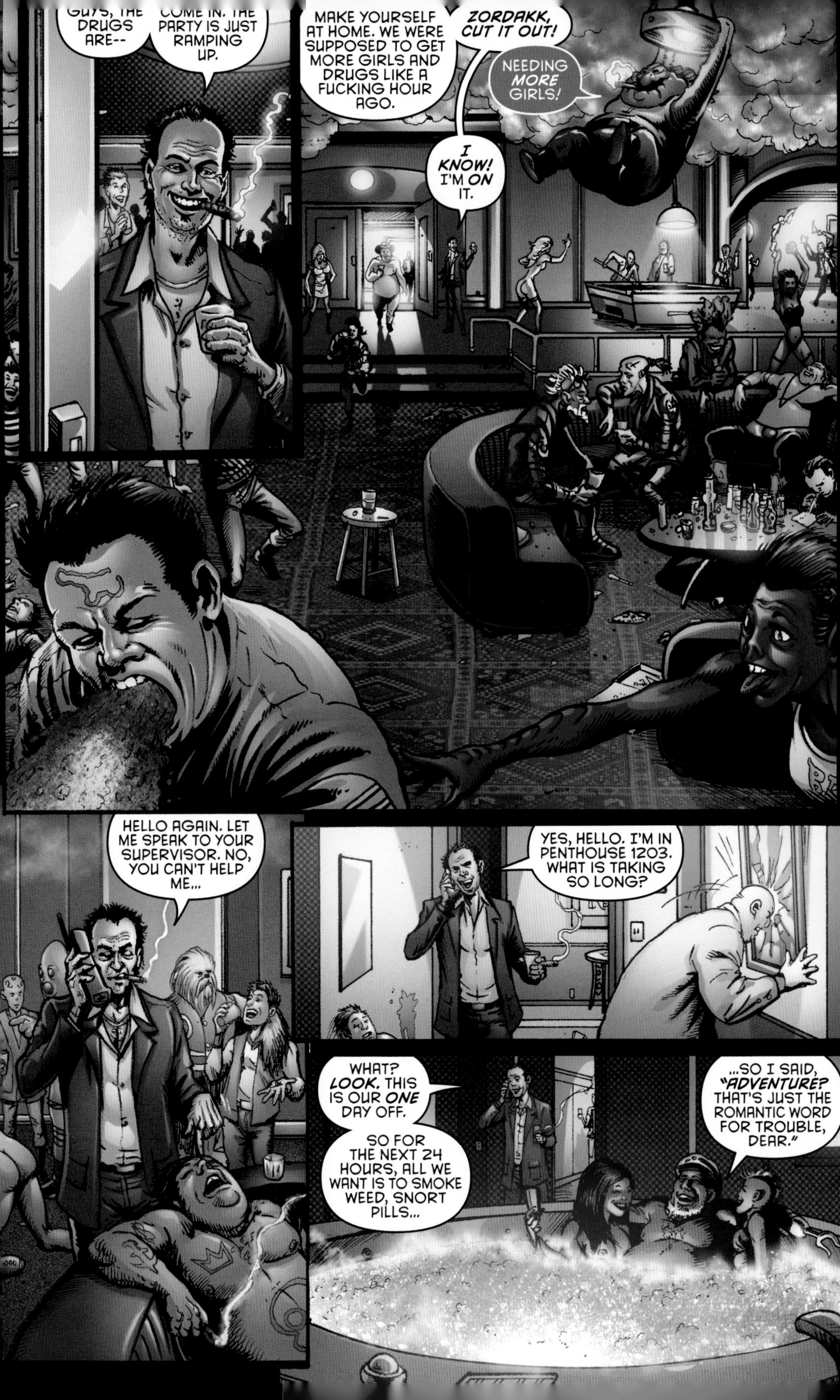
GUYS, THE DRUGS ARE--
COME IN. THE PARTY IS JUST RAMPING UP.
MAKE YOURSELF AT HOME. WE WERE SUPPOSED TO GET MORE GIRLS AND DRUGS LIKE A FUCKING HOUR AGO.
ZORDAKK, CUT IT OUT!
NEEDING MORE GIRLS!
I KNOW! I'M ON IT.
HELLO AGAIN. LET ME SPEAK TO YOUR SUPERVISOR. NO, YOU CAN'T HELP ME...
YES, HELLO. I'M IN PENTHOUSE 1203. WHAT IS TAKING SO LONG?
WHAT? LOOK. THIS IS OUR ONE DAY OFF.
SO FOR THE NEXT 24 HOURS, ALL WE WANT IS TO SMOKE WEED, SNORT PILLS...
...SO I SAID, "ADVENTURE? THAT'S JUST THE ROMANTIC WORD FOR TROUBLE, DEAR."

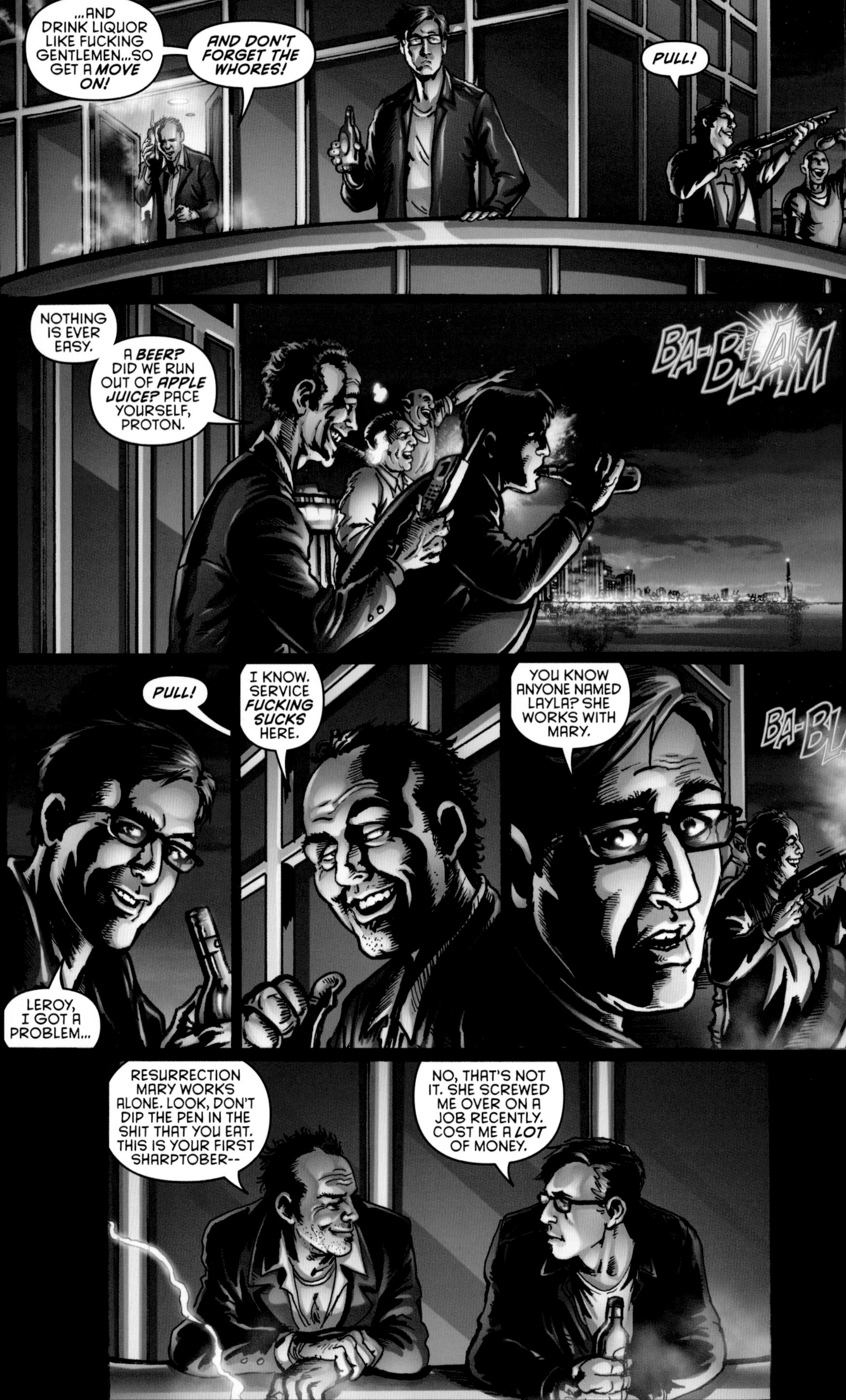

...AND DRINK LIQUOR LIKE FUCKING GENTLEMEN...SO GET A MOVE ON!
AND DON'T FORGET THE WHORES!
PULL!
NOTHING IS EVER EASY.
A BEER? DID WE RUN OUT OF APPLE JUICE? PACE YOURSELF, PROTON.
BA-BLAM
PULL!
LEROY, I GOT A PROBLEM...
I KNOW. SERVICE FUCKING SUCKS HERE.
YOU KNOW ANYONE NAMED LAYLA? SHE WORKS WITH MARY.
RESURRECTION MARY WORKS ALONE. LOOK, DON'T DIP THE PEN IN THE SHIT THAT YOU EAT. THIS IS YOUR FIRST SHARPTOBER--
NO, THAT'S NOT IT. SHE SCREWED ME OVER ON A JOB RECENTLY. COST ME A LOT OF MONEY.

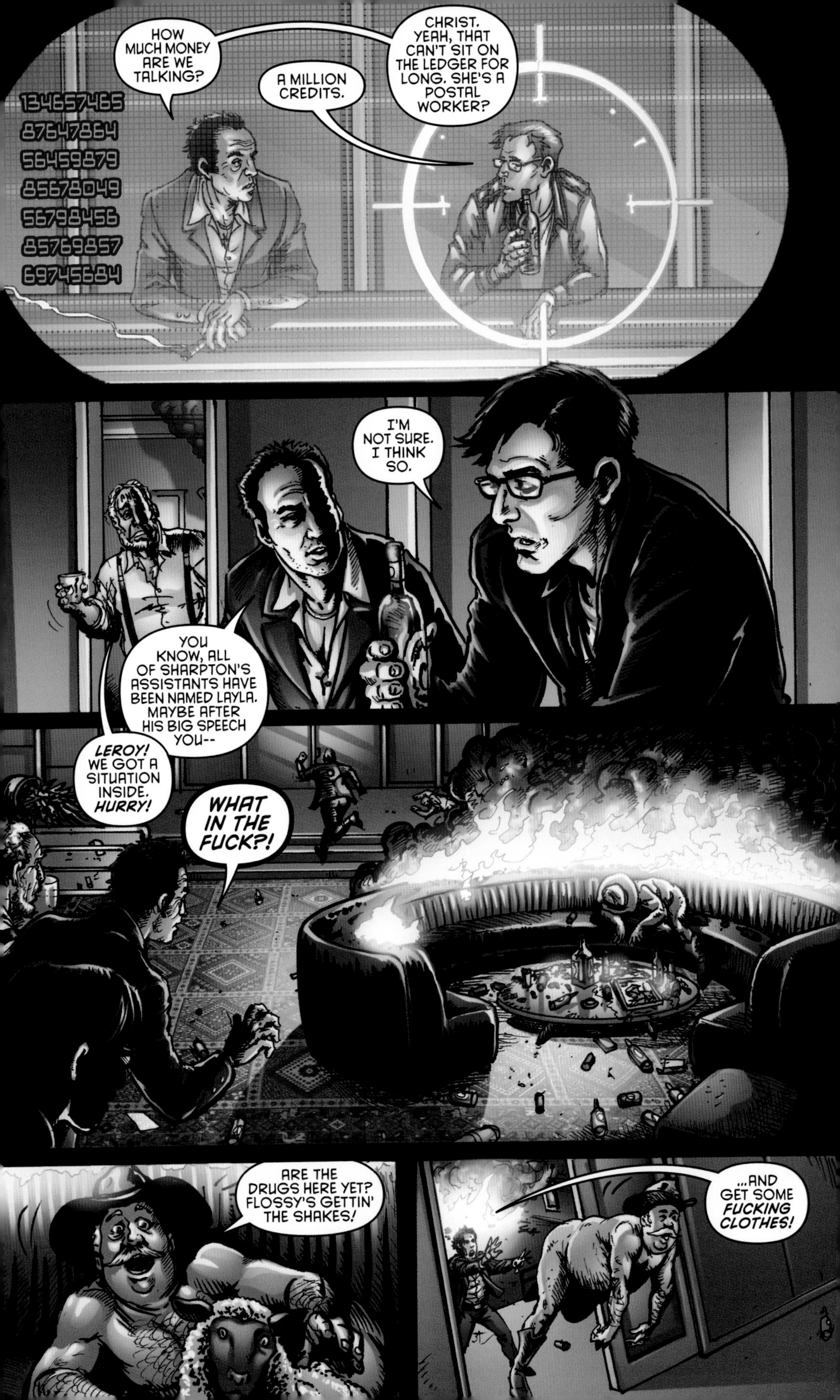

HOW MUCH MONEY ARE WE TALKING?
A MILLION CREDITS.
CHRIST. YEAH, THAT CAN'T SIT ON THE LEDGER FOR LONG. SHE'S A POSTAL WORKER?
134657465
87647864
56459879
85678049
56798456
85769857
69745684
I'M NOT SURE. I THINK SO.
YOU KNOW, ALL OF SHARPTON'S ASSISTANTS HAVE BEEN NAMED LAYLA. MAYBE AFTER HIS BIG SPEECH YOU--
LEROY! WE GOT A SITUATION INSIDE. *HURRY!*
WHAT IN THE FUCK?!
ARE THE DRUGS HERE YET? FLOSSY'S GETTIN' THE SHAKES!
...AND GET SOME *FUCKING CLOTHES!*

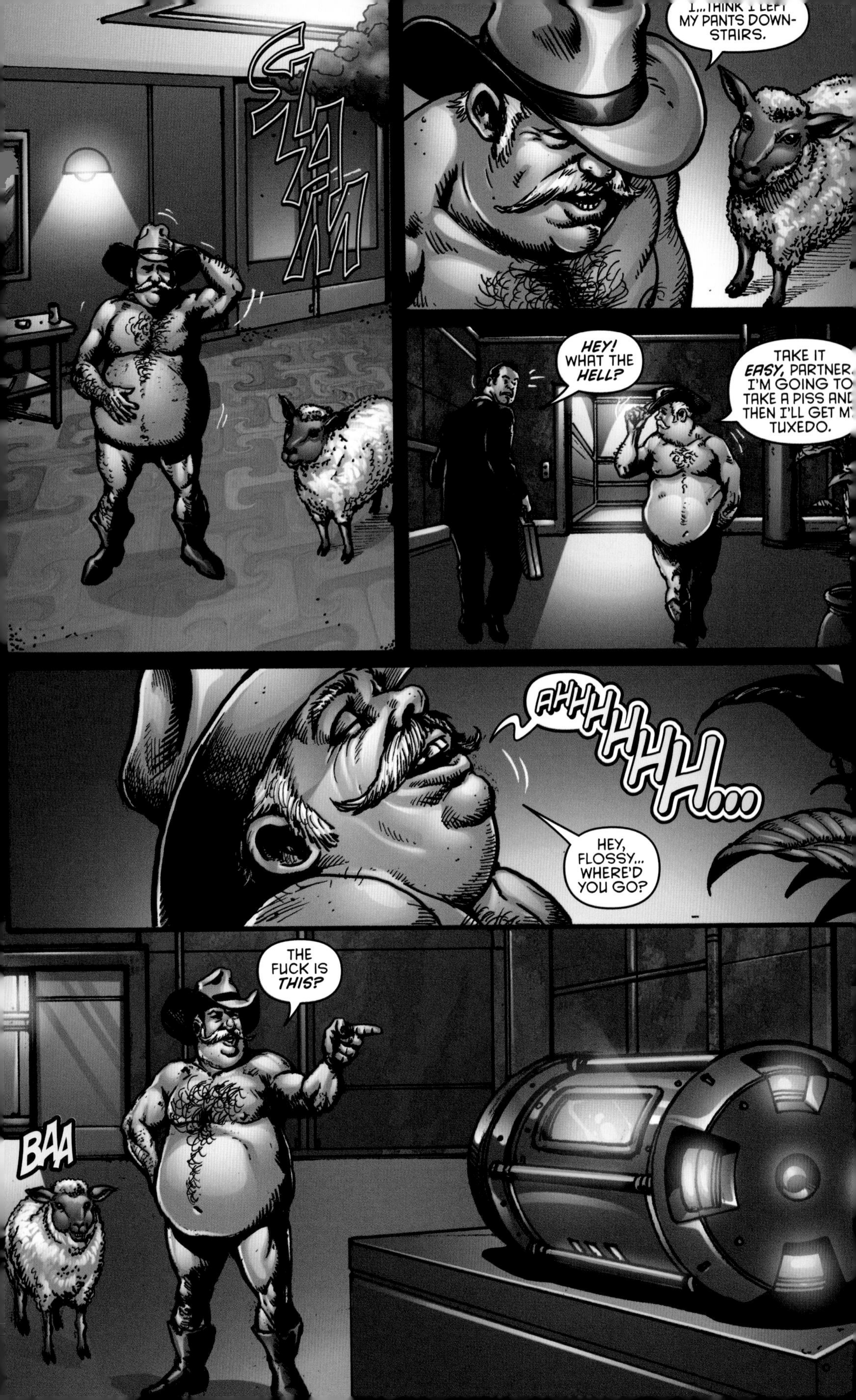
SLAM
I...THINK I LEFT MY PANTS DOWN-STAIRS.
HEY! WHAT THE HELL?
TAKE IT EASY, PARTNER. I'M GOING TO TAKE A PISS AND THEN I'LL GET MY TUXEDO.
AHHHHHHH...
HEY, FLOSSY... WHERE'D YOU GO?
THE FUCK IS THIS?
BAA

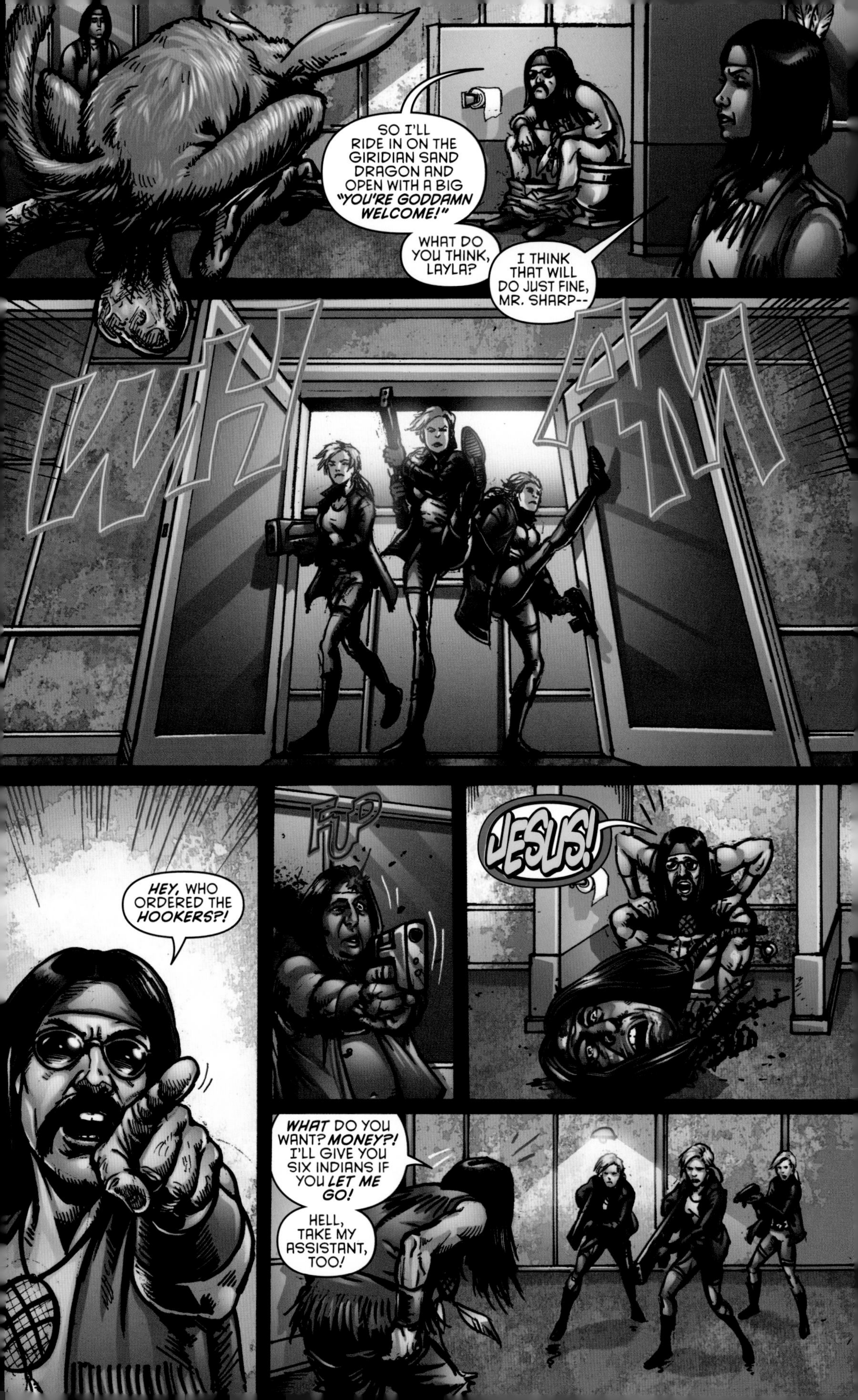
SO I'LL RIDE IN ON THE GIRIDIAN SAND DRAGON AND OPEN WITH A BIG "YOU'RE GODDAMN WELCOME!"
WHAT DO YOU THINK, LAYLA?
I THINK THAT WILL DO JUST FINE, MR. SHARP--
WHAM
HEY, WHO ORDERED THE HOOKERS?!
FTD
JESUS!
WHAT DO YOU WANT? MONEY?! I'LL GIVE YOU SIX INDIANS IF YOU LET ME GO!
HELL, TAKE MY ASSISTANT, TOO!

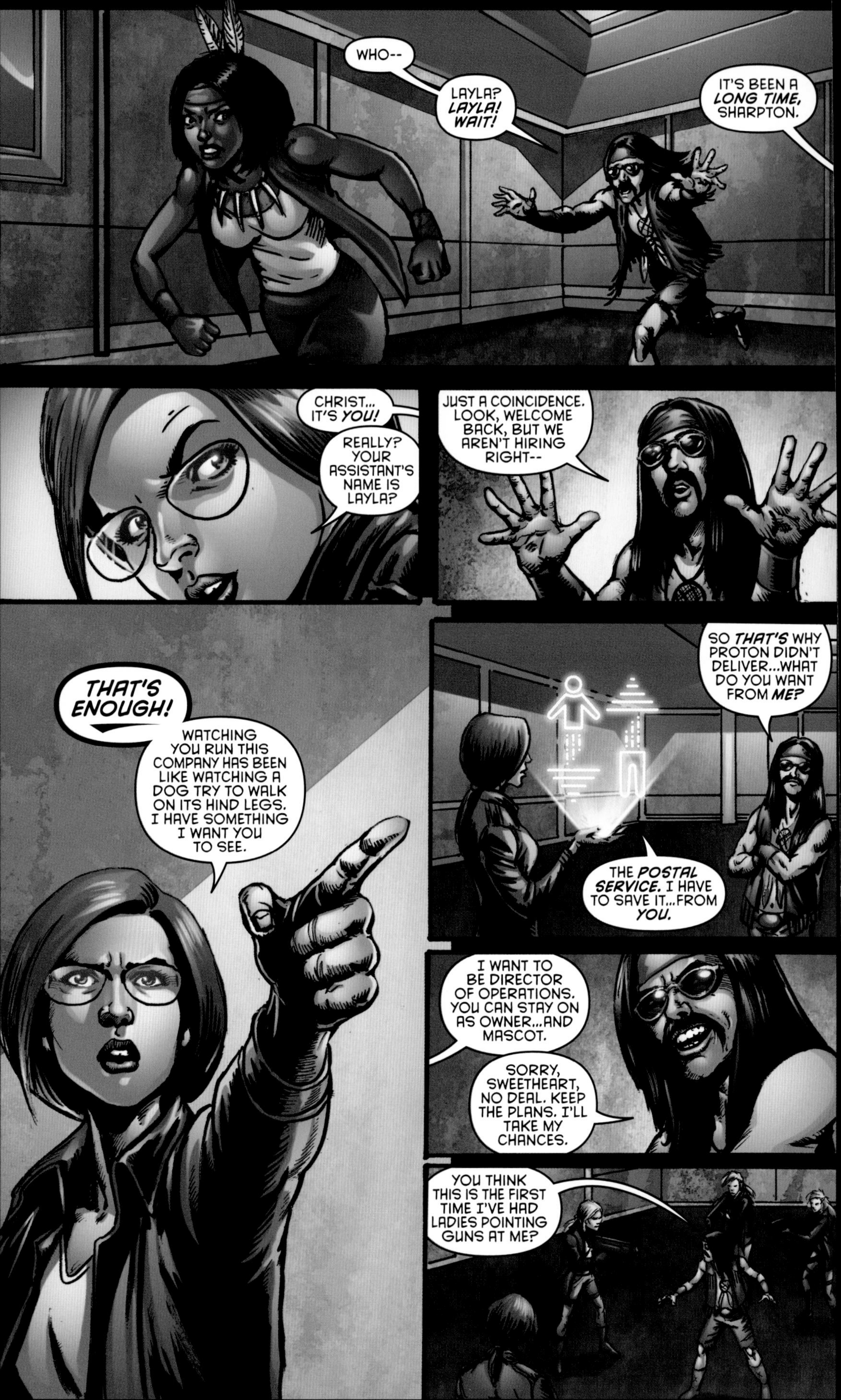

WHO--
LAYLA? LAYLA! WAIT!
IT'S BEEN A LONG TIME, SHARPTON.
CHRIST... IT'S YOU!
REALLY? YOUR ASSISTANT'S NAME IS LAYLA?
JUST A COINCIDENCE. LOOK, WELCOME BACK, BUT WE AREN'T HIRING RIGHT--
THAT'S ENOUGH!
WATCHING YOU RUN THIS COMPANY HAS BEEN LIKE WATCHING A DOG TRY TO WALK ON ITS HIND LEGS. I HAVE SOMETHING I WANT YOU TO SEE.
SO THAT'S WHY PROTON DIDN'T DELIVER...WHAT DO YOU WANT FROM ME?
THE POSTAL SERVICE. I HAVE TO SAVE IT...FROM YOU.
I WANT TO BE DIRECTOR OF OPERATIONS. YOU CAN STAY ON AS OWNER...AND MASCOT.
SORRY, SWEETHEART, NO DEAL. KEEP THE PLANS. I'LL TAKE MY CHANCES.
YOU THINK THIS IS THE FIRST TIME I'VE HAD LADIES POINTING GUNS AT ME?

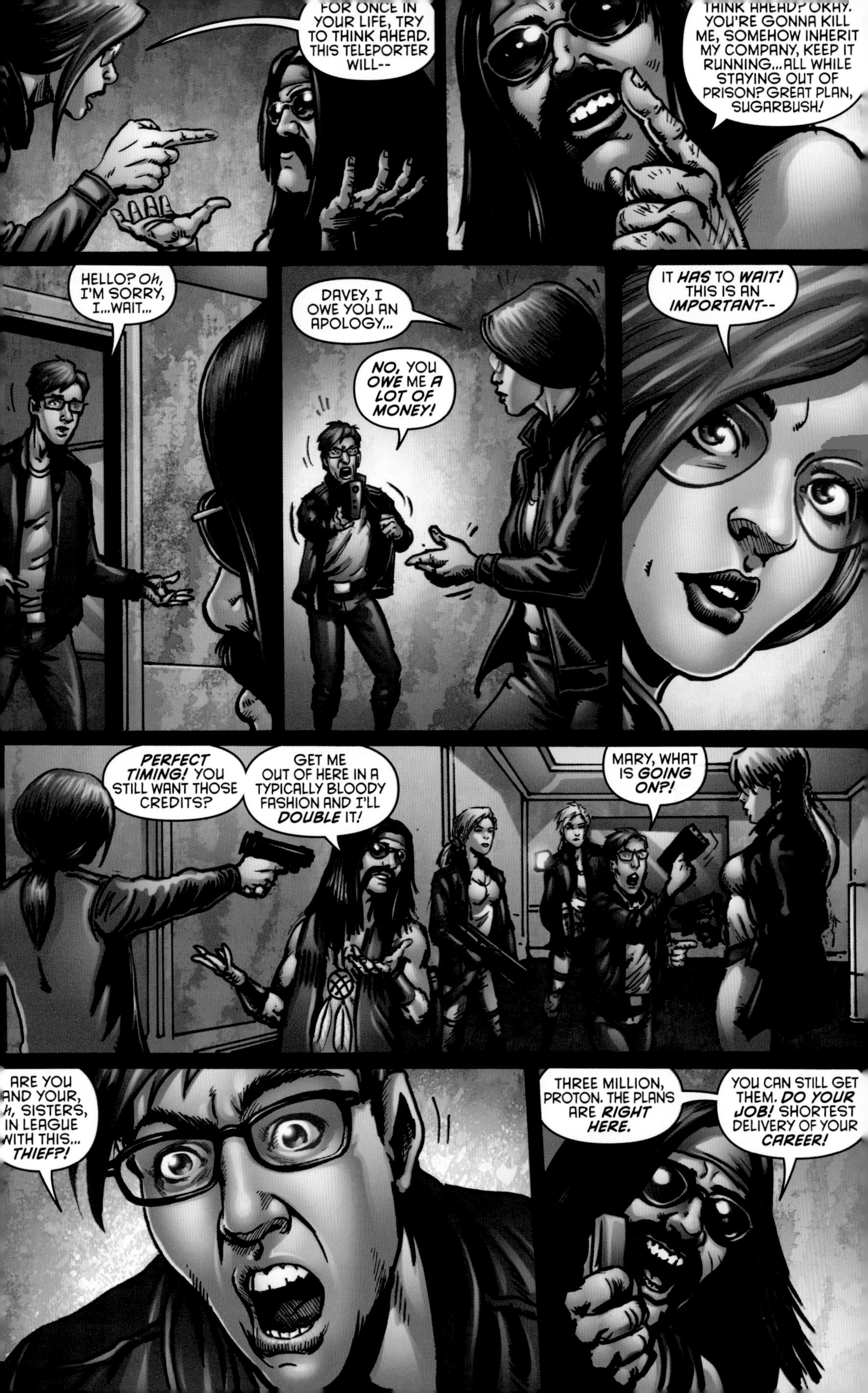
FOR ONCE IN YOUR LIFE, TRY TO THINK AHEAD. THIS TELEPORTER WILL--
THINK AHEAD? OKAY. YOU'RE GONNA KILL ME, SOMEHOW INHERIT MY COMPANY, KEEP IT RUNNING... ALL WHILE STAYING OUT OF PRISON? GREAT PLAN, SUGARBUSH!
HELLO? Oh, I'M SORRY, I... WAIT...
DAVEY, I OWE YOU AN APOLOGY...
NO, YOU OWE ME A LOT OF MONEY!
IT HAS TO WAIT! THIS IS AN IMPORTANT--
PERFECT TIMING! YOU STILL WANT THOSE CREDITS?
GET ME OUT OF HERE IN A TYPICALLY BLOODY FASHION AND I'LL DOUBLE IT!
MARY, WHAT IS GOING ON?!
ARE YOU AND YOUR, h, SISTERS, IN LEAGUE WITH THIS... THIEF?!
THREE MILLION, PROTON. THE PLANS ARE RIGHT HERE.
YOU CAN STILL GET THEM. DO YOUR JOB! SHORTEST DELIVERY OF YOUR CAREER!

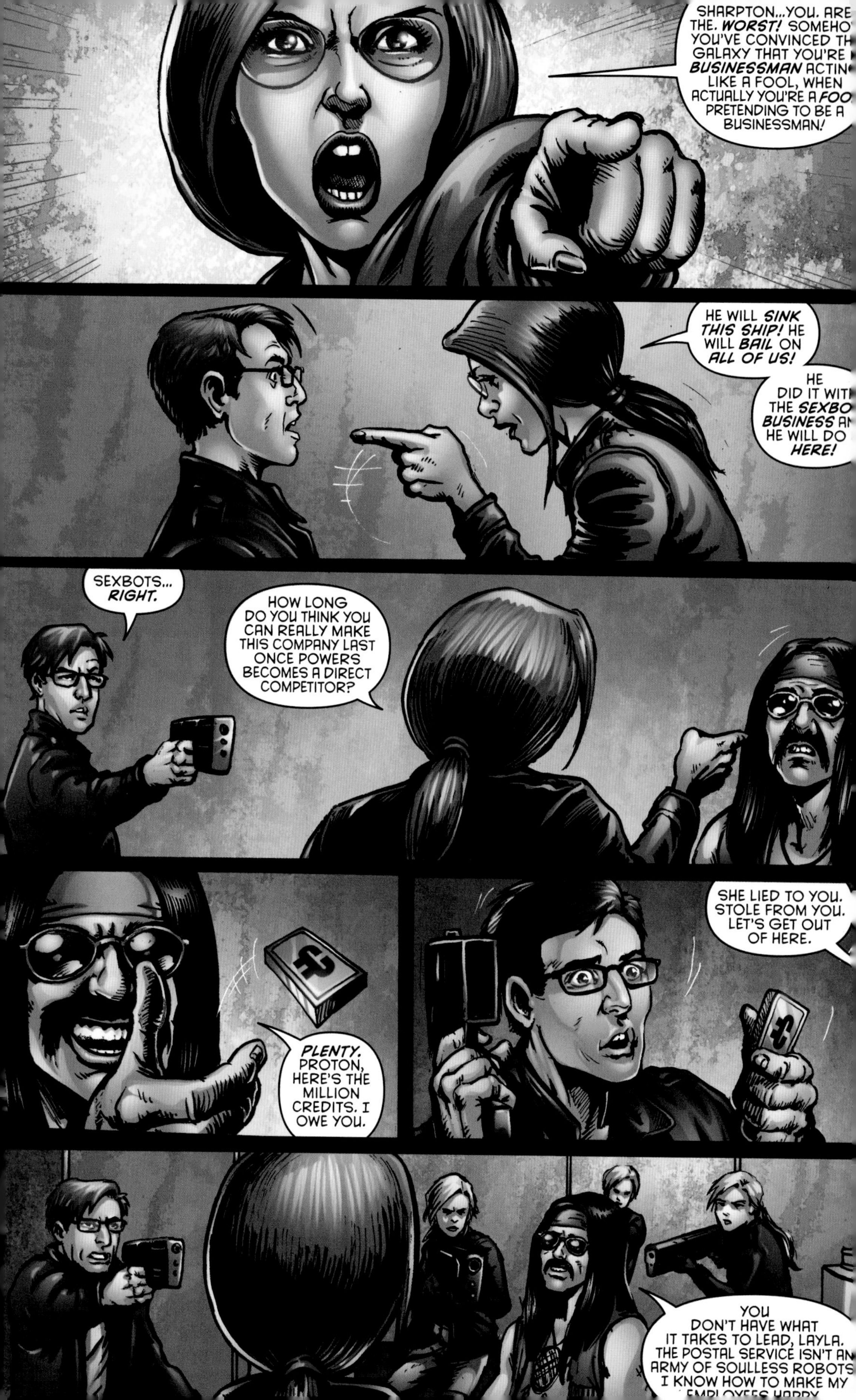
SHARPTON...YOU. ARE THE. WORST! SOMEHO YOU'VE CONVINCED TH GALAXY THAT YOU'RE BUSINESSMAN ACTIN LIKE A FOOL, WHEN ACTUALLY YOU'RE A FOO PRETENDING TO BE A BUSINESSMAN!
HE WILL SINK THIS SHIP! HE WILL BAIL ON ALL OF US!
HE DID IT WIT THE SEXBO BUSINESS AN HE WILL DO HERE!
SEXBOTS... RIGHT.
HOW LONG DO YOU THINK YOU CAN REALLY MAKE THIS COMPANY LAST ONCE POWERS BECOMES A DIRECT COMPETITOR?
PLENTY. PROTON, HERE'S THE MILLION CREDITS. I OWE YOU.
SHE LIED TO YOU. STOLE FROM YOU. LET'S GET OUT OF HERE.
YOU DON'T HAVE WHAT IT TAKES TO LEAD, LAYLA. THE POSTAL SERVICE ISN'T AN ARMY OF SOULLESS ROBOTS I KNOW HOW TO MAKE MY

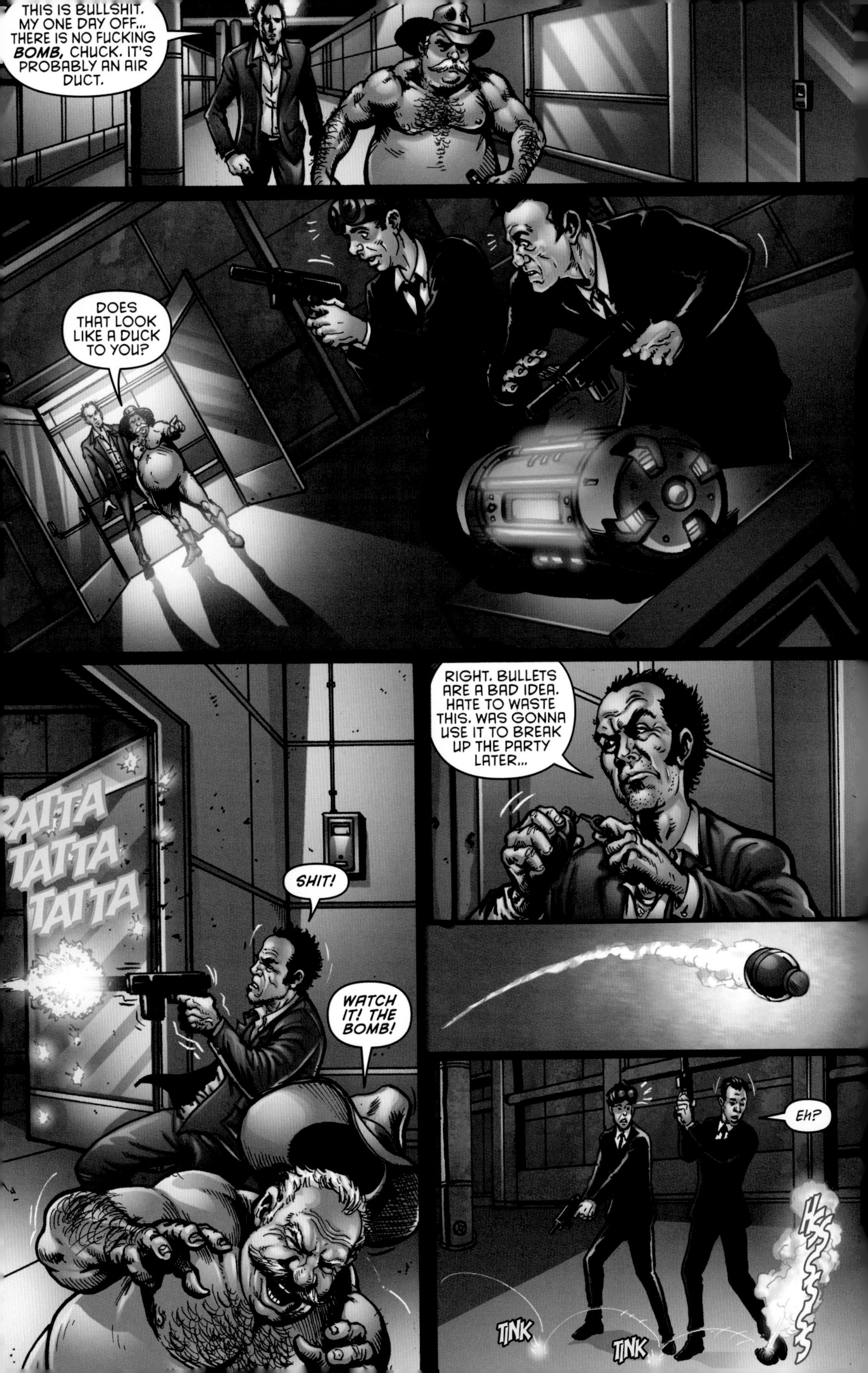
THIS IS BULLSHIT. MY ONE DAY OFF... THERE IS NO FUCKING BOMB, CHUCK. IT'S PROBABLY AN AIR DUCT.
DOES THAT LOOK LIKE A DUCK TO YOU?
RATTA TATTA TATTA
SHIT!
WATCH IT! THE BOMB!
RIGHT. BULLETS ARE A BAD IDEA. HATE TO WASTE THIS. WAS GONNA USE IT TO BREAK UP THE PARTY LATER...
Eh?
TINK
TINK

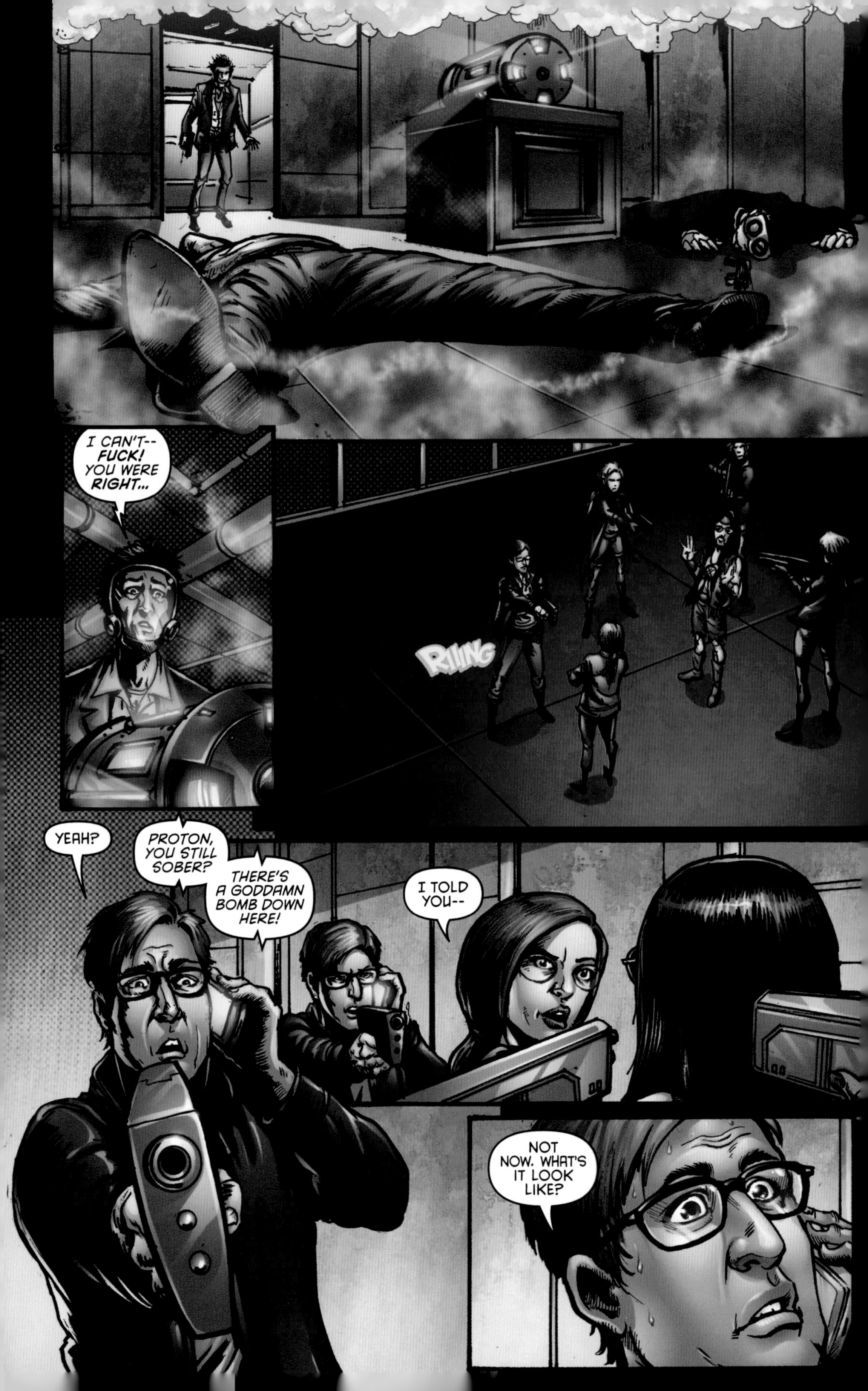
I CAN'T-- FUCK! YOU WERE RIGHT...
RIIING
YEAH?
PROTON, YOU STILL SOBER?
THERE'S A GODDAMN BOMB DOWN HERE!
I TOLD YOU--
NOT NOW. WHAT'S IT LOOK LIKE?

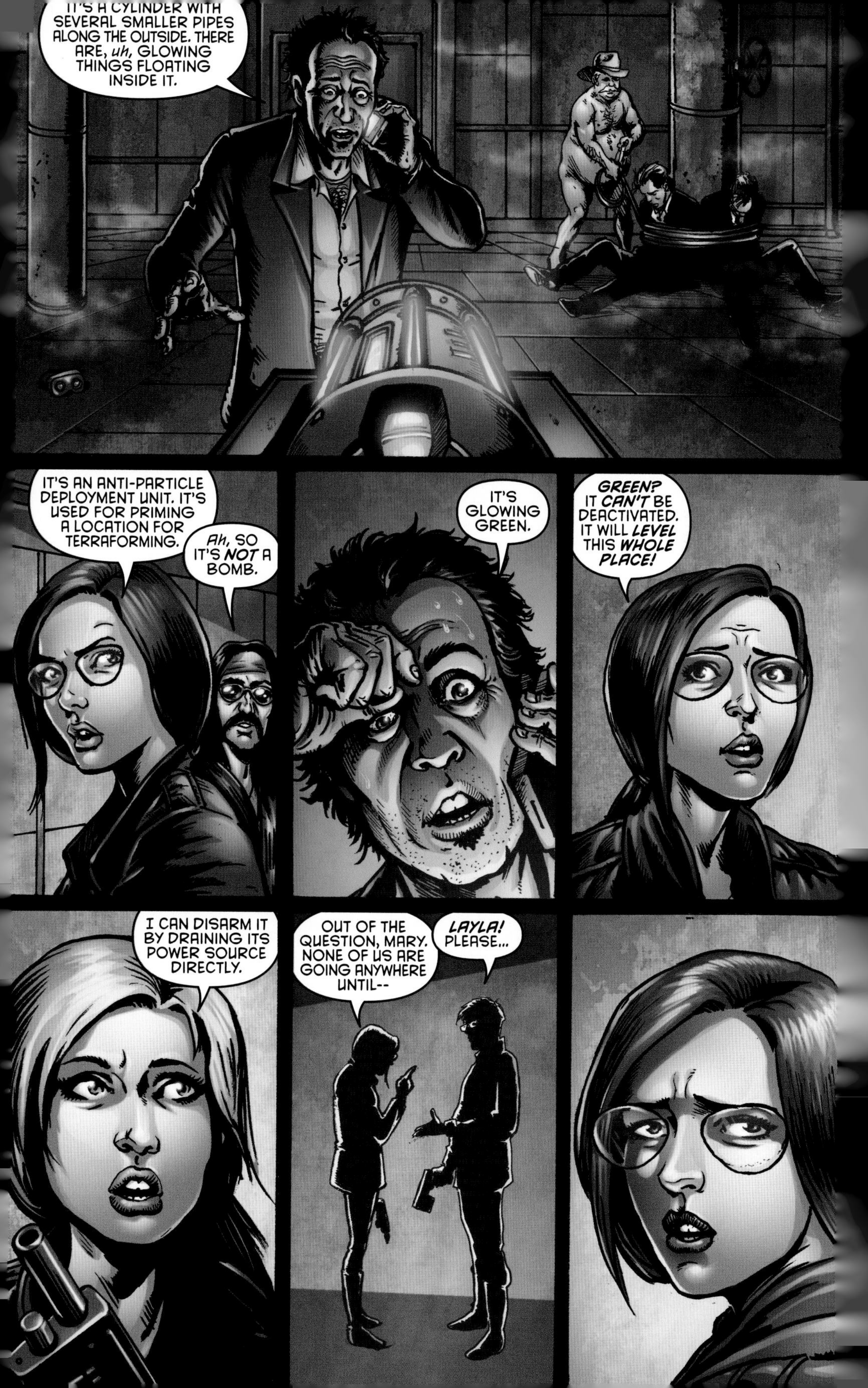
IT'S A CYLINDER WITH SEVERAL SMALLER PIPES ALONG THE OUTSIDE. THERE ARE, *uh*, GLOWING THINGS FLOATING INSIDE IT.
IT'S AN ANTI-PARTICLE DEPLOYMENT UNIT. IT'S USED FOR PRIMING A LOCATION FOR TERRAFORMING.
Ah, SO IT'S ***NOT*** A BOMB.
IT'S GLOWING GREEN.
GREEN? IT ***CAN'T*** BE DEACTIVATED. IT WILL ***LEVEL*** THIS ***WHOLE PLACE!***
I CAN DISARM IT BY DRAINING ITS POWER SOURCE DIRECTLY.
OUT OF THE QUESTION, MARY. NONE OF US ARE GOING ANYWHERE UNTIL--
LAYLA! PLEASE...

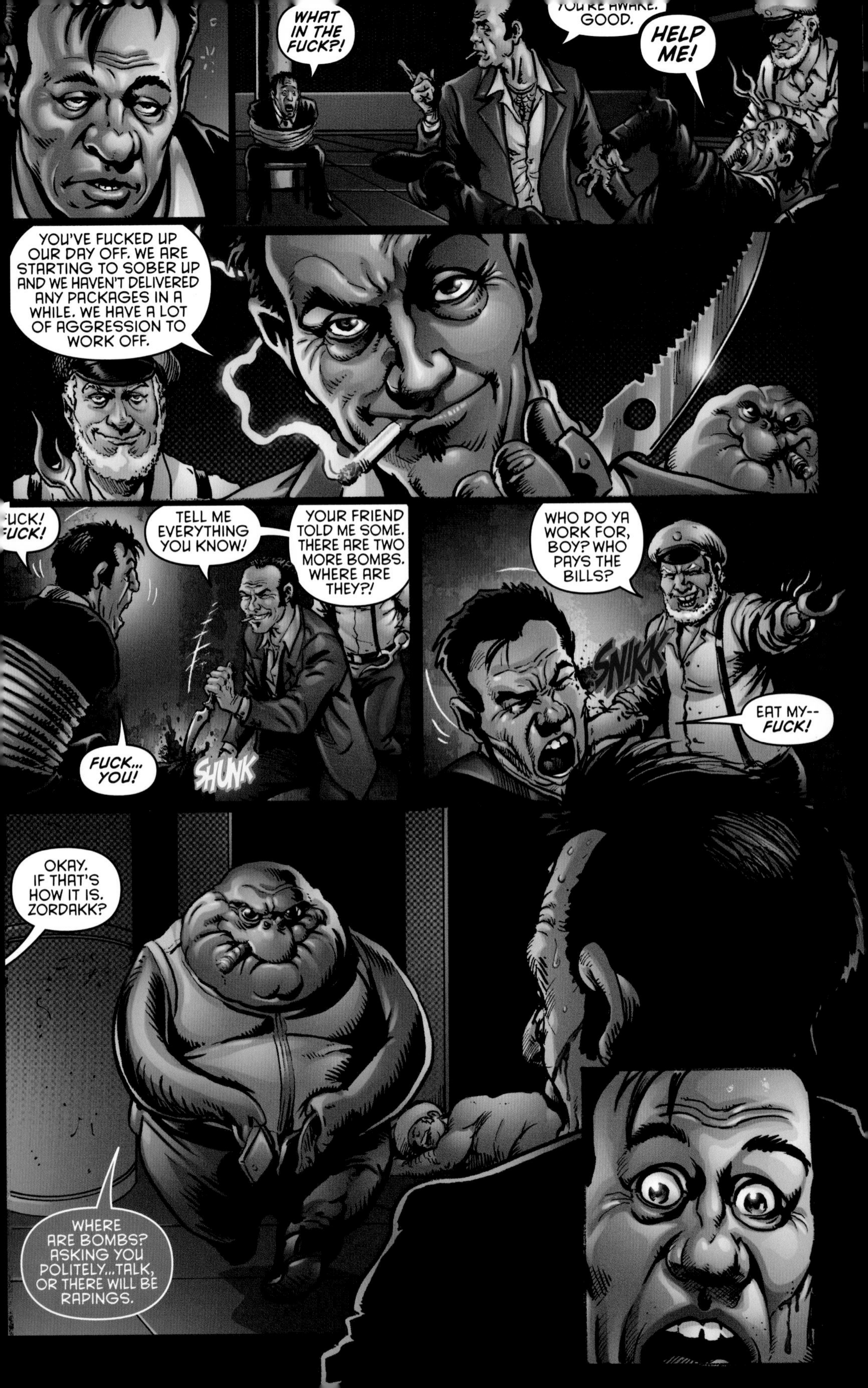
WHAT IN THE FUCK?!
YOU'RE AWAKE. GOOD.
HELP ME!
YOU'VE FUCKED UP OUR DAY OFF. WE ARE STARTING TO SOBER UP AND WE HAVEN'T DELIVERED ANY PACKAGES IN A WHILE. WE HAVE A LOT OF AGGRESSION TO WORK OFF.
UCK! UCK!
TELL ME EVERYTHING YOU KNOW!
YOUR FRIEND TOLD ME SOME. THERE ARE TWO MORE BOMBS. WHERE ARE THEY?!
SHUNK
FUCK... YOU!
WHO DO YA WORK FOR, BOY? WHO PAYS THE BILLS?
SNIKK
EAT MY-- FUCK!
OKAY. IF THAT'S HOW IT IS. ZORDAKK?
WHERE ARE BOMBS? ASKING YOU POLITELY...TALK, OR THERE WILL BE RAPINGS.

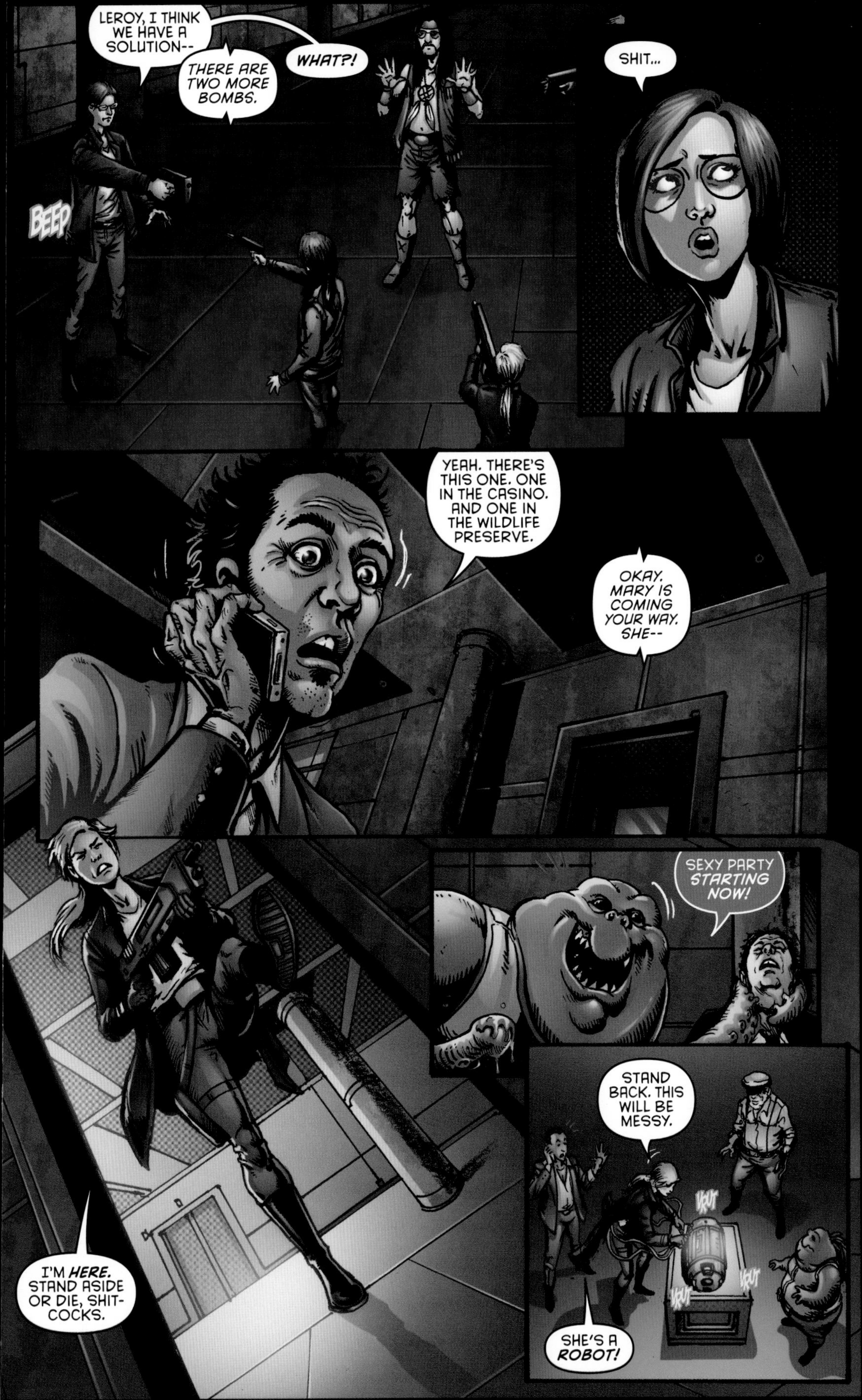

LEROY, I THINK WE HAVE A SOLUTION--
THERE ARE TWO MORE BOMBS.
WHAT?!
BEEP
SHIT...
YEAH. THERE'S THIS ONE. ONE IN THE CASINO. AND ONE IN THE WILDLIFE PRESERVE.
OKAY. MARY IS COMING YOUR WAY. SHE--
SEXY PARTY STARTING NOW!
I'M HERE. STAND ASIDE OR DIE, SHIT-COCKS.
STAND BACK. THIS WILL BE MESSY.
VRUT
VRUT
VRUT
SHE'S A ROBOT!

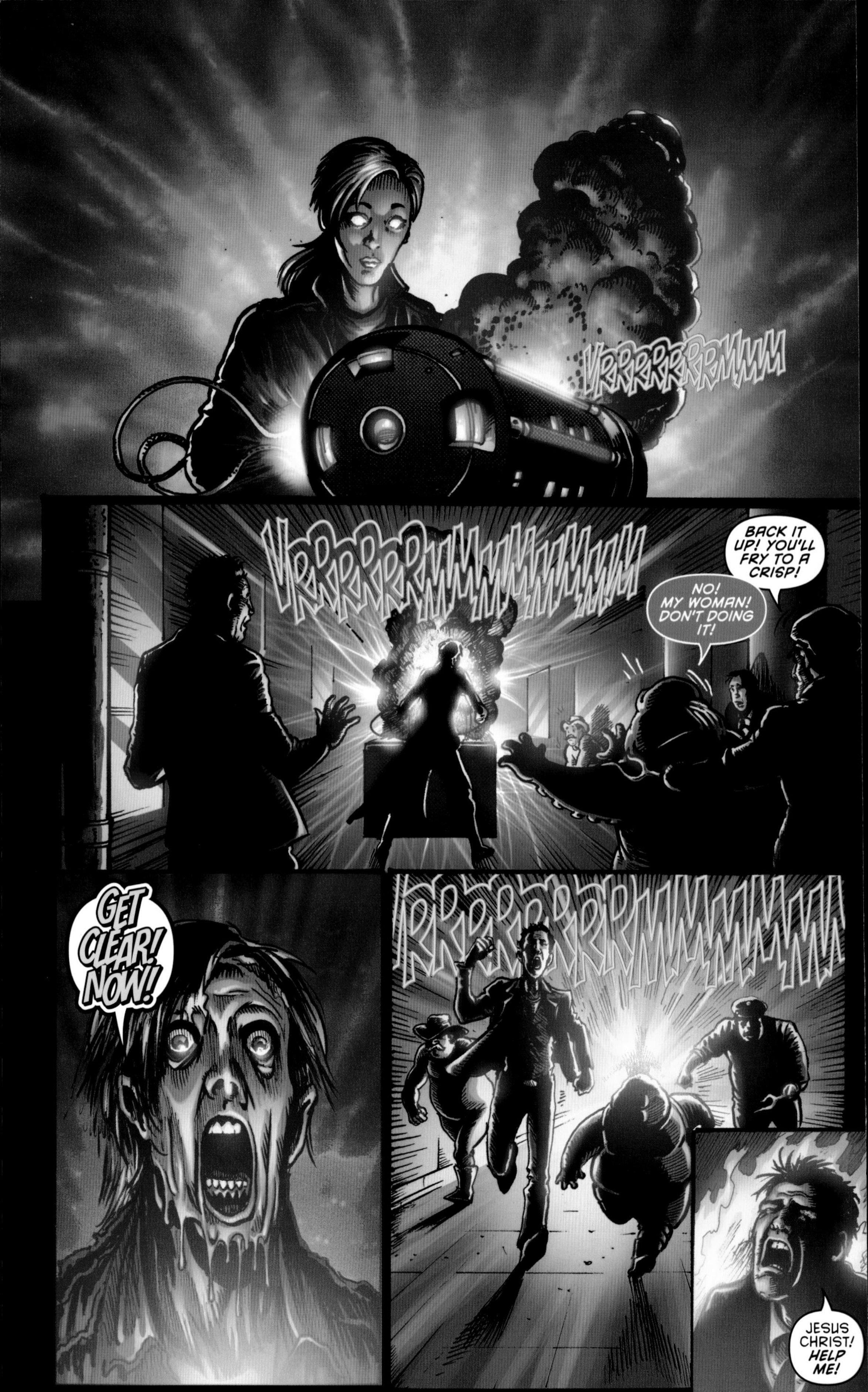
VRRRRRRRMMMM
VRRRRRRRMMMMMMMMMMMM
BACK IT UP! YOU'LL FRY TO A CRISP!
NO! MY WOMAN! DON'T DOING IT!
GET CLEAR! NOW!
VRRRRRRRRRMMMMMMMMM
JESUS CHRIST! HELP ME!

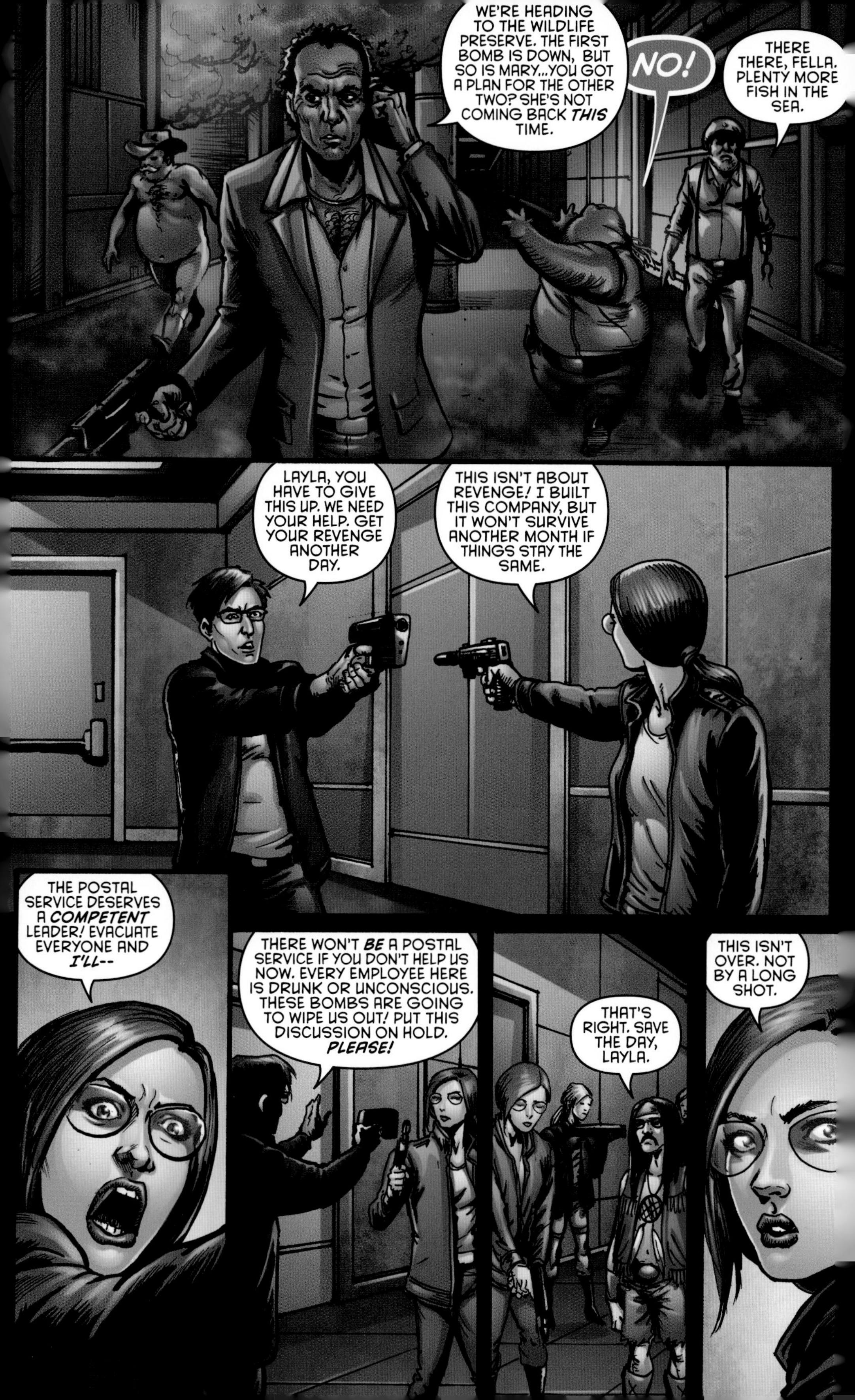
WE'RE HEADING TO THE WILDLIFE PRESERVE. THE FIRST BOMB IS DOWN, BUT SO IS MARY...YOU GOT A PLAN FOR THE OTHER TWO? SHE'S NOT COMING BACK THIS TIME.
NO!
THERE THERE, FELLA. PLENTY MORE FISH IN THE SEA.
LAYLA, YOU HAVE TO GIVE THIS UP. WE NEED YOUR HELP. GET YOUR REVENGE ANOTHER DAY.
THIS ISN'T ABOUT REVENGE! I BUILT THIS COMPANY, BUT IT WON'T SURVIVE ANOTHER MONTH IF THINGS STAY THE SAME.
THE POSTAL SERVICE DESERVES A COMPETENT LEADER! EVACUATE EVERYONE AND I'LL--
THERE WON'T BE A POSTAL SERVICE IF YOU DON'T HELP US NOW. EVERY EMPLOYEE HERE IS DRUNK OR UNCONSCIOUS. THESE BOMBS ARE GOING TO WIPE US OUT! PUT THIS DISCUSSION ON HOLD. PLEASE!
THAT'S RIGHT. SAVE THE DAY, LAYLA.
THIS ISN'T OVER. NOT BY A LONG SHOT.

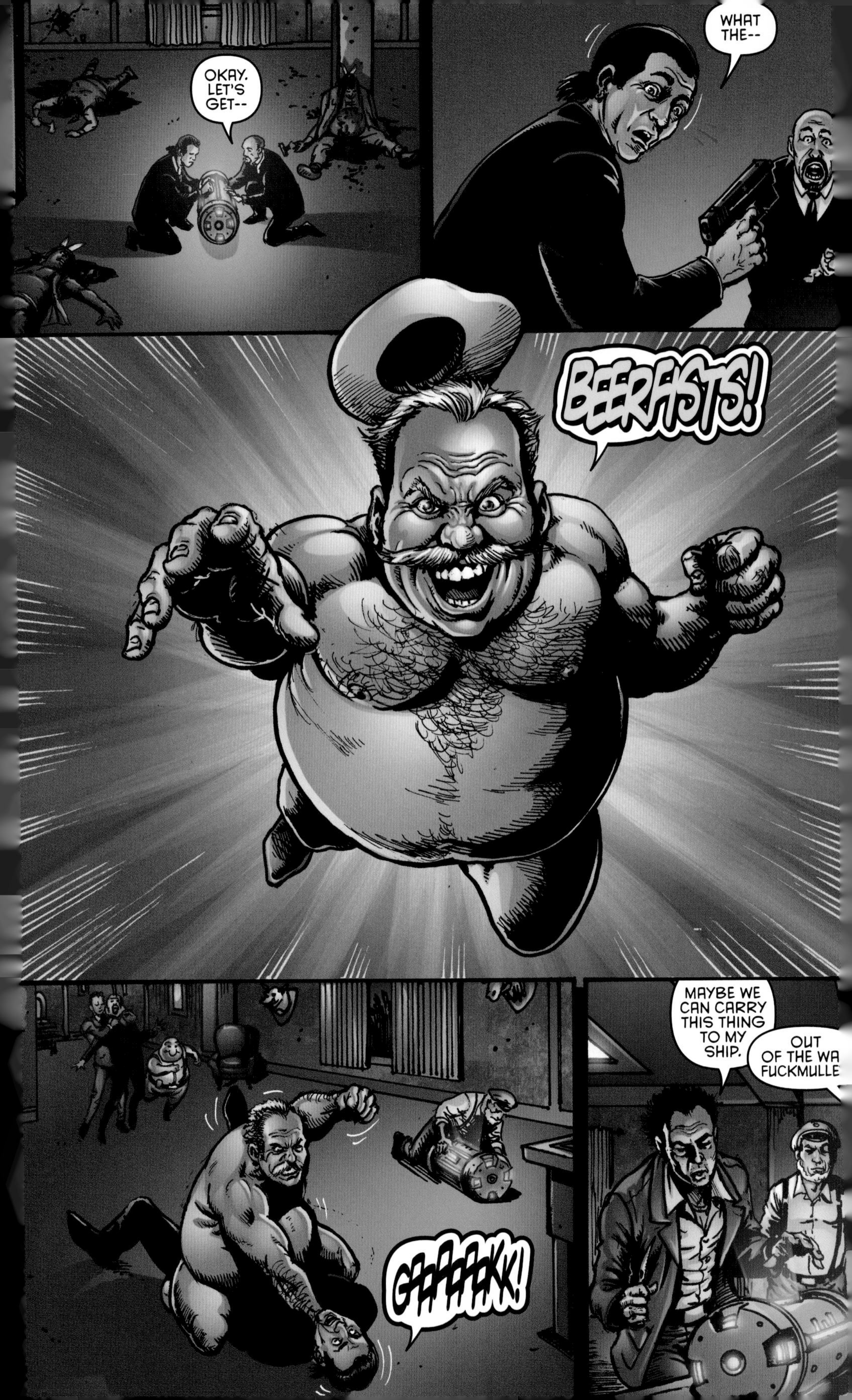

OKAY. LET'S GET--
WHAT THE--
BEERFISTS!
GAAAAAKK!
MAYBE WE CAN CARRY THIS THING TO MY SHIP.
OUT OF THE WA
FUCKMULLE

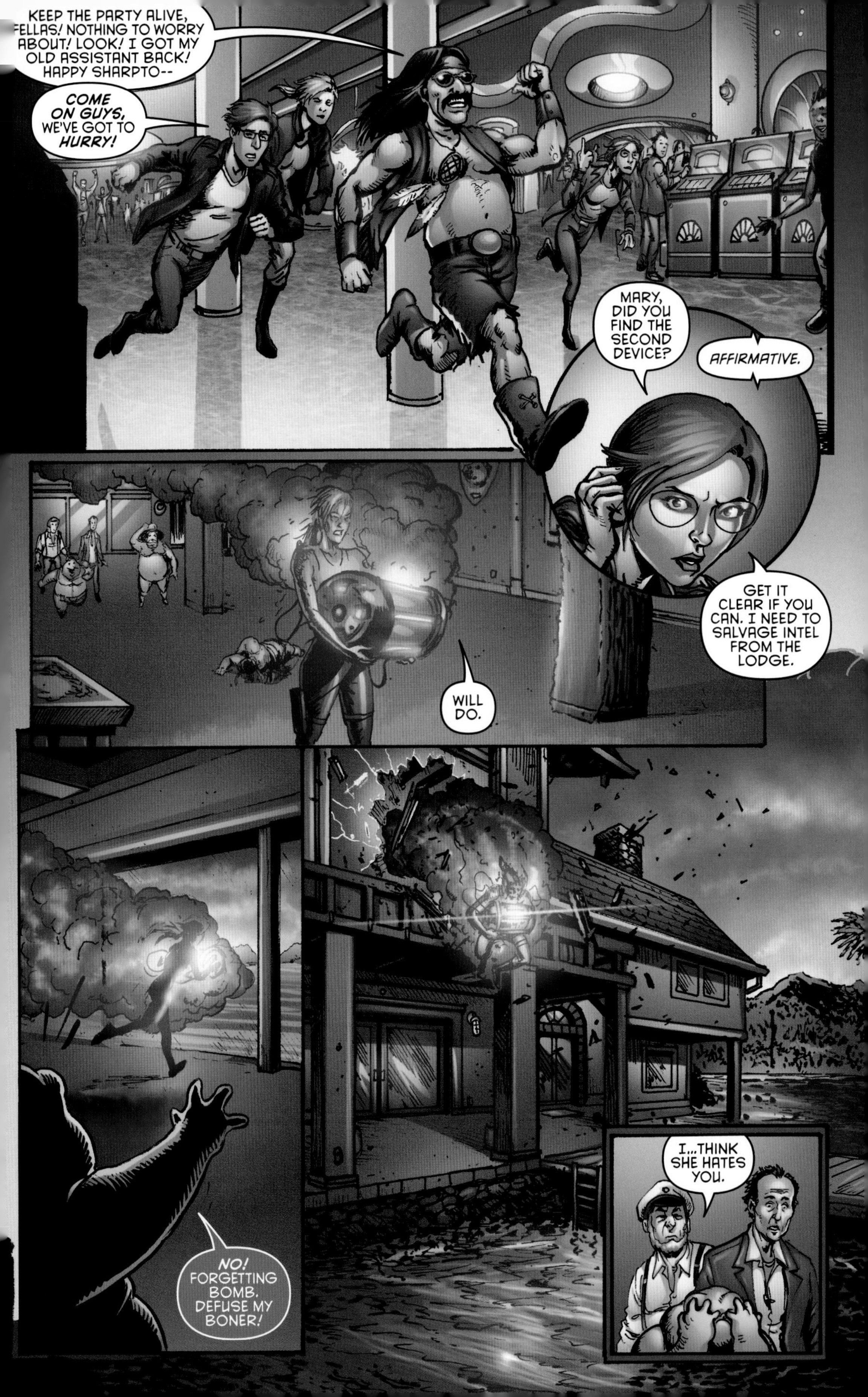

KEEP THE PARTY ALIVE, FELLAS! NOTHING TO WORRY ABOUT! LOOK! I GOT MY OLD ASSISTANT BACK! HAPPY SHARPTO--
COME ON GUYS, WE'VE GOT TO HURRY!
MARY, DID YOU FIND THE SECOND DEVICE?
AFFIRMATIVE.
GET IT CLEAR IF YOU CAN. I NEED TO SALVAGE INTEL FROM THE LODGE.
WILL DO.
NO! FORGETTING BOMB. DEFUSE MY BONER!
I...THINK SHE HATES YOU.

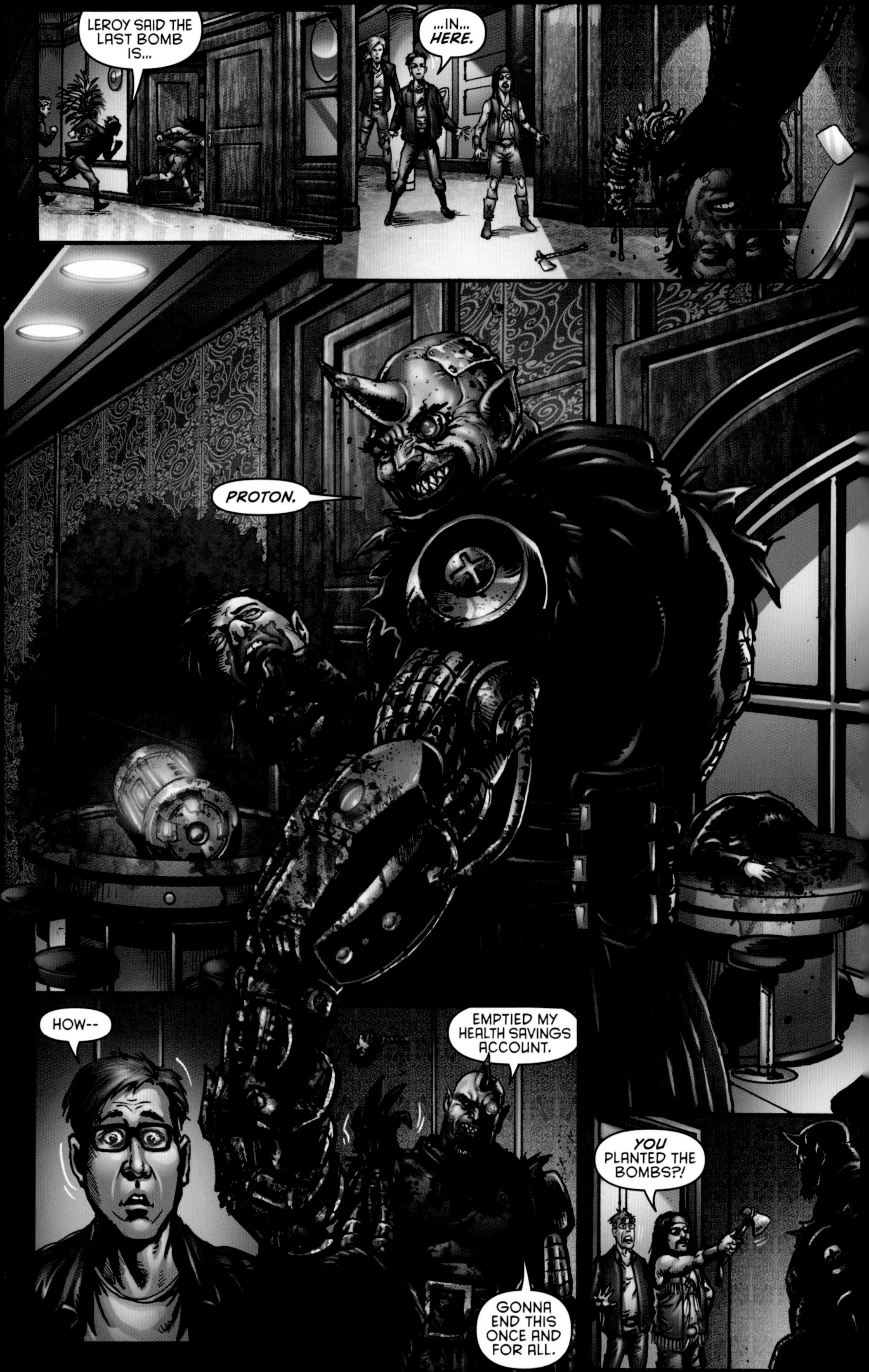
LEROY SAID THE LAST BOMB IS...
...IN... HERE.
PROTON.
HOW--
EMPTIED MY HEALTH SAVINGS ACCOUNT.
GONNA END THIS ONCE AND FOR ALL.
YOU PLANTED THE BOMBS?!

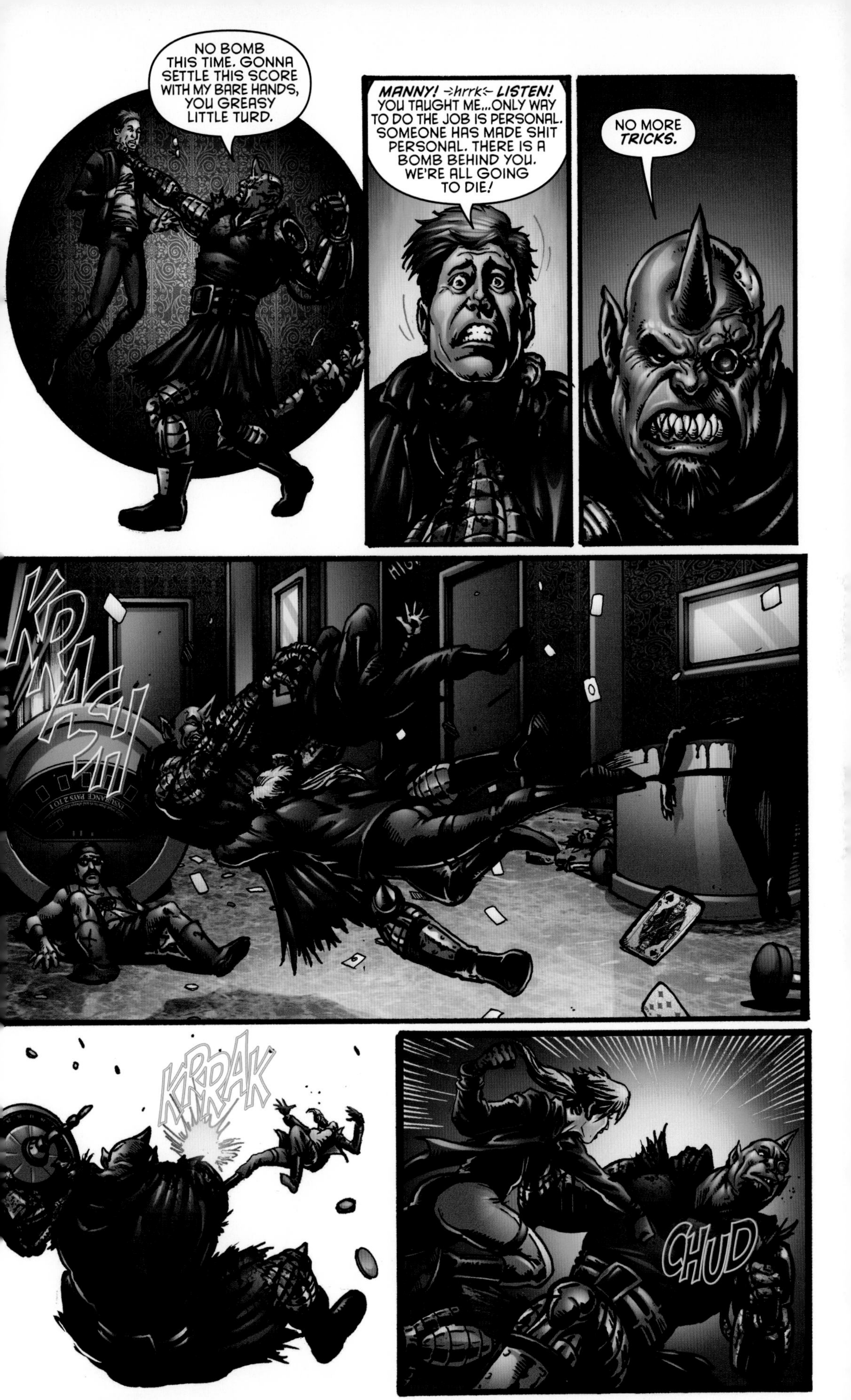
NO BOMB THIS TIME. GONNA SETTLE THIS SCORE WITH MY BARE HANDS, YOU GREASY LITTLE TURD.
MANNY! -hrrk- LISTEN! YOU TAUGHT ME...ONLY WAY TO DO THE JOB IS PERSONAL. SOMEONE HAS MADE SHIT PERSONAL. THERE IS A BOMB BEHIND YOU. WE'RE ALL GOING TO DIE!
NO MORE TRICKS.
KRAAGH
INSURANCE PAYS 2 TO 1
KRRAK
CHUD

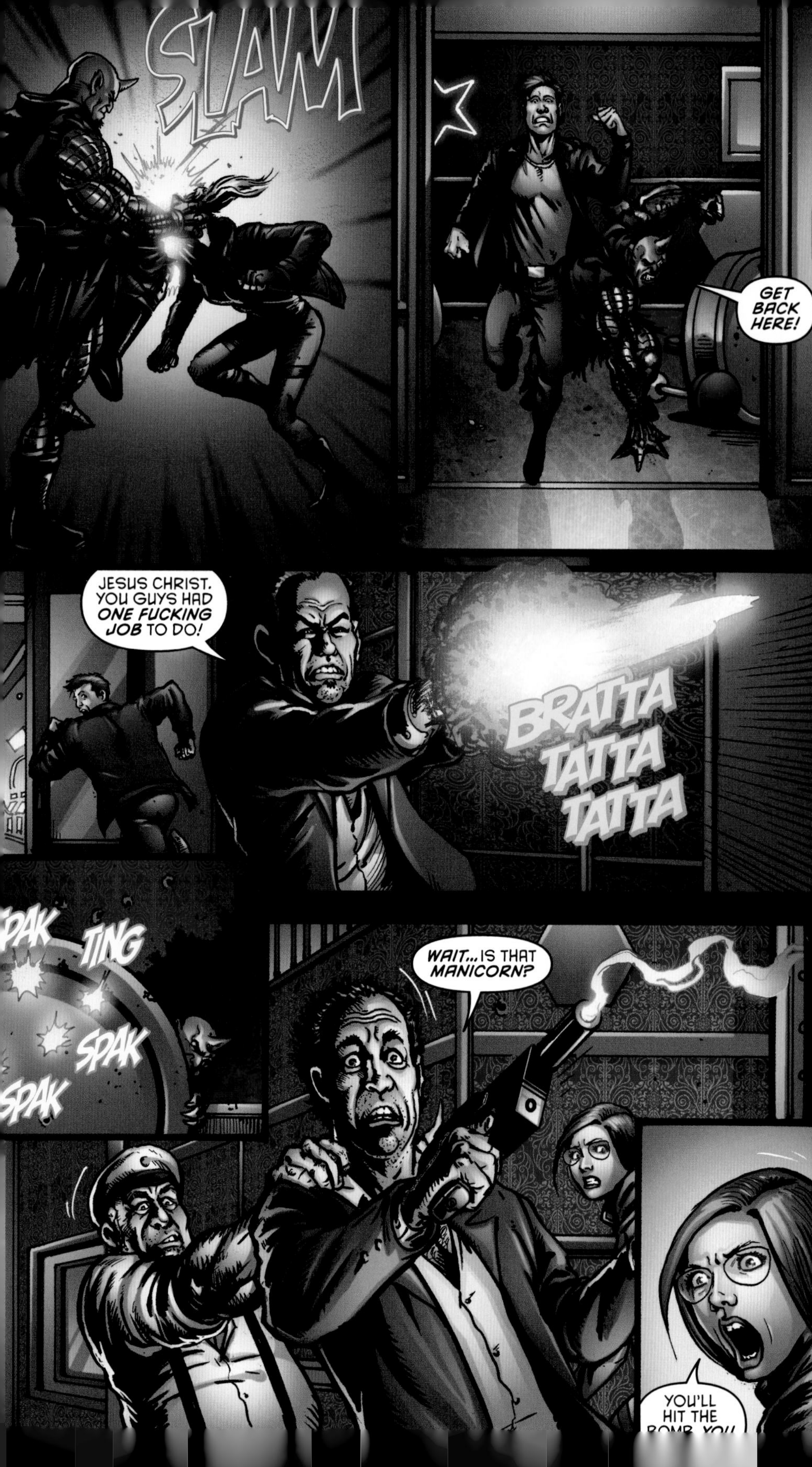
SLAM
GET BACK HERE!
JESUS CHRIST. YOU GUYS HAD ONE FUCKING JOB TO DO!
BRATTA TATTA TATTA
SPAK
TING
SPAK
SPAK
WAIT... IS THAT MANICORN?
YOU'LL HIT THE

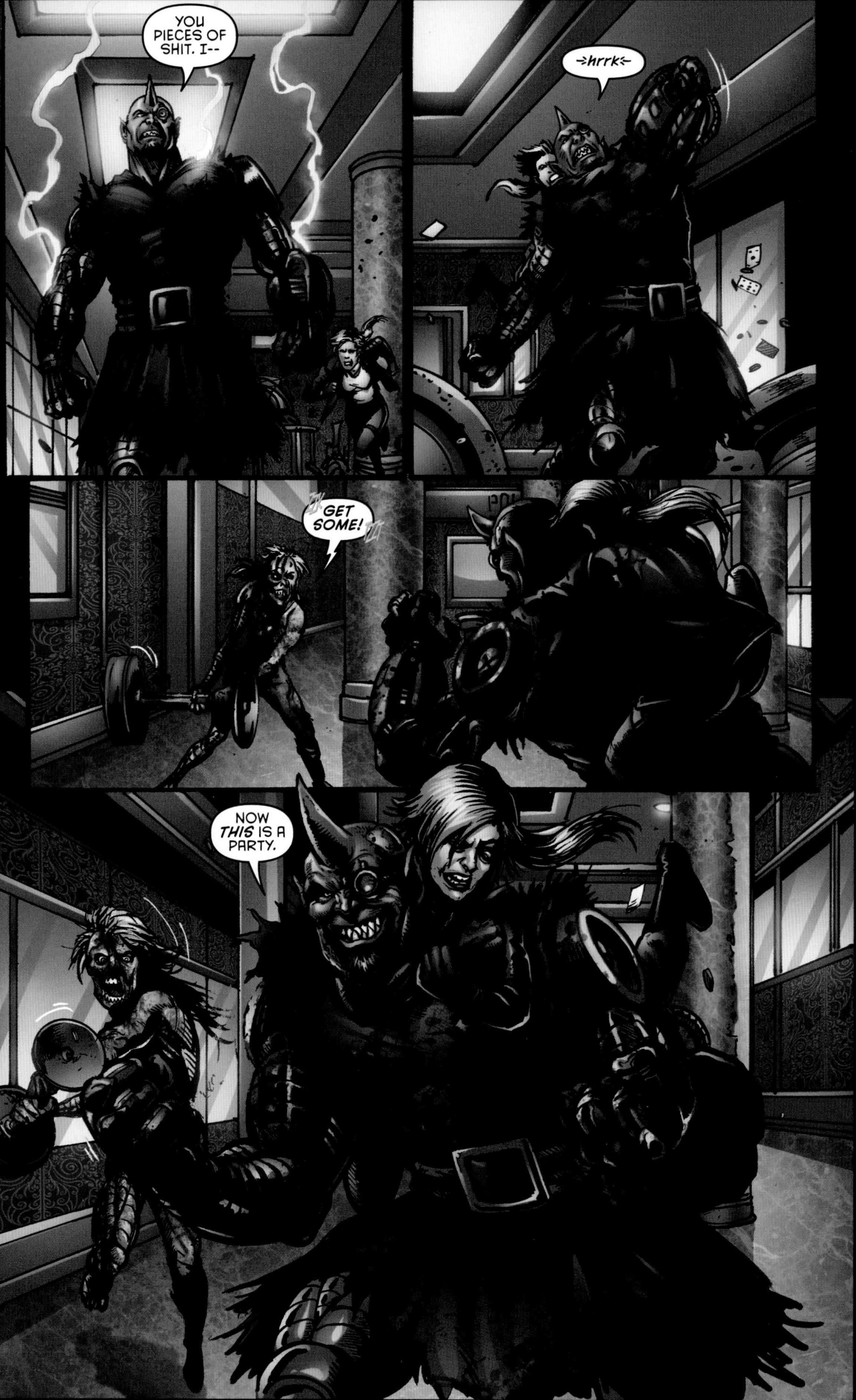
YOU PIECES OF SHIT. I--
-hrrk-
GET SOME!
NOW *THIS* IS A PARTY.

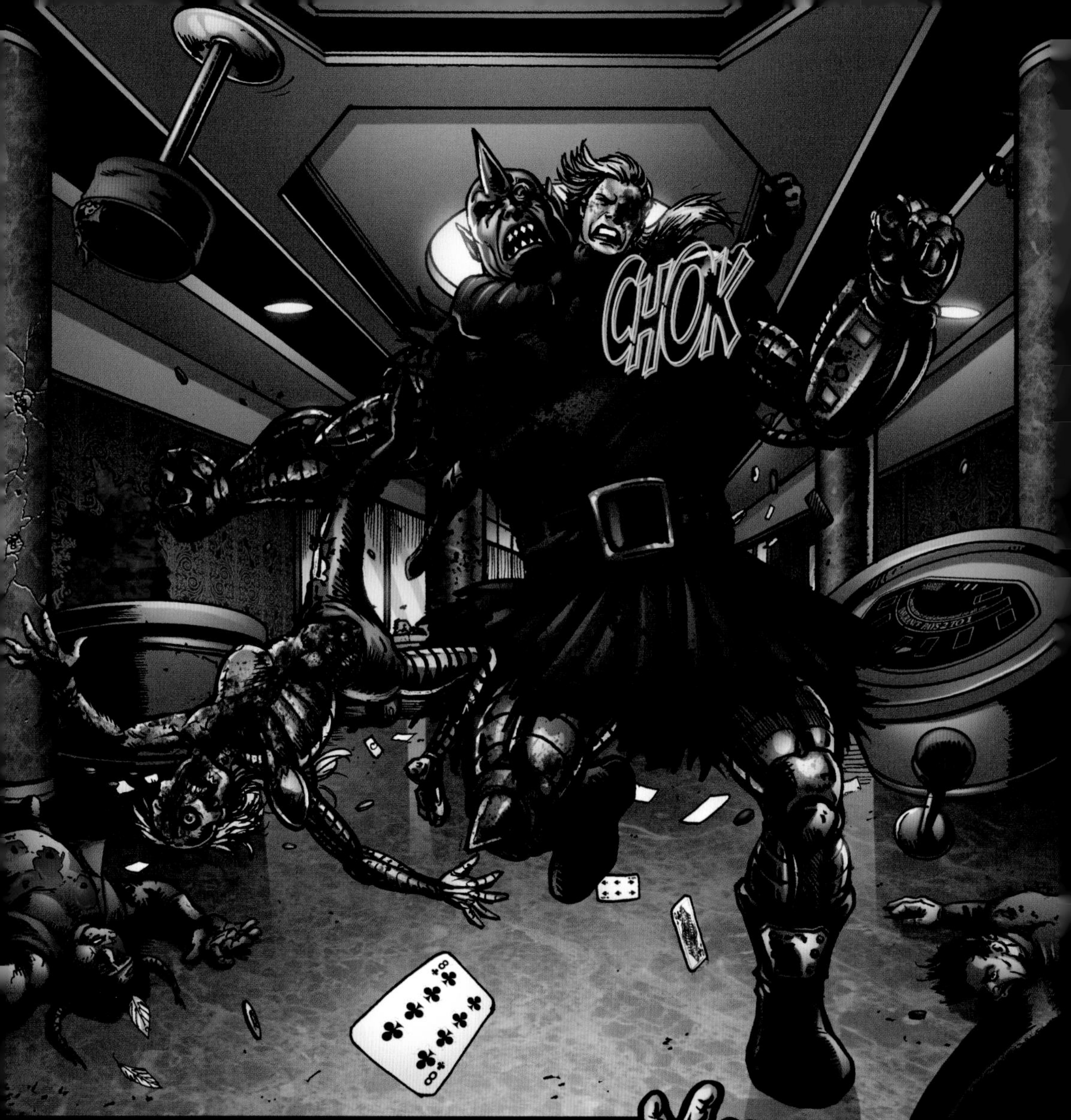
CHOK

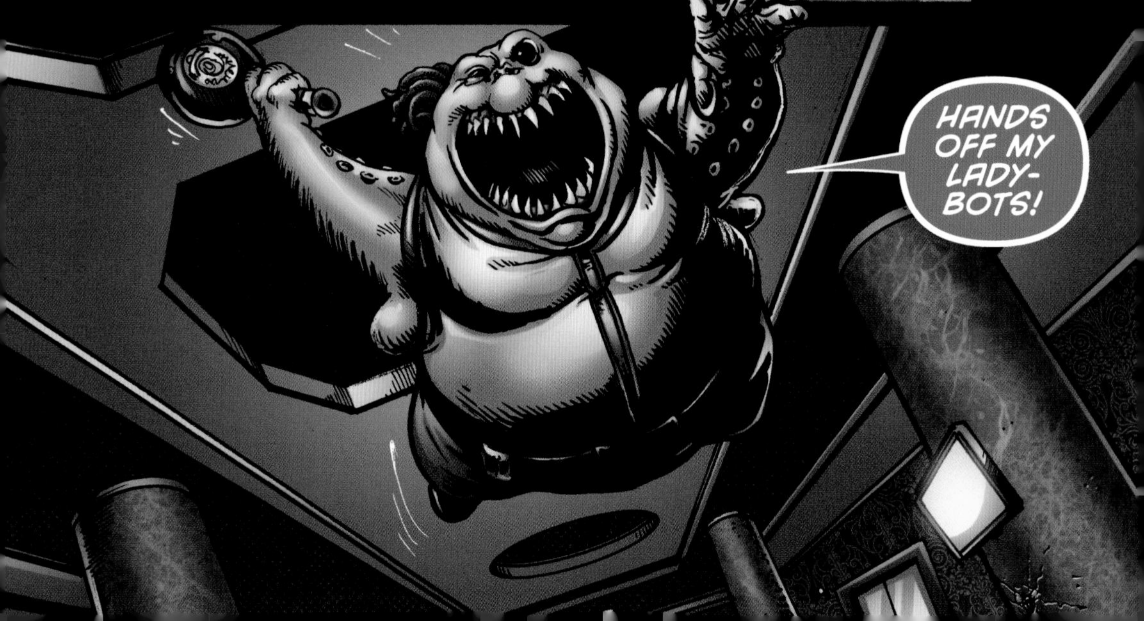
HANDS OFF MY LADY-BOTS!

WHAT ARE YOU DOING?!

GOTTA BUY US SOME TIME.

MARY! THE BOMB!

RAAAAGH!

SKREAWGHH

SEE YOU IN HELL.

WRRRRRRRR

NO!

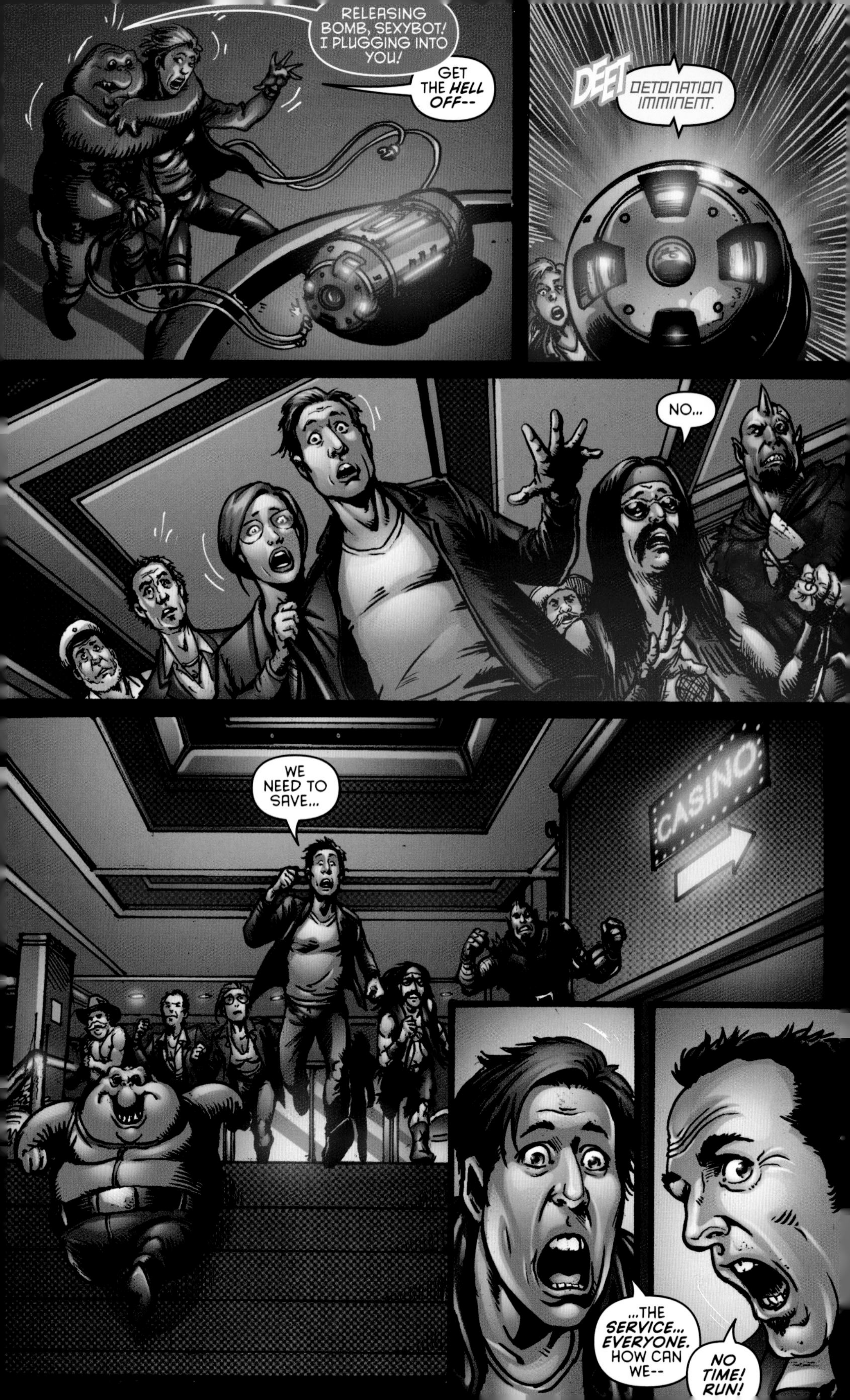
RELEASING BOMB, SEXYBOT! I PLUGGING INTO YOU!
GET THE HELL OFF--
DEET
DETONATION IMMINENT.
NO...
WE NEED TO SAVE...
CASINO
...THE SERVICE... EVERYONE. HOW CAN WE--
NO TIME! RUN!

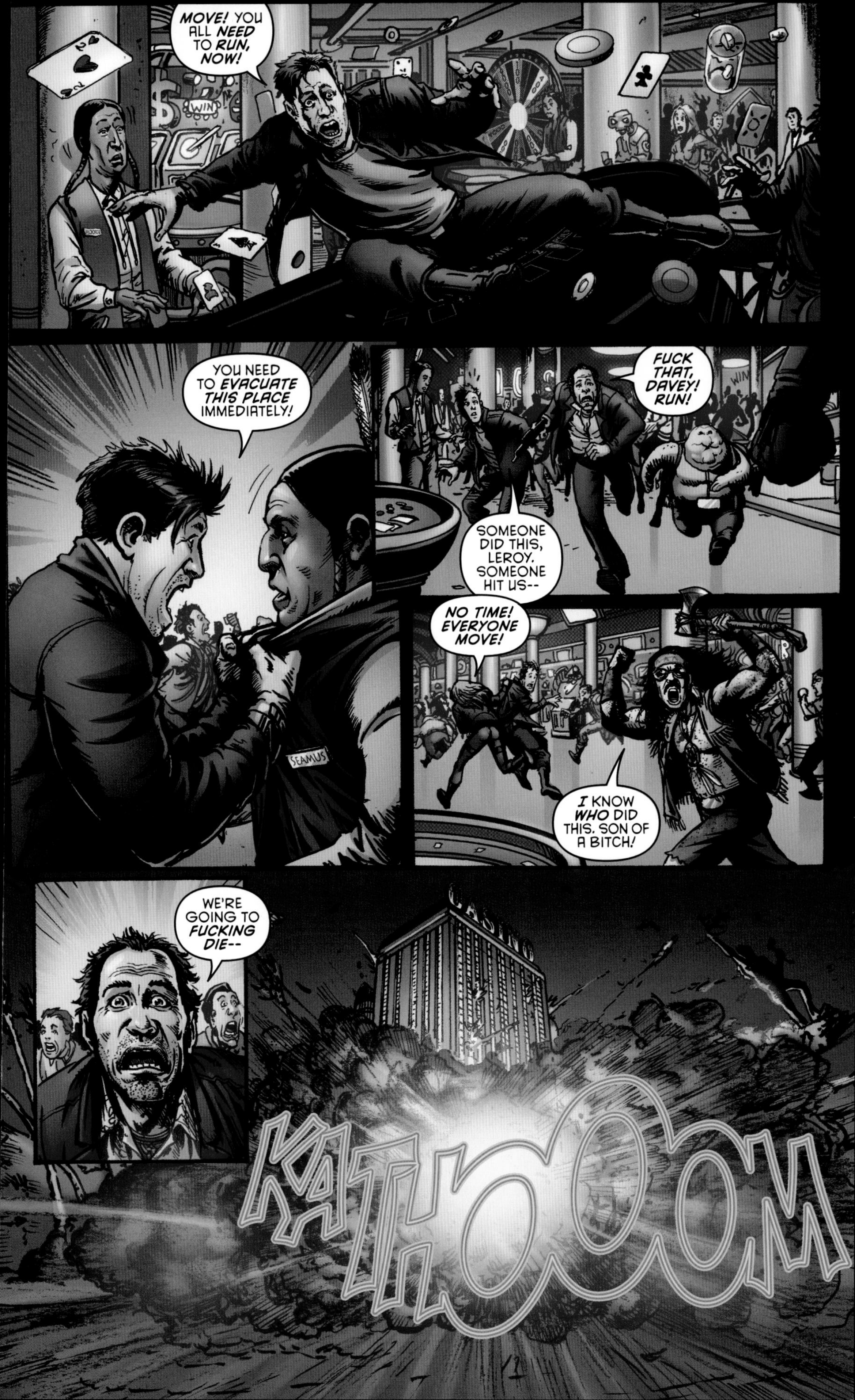

MOVE! YOU ALL NEED TO RUN, NOW!
WIN
YOU NEED TO EVACUATE THIS PLACE IMMEDIATELY!
SEAMUS
FUCK THAT, DAVEY! RUN!
SOMEONE DID THIS, LEROY. SOMEONE HIT US--
NO TIME! EVERYONE MOVE!
I KNOW WHO DID THIS. SON OF A BITCH!
WE'RE GOING TO FUCKING DIE--
CASINO
KATHOOOM

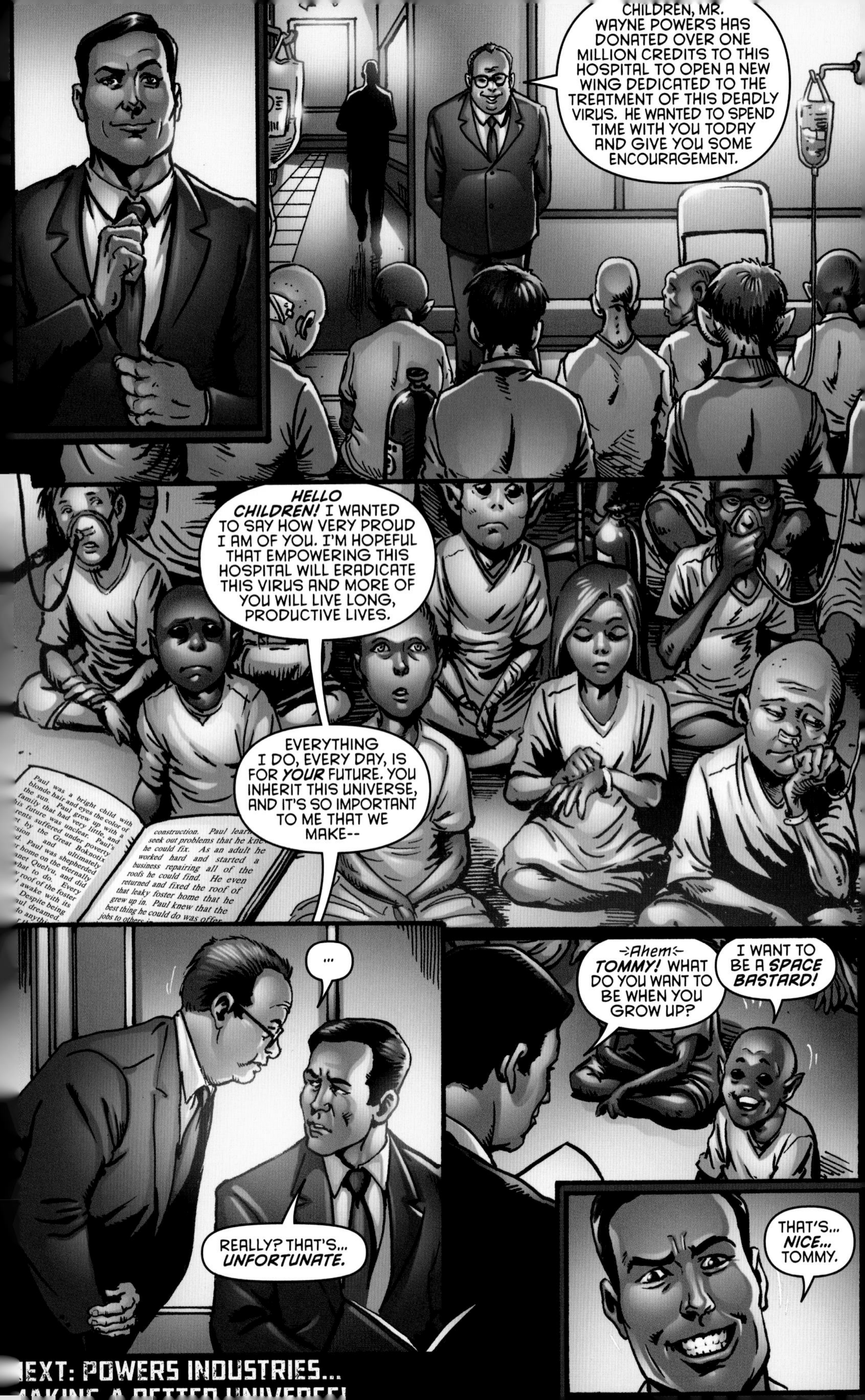
CHILDREN, MR. WAYNE POWERS HAS DONATED OVER ONE MILLION CREDITS TO THIS HOSPITAL TO OPEN A NEW WING DEDICATED TO THE TREATMENT OF THIS DEADLY VIRUS. HE WANTED TO SPEND TIME WITH YOU TODAY AND GIVE YOU SOME ENCOURAGEMENT.
HELLO CHILDREN! I WANTED TO SAY HOW VERY PROUD I AM OF YOU. I'M HOPEFUL THAT EMPOWERING THIS HOSPITAL WILL ERADICATE THIS VIRUS AND MORE OF YOU WILL LIVE LONG, PRODUCTIVE LIVES.
EVERYTHING I DO, EVERY DAY, IS FOR YOUR FUTURE. YOU INHERIT THIS UNIVERSE, AND IT'S SO IMPORTANT TO ME THAT WE MAKE--
-Ahem- TOMMY! WHAT DO YOU WANT TO BE WHEN YOU GROW UP?
I WANT TO BE A SPACE BASTARD!
...
REALLY? THAT'S... UNFORTUNATE.
THAT'S... NICE... TOMMY.
EXT: POWERS INDUSTRIES...

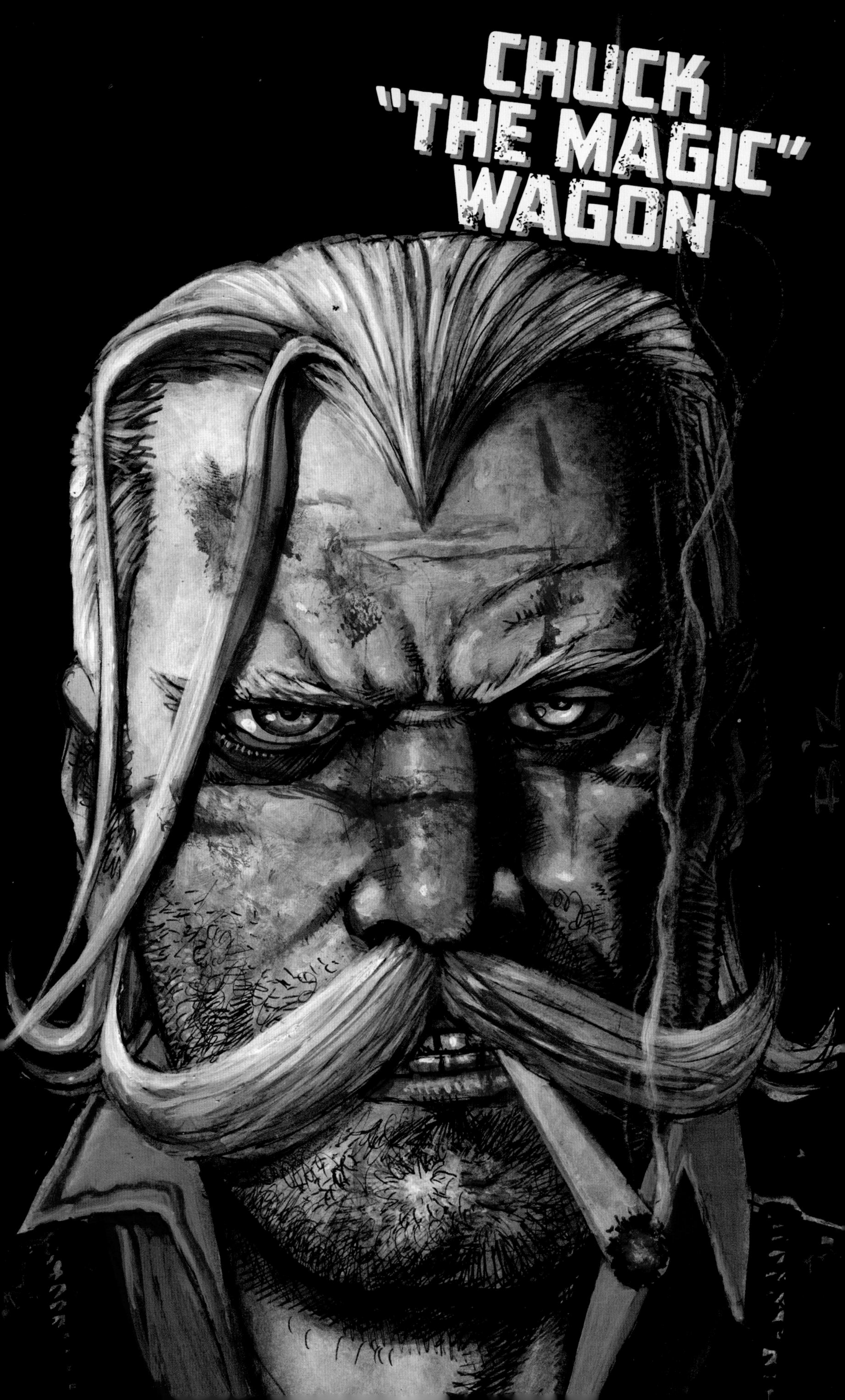
CHUCK "THE MAGIC" WAGON

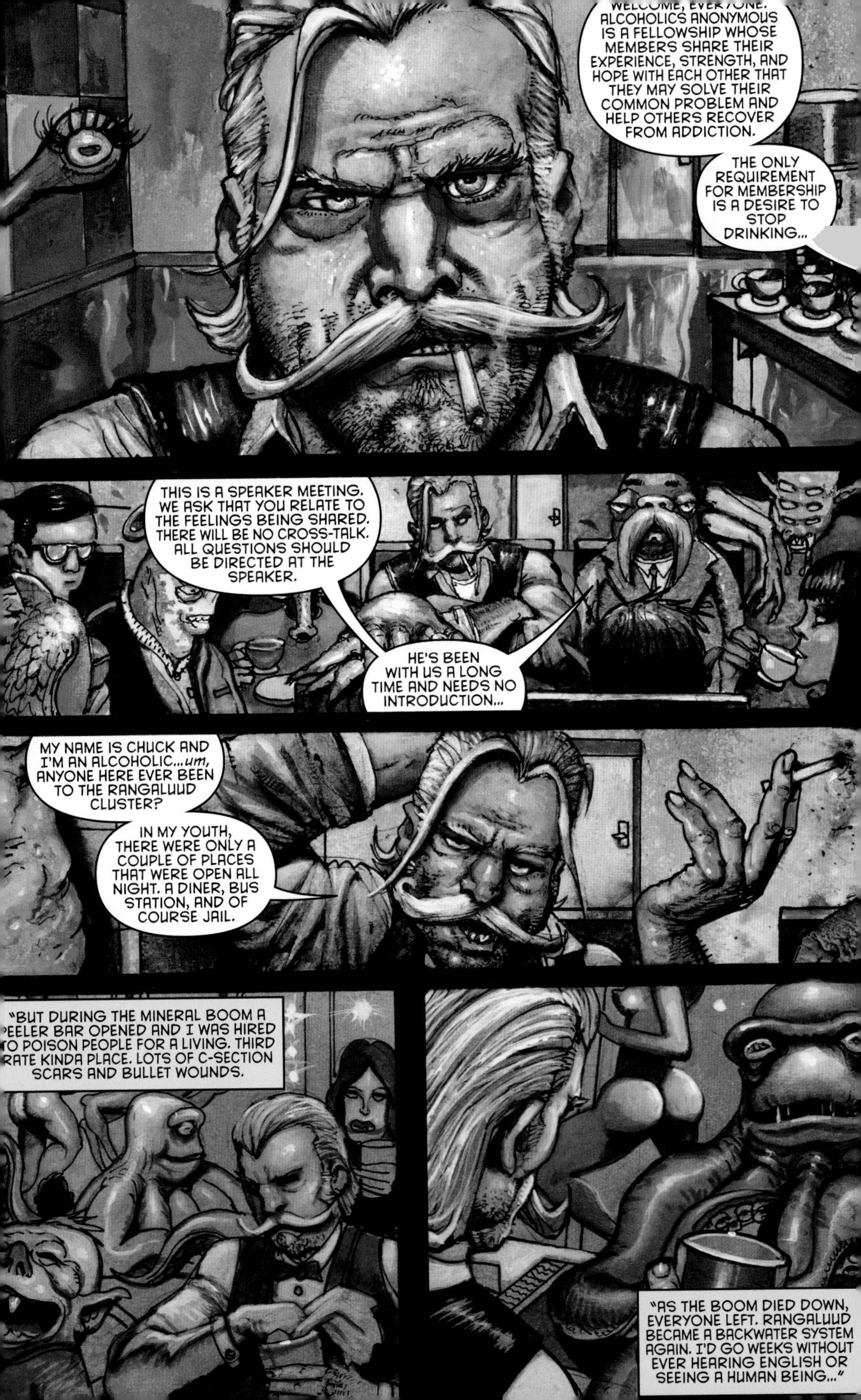
WELCOME, EVERYONE. ALCOHOLICS ANONYMOUS IS A FELLOWSHIP WHOSE MEMBERS SHARE THEIR EXPERIENCE, STRENGTH, AND HOPE WITH EACH OTHER THAT THEY MAY SOLVE THEIR COMMON PROBLEM AND HELP OTHERS RECOVER FROM ADDICTION.
THE ONLY REQUIREMENT FOR MEMBERSHIP IS A DESIRE TO STOP DRINKING...
THIS IS A SPEAKER MEETING. WE ASK THAT YOU RELATE TO THE FEELINGS BEING SHARED. THERE WILL BE NO CROSS-TALK. ALL QUESTIONS SHOULD BE DIRECTED AT THE SPEAKER.
HE'S BEEN WITH US A LONG TIME AND NEEDS NO INTRODUCTION...
MY NAME IS CHUCK AND I'M AN ALCOHOLIC...*um*, ANYONE HERE EVER BEEN TO THE RANGALUUD CLUSTER?
IN MY YOUTH, THERE WERE ONLY A COUPLE OF PLACES THAT WERE OPEN ALL NIGHT. A DINER, BUS STATION, AND OF COURSE JAIL.
"BUT DURING THE MINERAL BOOM A PEELER BAR OPENED AND I WAS HIRED TO POISON PEOPLE FOR A LIVING. THIRD RATE KINDA PLACE. LOTS OF C-SECTION SCARS AND BULLET WOUNDS.
"AS THE BOOM DIED DOWN, EVERYONE LEFT. RANGALUUD BECAME A BACKWATER SYSTEM AGAIN. I'D GO WEEKS WITHOUT EVER HEARING ENGLISH OR SEEING A HUMAN BEING..."

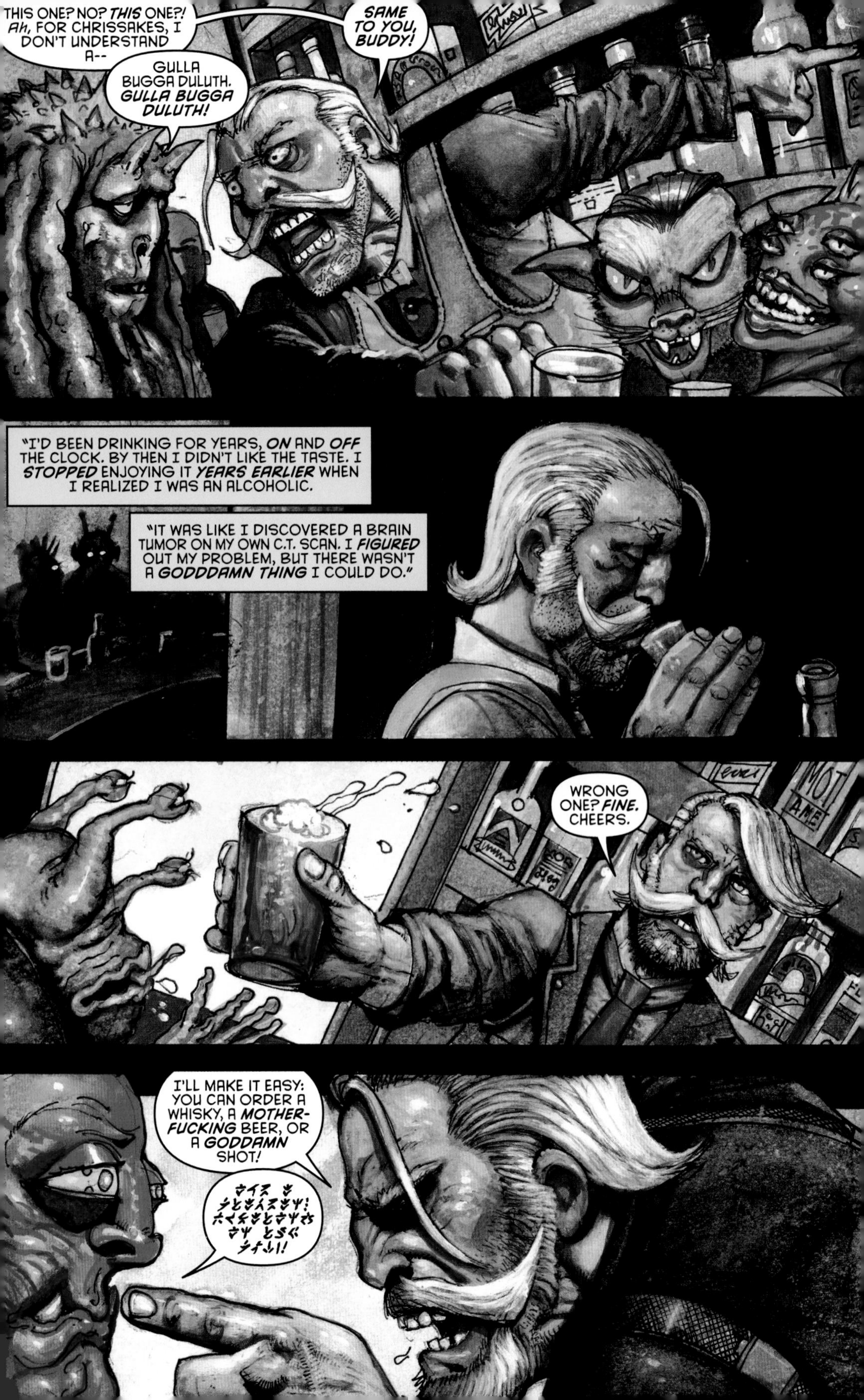
THIS ONE? NO? THIS ONE?! AH, FOR CHRISSAKES, I DON'T UNDERSTAND A--
GULLA BUGGA DULUTH. GULLA BUGGA DULUTH!
SAME TO YOU, BUDDY!
"I'D BEEN DRINKING FOR YEARS, ON AND OFF THE CLOCK. BY THEN I DIDN'T LIKE THE TASTE. I STOPPED ENJOYING IT YEARS EARLIER WHEN I REALIZED I WAS AN ALCOHOLIC.
"IT WAS LIKE I DISCOVERED A BRAIN TUMOR ON MY OWN C.T. SCAN. I FIGURED OUT MY PROBLEM, BUT THERE WASN'T A GODDDAMN THING I COULD DO."
WRONG ONE? FINE. CHEERS.
I'LL MAKE IT EASY: YOU CAN ORDER A WHISKY, A MOTHER-FUCKING BEER, OR A GODDAMN SHOT!

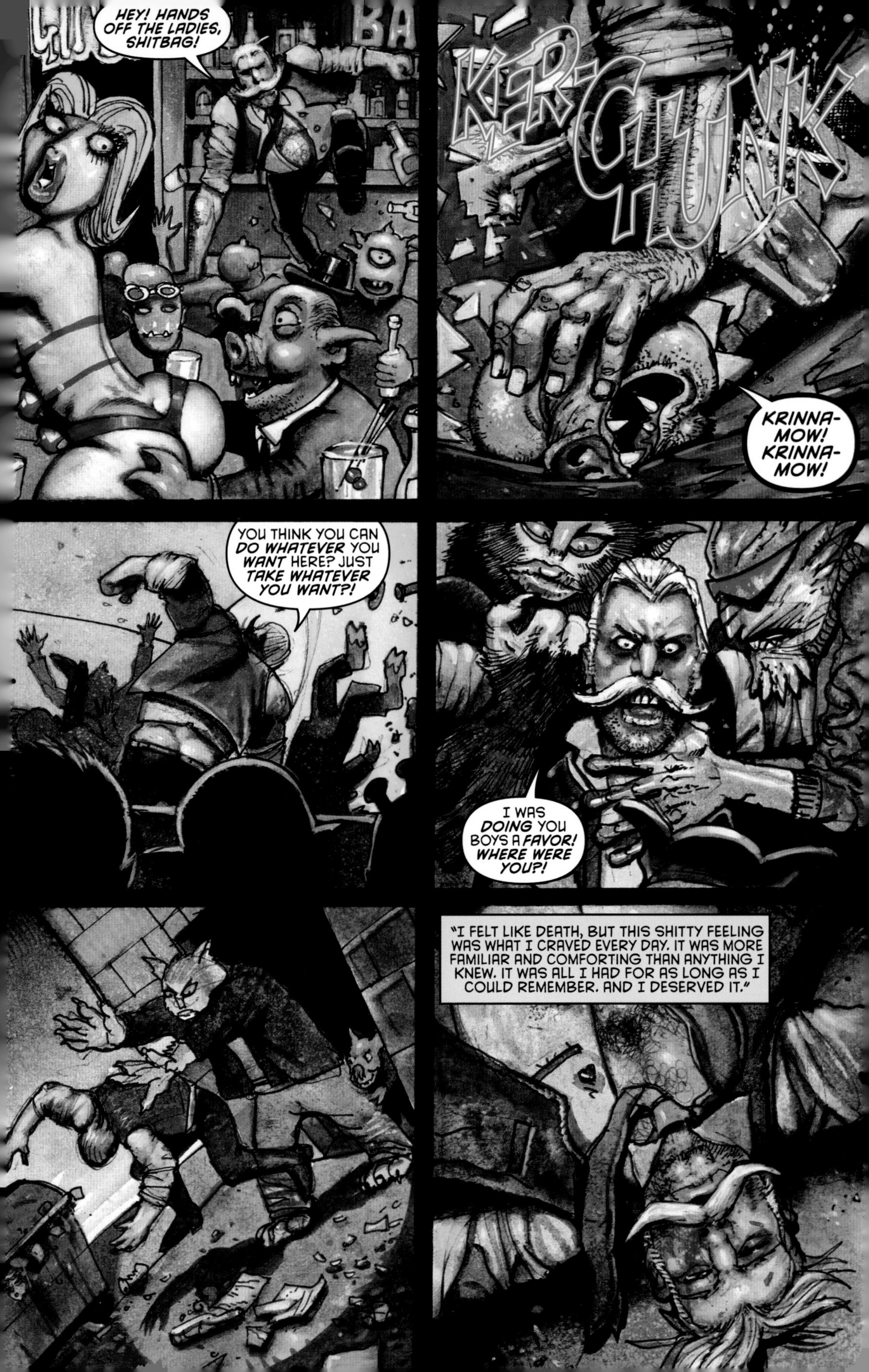
HEY! HANDS OFF THE LADIES, SHITBAG!
KER-CHUNK
KRINNA-MOW! KRINNA-MOW!
YOU THINK YOU CAN DO WHATEVER YOU WANT HERE? JUST TAKE WHATEVER YOU WANT?!
I WAS DOING YOU BOYS A FAVOR! WHERE WERE YOU?!
"I FELT LIKE DEATH, BUT THIS SHITTY FEELING WAS WHAT I CRAVED EVERY DAY. IT WAS MORE FAMILIAR AND COMFORTING THAN ANYTHING I KNEW. IT WAS ALL I HAD FOR AS LONG AS I COULD REMEMBER. AND I DESERVED IT."

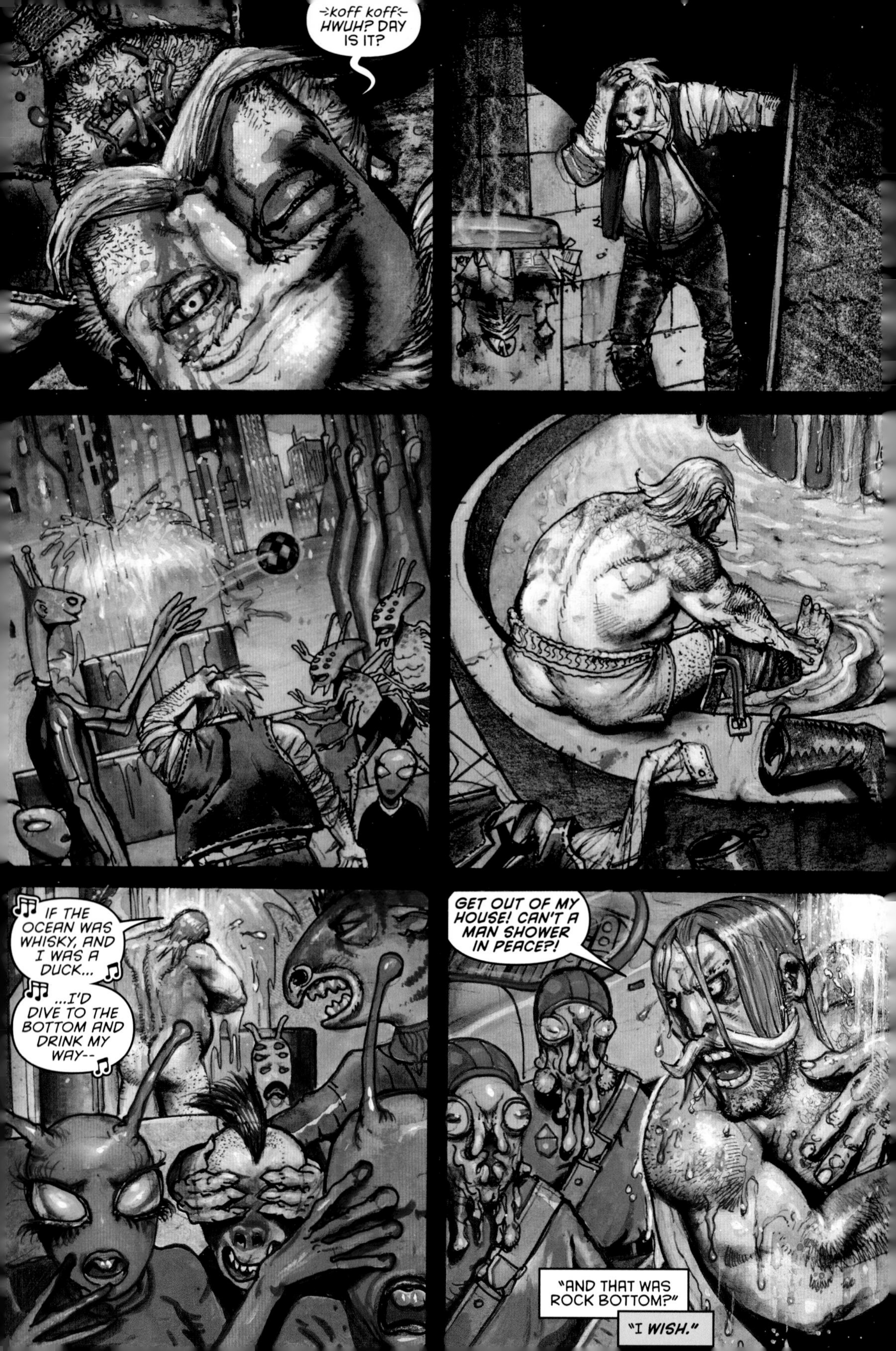

=koff koff=
HWUH? DAY IS IT?
IF THE OCEAN WAS WHISKY, AND I WAS A DUCK...
...I'D DIVE TO THE BOTTOM AND DRINK MY WAY--
GET OUT OF MY HOUSE! CAN'T A MAN SHOWER IN PEACE?!
"AND THAT WAS ROCK BOTTOM?"
"I WISH."

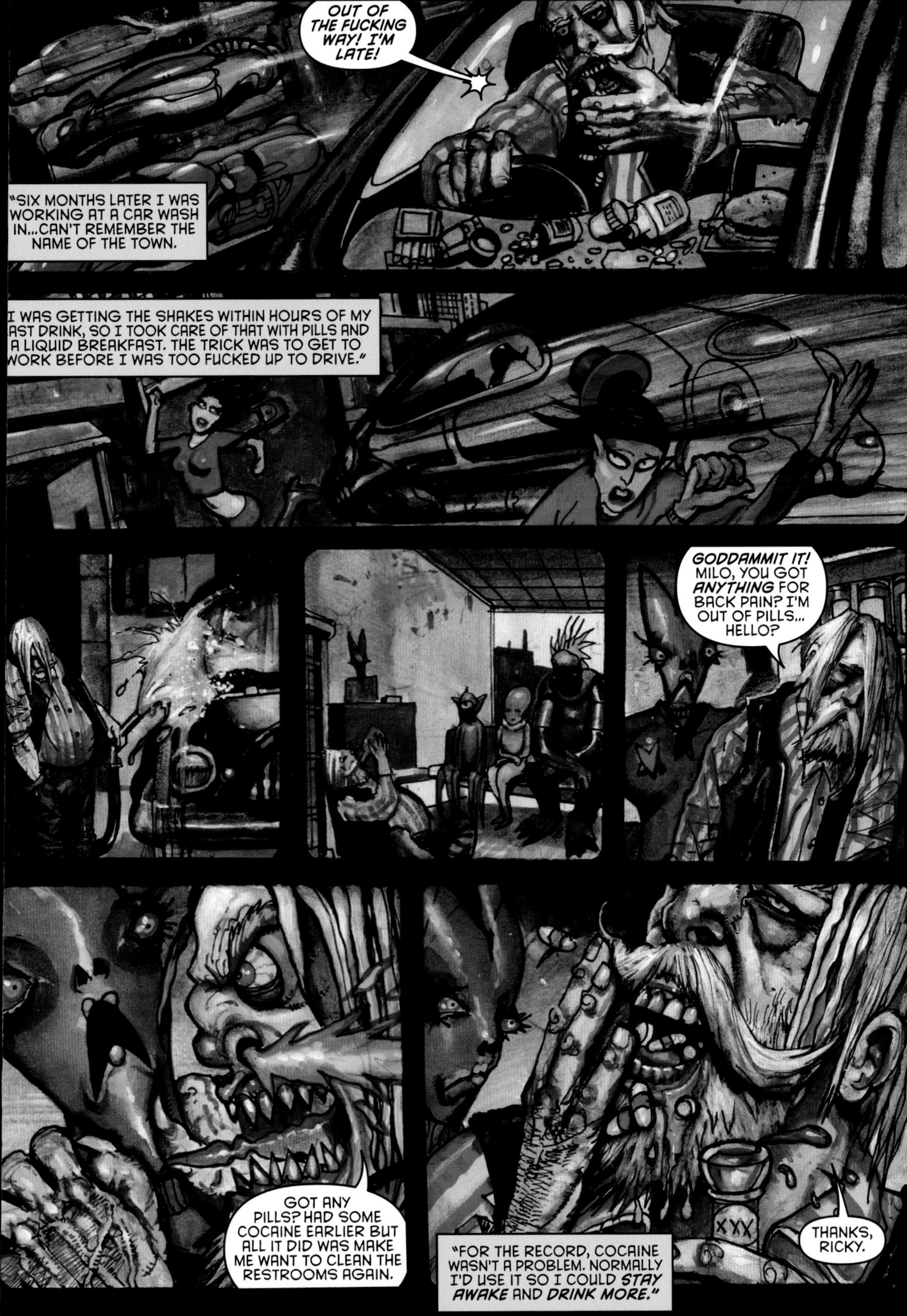
OUT OF THE FUCKING WAY! I'M LATE!
"SIX MONTHS LATER I WAS WORKING AT A CAR WASH IN...CAN'T REMEMBER THE NAME OF THE TOWN.
I WAS GETTING THE SHAKES WITHIN HOURS OF MY LAST DRINK, SO I TOOK CARE OF THAT WITH PILLS AND A LIQUID BREAKFAST. THE TRICK WAS TO GET TO WORK BEFORE I WAS TOO FUCKED UP TO DRIVE."
GODDAMMIT IT! MILO, YOU GOT ANYTHING FOR BACK PAIN? I'M OUT OF PILLS... HELLO?
GOT ANY PILLS? HAD SOME COCAINE EARLIER BUT ALL IT DID WAS MAKE ME WANT TO CLEAN THE RESTROOMS AGAIN.
"FOR THE RECORD, COCAINE WASN'T A PROBLEM. NORMALLY I'D USE IT SO I COULD STAY AWAKE AND DRINK MORE."
XXX
THANKS, RICKY.

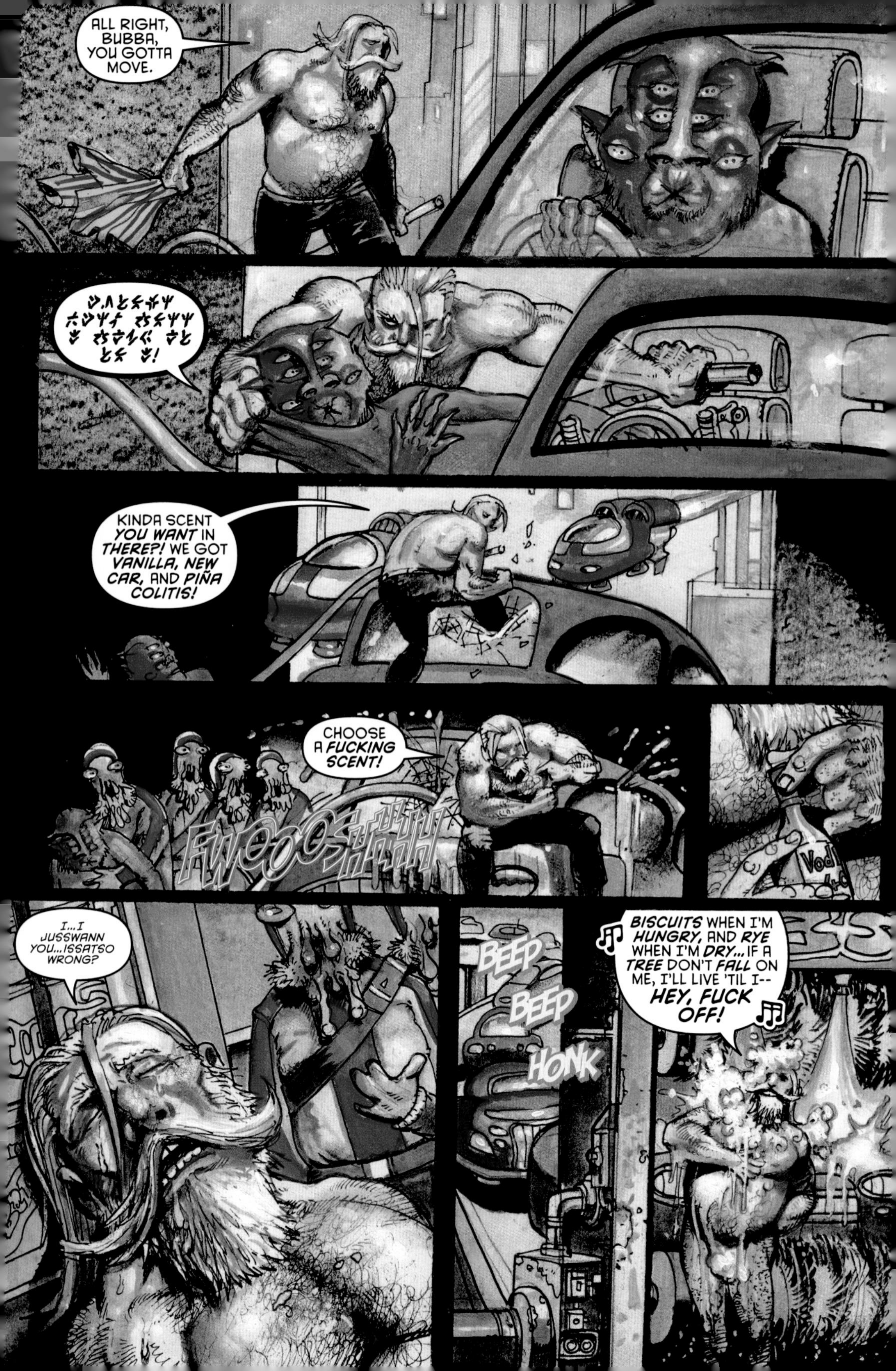
ALL RIGHT, BUBBA, YOU GOTTA MOVE.
KINDA SCENT *YOU WANT* IN *THERE?!* WE GOT *VANILLA, NEW CAR,* AND *PIÑA COLITIS!*
CHOOSE A *FUCKING SCENT!*
FWOOOSHHH
I... I JUSSWANN YOU... ISSATSO WRONG?
BEEP
BEEP
HONK
BISCUITS WHEN I'M *HUNGRY,* AND *RYE* WHEN I'M *DRY*... IF A *TREE* DON'T *FALL* ON ME, I'LL LIVE 'TIL I-- **HEY, FUCK OFF!**

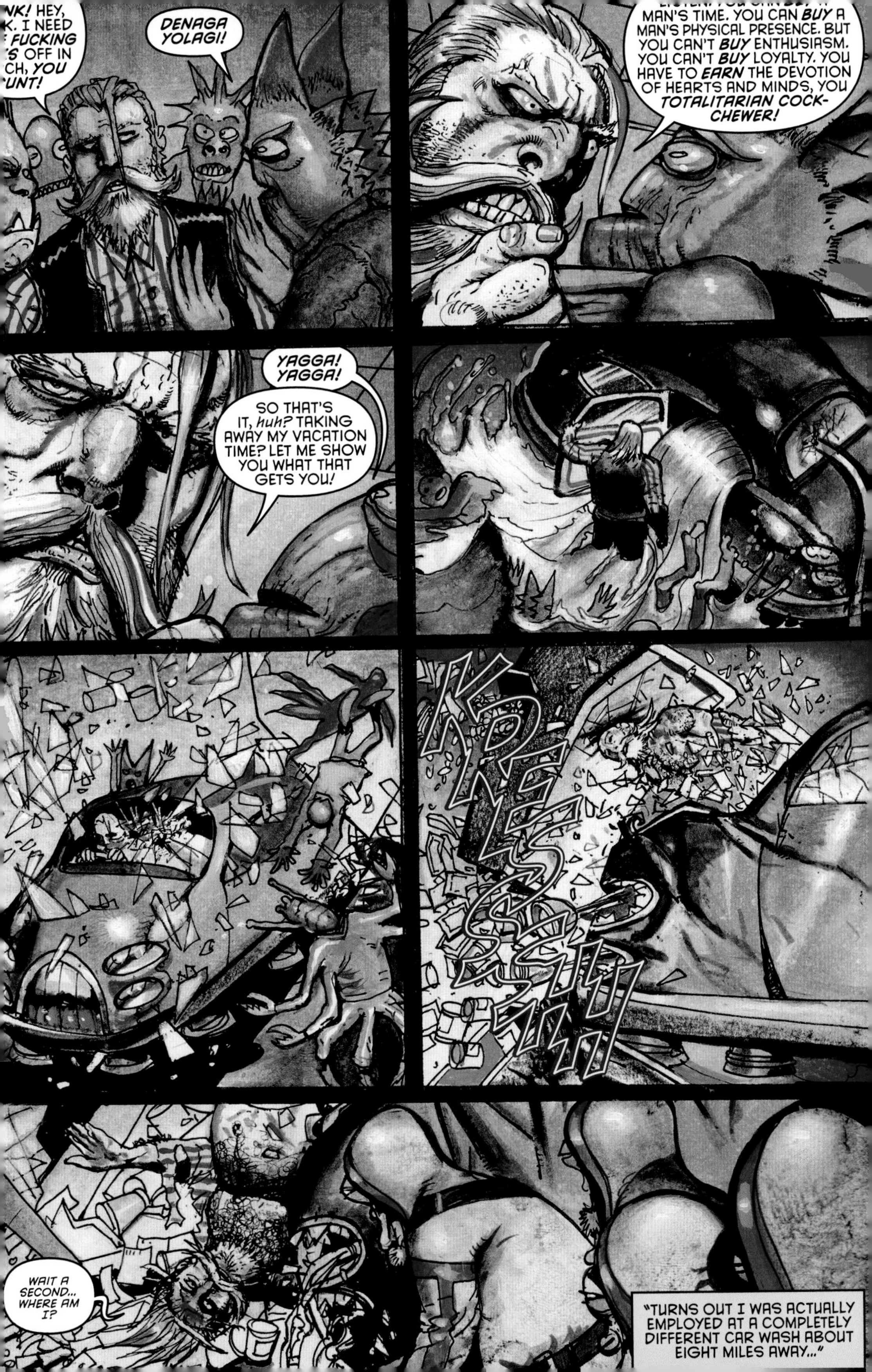

NK! HEY, K. I NEED FUCKING 'S OFF IN CH, YOU UNT!
DENAGA YOLAGI!
MAN'S TIME. YOU CAN BUY A MAN'S PHYSICAL PRESENCE. BUT YOU CAN'T BUY ENTHUSIASM. YOU CAN'T BUY LOYALTY. YOU HAVE TO EARN THE DEVOTION OF HEARTS AND MINDS, YOU TOTALITARIAN COCK-CHEWER!
YAGGA! YAGGA!
SO THAT'S IT, huh? TAKING AWAY MY VACATION TIME? LET ME SHOW YOU WHAT THAT GETS YOU!
KRESSSHHH
WAIT A SECOND... WHERE AM I?
"TURNS OUT I WAS ACTUALLY EMPLOYED AT A COMPLETELY DIFFERENT CAR WASH ABOUT EIGHT MILES AWAY..."

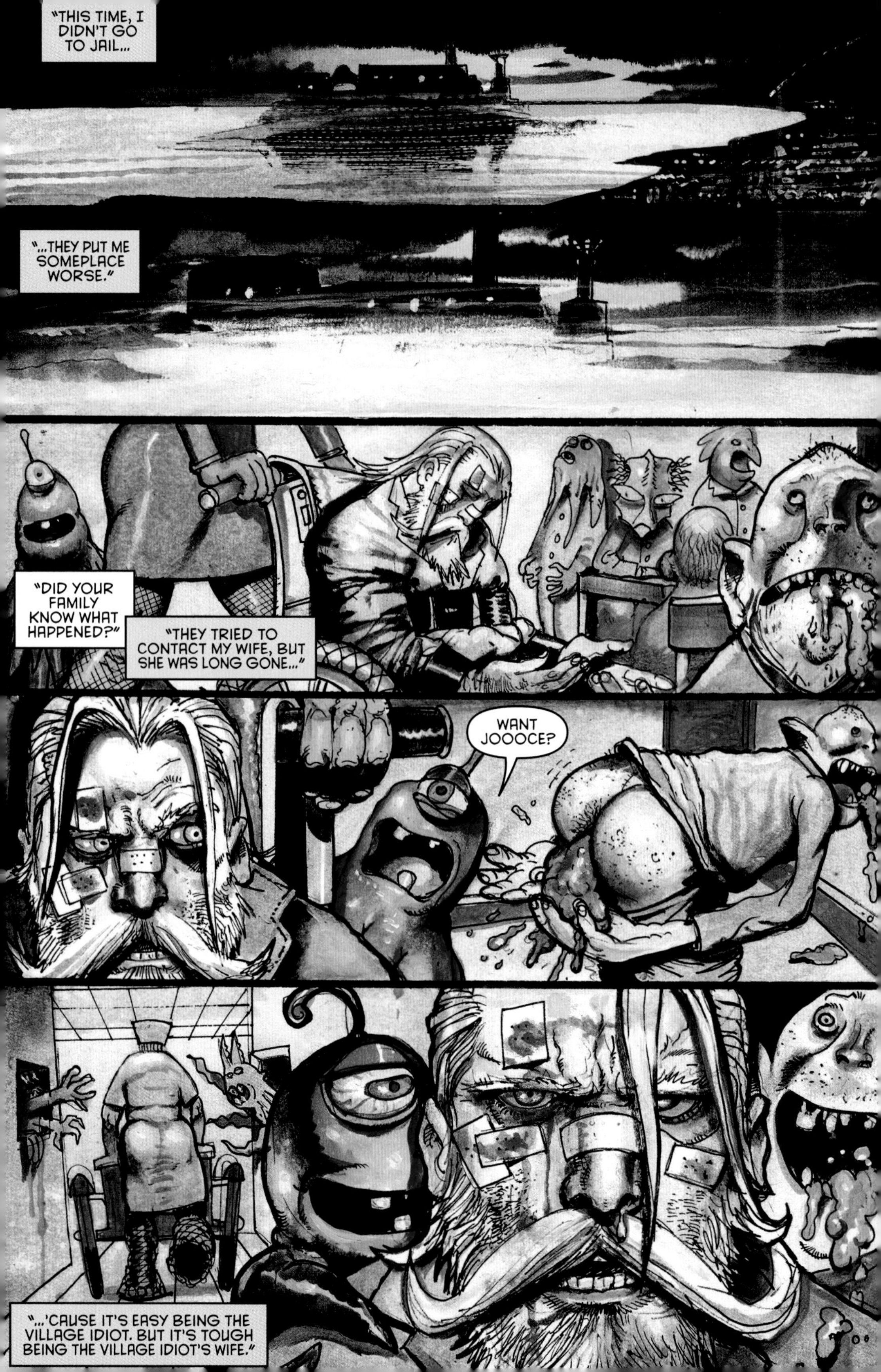
"THIS TIME, I DIDN'T GO TO JAIL...
"...THEY PUT ME SOMEPLACE WORSE."
"DID YOUR FAMILY KNOW WHAT HAPPENED?"
"THEY TRIED TO CONTACT MY WIFE, BUT SHE WAS LONG GONE..."
WANT JOOOCE?
"...'CAUSE IT'S EASY BEING THE VILLAGE IDIOT. BUT IT'S TOUGH BEING THE VILLAGE IDIOT'S WIFE."

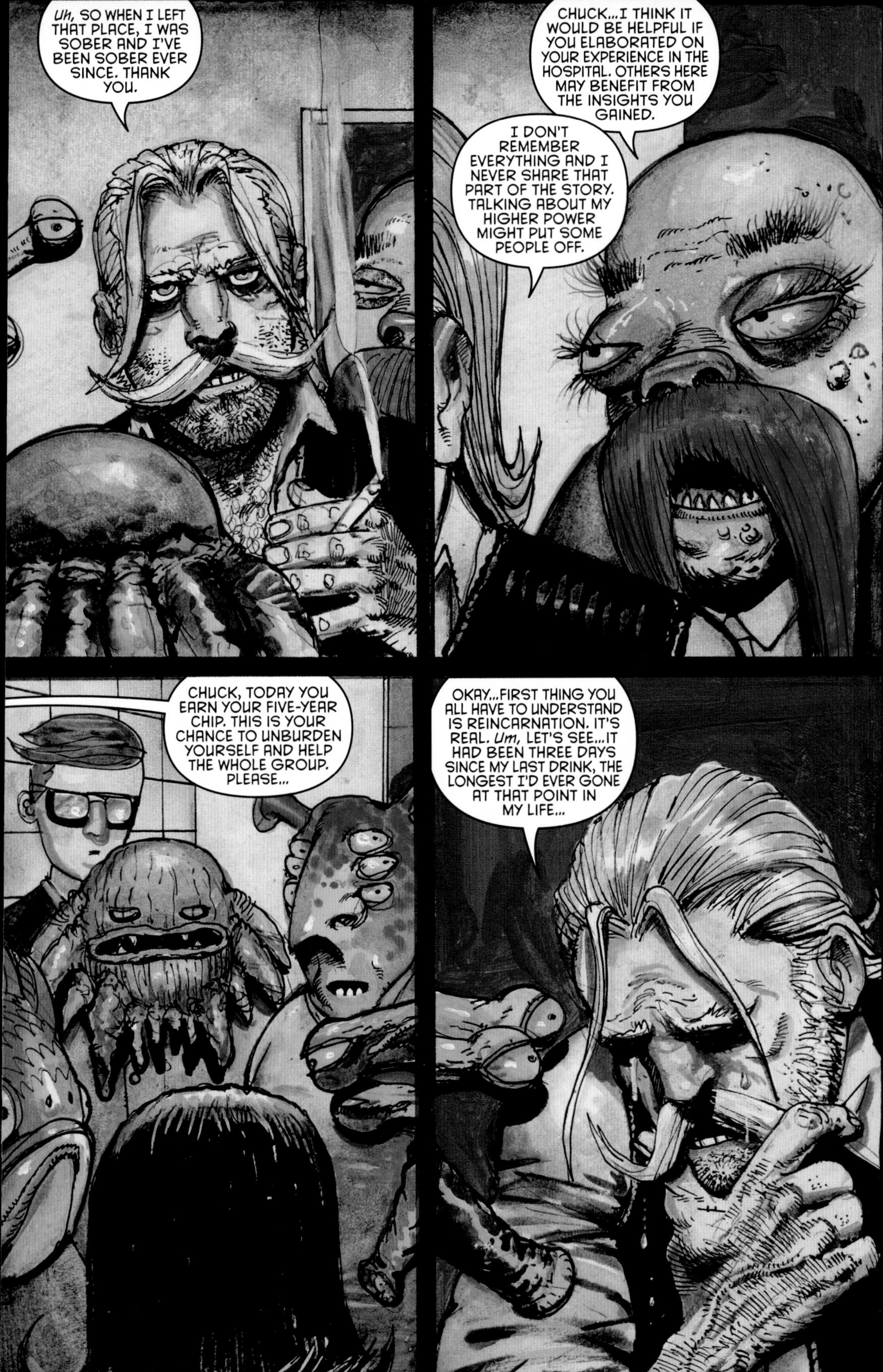

Uh, SO WHEN I LEFT THAT PLACE, I WAS SOBER AND I'VE BEEN SOBER EVER SINCE. THANK YOU.
CHUCK...I THINK IT WOULD BE HELPFUL IF YOU ELABORATED ON YOUR EXPERIENCE IN THE HOSPITAL. OTHERS HERE MAY BENEFIT FROM THE INSIGHTS YOU GAINED.
I DON'T REMEMBER EVERYTHING AND I NEVER SHARE THAT PART OF THE STORY. TALKING ABOUT MY HIGHER POWER MIGHT PUT SOME PEOPLE OFF.
CHUCK, TODAY YOU EARN YOUR FIVE-YEAR CHIP. THIS IS YOUR CHANCE TO UNBURDEN YOURSELF AND HELP THE WHOLE GROUP. PLEASE...
OKAY...FIRST THING YOU ALL HAVE TO UNDERSTAND IS REINCARNATION. IT'S REAL. *Um,* LET'S SEE...IT HAD BEEN THREE DAYS SINCE MY LAST DRINK, THE LONGEST I'D EVER GONE AT THAT POINT IN MY LIFE...

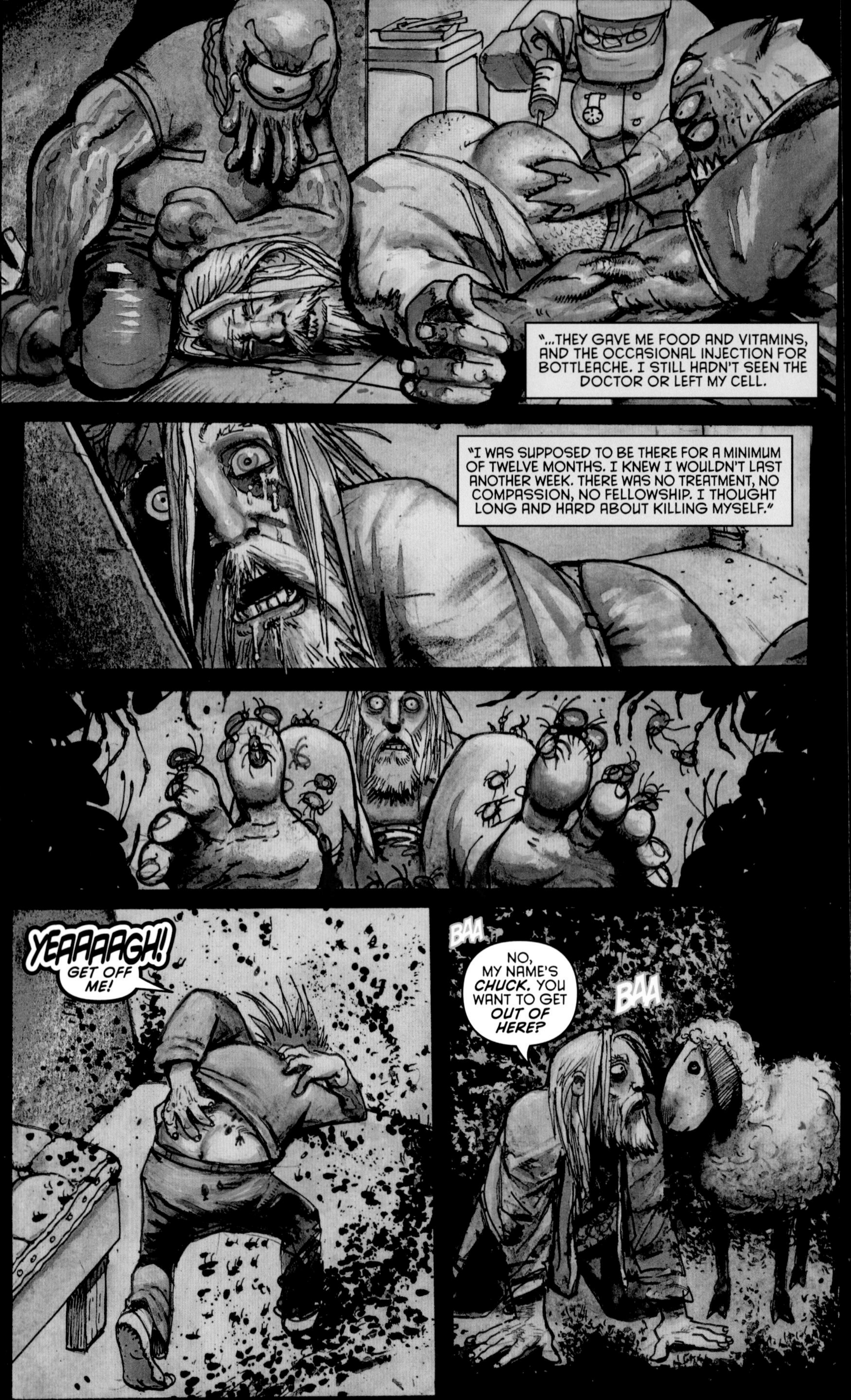
"...THEY GAVE ME FOOD AND VITAMINS, AND THE OCCASIONAL INJECTION FOR BOTTLEACHE. I STILL HADN'T SEEN THE DOCTOR OR LEFT MY CELL.
"I WAS SUPPOSED TO BE THERE FOR A MINIMUM OF TWELVE MONTHS. I KNEW I WOULDN'T LAST ANOTHER WEEK. THERE WAS NO TREATMENT, NO COMPASSION, NO FELLOWSHIP. I THOUGHT LONG AND HARD ABOUT KILLING MYSELF."
YEAAAAGH! GET OFF ME!
BAA
NO, MY NAME'S CHUCK. YOU WANT TO GET OUT OF HERE?
BAA

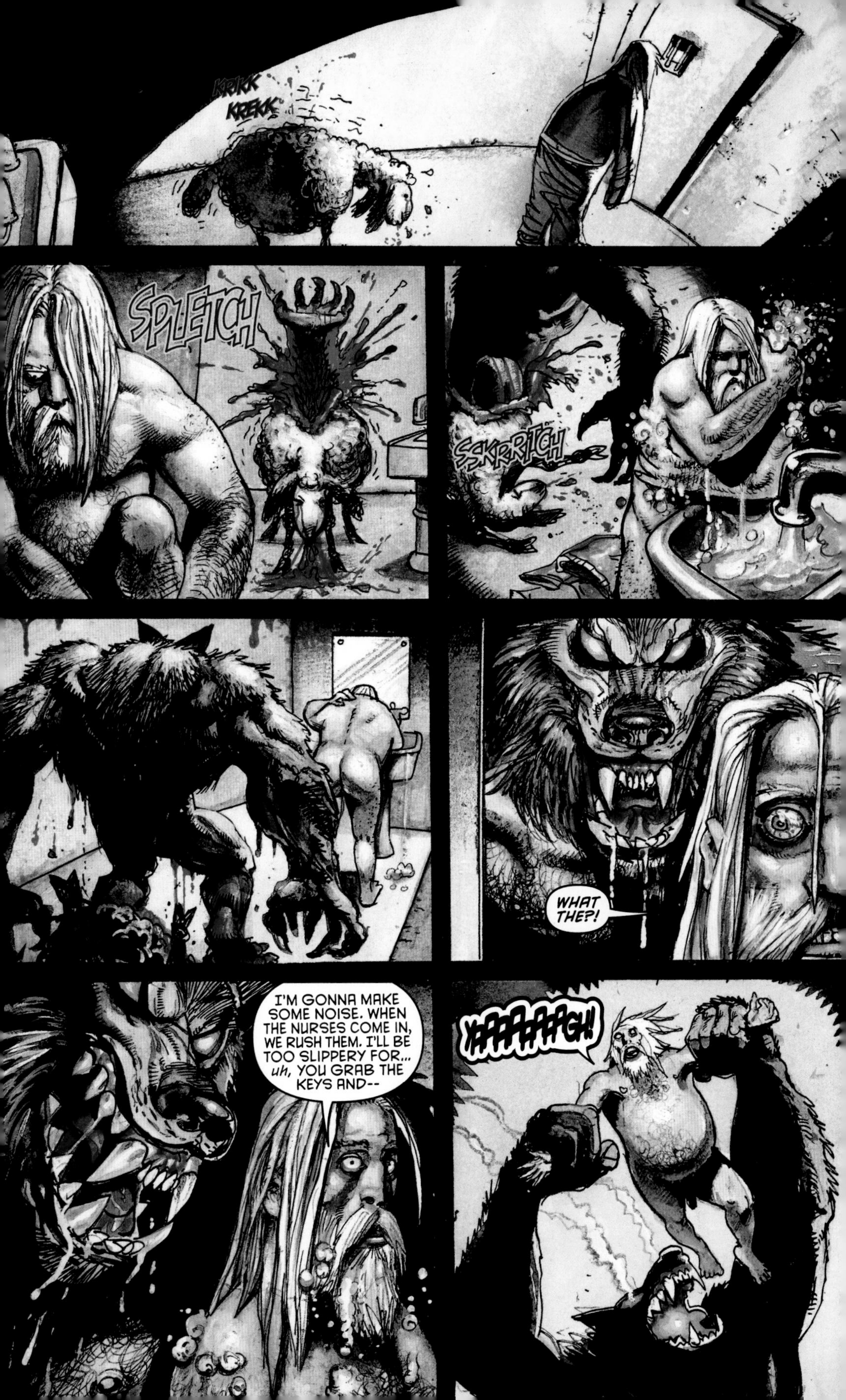
KRIKK
KREKK
SPLETCH
SSKRRITCH
WHAT THE?!
I'M GONNA MAKE SOME NOISE. WHEN THE NURSES COME IN, WE RUSH THEM. I'LL BE TOO SLIPPERY FOR... uh, YOU GRAB THE KEYS AND--
YAAAAAAAAGH!

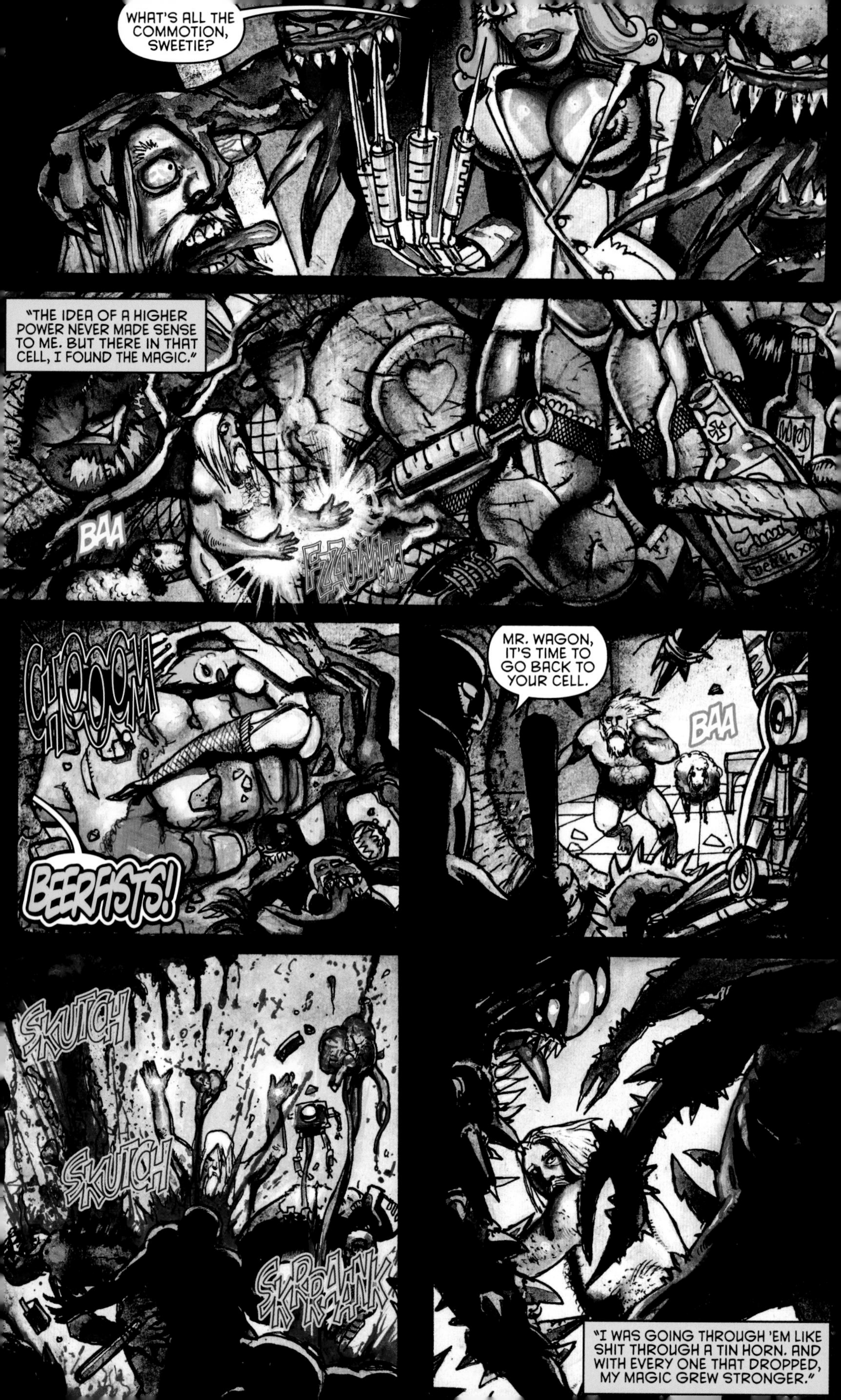
WHAT'S ALL THE COMMOTION, SWEETIE?
"THE IDEA OF A HIGHER POWER NEVER MADE SENSE TO ME. BUT THERE IN THAT CELL, I FOUND THE MAGIC."
BAA
FZZUMMM
CHOOOOM
BEERFISTS!
MR. WAGON, IT'S TIME TO GO BACK TO YOUR CELL.
BAA
SKUTCH
SKUTCH
SKRAANK
"I WAS GOING THROUGH 'EM LIKE SHIT THROUGH A TIN HORN. AND WITH EVERY ONE THAT DROPPED, MY MAGIC GREW STRONGER."

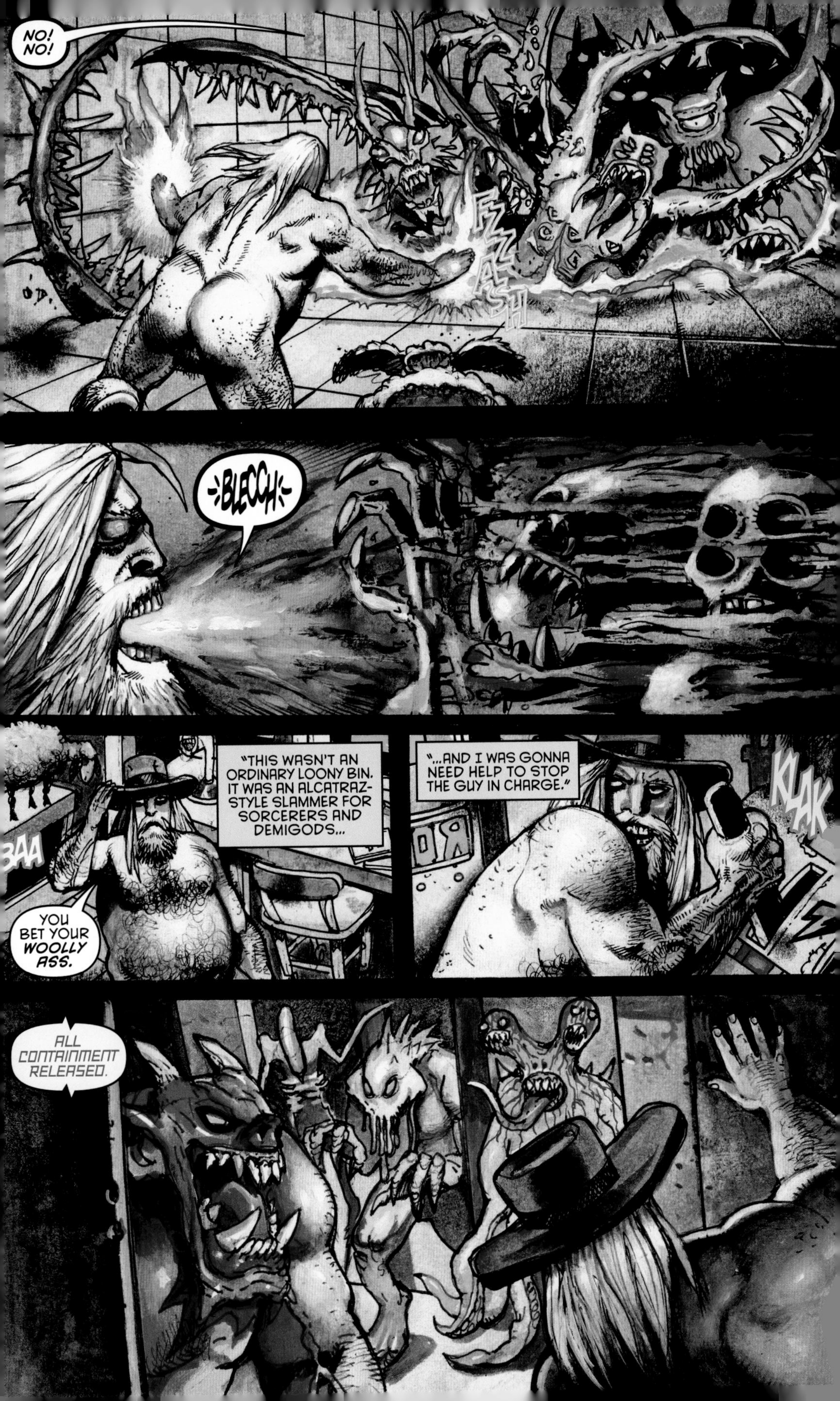
NO! NO!
FZZASH
BLECCH
BAA
"THIS WASN'T AN ORDINARY LOONY BIN. IT WAS AN ALCATRAZ-STYLE SLAMMER FOR SORCERERS AND DEMIGODS...
YOU BET YOUR WOOLLY ASS.
"...AND I WAS GONNA NEED HELP TO STOP THE GUY IN CHARGE."
KLAK
ALL CONTAINMENT RELEASED.

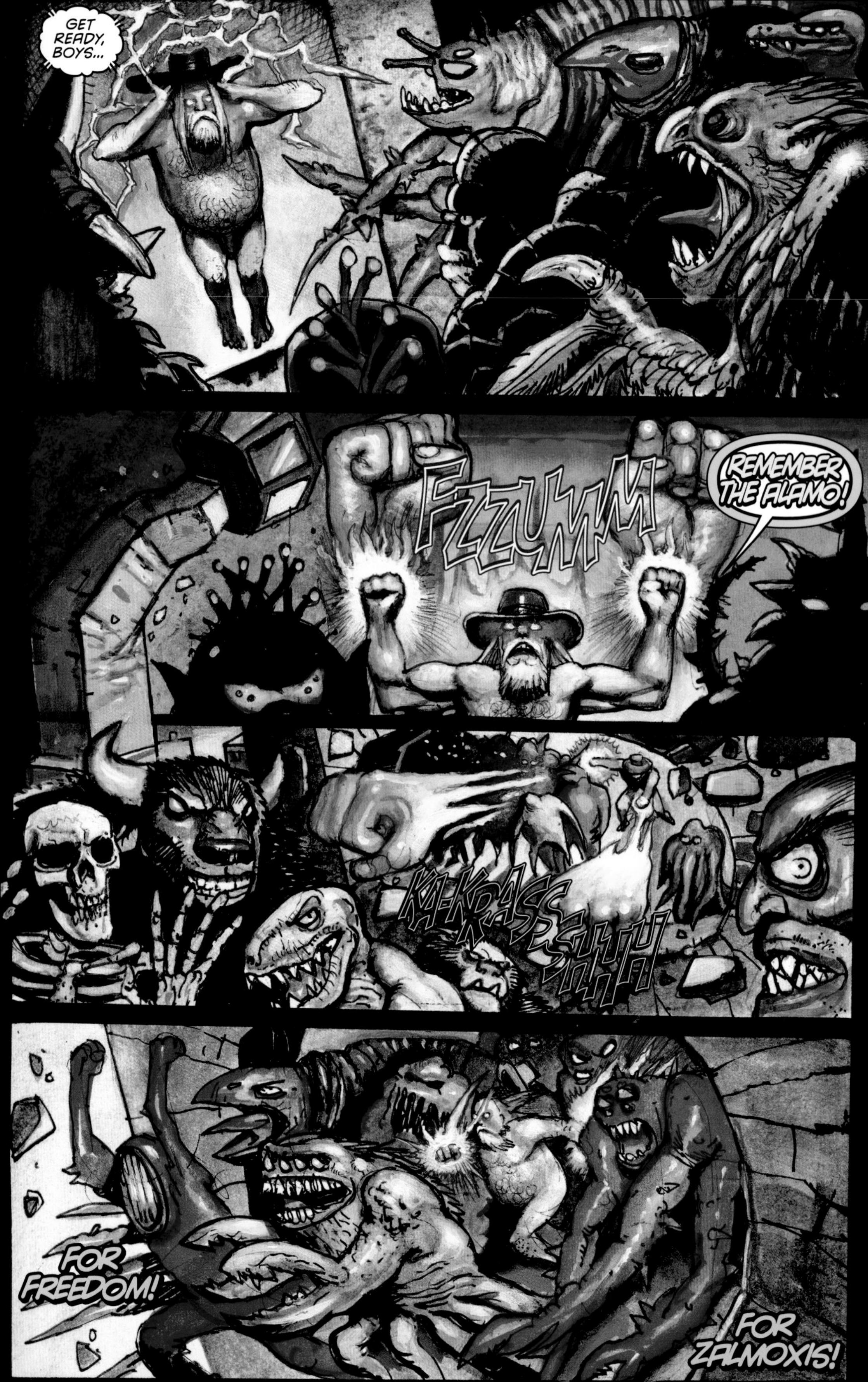
GET READY, BOYS...
FZZUMM
REMEMBER THE ALAMO!
KA-KRASSSHHH
FOR FREEDOM!
FOR ZALMOXIS!

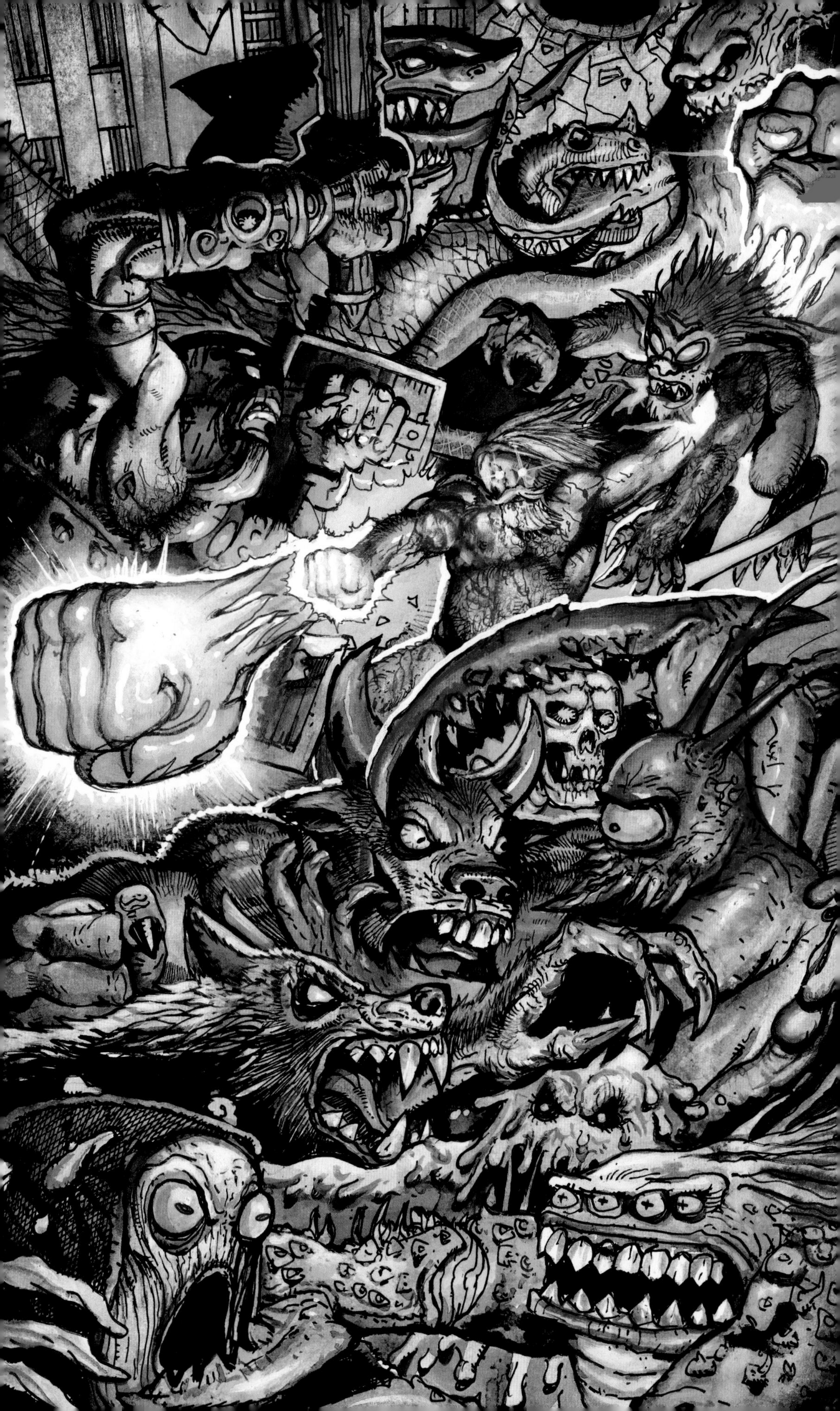

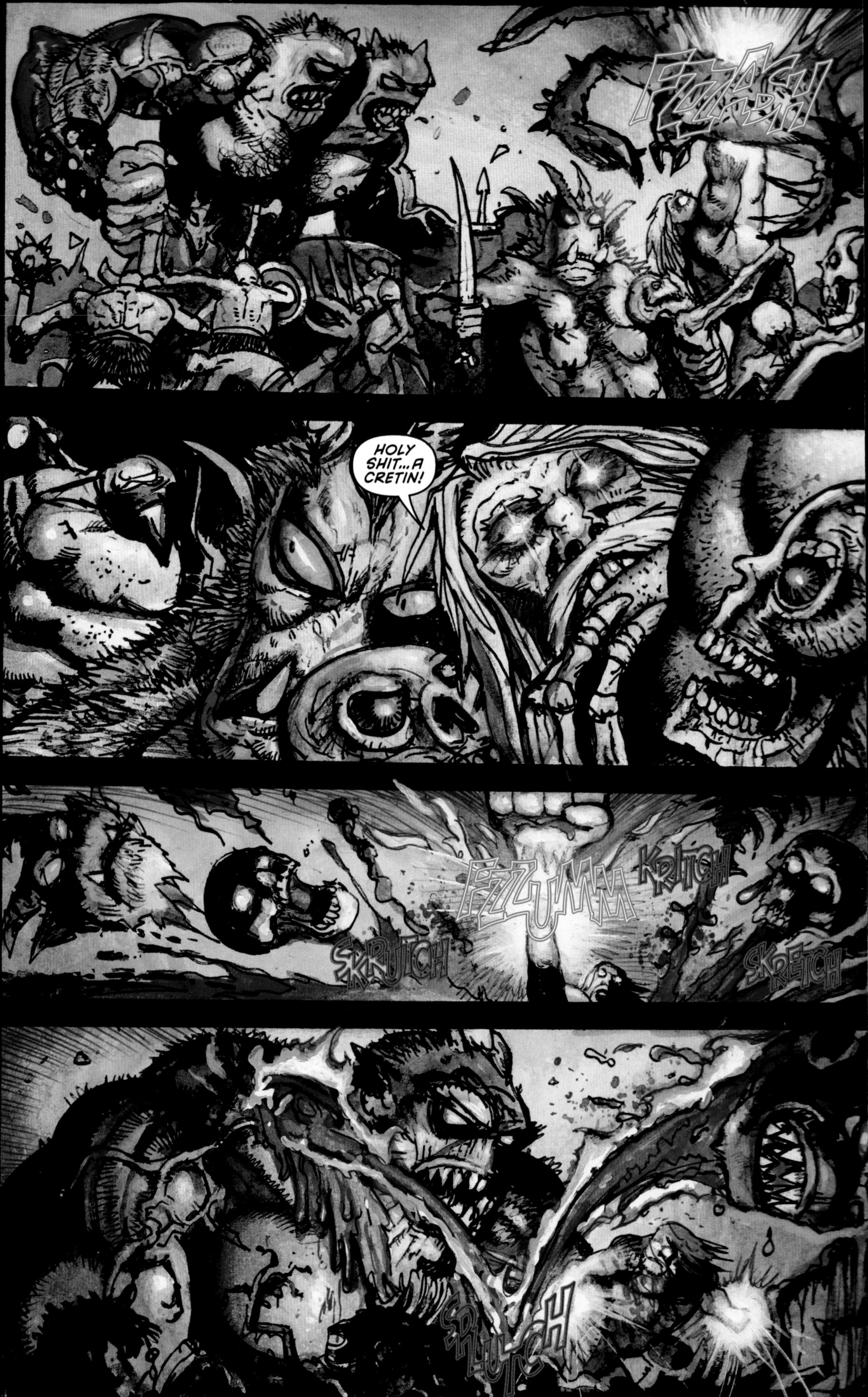
FZZAGH
HOLY SHIT...A CRETIN!
SKRUTCH
FZZUMMM
KRUTCH
SKRETCH
SPLUTCH

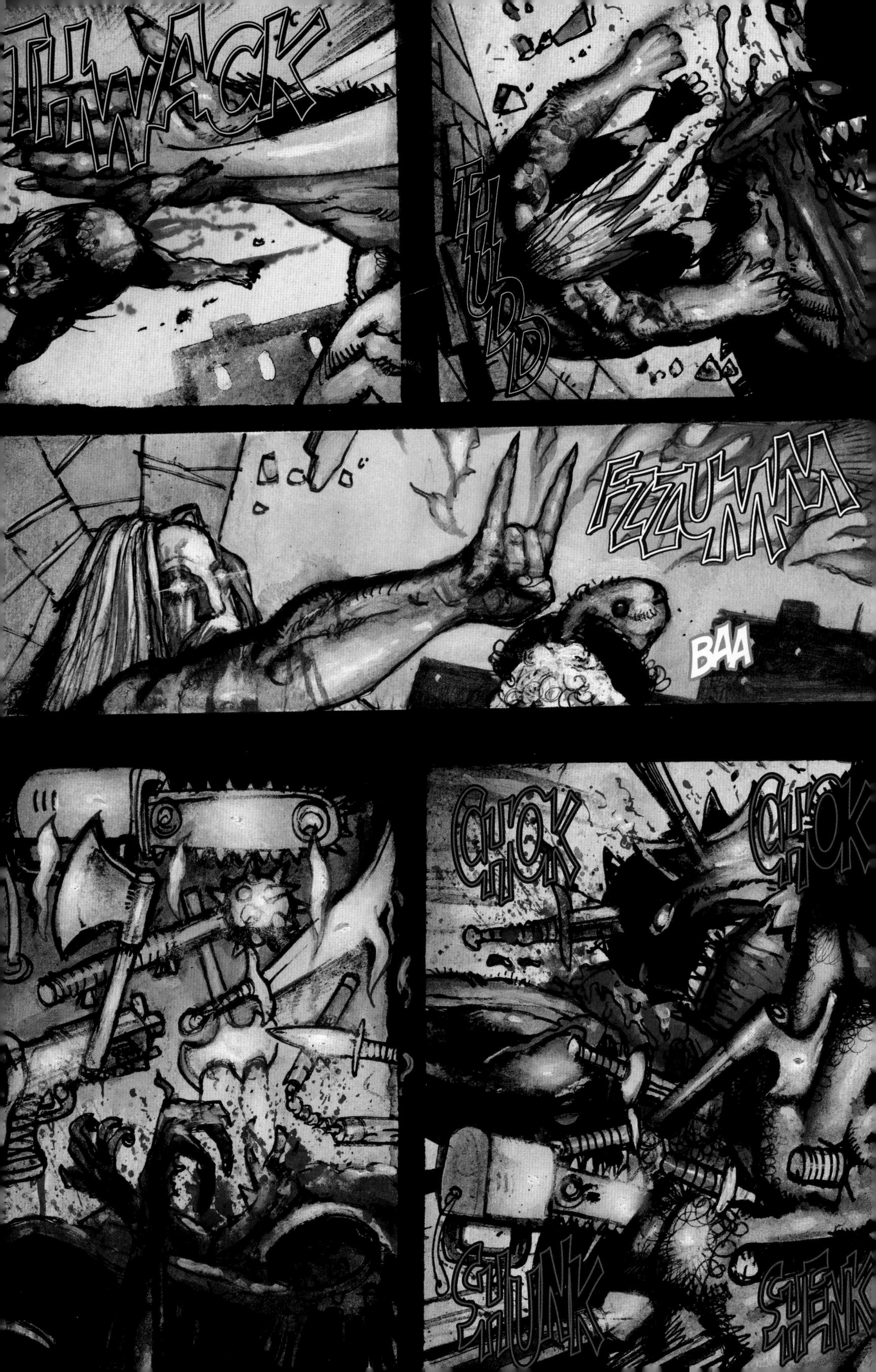
THWACK
THUDD
FZZUMM
BAA
CHOK
CHOK
CHUNK
SHENK

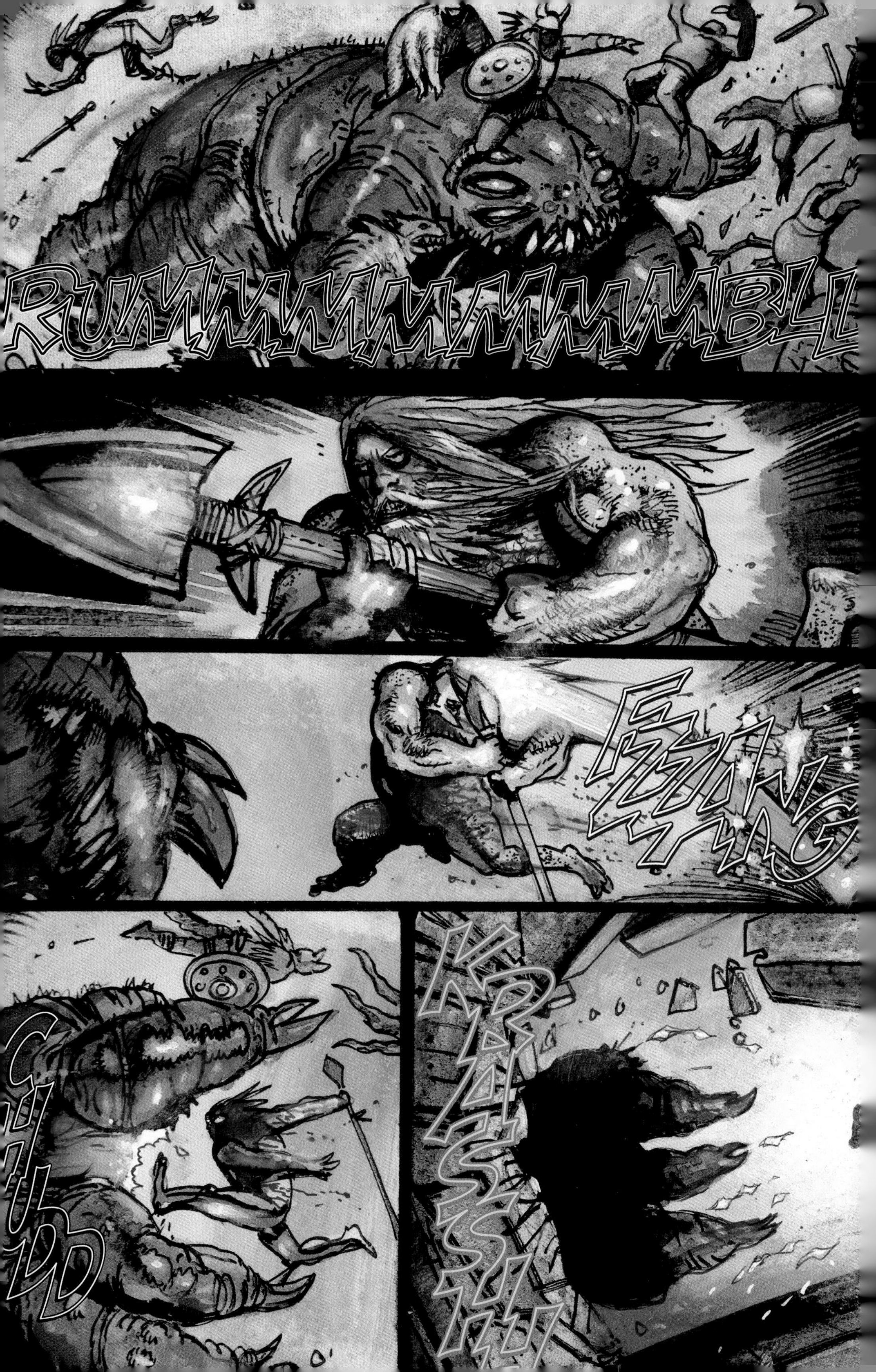
RUMMMMMMMMBLL
FZZANG
CHUDD
KRASSHH

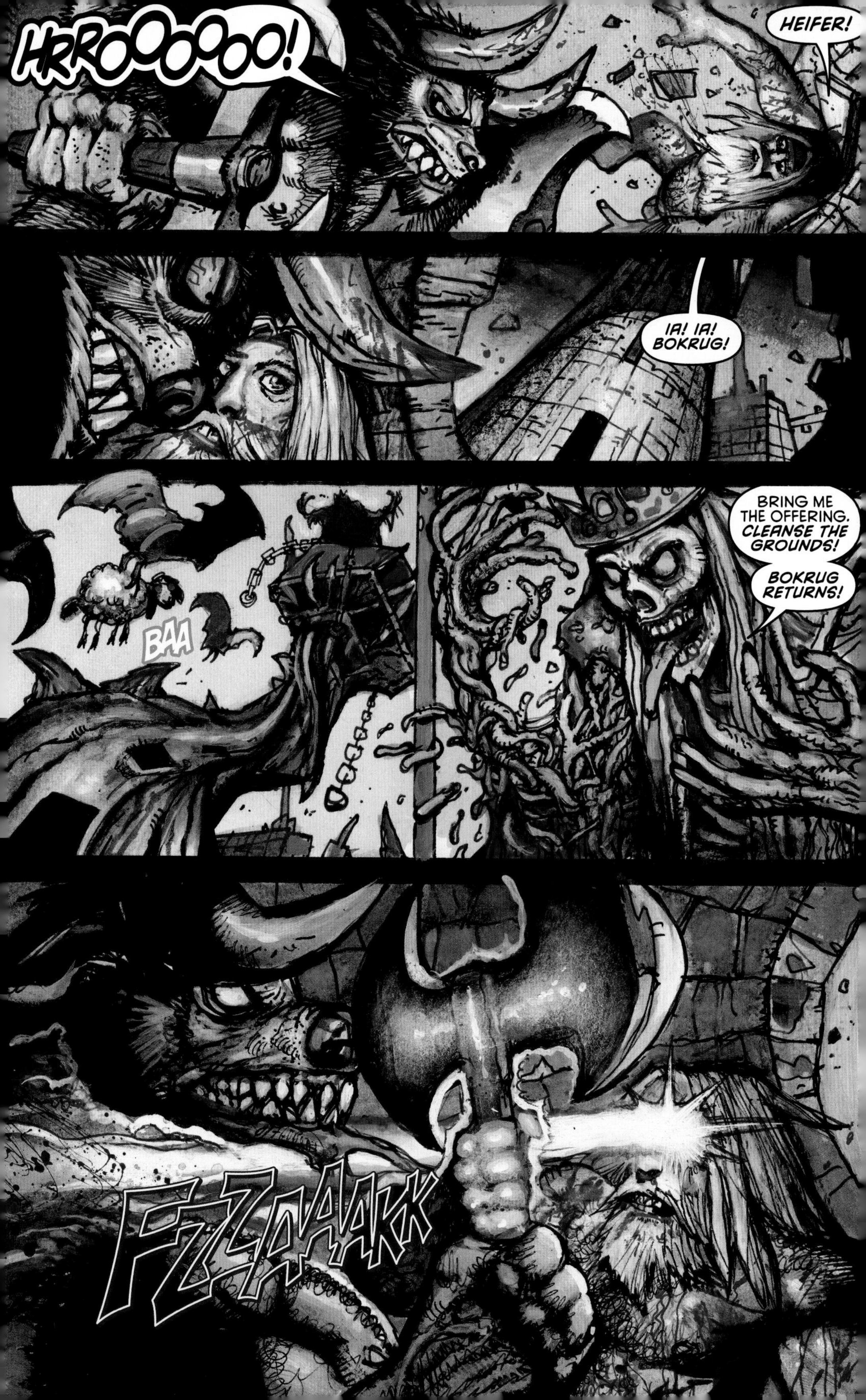
HRROOOOOOO!
HEIFER!
IA! IA! BOKRUG!
BAA
BRING ME THE OFFERING. CLEANSE THE GROUNDS!
BOKRUG RETURNS!
FZZAAAKK

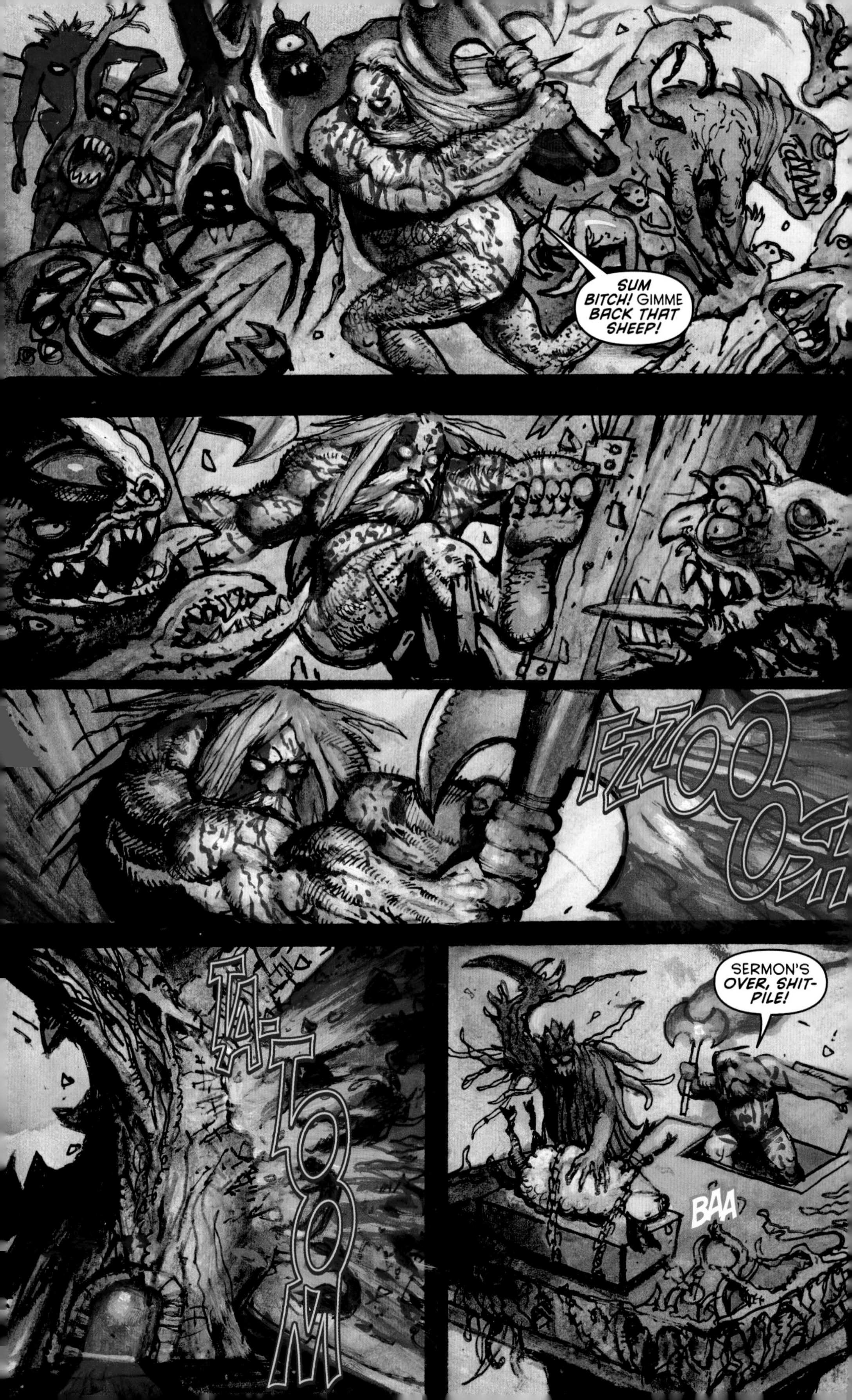
SUM BITCH! GIMME BACK THAT SHEEP!
FZZOOOOOM
TA-TOOOM
SERMON'S OVER, SHIT-PILE!
BAA

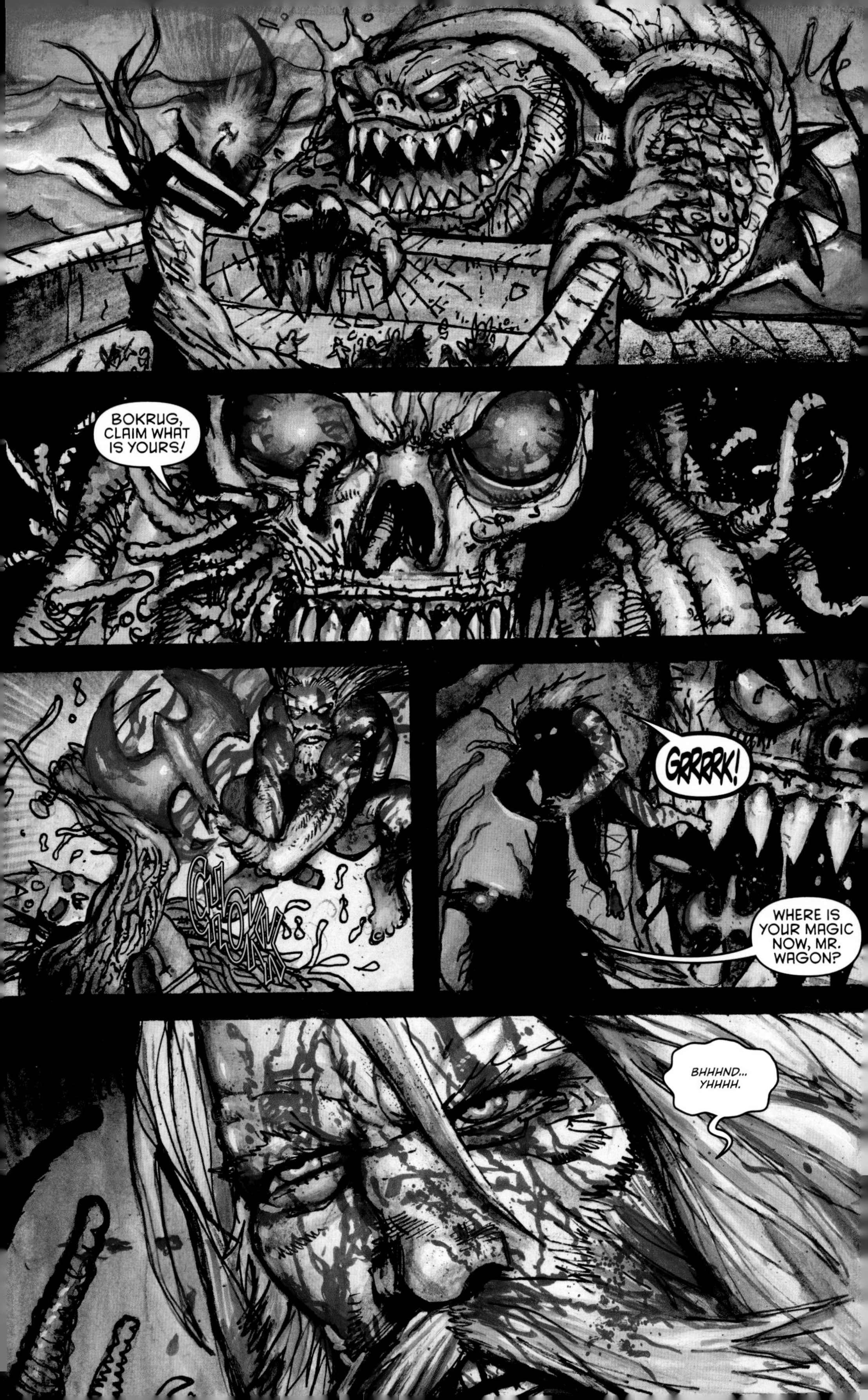
BOKRUG, CLAIM WHAT IS YOURS!
GRRRRK!
WHERE IS YOUR MAGIC NOW, MR. WAGON?
BHHHND... YHHHH.

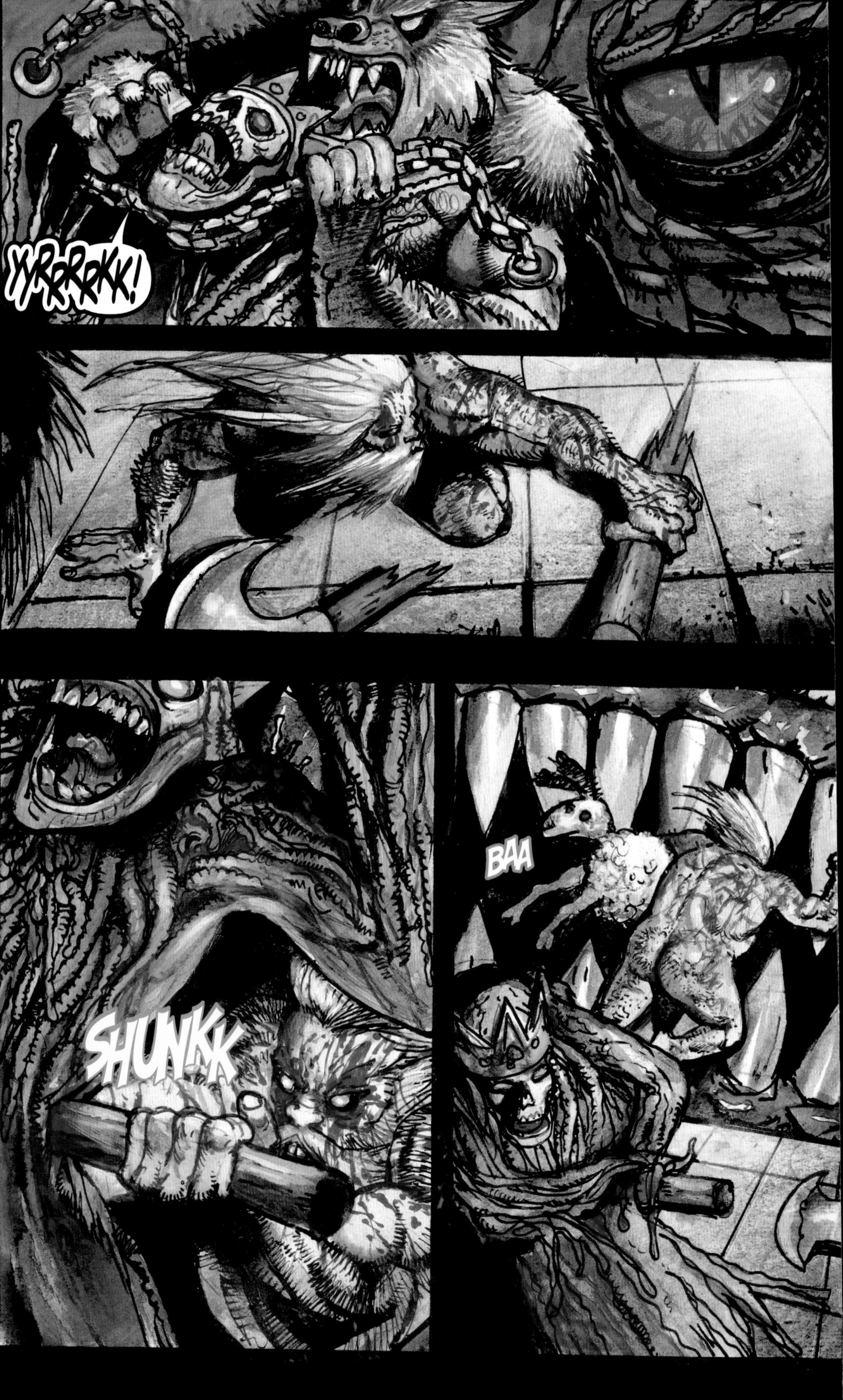
YYRRRRKK!
SHUNKK
BAA

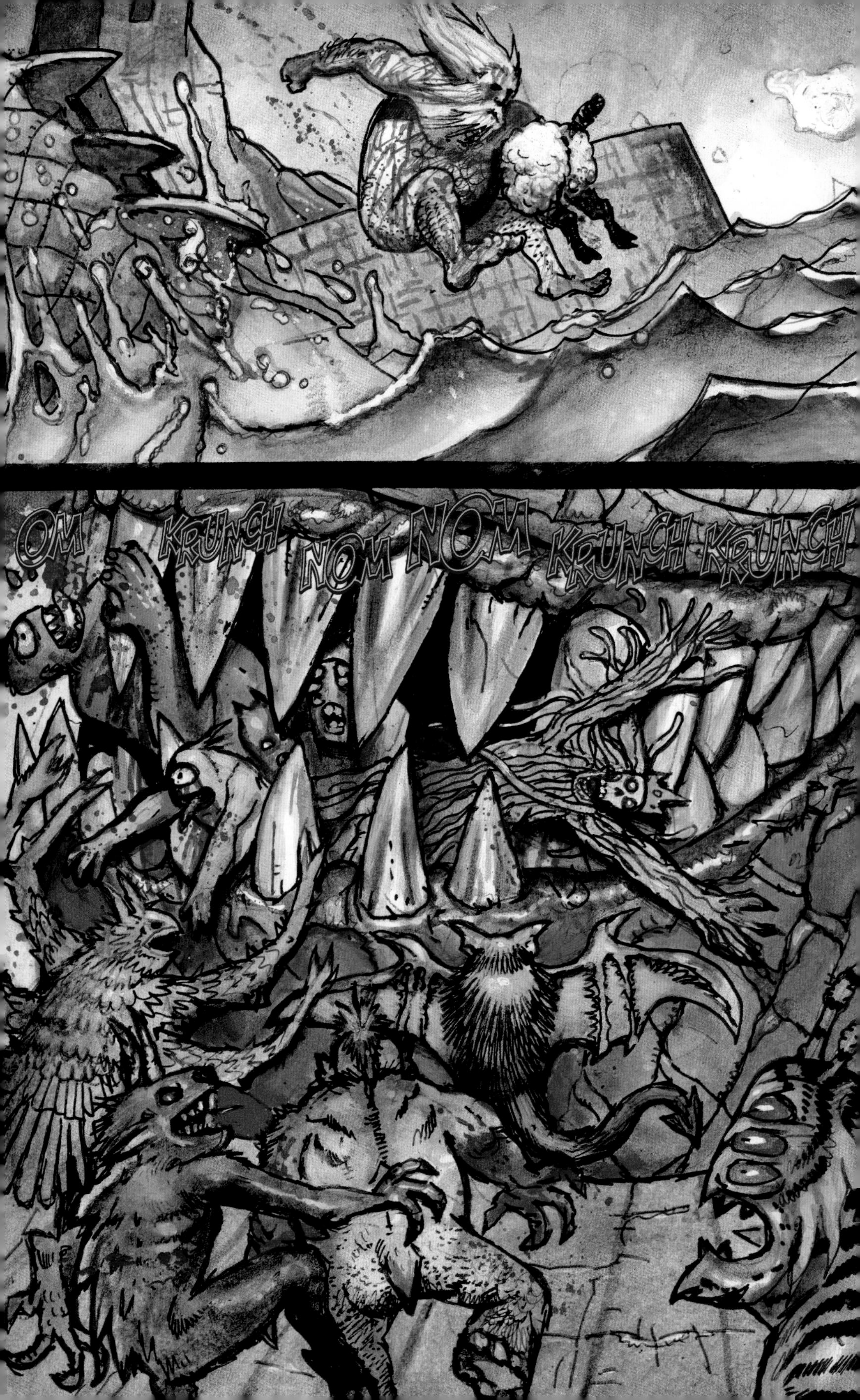
OM
KRUNCH
NOM NOM
KRUNCH
KRUNCH

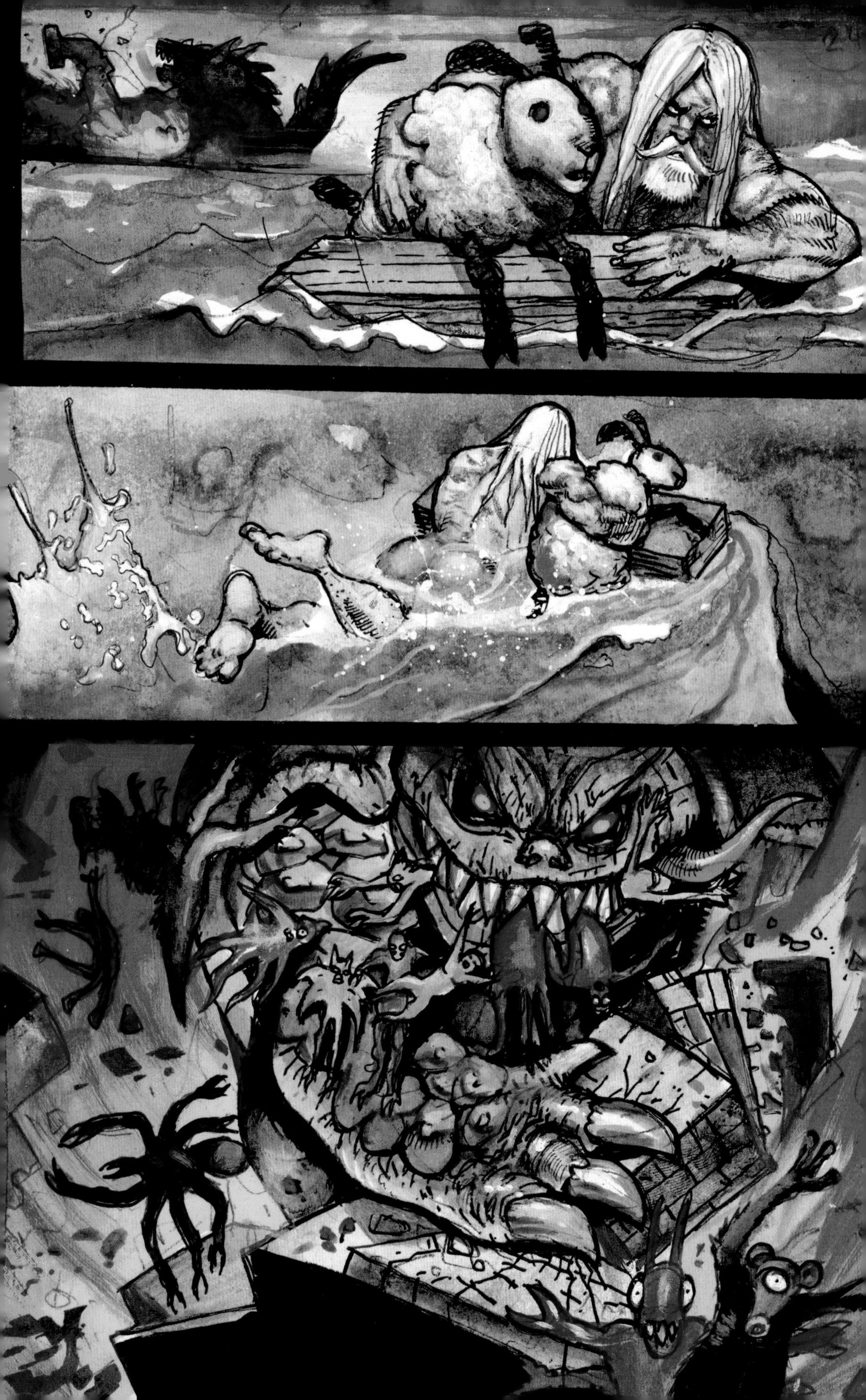

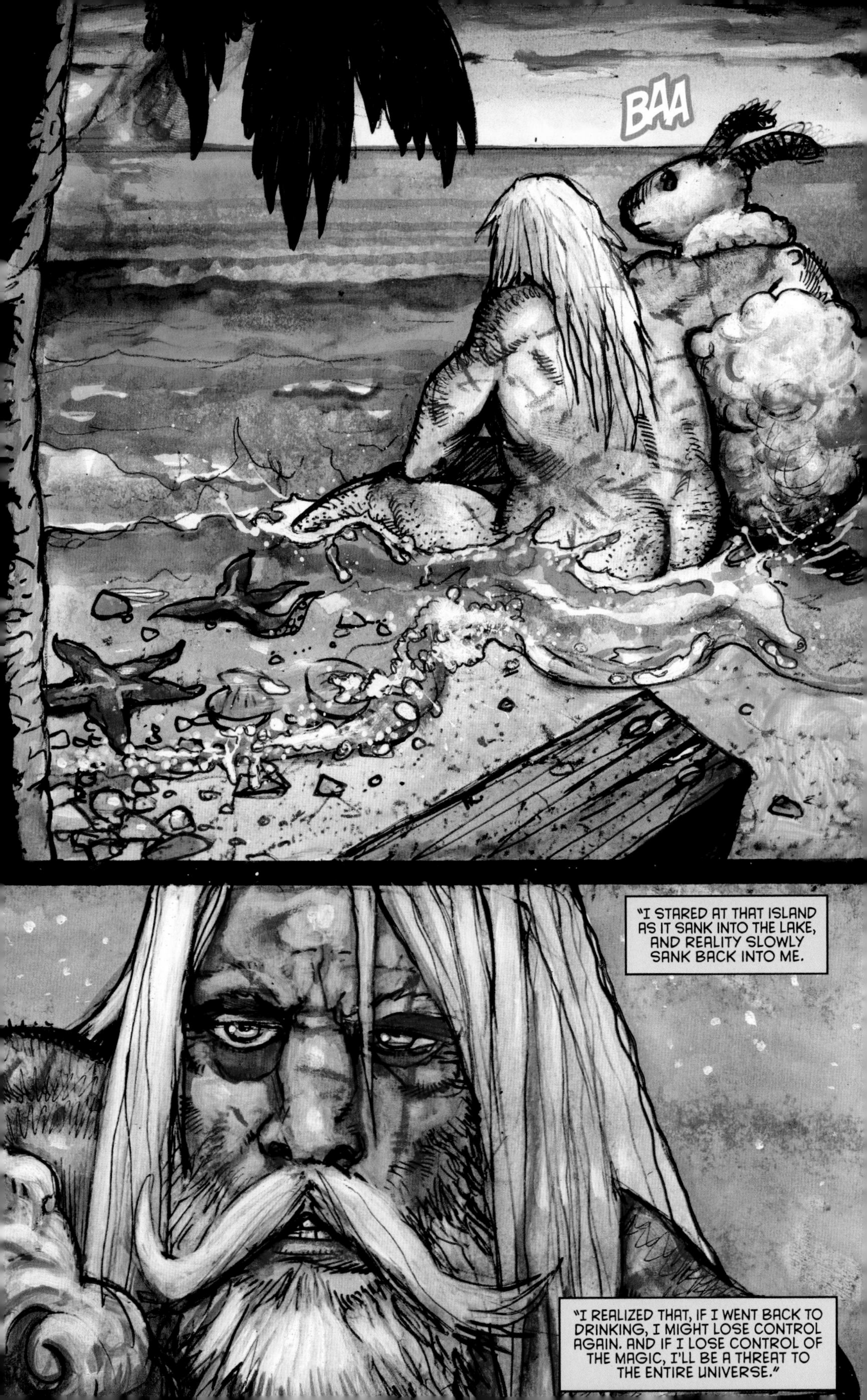
BAA
"I STARED AT THAT ISLAND AS IT SANK INTO THE LAKE, AND REALITY SLOWLY SANK BACK INTO ME.
"I REALIZED THAT, IF I WENT BACK TO DRINKING, I MIGHT LOSE CONTROL AGAIN. AND IF I LOSE CONTROL OF THE MAGIC, I'LL BE A THREAT TO THE ENTIRE UNIVERSE."

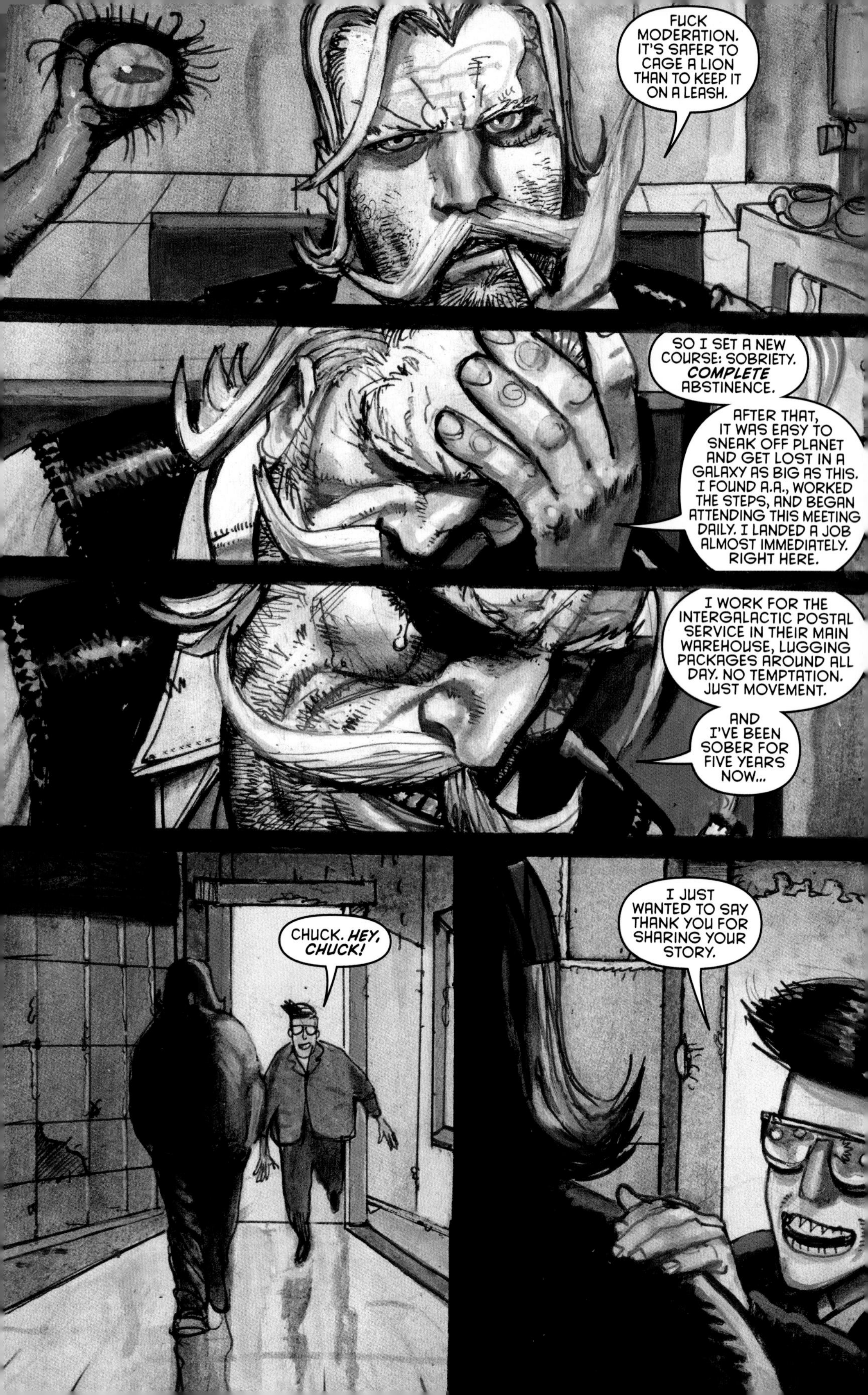
FUCK MODERATION. IT'S SAFER TO CAGE A LION THAN TO KEEP IT ON A LEASH.
SO I SET A NEW COURSE: SOBRIETY. *COMPLETE* ABSTINENCE.
AFTER THAT, IT WAS EASY TO SNEAK OFF PLANET AND GET LOST IN A GALAXY AS BIG AS THIS. I FOUND A.A., WORKED THE STEPS, AND BEGAN ATTENDING THIS MEETING DAILY. I LANDED A JOB ALMOST IMMEDIATELY. RIGHT HERE.
I WORK FOR THE INTERGALACTIC POSTAL SERVICE IN THEIR MAIN WAREHOUSE, LUGGING PACKAGES AROUND ALL DAY. NO TEMPTATION. JUST MOVEMENT.
AND I'VE BEEN SOBER FOR FIVE YEARS NOW...
CHUCK. *HEY, CHUCK!*
I JUST WANTED TO SAY THANK YOU FOR SHARING YOUR STORY.

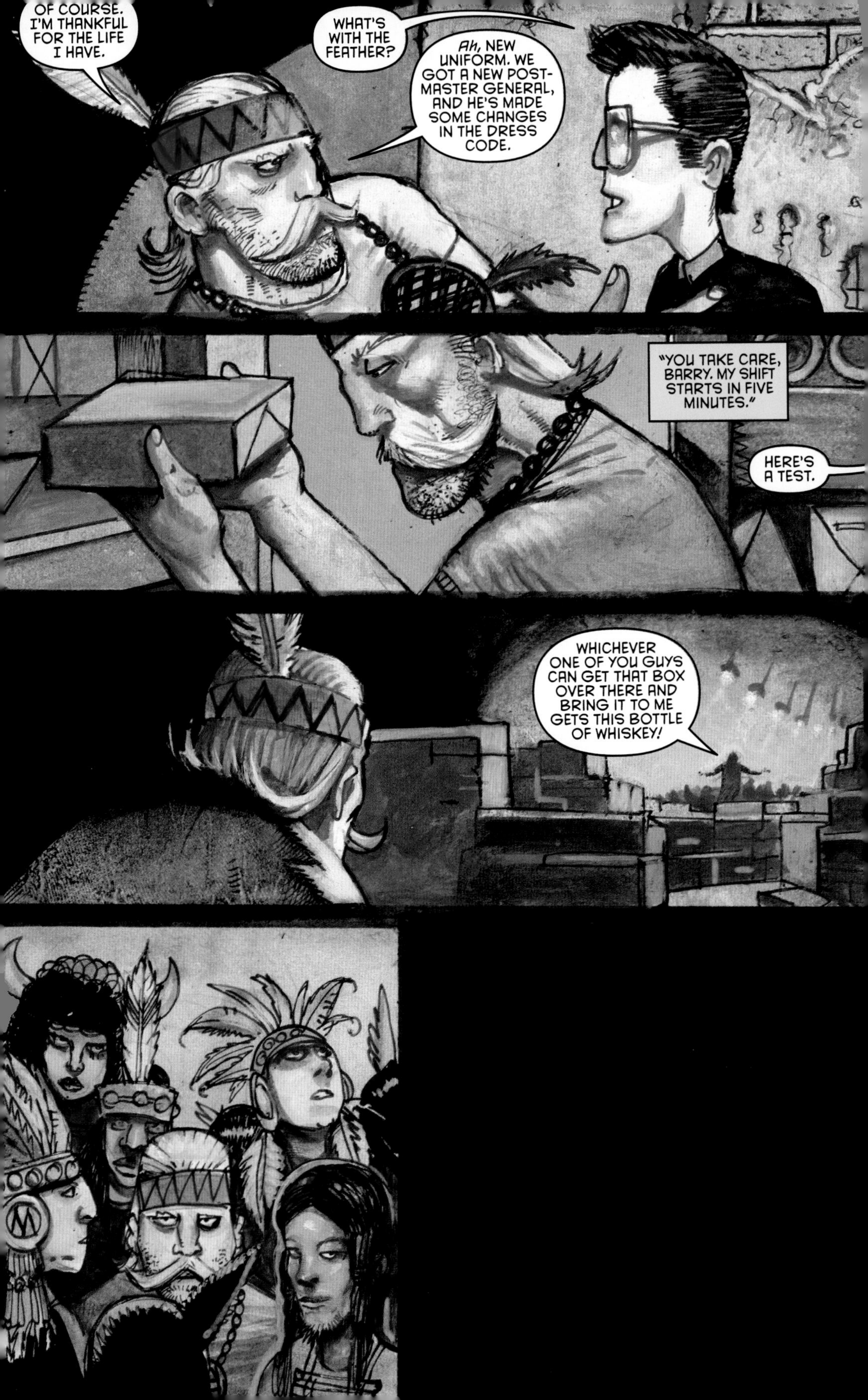
OF COURSE. I'M THANKFUL FOR THE LIFE I HAVE.
WHAT'S WITH THE FEATHER?
Ah, NEW UNIFORM. WE GOT A NEW POST-MASTER GENERAL, AND HE'S MADE SOME CHANGES IN THE DRESS CODE.
"YOU TAKE CARE, BARRY. MY SHIFT STARTS IN FIVE MINUTES."
HERE'S A TEST.
WHICHEVER ONE OF YOU GUYS CAN GET THAT BOX OVER THERE AND BRING IT TO ME GETS THIS BOTTLE OF WHISKEY!

SPACE BASTARDS PRESENTS:
CHUCK "THE MAGIC" WAGON

written by ERIC PETERSON and JOE AUBREY
artwork by SIMON BISLEY lettering by TAYLOR ESPOSITO
created by ERIC PETERSON · JOE AUBREY · DARICK ROBERTSON

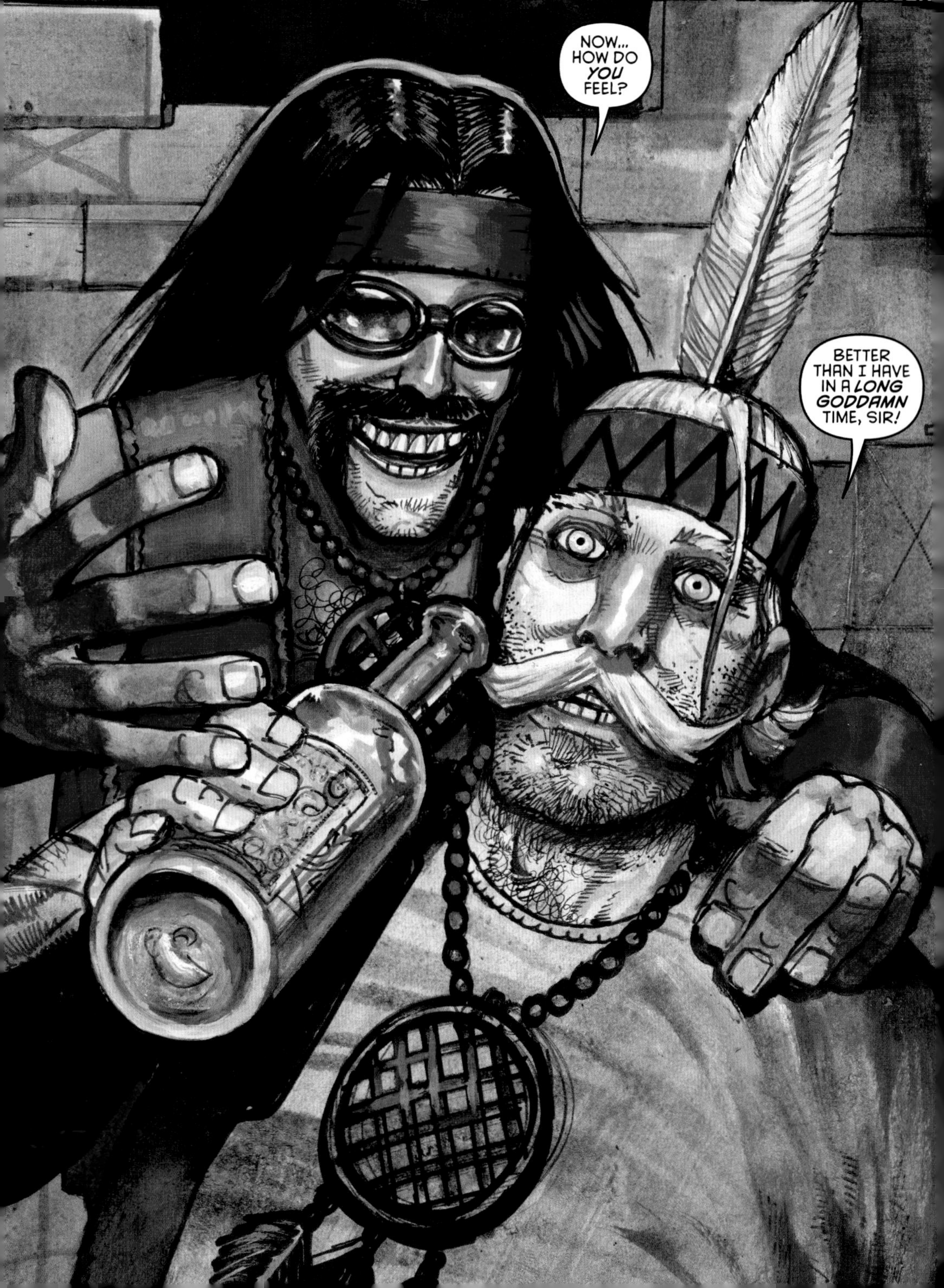
NOW... HOW DO *YOU* FEEL?
BETTER THAN I HAVE IN A *LONG GODDAMN* TIME, SIR!

SPECIAL DELIVERY

BEHIND THE SCENES OF SPACE BASTARDS

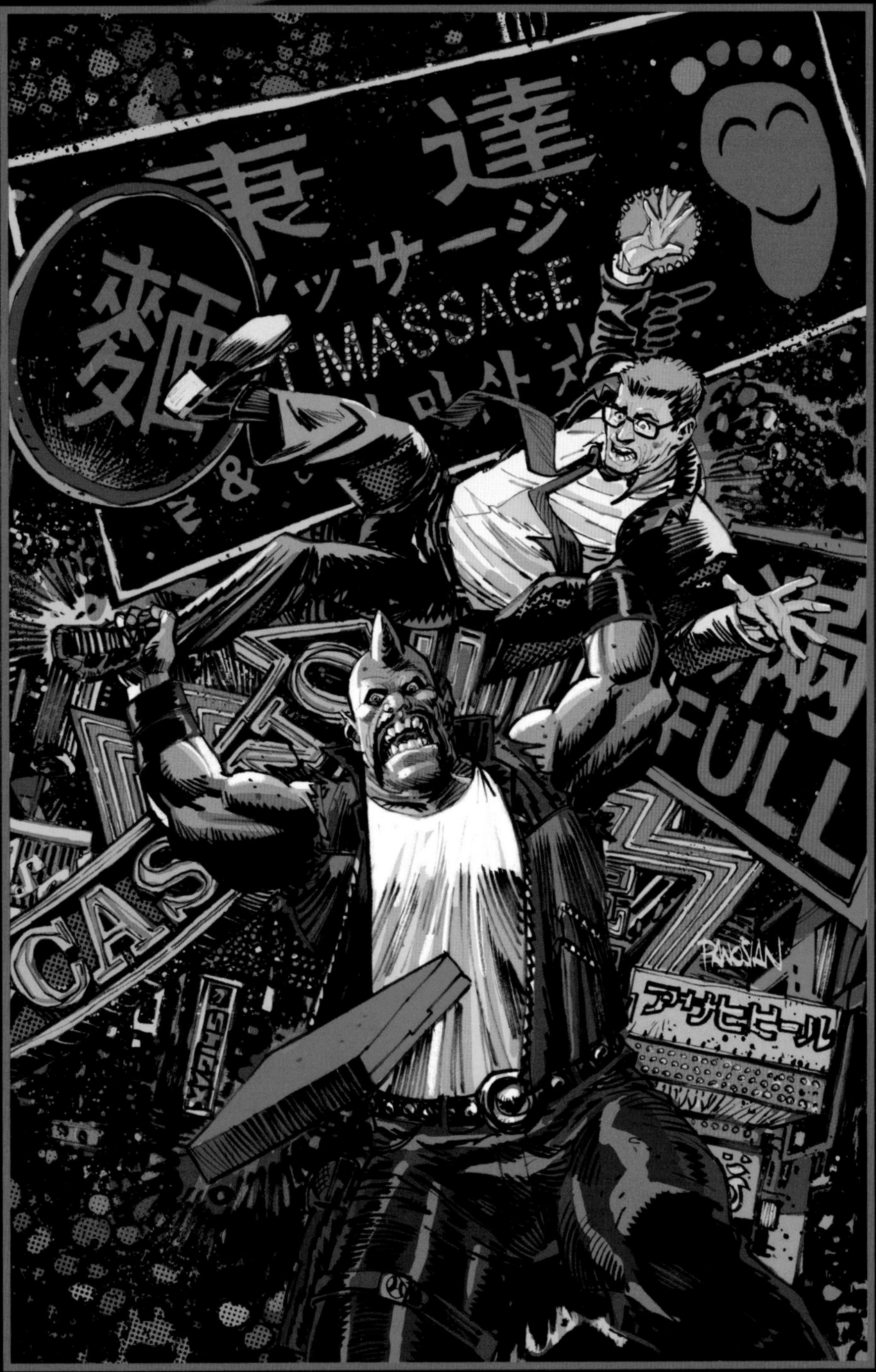
達
ッサージ
MASSAGE
FULL
CAS
PANOSIAN
アサヒビール

Space Bastards #1 Incentive Fluorescent Variant by **Dan Panosian**

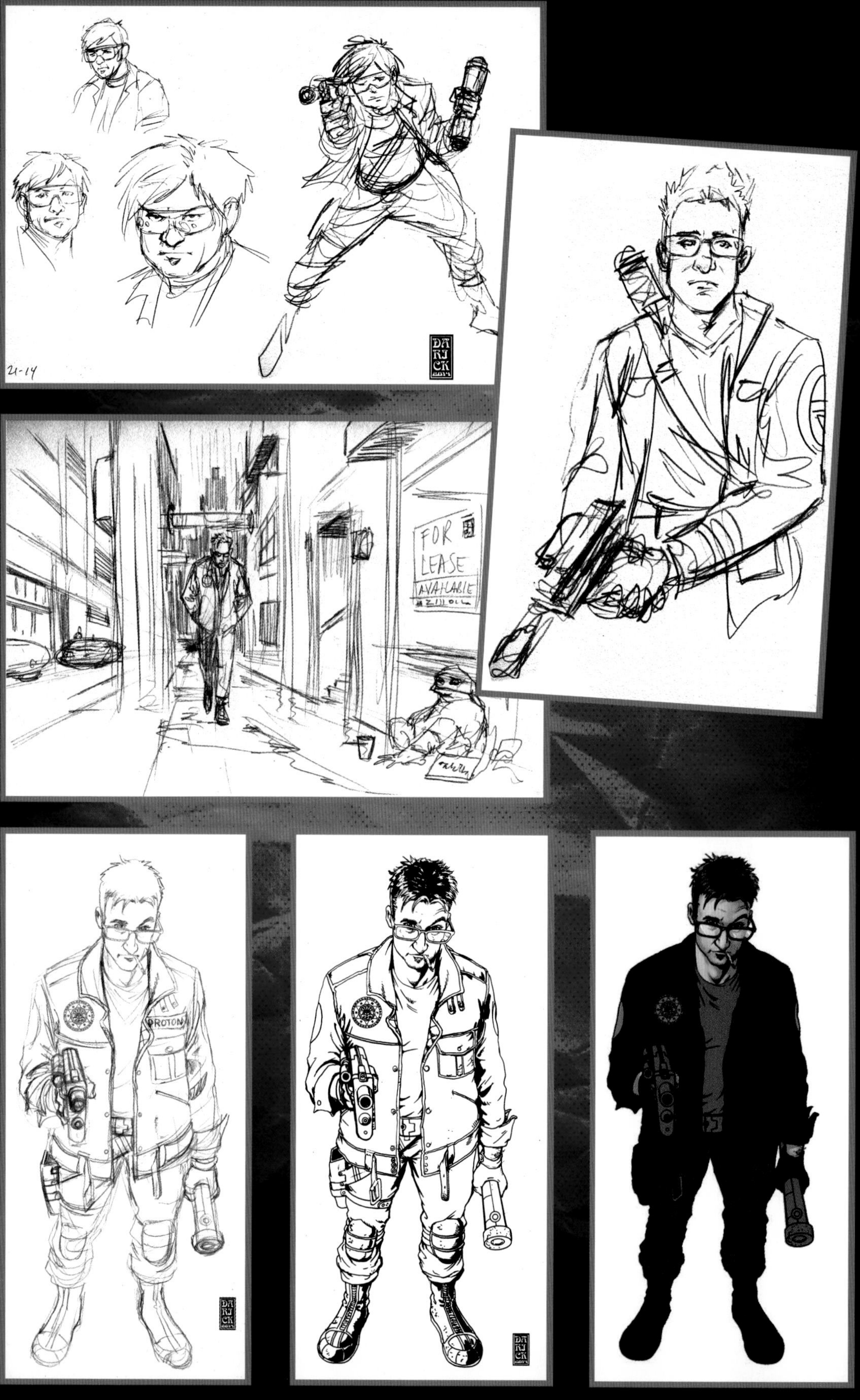
21-14
FOR
LEASE
AVAILABLE
PROTON

Darick's designs for **David S. Proton**

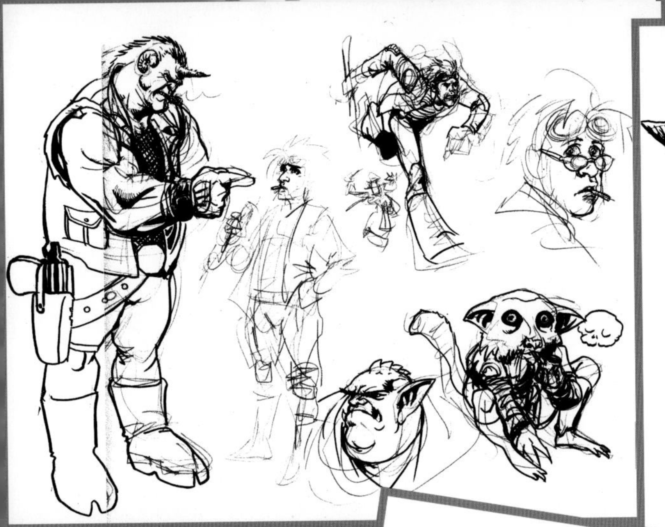
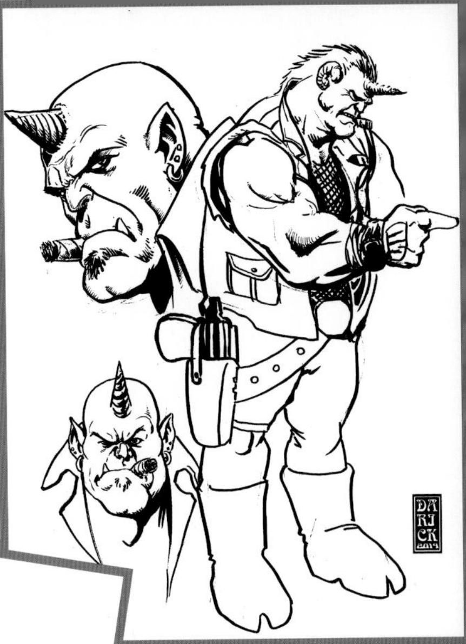
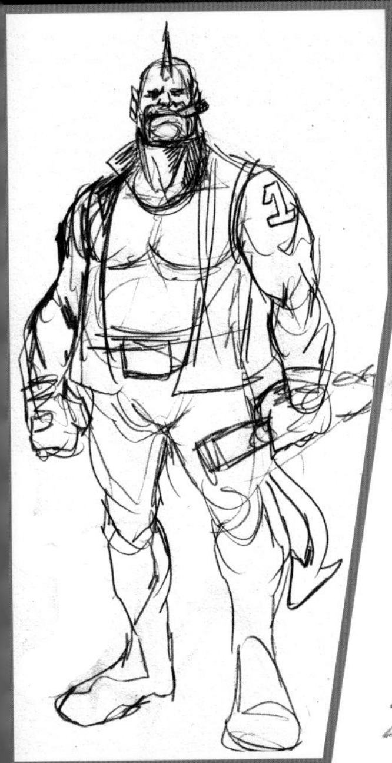
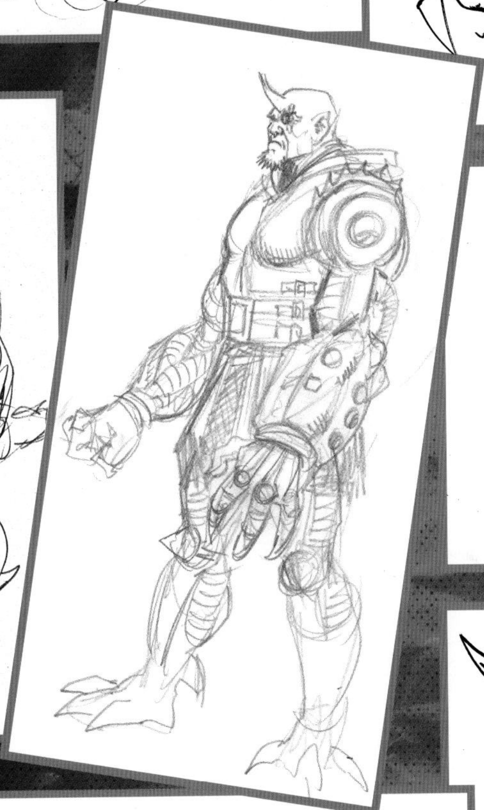
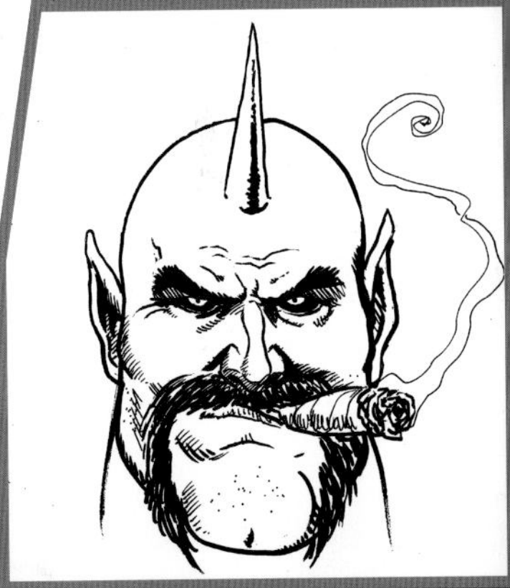
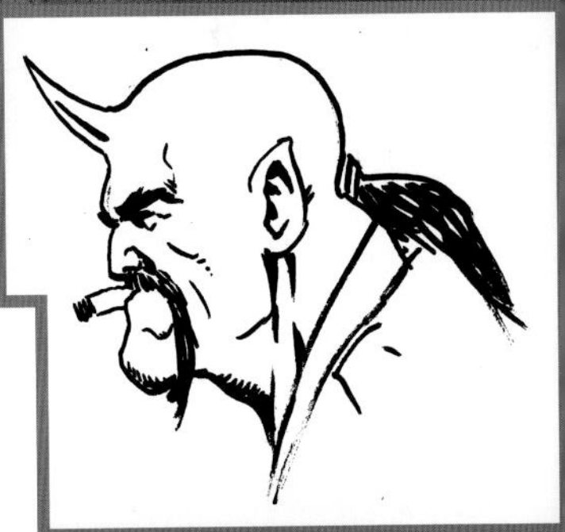
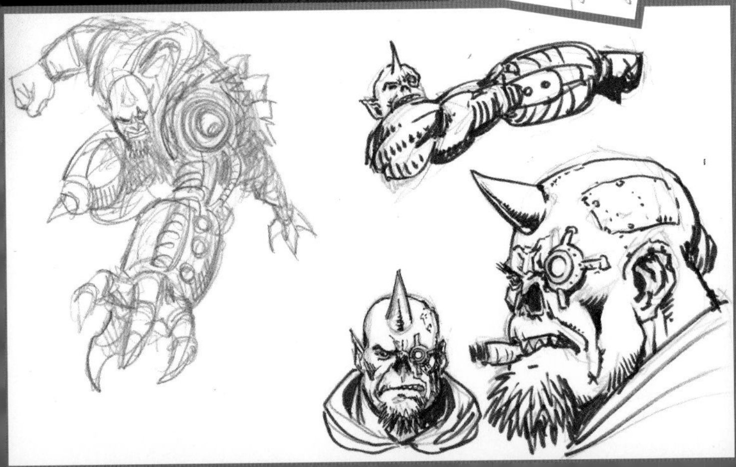

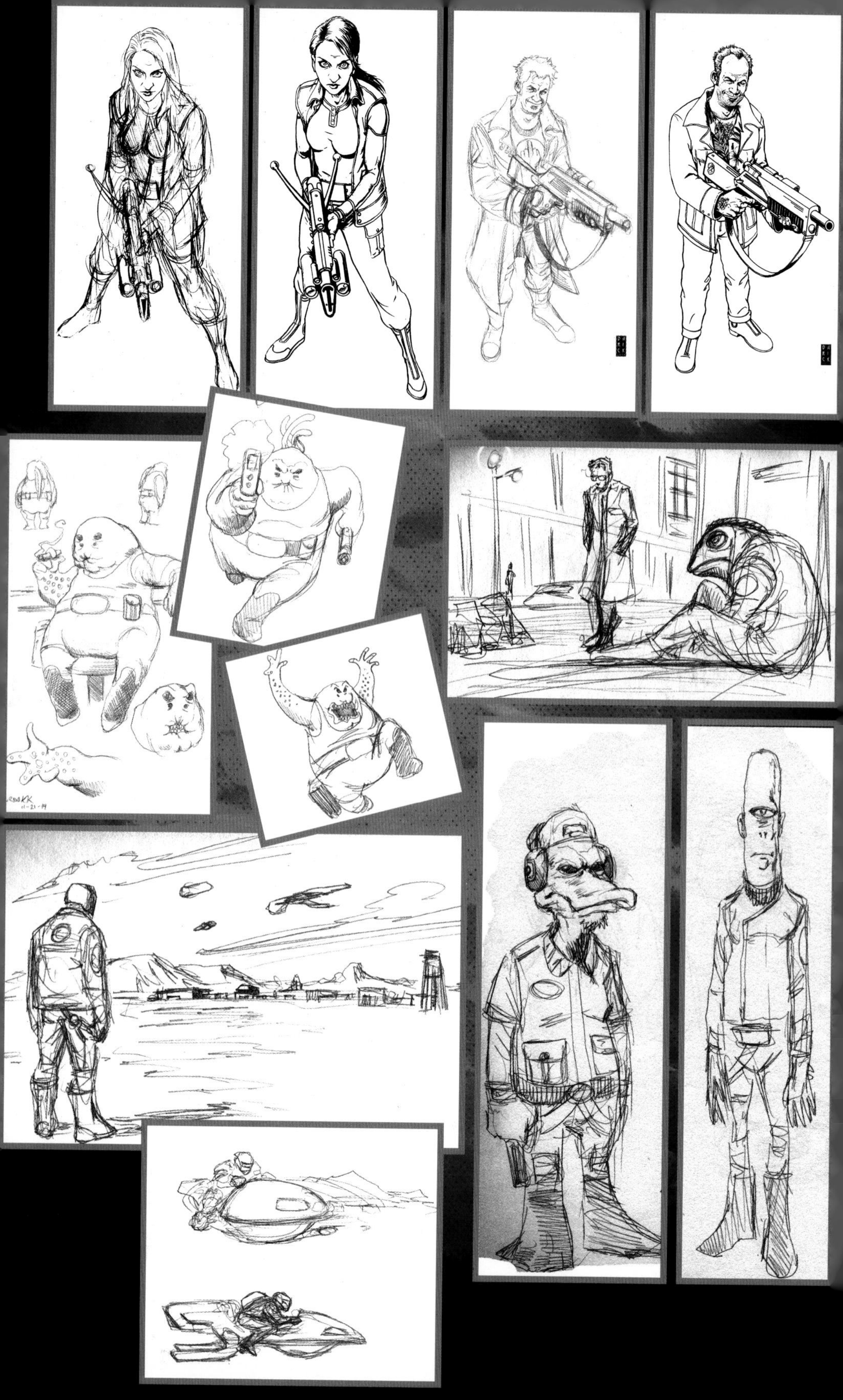

Darick's designs for **Layla Fontane**, **Leroy Palestine**, and **Zardakk** [illegible]

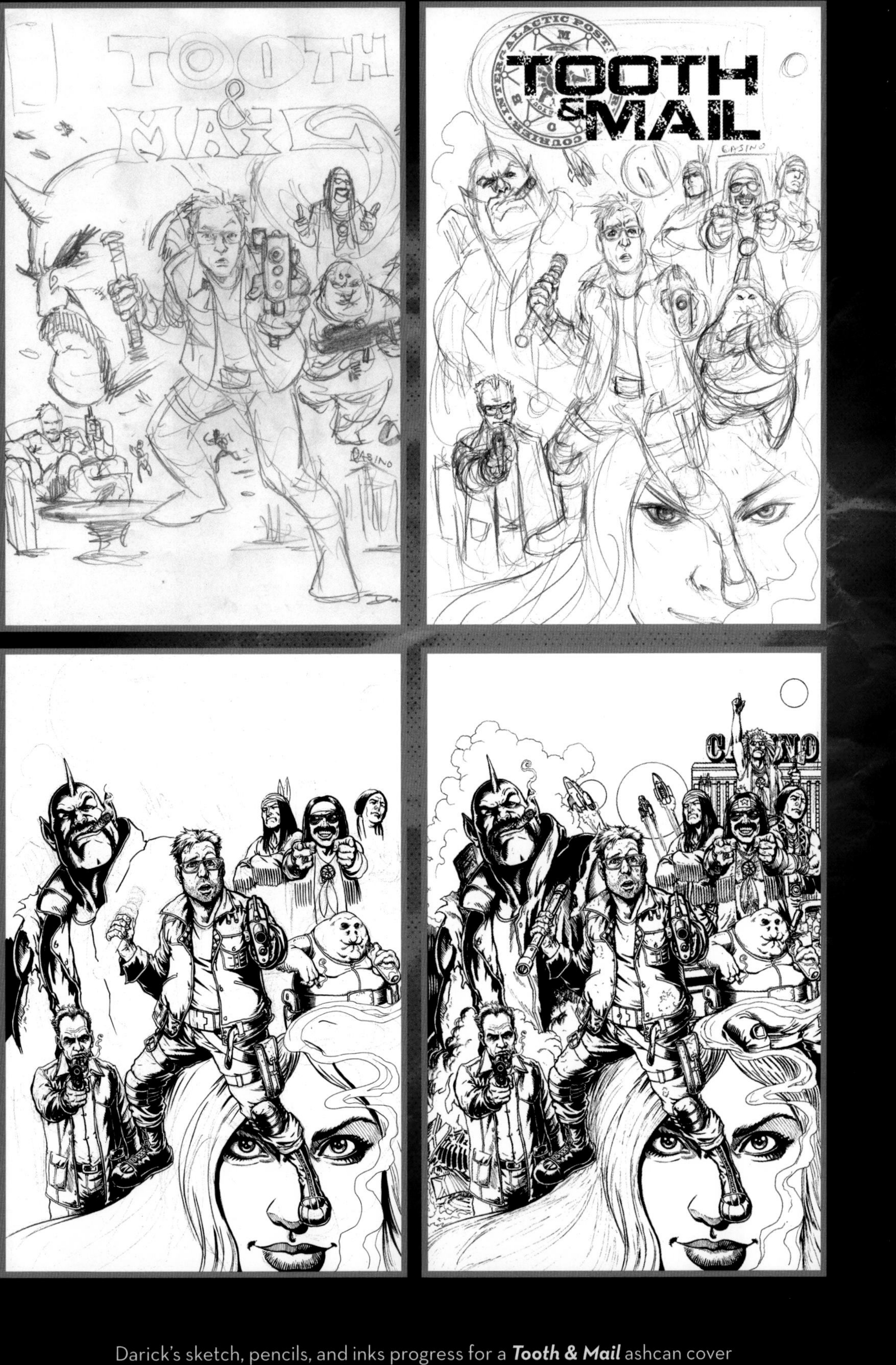
TOOTH & MAIL
CASINO
TOOTH & MAIL
CASINO

Darick's sketch, pencils, and inks progress for a ***Tooth & Mail*** ashcan cover

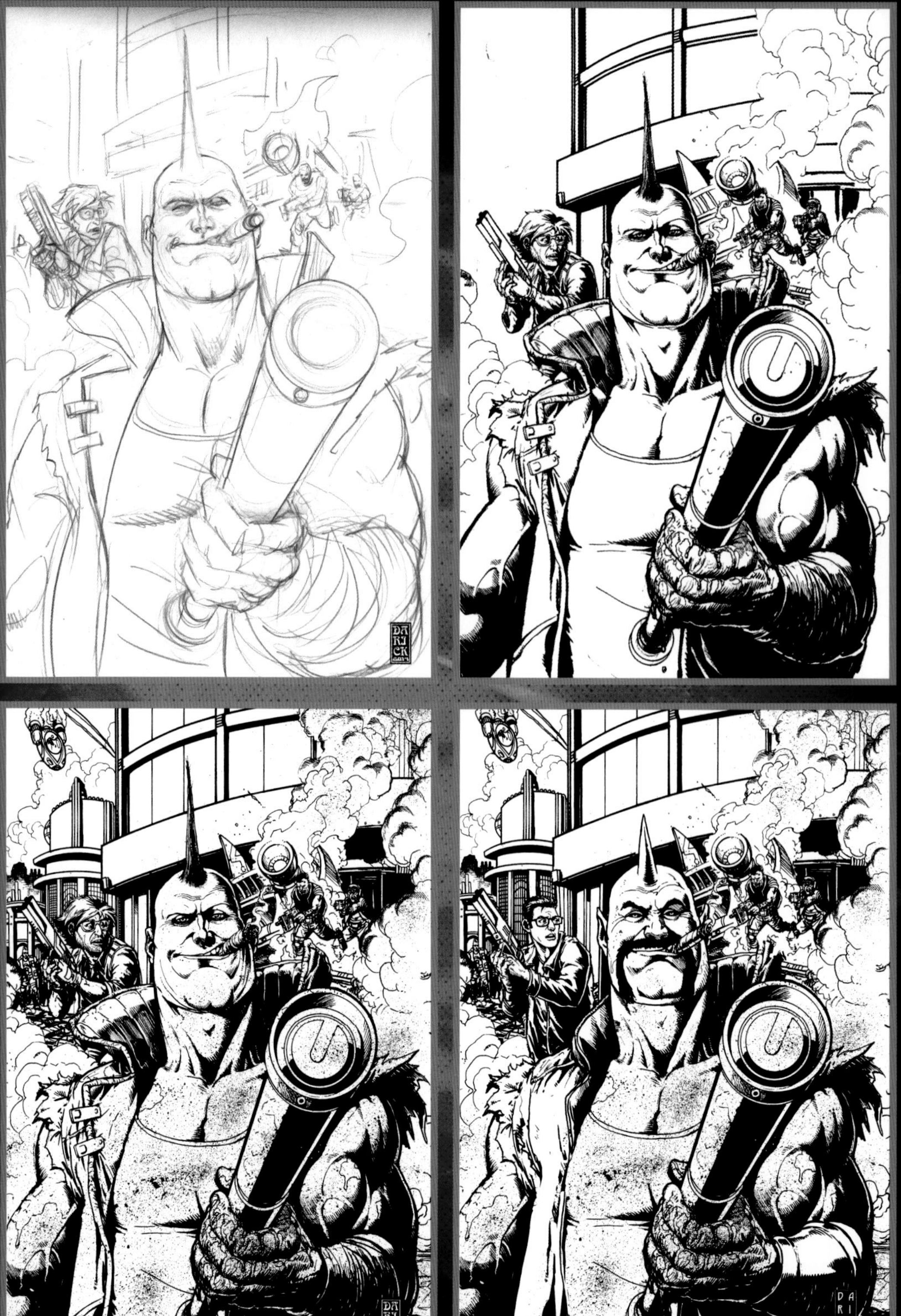

Pencils and inks for Darick's ***Space Bastards #1*** cover, featuring very different looks for

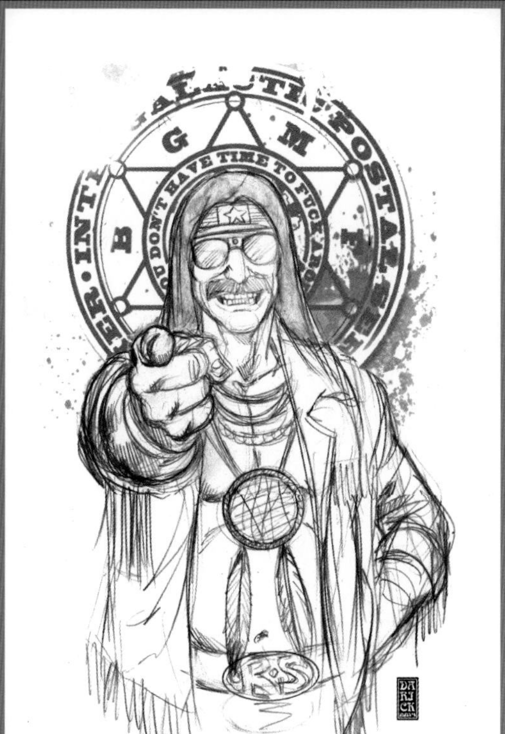

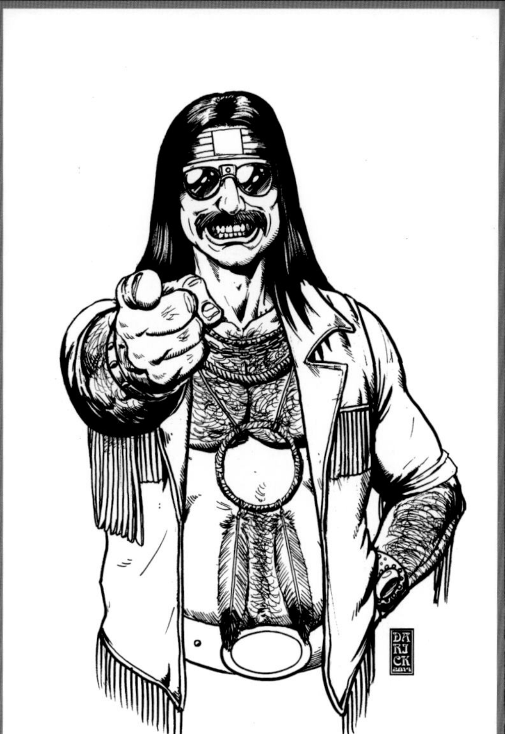

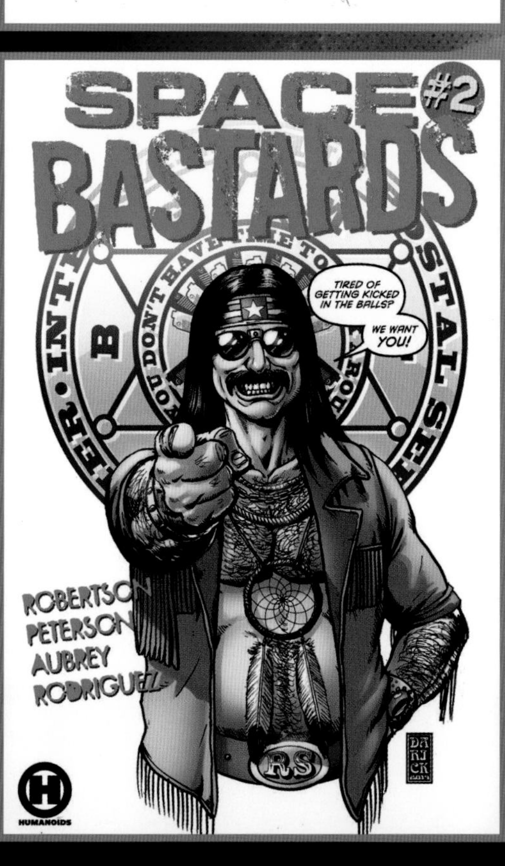
SPACE #2
BASTARDS
TIRED OF GETTING KICKED IN THE BALLS?
WE WANT YOU!
ROBERTSON
PETERSON
AUBREY
RODRIGUEZ
HUMANOIDS

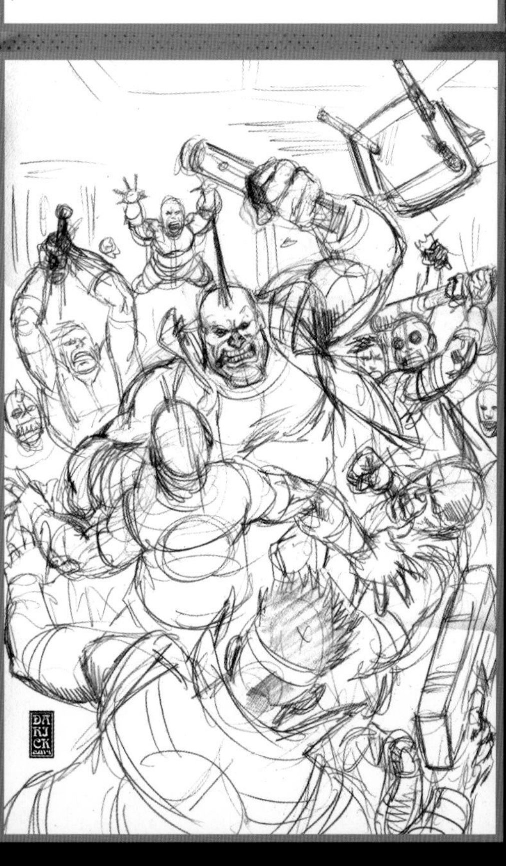

Pencils and inks for Darick's ***Space Bastards* #2** cover, as well as the color version by **Diego Rodriguez** which also features a censored IPS logo; sketches for an alternate take on #3's cover

NEW PAGE

1) Wide - Aerial view of one man running across the top of a skyscraper, with hordes of other men on his tail. The man in front is Davey Proton, several months after issue 1. He should look more settled in. In fact, he is rocking this shit (as we'll soon see). But this should evoke Indy running with the natives hot on his ass.

2) Wide. Straight on shot. We see Davey, package in his hand, eyes wide and his face filled with adrenaline, running right towards us. Behind him we see twelve or so postal workers running after him, firing guns.

3) Medium. Davey slams on the brakes as an alien with an elephant head appears at the end of the skyscraper's roof (with a jetpack), with a plasma-gun pointed at Davey. NOTE: Plasmagun should be like a flamethrower, but with a wider nozzle. Shoots "Godzilla breath."

                EPHANT MAN
    End of the fucking line, proton.

4) Medium. Davey takes a few steps back from the ledge. He's smiling, posed like he's about to jump.

                DAVEY PROTON
    You want this package? This one
    right here?

5) Wide. A business board room, with wall length glass windows. A bunch of guys in some shareholders meeting. Through the huge glass windows we can see the building across the way is just slightly higher. We see vaguely in that space out there Davey tackling the jetpack man in mid-air and the two of them flying towards us. The plasmathrower is engaged, but Davey is pushing the jetpack guy's hands upward. So the two of them are twisting toward the board room, leaving a spiraling fiery trail, one end from the jetpack exhaust and the other from the plasmathrower. Behind them, on the roof, is the row of other mailmen all halted at the edge.

                BUSINESS MAN
        there is increasing demand for our
        products on Betelgeuse IV.
        Profits will continue to climb as
        we improve our margins...

NEW PAGE

1 - Huge. Sideways view of the board room. Davey and the flamethrower Elephant Man careen through the glass, and onto the conference table, which is knocked off kilter.

The business men are out of their seats, completely surprised.

                BUSINESS MAN
    -- the fuck?!

2 - Medium. Davey picks himself up. The elephant man's head is in the foreground, on fire. Davey is covered in glass splinters. One wall has caught fire along with the carpet and some fake plants in the corner.

3 - Medium. Davey turns to face one of the board members, extending the package. The board member looks horrified, but reaches out to "sign" for the package.

                DAVEY PROTON
    Package -- *hnnh* -- for mr. Zoon.

                SOUND EFFECT
    Parcel delivered. Thank you.

4 - Wide. Davey walks through the indoor lobby on the ground floor, completely dirty. Completely smug.

                DAVEY PROTON
    Sixty-five thousand credits. Time
    for some new engines...

NEW PAGE

1 - Wide, almost. The whole building explodes. In the foreground is a silhouette of a large familiar character with a lone spoke of bone jutting from the top of his bulbous head. He's holding a detonator with his thumb pressed on the trigger.

                SOUND EFFECT
    Ba-boom!

2 - Small. Manicorn in full view, smiling. Detonator, depressed, in frame.

                MANICORN
    Eat shit, proton.

3 - Wide. A weasely looking HR guy (white) in glasses wearing Native American regalia sits in a room filled with other similarly dressed personnel. He is holding a datapad handed to him from a brunette big-breasted alien assistant and speaking to another HR guy in Native American regalia.

                JERRY
    Thanks, tiff. Allllrighty. Mark?
    Looks like one of the boys got a
    bit too overzealous again.
        (MORE)

                JERRY (CONT'D)
    Heavy collateral damage, multiple
    casualties, and the package was
    already delivered. Not in play.

                MARK
      (typing into a computer)
    You got it, jerry. Sending him to
    time out.

4 - Medium. Manicorn walks down a street with a big machine gun over his shoulder. Cigar in mouth. Smiling. Peacocking. He's in a great mood. He speaks into his bracelet.

                MANICORN
    All right. time to get back to
    work.

                BRACELET
    Login declined.

                MANICORN
    Fuck you. Retry.

5 - Medium. Close-up of Manicorn's face. One eye is twitching.

                BRACELET (O.S.)
    Login declined. Account
    suspended.

6 - Wide. Roll credits.

                TITLE
    Issue 3. Manicorn's day off.

NEW PAGE

1 - Wide. Roy's compound exterior. Log cabin that we saw him in at the end of issue 2. It's next to the wildlife resort, casino, and postal HQ.

                LAYLA V (O.S.)
    Sir? Do you have any statement
    you wish to make about the
    bombing?

2 - Wide. Inside. Roy is shooting with an elephant gun (complete with targeting reticle propped up) at a cardboard cut out of "ancient Indian enemies" (Davey Crocket, other Alamo guys). He is missing quite frequently. He is wearing his typical Native American regalia. There are holes everywhere.

His alien assistant (Layla V, named after his original assistant) from the first and last pages of issue 2 is present. The large rare companion animal of Roy's (seen in previous issues) sleeps in the corner of the room.

                ROY SHARPTON
    What? no. Jesus christ, no.

                LAYLA V
    Are you sure, sir?

                ROY SHARPTON
    Layla, boys will be boys. no
    biggie. We have--

3) Medium. Manicorn kicks open the door, and is shoving a thumb over his shoulder at the assistant.

                MANICORN
    You. Leave. Me and your boss
    need to talk.

4) Medium. On Roy. The alien girl rolls her eyes as she leaves Roy. Roy is in sales mode. He already knows what this is about. He puts down the gun.

                ROY SHARPTON
    Goddamn, Manny! Good to see you.
    we don't see each other enough.

5) Wide. Manny is ON Roy, jutting a finger into Roy's forehead.

                MANICORN
    Can it, Roy. Reinstate me.

                ROY SHARPTON
    I can't do that, Manny.

                MANICORN
    Reinstate me or i will rip out
    your eyes and piss on your brain.

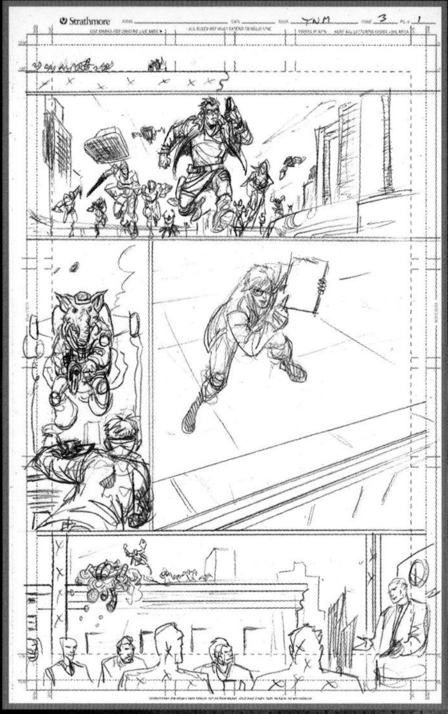
Strathmore

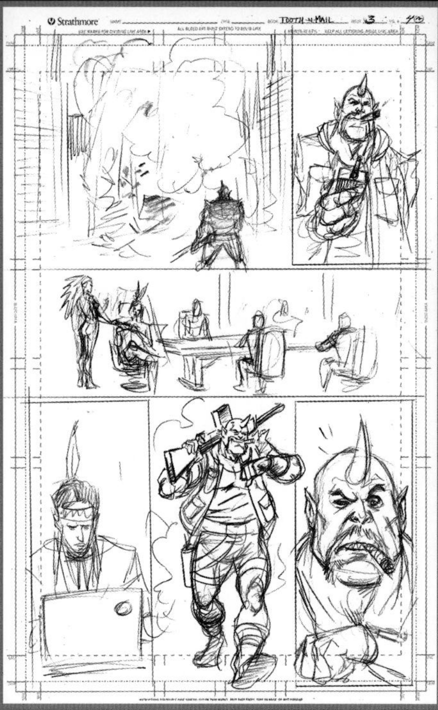
Strathmore

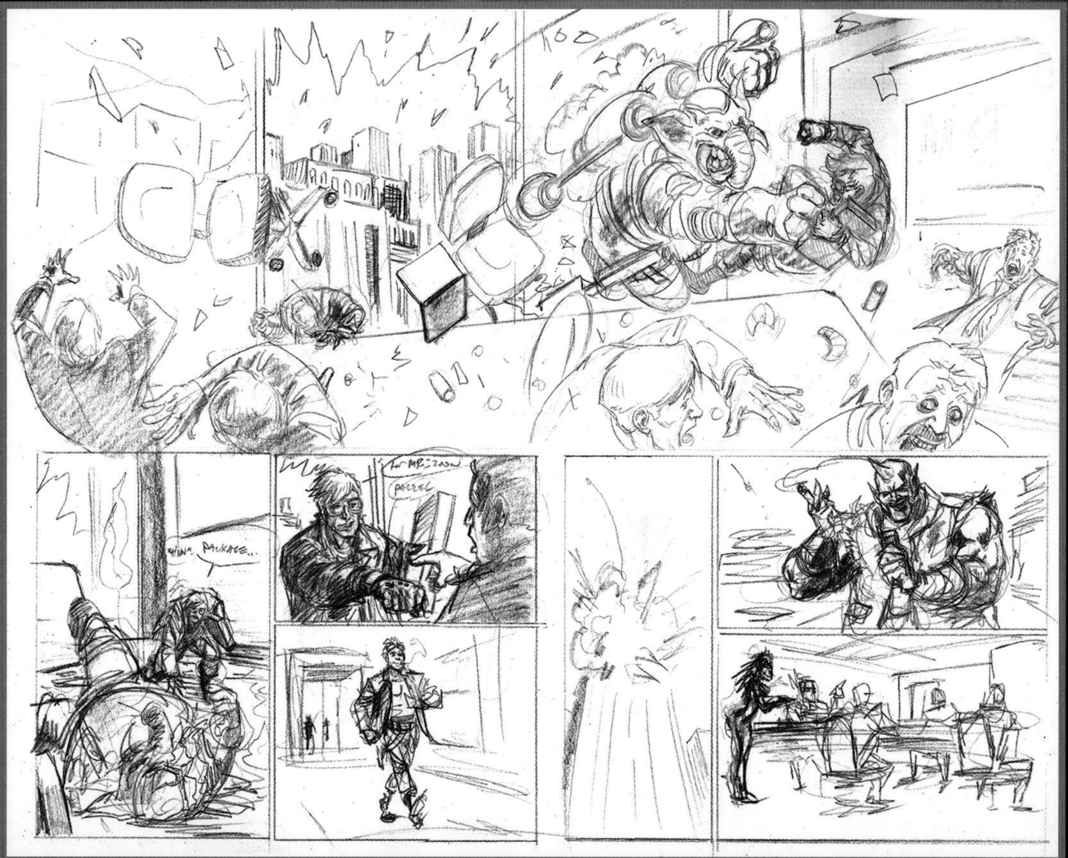
PACKAGE...

Darick originally attempted to combine pages 2-3 as a double-page spread before the gang decided it would work better to give Davey and the Elephant Man an even grander entrance on page 2.

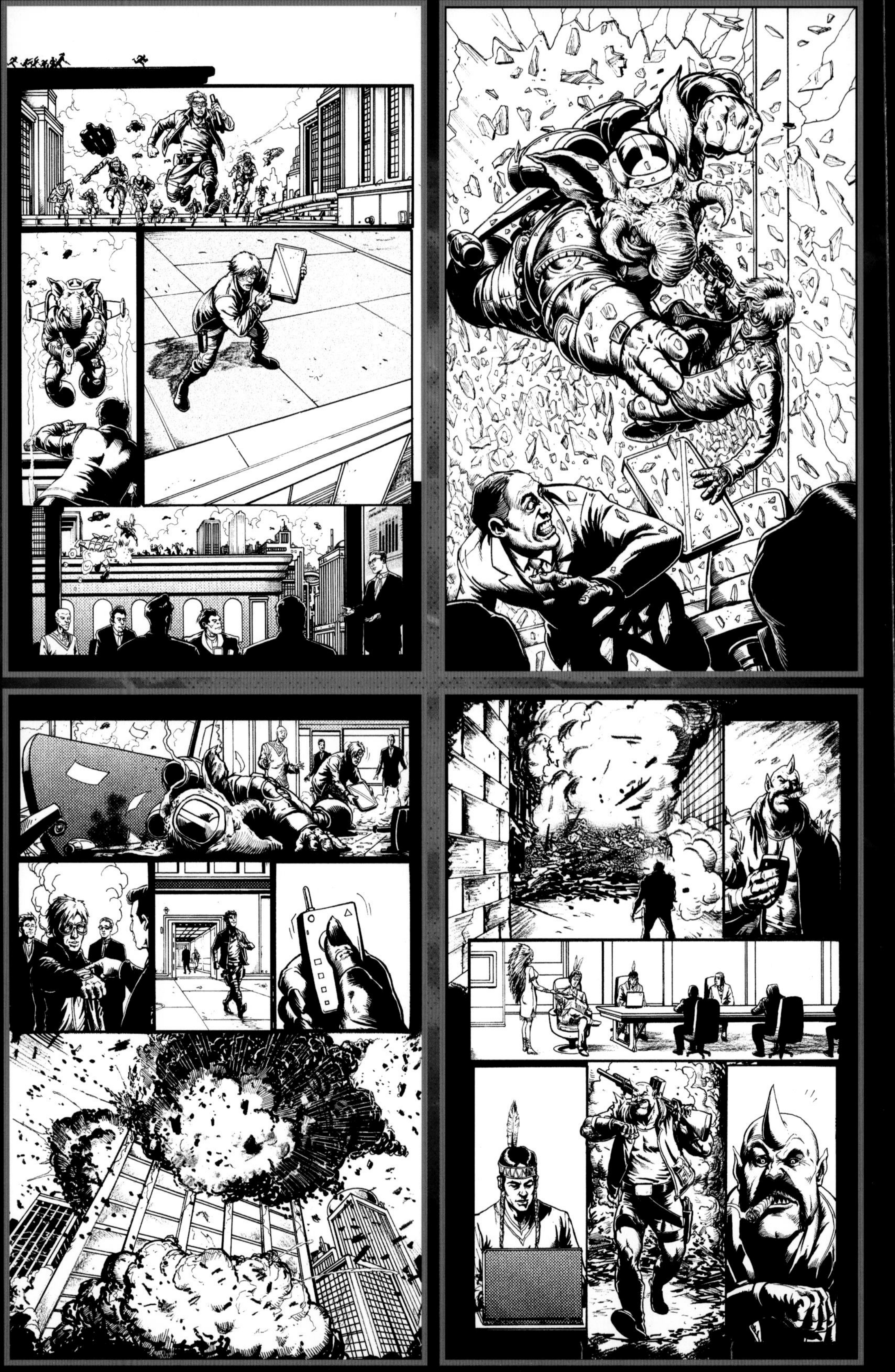

As Darick revised and moved to inks, page 2 became a splash page.

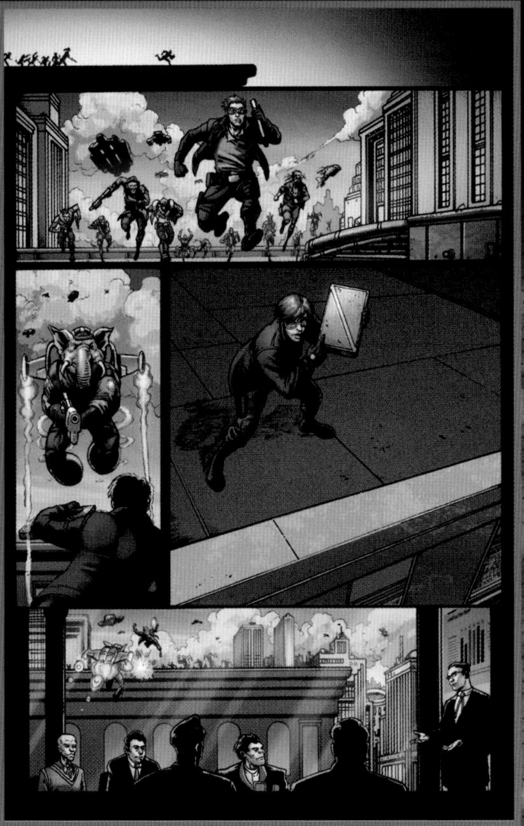
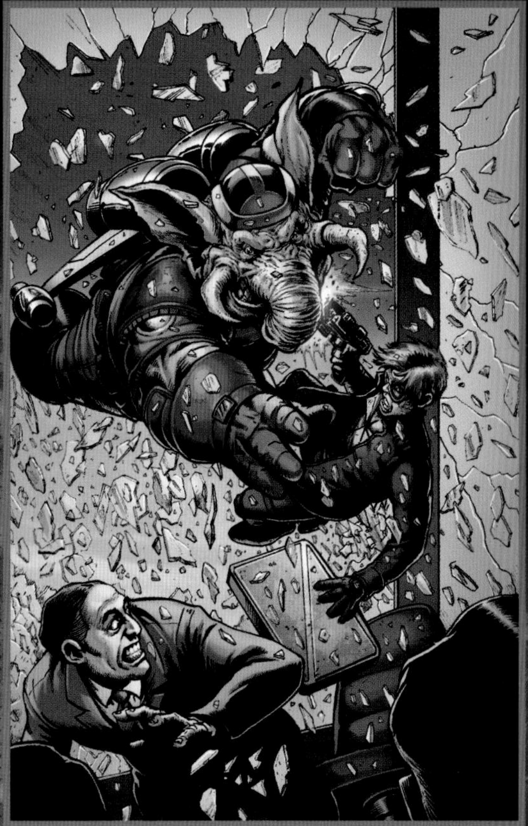
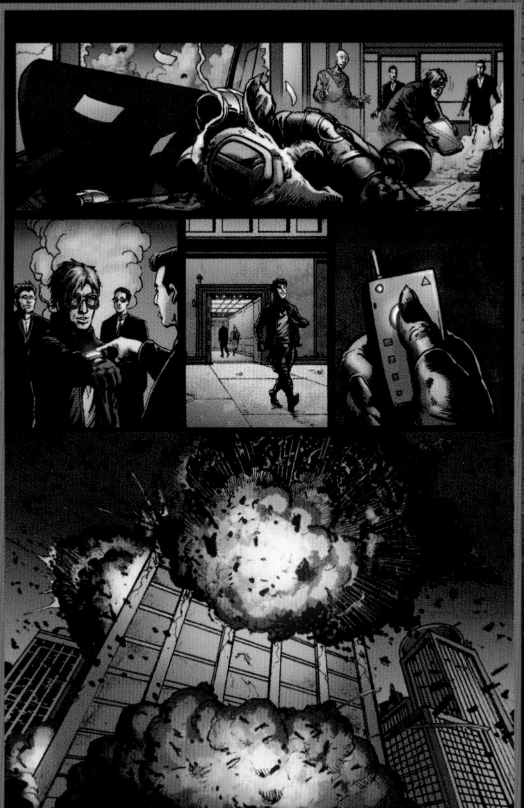
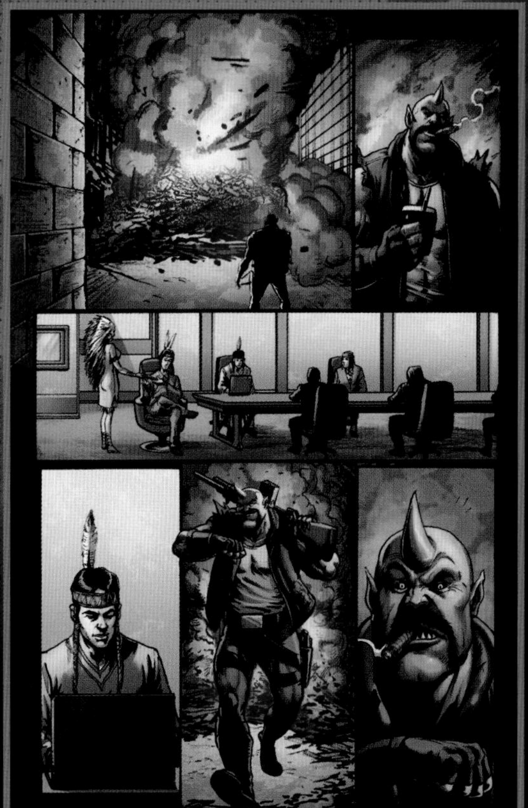

Diego's colors then brought even more drama to the sequence.

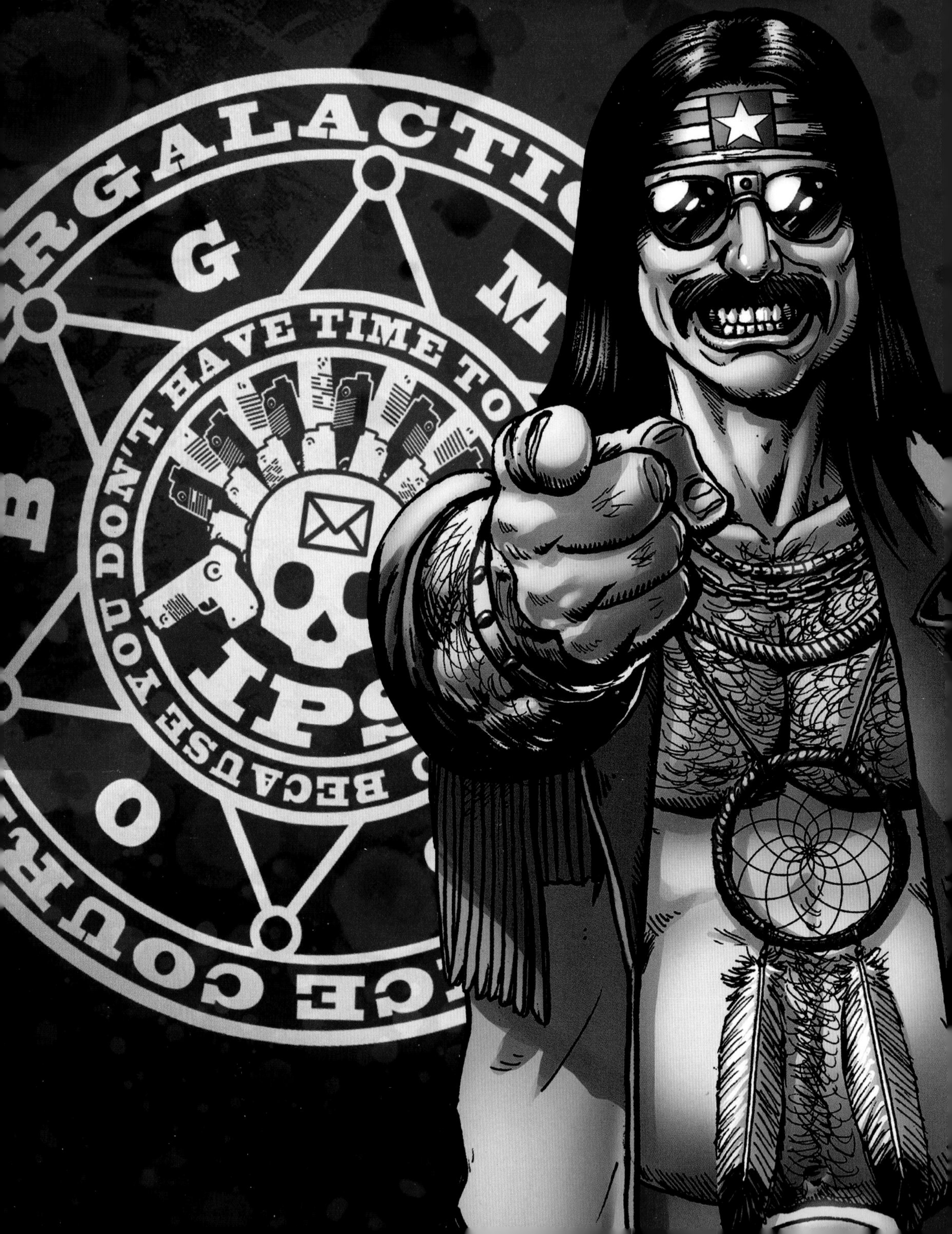
BECAUSE YOU DON'T HAVE TIME TO
G
M
IPS